HER

CATHERINE CLARKE

BOOK

ANGELS AND MEN

CATHERINE FOX

Angels and Men

HAMISH HAMILTON · LONDON

HAMISH HAMILTON LTD
Published by the Penguin Group
Penguin Books Ltd, 27 Wrights Lane, London w8 5TZ, England
Penguin Books USA Inc., 375 Hudson Street, New York, New York 10014, USA
Penguin Books Australia Ltd, Ringwood, Victoria, Australia
Penguin Books Canada Ltd, 10 Alcorn Avenue, Toronto, Ontario, Canada M4V 3B2
Penguin Books (NZ) Ltd, 182–190 Wairau Road, Auckland 10, New Zealand

Penguin Books Ltd, Registered Offices: Harmondsworth, Middlesex, England

First published 1995

First published in Great Britain by Hamish Hamilton Ltd 1995
1 3 5 7 9 10 8 6 4 2

Filmset in 11.5/13.75 pt Monophoto Bembo
Typeset by Datix International Limited, Bungay, Suffolk
Printed in Great Britain by Clays Ltd, St Ives plc

A CIP catalogue record for this book is available from the British Library

ISBN 0–241–13505–2

FOR PETE

Michaelmas Term

CHAPTER I

The City is a galleon sailing on the river. Listen to the wind thrumming in the trees and singing round the chimney-pots. High on the crow's nest of the cathedral hear the ping-ping-ping of rope against flagpole. This is where the angels pass by. These are the angel paths, the windy walkways. They are clothed with polished air and their faces are the faces of statues, bright as sunlight off water. No one sees them.

Down below on the streets people are walking to and fro, going about their business. They come in and out of the doors of the houses and colleges, through archways, across cobbles, down the steps and the steep pathways that lead to the river. Sometimes they look back up at the cathedral and castle against the sky, wondering.

Aunt Jessie could see angels; but then, she was mad. Ran mad in the Welsh revival in 1904. She lies now in a quiet graveyard. Her tombstone says: *Nearer my God to thee.*

A few years ago, when Aunt Jessie would have been ninety-something if she had lived, her great-niece, Mara Johns, stepped out through the door of one of the colleges and looked up at the sky. High above in the cathedral tower the clock chimed midday. The notes trembled in the air, and a pigeon rose clapping into the blue October sky before wheeling away behind a rooftop. Mara paused, her face bleached white in the brightness, pale against her dark hair and clothes.

Ah, this is a day for walking on air and climbing the wind, not for studying. With this thought she was about to run down the steps and off along the street where leaves scratched past on the wind, but the door behind her opened. She turned and saw a priest standing there. Damn. The Principal. He came down the steps towards her, smiling.

'Mara. Settling in all right?' She nodded. Too late to escape. He began to walk down the street with her. Her mind bobbed impatiently against the sky, a balloon tethered to the ground by his string of urbane small talk. Her work was going well, he trusted; and had she located the libraries, made contact with her tutor, met up with her fellow postgrads? Yes, yes, yes, no. The wind tugged at her skirt. Come on, come on. She saw her chance as they approached the archway which led into the cathedral close. They drew level with it and she stopped. The Principal paused too.

'Off to the cathedral?'

'Yes.'

'Good. Good.' Well, bugger off, then. But he hovered, frowning slightly. 'You're not Morgan Johns' daughter, are you?' She scowled.

'Yes.'

'Aha.' That would explain it, said his expression. 'I've just been reading his article on women's ordination. Excellent piece. Fine scholar, your father.' He paused, but she made no comment. 'He'll have his enemies, no doubt. Still in parish ministry?'

'Yes.' Yes, yes. Her mind raced off, following the flight of a sea-gull as it circled high overhead. She scarcely heard his next sentence. Something about a sherry reception. 'Yes. Thanks. Goodbye.' He raised his hand graciously as though bestowing a priestly blessing and she turned and ran through the archway.

She came out into the sunlit cathedral close. Her heart rose. There was nothing but the wind rushing in the trees and wires. The whole City was alive with it, a vast harp played by an unseen hand. People turned to glance at her as she passed. She watched them, seeing them wonder: Is that the newest fashion, those long dark skirts and black hat? Or is she just a bit odd? She broke into a run again, rounding the corner that led to the cloisters. The sun cast short arches across the floor as she slipped through: dark, light, dark, light, until she reached the great door.

I'll never go to Church again. It was her own voice speaking in her memory on the day she had broken with the sect. She felt her face harden, her pale eyes glinting, and saw her father turning away and saying nothing at all. If I had been any poxy parishioner of his he would have argued with me, or asked me why. He was just giving her room, of course. Letting her make her own choices. But it always left her feeling as if she could have been dead to him. It was over three years ago, but she still felt the coldness of it.

Some people passed out through the door. Suddenly she stepped forward. Why must everything be done with reference to her father? She squeezed past a woman in the doorway and entered. This year is for myself, not for him. She was in the cathedral.

It swallowed everything, all noise and hurry, muffling the footfalls and voices. The sounds rose to the great vaulted ceiling and vanished. The stones of the floor were worn by countless forgotten feet, the centuries of the faithful. She listened for a whisper of them in the huge cave of the cathedral as it echoed with its tide of visitors.

Then she began to walk towards the chancel. It felt like visiting the house where you grew up. Everywhere there were touches of recognition: I remember that smell, that colour, that ray of light. A tall clergyman inclined his head at her as she entered the chancel. She shot him a look: *Leave me alone.* He read the message and blinked. She walked on. This was where the choir sat service by service in their carved wooden stalls. Behind them the organ pipes rose up, decorated bright with red and gold. At that moment someone began to play. The notes climbed higher and higher, lingering and merging until the whole chancel was one mounting sound. The playing stopped as suddenly as it had begun, but the chords echoed on for a moment like the sound of the sea in a shell. Then the silence ebbed back.

By now she had reached the communion rails and was standing looking at the altar. How empty it was, as though God had been called temporarily away. Was that the faint smell of wine lingering? The sun came blazing through a south window, and she walked into it away from the roped-off altar.

At last her eyes wandered back down the chancel. A young man was kneeling in one of the choir stalls in a shaft of sunlight. She had not noticed him earlier. His hands were grasping the pew in front, and his dark head was bowed, resting on them. She looked away in embarrassment, as though she had caught sight of some intimate act; but then her eyes strayed back again, and suddenly he raised his head, fixing dark eyes on the source of light. For a moment he was still, burning in the sun like an icon, then he sat back into the shadow.

She turned and slipped away, making for the door as swiftly as she could, leaving the cathedral and heading for the college. She could feel her heart pounding again. Had she ever seen him before?

The bells called out once more across the City. Mara disappeared into a building. *Jesus College,* said the stone above the door. The windows stared. Behind some of them students were walking back and forth unpacking books and clothes. Halfway up the building Mara appeared briefly at another window as she climbed the stairs. Across the street, other windows stared back from one of the houses on the cathedral close. A large geranium stood in a quiet room. At another window the Canon rinsed a teacup at his sink. A pigeon swept past, then up, up, and over the rooftop where it glided along the backs of the college buildings that looked down over the river far below.

Mara was back in her room on the top floor, her dark head bent over a book. The pages were blank, and in her left hand she held a pencil. She was drawing. On the page tiny figures began to form. Some were like mythical beasts or parts of architectural plans, other like old alchemical drawings. It could almost have been writing, secret hieroglyphs, a record of her thoughts in a language of her own.

An apple tree. The fruit nestled in the wreaths of leaves like jewels in an ornate setting. I could see an apple tree out of my bedroom at the vicarage at home. The wasps ate the fruit that fell. This was one of the garden's secret horrors – the perfect skin gleaming on the lawn, but when you rolled it over it was gnawed out and empty, like the head of a doll with empty eye-sockets hiding in the grass.

The tree stood complete on the page. It looked like a woodcut from a seventeenth-century pamphlet. A pamphlet called something like 'The Fruit of the Tree of LIFE: *Or* The Way Back through the *Flaming Sword*, being a Reply to So-and-so his Book . . .' Too much reading. I need to be with people. She began drawing a branch of a tree with a bird roosting there. She needed people; not for company, but to define herself against, as markers for the boundaries of her personality.

She flipped back through the pages, reminded of the first time she had used this as a method of sorting her thoughts out.

'Why don't you draw me something?' the psychiatrist had asked. Maybe he'd been worn out by this silent obstinate fourteen-year-old. 'Draw me a picture of your father.' But she wasn't going to be caught out that easily. To foil him she scribbled a little stick man. 'Draw your mother.' Another stick man. She drew him her sister, her teacher, a nurse, a farmer, a stranger. A row of little identical stick men. There was a long silence. She folded her arms smugly.

'Look at what you've done,' he said. She looked. Suddenly the significance leapt out. All the same. Blank. Interchangeable. A stranger meant as much to her as her mother. Her hand holding the pencil had started to tremble.

Surely I've changed a little since then? She sat frowning for a moment, then closed the book and walked across to the open window. Down on the terrace below small groups of people were standing. They looked awkward. New students just arrived, some still accompanied by their parents. It was like an airport. Just go. Wave them off and go. Don't stand around drinking tea from the college cups delaying your children's departure. Wave them through passport control and on to the plane and off, up through the clouds to a new world.

She looked down on them, seeing the tops of their heads. Voices were murmuring, but no words reached her. In her mind she floated down until she was hovering above the talking groups. Back and forth go the questions in a kind of desperate, verbal gavotte, grouping, moving on, regrouping. I remember it from Cambridge. How terrible to be an undergraduate. A fresher. This time I'll stay out of the way until it is all over. All alone like a princess in an iron tower. Unless I make a new beginning here, take a risk and try to make some friends for a change?

Almost at once there was a knock at the door, as though someone were coming to test this tentative thought. Mara went to open it. A breathless girl stood there holding out an invitation card.

'Hi! Welcome to Jesus College. My name's Sue and I'm from the Christian Union.' Mara felt herself tense. 'We're having a tea party, and I wondered if you'd like to come?'

'I'm not interested.'

The girl flushed, but managed to hold out a different card to Mara. 'Well, maybe I can leave you this? It's a programme of this term's events.'

'I said I'm not interested.'

The girl gave a little bubbly laugh. Mara could see tears starting in her eyes. Take it. Just take the card, for God's sake. You can always throw it away. But she couldn't bring herself to accept it.

'Well, sorry to have bothered you.'

The girl's footsteps scurried off down the stairs. Mara shut the door. Her scalp was prickling at her unnecessary harshness. But I can't help it. If it had been any other group – the Students' Union, the Boat Club, even the sodding Tolkien Society . . . Why am I still so hysterical about it all?

She crossed back to her desk and sat with her head in her hands. Gradually she admitted that the girl's earnest manner had reminded her of her twin sister. She could picture that same look on Hester's face as she had begged her to go to those praise meetings. Miracles, healings, baptism in the Holy Spirit. Please, Mara. Just try it. Eventually she went, sneering at first, then suddenly and violently convinced. She saw a vision. For two months she had walked on air, a handmaid of the Lord. But somehow it had not lasted. Lies. All lies. Over three years ago.

Mara went back to the window again. She could freeze off the self-assured without a pang, but people like Sue were different. She hated herself for snubbing them. There were two of the same type living in the room next door, quiet studious young women in their Finals year who had smiled nervously at her and said 'Hello' before darting back into their room again. Field mice. Suddenly a thought struck her, and her lips twisted a little. What if she had been put on the same corridor because someone saw her in that light? The studious mousy postgraduate next to the serious mousy Finals students. A little murine blue-stocking enclave, books and cocoa and early nights.

There was a loud and naughty laugh from the lawn below. She looked down and saw a tall, red-haired girl with a small crowd around her. Beside her was a shorter girl with brown curly hair and a wide-eyed pretty-pretty look, like an Edwardian china doll. The tall red-head said something, and the other laughed. Now the red-head laughed again. It was the sort of laugh that drew others in, and soon even those not close enough to hear what was being said were smiling. Put them in the hyena section. They don't belong up here. But then Mara felt a pang, like the little match-girl outside in the cold watching Christmas through the windows. What would it be like to have those two as friends?

Look, they must have been called in. She watched as the last students and their parents disappeared beneath her into the college. Someone closed the French windows and the murmuring voices were hushed. The wind worried on through the trees. She found herself thinking about the curly-haired girl. A china doll, smiling and showing its pearly little teeth. A row of china dolls, she thought suddenly. Then she knew. The girl was the oldest daughter of the vicar of a parish near her father's. She probably even went to the same school as I did. What will she know about me? What will she have heard? This year will not be the blank volume I have designed for myself. There is already a preface. She stood up and closed the window, and walked back to her desk. As the light gradually faded she was still there, reading and making notes with close concentration.

8

The cathedral clock chimed the passing hours, three, four, five, six. All around the roofs and chimney-pots the wind rushed free.

At about eight she sat back and told herself to do what she had been avoiding. Go and ask for that book. She had looked for a particular volume in the college library only to discover that it had been taken out by one of the tutors in Coverdale Hall, the City's Anglican theological college. Mara had realized to her dismay shortly after arriving that Coverdale was not only next door to Jesus, but it was actually part of the same foundation. Was there no escaping the long arm and limp wrist of Anglicanism? Her door swung shut behind her.

I hate going to meet people, she thought as she ran down the stairs. Even the simplest utterance seems to take on a peculiar ring. The more I try to be normal the more dangerous I feel, like Morgan le Fay interrupting a sherry party. She passed through several corridors, moving, she supposed, roughly parallel to the street outside. This must once have been a series of different houses. She thought of the previous occupants – what if they had looked up from their papers in the breakfast room one morning and seen into the future? Dozens of strangely dressed young people appearing suddenly through one wall, hurrying past, and vanishing through another. Up another set of stairs she went, peering at doors until she found one which said 'Rev. Dr James Mowbray'.

'Do try to be nice, darling,' pleaded her mother's voice in her mind. Mara knocked. Someone called her in, and she entered the flat. It was like the study of some eighteenth-century intellectual. Her glance took in green walls with framed prints, faded rugs, rank on rank of books, and an old brown globe. A man stood under a light like a portrait of himself, an old seafarer, maps and charts about him. Outside the wind was a restless sea. He greeted her inquiringly. On the sofa facing her was a young man. A flash of recognition – the man in the cathedral.

'How can I help you?' Dr Mowbray asked. The young man burned on the edge of her vision.

'Do you have *Seven Reasons why God Used Dwight L. Moody*?' A pause.

'Not off hand.' She saw he was laughing at her. A snarling look came across her face.

'It's a book.' All the time the young man was lounging on the sofa. She could see the insolence of his posture without looking at him, and his presence somehow made it impossible for her to be *nice*.

'Yes. I'm sorry. I have the book. And you, I take it, would like to borrow it. Let me see – you're one of the new postgrads, aren't you? Women and sectarianism?' She inclined her head.

'Well,' he began when she said nothing. The word teetered. He sprang on to a secure phrase: 'And how are you settling in?'

'All right.' Another silence yawned like a mineshaft. He looked around as if wondering where the next piece of solid ground might be. Why did he remind her of an old sea captain?

'And your name is?'

'Mara Johns.'

'Mara,' he confirmed. 'I'm James Mowbray, and this is . . .' He stopped in the act of turning to the young man on the sofa. She could see a sentence forming in his mind as clearly as if he had a cartoon thought-bubble drifting out of his head. *You must be Morgan Johns' daughter*, it said. Her expression became very nasty indeed.

'You must be' – and, catching sight of the expression, he changed tack – 'a person in your own right.' A rare smile flashed across her face. It vanished just as suddenly.

'I'm Morgan Johns' daughter,' she said.

He laughed. 'Yes, I'm afraid I realized that. How is your father these days? A bit of a lone voice crying in the wilderness, I'd have thought. High churchmen in *favour* of women's ordination are a rare breed. I've just read his latest article.' He paused, perhaps to see if she had any comment to make, then leapt on to another solid-looking idea: 'He and I were at theological college together, you know.'

She made no reply. The conversation disintegrated beneath him, and they stood in silence. She could see he wanted a cosy chat about the Johns family and she dared not encourage him.

'Well, well, well,' he said at length. 'We have met before, actually, only you won't remember it. You would have been about seven. It was in Lyme Regis.'

Suddenly she remembered and spoke involuntarily. 'Do you have a boat?'

He smiled. 'I used to have a very small yacht. No longer, sadly. Yes. You were wild about the sea.'

She could hear the ropes slapping on the masts all around, each giving a different note, as though they were bells not boats rocking and cockling on the waves. Her face softened at the memory. I was going to run away to sea.

'You grilled me on the names of the sails on square-rigged vessels,' Dr Mowbray continued. 'I was a sad disappointment to you.' She hardened herself and there was another silence.

They stood for a while. Then, having clearly just asked himself 'Where were we?' Dr Mowbray said, 'I'm so sorry. This is John Whitaker. Training for the ministry here at Coverdale Hall.'

Mara turned at last to look at him. He made no effort to stand, merely gave a slight ironic salute and smiled at her. She stared briefly, then looked back at Dr Mowbray. Good God. Not my mental picture of an ordinand.

'If ever you're locked out of your car, John's your man. I'll get that book for you.' Dr Mowbray walked towards a shelf and began to run his finger along the spines.

What's this? thought Mara. An ordinand with a shady past? She couldn't prevent herself sneaking another glance at the young man. He was ready for her, and winked. She looked away again, flushing angrily.

'Do you have enthusiasm?' asked Dr Mowbray.

Enthusiasm? 'In my way.'

'The book – oh, ah yes. Very good. *Touché.*' He handed her a volume. *Enthusiasm*, she read on the spine. Ah. She bit on a smile. This was going to be one of the problems with having read English and not theology. She had done as much frantic reading as she could over the summer, cantering briskly through centuries of church history, slowing to a trot over rocky doctrinal countryside, collapsing at last in despair in the vast trackless wastes of German liberal protestantism. Despite all this, parcels of unexploded ignorance lay concealed on all sides. Even the most innocent-seeming question – Who is so-and-so? – could go off in your face. You might be asking the equivalent of 'Who is Shakespeare, exactly?' Or, on the other hand, the unknown theologian might be an obscure Restoration dramatist, as it were, that nobody could expect you to know about. Dr Mowbray continued to hand her books. Out of the corner of her eye she thought she could see the young man grinning. Maybe he had seen through her. Or maybe he was amused at the number of books she was now holding. This thought seemed to strike Dr Mowbray.

'Well, I'm sure that will keep you going for a few days.' He smiled. 'Would you like some coffee?'

'No thanks.' She began to make a move towards the door.

'Sure? Well, give my regards to your father when you next speak to him.'

When they serve ice-cream in hell. She gave a nod. Why wouldn't he let her go? He was like the person who keeps raising points of information when other people want the meeting to finish.

'And to your mother, of course.'

Another nod. Yes yes yes.

He walked with her towards the door. 'Does your father still have his legendary violent temper, I wonder?'

Her hand was on the handle, but this brought her back sharply. 'No,' she said in astonishment.

'Really?' He seemed surprised himself. 'He had the worst temper I've ever come across.' The words 'present company excepted' seemed to hang in the air unspoken. Mara's glance darted involuntarily towards the man on the sofa again. He was lighting a cigarette, and appeared to be paying no attention.

'I'm afraid Morgan-baiting was something of a college sport,' went on Dr Mowbray. 'To see how quickly he could be made to explode. He was always so passionate about everything.'

Mara stood as still as a stone. Why was I never told this before? Why have I always been made to feel like a changeling? In her mind she heard the adult voices: Why can't you be nice like Hester? . . . What a face! . . . Dear me, what a naughty temper. I don't know where she gets it from.

'I've never heard him raise his voice.'

'Well, people change,' said Dr Mowbray. His tone had a summing-up quality.

'Thanks for these.' She made a gesture with the pile of books.

'You're welcome. If there's anything else . . .' She had the door open. 'It's been good to meet you, Mara.' She could leave. But no – one small item of any other business to finish. He dropped his voice, and began to say, 'I was sorry to hear about your –'

'*Thank you.*' She snuffed out his sentence.

Instantly the young man's attention was on her. This was what she had been dreading. Dr Mowbray eyed her cautiously.

'Goodbye,' she said before he could try again. She left the two of them with a surprised silence twanging in the air.

Forget it. Forget it, she told herself as she made her way down the stairs. She went out of the back of the building and began to walk along the terraces and through the gardens that ran behind the college. The sky above the rooftops was a deep dark blue, and a cathedral tower was just visible beyond the chimneys, ghostly in the floodlights. She hugged the books in her thin arms. Something like glee seized her. She could drop the books and, raising her arms, be lifted on the steady wind, treading higher and higher until she looked down on the City twinkling beneath her. Tree shadows danced on the walls. She heard the water running over the weir deep in the river, over and on and out to the distant sea. Some of the college windows were lit up, bright as pictures on a black wall. As she walked, the sound of music came from various rooms.

She entered the hallway and passed through a group of students as they exclaimed and talked. I might be a ghost, she thought. What a strange twilight realm we postgraduates inhabit. Pale figures haunting the libraries long outside term-time. She began climbing the stairs leaving their voices behind. This hall must have been majestic once. The frou-frou of long-gone petticoats rustled in her mind. Maybe she would meet her fellow ghosts one day on these steps. A Victorian maid, the one who polished these banisters a hundred years ago. We would stare at one another, wondering who was haunting whom. Mara stood feeling in her pocket for her keys, balancing the pile of books with her chin. There was a sudden noise as someone came out of the next room. She looked up to see an entirely different manifestation confronting her: a dark young man with a look of languid contempt on his face.

'Jesus Christ. Another bloody woman.'

She straightened up slowly and stared into a pair of cold grey eyes. No need to be *nice* here. One of her fellow postgrads? He looked about twenty-four or -five.

'I came back thinking I was on an all-male corridor, and what do I find? It's overrun with *girls*, buggering up my morning routine and clogging the bathrooms with their toiletries and tampons.'

She continued to stare at him, fixing her eyes with offensive blankness on the bridge of his nose.

'Let's try and understand one another, shall we?' he continued. '*That*' – pointing at a door – 'is the bathroom I intend to use. You *girls* can use the other one.'

She raised an eyebrow and let her gaze travel down to his feet, then back up to his face. He was around six feet tall, about her own height. He looked tailored and expensive from black hair to black brogues. The statement was unambiguous: Don't fuck with me – you're not in my league. Her eyes rested on him a while longer, then she turned indifferently and put her key in the lock. The last glimpse she had was of his astonished face as she closed him out. A smile struggled on her lips. She stood looking at the door. Was he standing staring at the other side of it, thinking – what would he be thinking? Why the hell didn't she say anything? Or: Stuck-up bitch! She heard his footsteps walking away at last, then going into the room next door. So she was stuck between him and the field mice. Some music began to play. Tallis, she thought. How inappropriate. She tried to picture Sue from the Christian Union inviting him to a tea party. Then an idea occurred to her and a smile burst out before she could stop it. The joker that had arranged this menagerie of a college had been uncertain about her. Somebody had looked at her and not known whether she would prove to be a field mouse or a half-starved feral mink.

CHAPTER 2

Mara lay on her back with her hands and ankles crossed like a stone effigy on a tomb. The cathedral clock had just struck half-past-two. Am I going to hear every bloody quarter of the whole twenty-four hours? At once she tried to unknot her impatience and soothe it away. 'Just think nice thoughts, darling,' her mother used to say. It was never that easy. Take counting sheep, for instance. As a child she had never understood why people did this. The sheep kept wandering about the hillside, disappearing behind rocks or making stupid rushes towards the stream until she was ready to dance with frustration. Stand still while I count you!

Instead she began to imagine a hillside bare of sheep. It was moorland dark with heather under a late-winter sky, white and low, pressing on the earth. Maybe it would rain. A touch of mildness was in the air – surely the spring would not be long? Listen to the stream over the stones, hush, hush; hear the wind rattling a sigh through the dead heather. Then with outstretched arms she rose into the sky, the moor wheeling and sliding away beneath her. Soon it will be spring . . .

In the last moment before sleep came, her mind was full of voices speaking Welsh, her uncle's family murmuring words she almost understood, a language she could speak in her dreams but forgot when she woke.

She was in a dark house with many rooms. Their doors were locked. On and on she walked, looking for her sister's baby. Why wouldn't her legs work properly? Each step was harder than the last. Come on, she urged herself, forcing one foot in front of the other. Here was a door. She tried the knob. It opened and she entered a room. In the corner was a cradle. She struggled over to it and looked inside. There was a mound under the cover – the baby was there. She pulled back the blanket and there lay a doll's body, its head missing.

Dear God! She sat bolt upright with the sweat pouring off her. The bell chimed five. Gradually the horror receded. All hope of sleep was gone, but she lay down again anyway. Just forget it. It's only a dream, she told herself. You know that. Her breathing grew steadier at last. Quarter past five.

By half-past she had given up and was pulling some clothes on. She wrapped her black wool clerical cape around her. It had belonged to her grandfather before he was made bishop. She made her way quietly down the stairs then out on to the dark street. The wind had dropped. Nothing. She began to walk along the cobbled street away from the cathedral, down towards the old bridge that spanned the river. Her footsteps sounded as she walked past the college buildings. Their eyes were closed and dreaming as the revolving stars slid across their panes.

Soon she was standing on the high bridge looking downstream, a watchman on a city wall longing for morning. She hugged her cloak around her. In the distance she could see street lights on another bridge, with their partners shivering on the water below. The weir rumbled on like one eternal wave breaking on the shore. When would all this pass? The bells chimed quarter to six. They sounded different out there, cold and clear.

Then came the distant whine of a milk-float as it toiled up a street over to the left. It stopped with a rattle of bottles. The world was waking up. Maybe that was the first hint of dawn in the east. Her eyes could just make out the dark shape of the cathedral as it loomed over the City. She leant forward and rested her arms on the stone parapet of the bridge, and gazed at the black towers.

They grew more distinct in the gathering light as she watched, quarter by quarter, until behind her on the river she heard the call of the first cox as a college eight pulled towards her on the water below. At this she crossed over to the other side. They came steadily on, with a ghostly underwater crew keeping time upside down beneath them. The tips of the blades met, then skimmed back through air or water. The boat passed under the central archway below her. Now that it was light she could pick out a fisherman sitting patiently on the bank. A seagull circled slowly. All around her the colours gained in intensity; the white of the bird, the dying blaze of the trees, red or gold against black bark, and the green of the undergrowth along the banks. She sighed. Another day.

The crew had turned and was sliding back up river. 'One! Two!' roared the cox. 'Eyes in the boat, men!' crackled a voice. She turned and saw someone cycling along the bank with a megaphone. The boat emerged through the archway down below. This time she could make out the faces twisted in exertion as they pulled away from her. Mad. But they at least had some reason to be out in the cold. The sun began to touch the cathedral walls and the highest treetops and she wandered back for college breakfast.

The noise of voices and clashing crockery filled the dining-room. Mara felt stupefied by it after the silence of the morning outside. Mercifully there was a 'quiet' table where the antisocial or overhung could breakfast without the threat of conversation. She carried her toast and coffee over to it, draped her cloak over the chair back, and sat down. The smell of bacon and eggs hung about. She could pick out the new First Years as they wandered uncertainly in. Spoons clattered in bowls. Before long Mara was joined by the polecat from the room next door. He was wearing the same supercilious sneer that he had turned on her the previous night, drinking his coffee and looking around the room in disdain. Caffeine alone could not mitigate the outrage of having to breakfast in a zoo.

Mara sat drinking and watching those around her. From the doorway came the sound of hearty conversation. Some young men in tracksuits entered. Their faces were red with fresh air and exercise, and their voices had not yet lost their outdoor loudness. One threw his head back and roared, beating his fists on his chest like a gorilla.

'Shut up!' snarled the polecat. Silence fell. The gorilla hung his head and slunk off. It was a while before conversation returned to normal. Well, well. Who was this man who must not be crossed? Mara went to get another cup of coffee, flicking him a contemptuous glance as she passed. His eyes narrowed. When she got back, he had gone.

She sat again and resumed her watching. Before long she saw the tall red-head and the china doll at the far side of the room. There was an air of mischief at their table. 'Shut up!' barked a voice. The red-head. Everyone laughed, for it was a very fair imitation of the polecat. Mara felt her lips twitch. A pity she hadn't dared to do it while he was still in the room. She drank some more coffee. The field mice crept past and smiled at her. She nodded at them. Then from across the room she saw a pair of big blue eyes fixed on her. She stiffened. The china doll had recognized her. Mara saw her lean across and say something to the red-head. Before they both had a chance to look at her, and perhaps come across for some kind of introduction, Mara left the hall.

The common room was quiet. People sat reading newspapers or opening their post. There was an occasional yawn, or the sound of a newspaper being batted into shape, and now and then a murmured comment. In one corner a girl sat filling in the *Times* crossword. It was little Sue from the Christian Union. Mara felt a twinge of guilt and picked up another paper and began glancing through it. Before long the red-head and her friend came in. Mara continued reading, alert to their movements, but the two of them settled on the other side of the room without appearing to see her.

After a moment she put down the paper and went across to the pigeon-holes to see if there were any letters for her. The polecat came in. People seemed to flinch a little. His glance swept around the room. He was looking for something – *The Times*? Yes. He located Sue in the corner filling in the crossword and bore down on her. She looked up at him, read the expression on his face, and thrust the paper towards him. He seized it, and after a glance, held it up between finger and thumb.

'What,' he asked, 'is *this*?' The attention of the whole room was on him. Mara put the letters back, folded her arms, and watched. The girl looked like a rabbit that sees the hawk and forgets how to run.

'The crossword,' she said desperately.

'I know that, for Christ's sake.' He waited. The whole room waited.

'Is this going to happen every day?'

'I was only . . .' Mara thought there were tears in Sue's eyes. Was no one going to do anything? She looked around. People were buried unconvincingly in their papers. Who the hell does he think he is? The hair on the back of her neck began to prickle. He's no worse than you are, her conscience accused.

'If you want to deface a paper, I suggest you confine yourself to one of the *tabloids*.' With that, he crossed the room and sat down. Utter silence.

'What a wanker,' said Mara, and walked out of the room. The silence, broken only by her footsteps, lasted the full length of the corridor until she reached the stairs. Then came the sound of laughter. The red-head, followed after a moment by everyone else. In her mind Mara heard the satisfactory sound of an arrow whizzing with a thud into its target. Twang! She strode up to her room.

High up on the tower's face the men were working. The City lay spread like a map beneath them, narrow streets with tiny people going back and forth about their business. Students streaming over the bridges, off to libraries and lectures, and the shoppers milling in the marketplace. The men toiled on, whistling in the wind and hearing the crooning pigeons that clustered in the stone crevices all around. The clock chimed three, and a pigeon took off, glided down, then landed on the builders' sign halfway up the scaffolding. It sidled along the top and began preening itself. *Allinson, Whitaker and Sons,* said the letters.

Back down in the college Mara sat at her desk working. She heard the bells and leant back and stretched. From the other side of the wall she could hear classical music playing. She bared her teeth in a death's head grin, picturing the polecat sitting at his desk facing her only feet away in the next room. The half-expected confrontation – face thrust in hers: *Bitch!* – had not occurred. Maybe he was biding his time. There had been something odd in people's faces at lunchtime. She had the feeling that word had got round. That's her – that's the one who called whatsisname a wanker in the Junior Common Room. What *is* his name? she wondered now, but could not be bothered to go and look at his door to find out. Instead she reached for a pencil and her black book.

A face flowered in the centre of the page. A jester, perhaps, or the Joker from a pack of cards. She continued drawing. Around the face danced a circle of morris men. They always made her want to cry as a child, for all their bells and pig's bladders and silly antics. Maybe it was the music. The trailing ribbons furled and unfurled until a wheel of dancers writhed around the Joker.

Her pencil continued to scratch, leaving behind another ring of tiny characters. They looked like figures from the margin of a medieval manuscript. Round the wheel they trudged with their buckets and ladders and tools. The cathedral builders. And outside them, so faint they could hardly be seen, were the seraphim. Each had six wings, burning, burning, and the wings of one touched the wings of the next and the whole wheel spun in fire around its focus.

Mara stared at what she had drawn. It depicted the ultimate silliness of the universe. This was how the world had seemed to her since she had turned her back on her faith. And yet she had a recurring sense that it all meant something, that it was worth working, building cathedrals, and that the whirling chaos was enclosed in the wings of the watchful seraphim. Ah, but that could be the last trick of all. At the very end your fingers would turn up the Joker again. But did it matter, even? Life might be everything, or it might be nothing at all.

There was an abrupt knock. Mara jumped. The Christian Union again? She sat motionless for a moment, tempted not to answer, but curiosity eventually drew her towards the door. She opened it, and there stood the red-head and the china doll.

'Do you have any milk?' asked the red-head. Was this a gambit, a sort of borrowing-a-cup-of-sugar from the new neighbours?

'Yes,' Mara said, watching them carefully.

'She has milk,' said the red-head in an undertone to her friend. She turned to Mara again. 'And do you have any tea?'

Mara's hand quivered to close the door. But no, she would just see what they were up to. 'Yes,' she answered, a hint of nastiness creeping into her voice.

The red-head turned to the other again and whispered, 'She has tea as well!'

The china doll widened her blue eyes. 'Tea!' she breathed.

What were they playing at?

'How very odd,' said the red-head, 'because we have cakes.' She held up a box.

'And biscuits,' said the other, showing the packet.

'I have a terrible sense of foreboding,' continued the red-head. 'It's almost as if *something is about to happen*. Do you think this strange coincidence of tea things is significant?' She turned to her friend. 'I sense an impending tea party.'

They both turned to Mara and asked, 'What do you think?'

Mara stood and considered. She could close the door in their faces, or open it and let them in. If she let them in, nothing would ever be the same again. Fear touched her. Shut the door! But a memory rose up and swallowed her mind; and there she was again, aged fourteen, turning the corner in the grounds of the clinic, the stitches still prickling in her slashed wrist. Sunlight was slanting down through the trees with smoke from the bonfire hanging in its shafts, and in that moment came the thought: *I choose to live*. This was another such moment. She opened the door.

'Oh frabjous day!' exclaimed the china doll, and the two of them burst in. Mara watched their gaze sweeping around looking for clues or demonstrations of her personality.

'But you've done nothing to your room!' protested the red-head. 'No pictures, no plants, no nothing.'

Mara began to fill the kettle and make the tea, moving between them as they talked and snooped, as alien as a foreign maid.

'She has nice cups, though,' said the china doll.

'Yes, I'll admit she has nice cups.'

Mara glanced at the pretty blue and white china. Her mother had bought them for her. For a moment there was silence, and the three of them stood as though listening to the kettle.

'You may be wondering who we are,' said the red-head suddenly.

Mara raised an eyebrow. In fact, she had been wondering nothing of the sort, since their beings were fixed in her mind by the labels she had attached to them.

'May was at school with you,' said the red-head, indicating the other girl.

'Only I was several years younger,' said the china doll, 'so you won't remember me. And anyway, we moved house years ago when Papa was made vicar of St Botolph of the Holy Nails.' Mara said nothing, and the girl went on: 'You were brilliant at drawing. We used to have RE lessons in your form room after lunch on Fridays, and there were always rude pictures of the staff on the blackboard.'

With these words the girl leapt into life in Mara's mind. She was no longer a doll, but another young woman with a memory, a past that included both of them. So the family had moved. Good. I must have forgotten that.

'May Poppett,' she said, and saw the girl's face light up.

'You remembered!' How easy it was to please. 'Do you still draw?'

Mara shook her head.

'I'm Maddy,' said the red-head. 'Madeleine. Only don't call me that, or I'm afraid I shall have to kill you.'

A pause followed. 'I'm Mara Johns,' she said at last, as though hauling the phrase up from her memory. She made the tea.

'Yes, yes. We know that,' said Maddy. 'Mara Johns, the one who dared to call Andrew Jacks a rude word in the JCR. You're famous.'

So that was his name. She wondered if he was listening through the wall at that very moment.

'I thought I'd *die*,' Maddy went on. 'Laugh? I haven't laughed so much since Grandma's left tit got caught in the mangle. Where's the tea, then? I'm gasping.' She seized the pot and began to pour. 'Milk?' Mara felt dazed but, collecting herself, went outside and along the corridor to the fridge. She stood for a moment with the bottle in her hand. Why did I let them in? I could just walk away now and leave them. But she knew she would not.

Maddy and May had opened the cakes and biscuits, and there was a Sunday school party smell in the air. Mara poured milk into the tea and they began to eat and drink. In the silence Mara began to call back her empty moorland. I'm flying. The heather stretches beneath me.

'Do you know what the three of us have in common?' asked Maddy through a mouthful of cream slice. 'How rude,' she commented, smacking her lips. 'Yum, yum. Well?' She rounded on Mara. 'What do we have in common?' she repeated.

Nothing in this world, thought Mara. But they were both waiting for her answer.

'X chromosomes?'

'She doesn't know,' said Maddy. 'We're going to have to tell her.'

'Our fathers are all clergymen,' said May.

The wind shivered in the empty heather bells.

'This place is literally riddled with the sons of the clergy,' remarked Maddy, reaching for another cake.

'*Brightest and best of the sons of the clergy*,' sang May. 'There's a bishop's son training for the ministry at Coverdale Hall. Rupert Anderson, he's called. Keep nepotism in the family, as my father's uncle used to say. He was a Canon. Until the court case, of course.'

'O Rupert the Fair, Rupert the Brave,' said Maddy. 'Have you met him yet? His father is May's father's Bishop, and he's quite, quite wonderful.' Their conversation went on, drifting up to her as she flew by, as though they were picnicking on the edge of her dream with the radio turned up too loud. 'It's a shame Rupert's such a sissy name. It makes me think of Wupert the Bear. He looks more like a William to me. You know – dependable rugger bugger type.'

'Oh, definitely,' agreed May. 'He's probably got an Oxford Blue for looking like a dependable rugger bugger type called William.'

'"Rupert"? Never! There was obviously a cock-up with his birth certificate,' said Maddy.

'*And*,' said May, 'he has a wonderful friend with dark eyes, whose name we haven't discovered yet. One of those smouldering animal types.'

Mara's attention came back with a jolt. John Whitaker. It had to be.

'Yes. He probably has to keep a fire extinguisher strapped to his leg in case of spontaneous combustion,' agreed Maddy.

'Is that a fire extinguisher in your pocket, or are you just pleased to see me?' said May. They were both giggling.

'I wonder how old they are?'

Too old for you, thought Mara.

'Rupert's twenty-eight. I just happen to know that,' said May. 'I did some careful angling when his father last came to do a confirmation. "So how old's your son then, Bishop?" I asked subtly. I expect his friend's the same age.'

'Younger. Twenty-six, I'd say. He looks a bit like a workman, though,' said Maddy with a frown. 'He has an ear-ring. Could you marry a man with an ear-ring?'

'Shakespeare had an ear-ring,' said May.

'Shakespeare was a pederast,' said Mara. A slight pause followed this contribution.

'Which Rupert's friend isn't, we devoutly pray and hope,' said May. 'We admire him from afar.'

'Admire, my arse,' said Maddy. 'We lust, my dear, we lust. Our room overlooks the street, so we can hang out of the window and watch the men come and go.'

'Talking of Michelangelo,' added May.

'Ignore her. She's an English student.'

Mara looked at Maddy. She's as tall as I am, only she has coped with it differently, growing an extravagant personality to match.

'And I am a music student,' continued Maddy, and let forth a tremendous arpeggio.

There was an angry thump from the other side of the wall.

'What was that?' asked Maddy and May together.

'The polecat,' said Mara. They looked around in alarm, as though they believed she might well keep one in a box under her desk. 'Next door,' she said, pointing at the wall. 'Whatsisname. The wanker.' They stared at her in astonishment, then laughed long and hard. Mara covered her smile with her hands.

'Shut up!' snarled Maddy, breaking into an impersonation of him. 'Some of us are trying to work, for Christ's sake! Oh, howl, howl. The polecat. I think that's wonderful.'

Their laughter died away as the cathedral bell began tolling for evensong.

'Is that the time?' asked Maddy. 'We'll be late for choir practice. Come along, Poppett.'

'All right, Darling.' Maddy caught Mara's questioning look.

'It's my surname: Darling. You cannot conceive how I have suffered. Isn't it bizarre that we should have ended up sharing a room? Rumour has it that the Principal arranges everyone into an amusing order. There's a whole corridor of men called James and John. But can you *really* imagine the Principal doing anything amusing?' She folded her hands piously. 'Welcome to Jesus College. I trust –'

'Oh, come on,' said May breaking into Maddy's impersonation. They bundled out of the door.

'Come for coffee before lunch tomorrow,' said Maddy sticking her head back into the room. 'It's very important. Bye.'

They rushed off along the corridor. Mara listened to their footsteps thundering down the stairs. Poppett and Darling. She sat at her desk neither reaching for her books, nor tidying away the remains of the tea. The bell called on and on, and outside the sky faded and streetlights flicked awake. From a hidden tree a robin sang. The tolling stopped and the clock chimed five, but she continued to sit, until darkness filled the room, wondering what she had done. Down on the riverbank the robin continued to sing. My friends, Maddy and May. She experimented with the sound. Maddy and May, friends of mine. It won't last.

After dinner Mara roused herself, picked up a file and made her way to the college library. It was empty. Everyone else had better things to do with their evening. The university would be alive with music and talk. All those Freshers' events. She found the book she was looking for and tried to settle down to work. Her thoughts wandered to Maddy and May. Where would they be now? What mischief would they be making? For a moment she wondered whether she was missing out by refusing to attend student parties, but then she pictured the humiliation of trying and failing to fit in. It would be like Primary School all over again. Hanging around on the edges waiting to be picked. Grammar School had been marginally better. At least the other girls had only ignored her, not baited her.

It was ten o'clock by the time she was climbing the stairs back to her room. As she crossed the first landing, a door burst open and a group of young men staggered through, arms round one another's shoulders, bellowing a song. Drunk, thought Mara. She shrank back to let them pass.

'Get stuck into *that*,' said one. Suddenly they were on to her. Her file was knocked from her grasp as they bundled her up against the wall. A hand grubbed around at her crotch. Beery breath in her face, a slobbering mouth. Then just as suddenly they released her, and stood jeering as she scrabbled on the floor for her notes and stumbled off.

She reached her room sick with shame and fear. Oh Jesus – what if they follow me? Keys, keys! A noise made her whirl round. The polecat emerged from the bathroom still doing up his flies. His cold eyes travelled over her.

'What, sweeting, all amort?'

'Fuck off.' But her voice shook. He came and leant on the door frame. She caught a whiff of whisky. Not him too! He was watching as she fumbled at the lock.

'Having difficulty putting it in?' Her face burned. 'Calm down, little one. Deep breath. Just let it slip in – there.' Somehow she got the door open. 'Relaxation,' he drawled. 'Always works for me.' She shut out his loathsome face and stood in the room trembling and trying not to cry.

Why me? What is it about me? She hugged herself to stop the shaking. I'm not even attractive. I must smell like a victim. Men come sniffing round like dogs and piss on me. She longed for a bath to wash their foulness off her, but what if the polecat was still out there with his disgusting, sneering innuendoes and undone flies? She sat at her desk and tried to read. Tears rolled down her cheeks. She told herself she was safe, but it was a long time before she dared try to sleep.

CHAPTER 3

'And how are you settling in, Mara?' The last chime of eleven died away as Mara sat down.

'All right,' she said. Then, catching herself, added, 'Thank you.'

'Tell me what you've managed to read.' It was all so low-key. 'What you've *managed* to read', as if having read anything at all would be admirable in the circumstances. What circumstances? She's looking at me as though my entire family have just been tragically killed. Mara listed the books she had read, outlining her thoughts on what she had discovered.

'Well, that sounds like a good beginning.'

There was a pause, and Mara began to feel that her tutor was allowing the silence, reading her in it, and reflecting on what she read. A strange sensation. Mara was used to observing other people's growing discomfort in the face of her own silence. Dr Jane Roe. She can only be about ten years older than I am. Church historian.

'I wonder why you want to study this subject?' Mara made no reply. 'I read your father's article, by the way. What do you make of it?'

'It's very good,' said Mara lamely. This was the problem. She agreed with his conclusions, and was now haunted by the fear that whatever she wrote people would simply say, 'Well, of course, she would think that. She's Morgan Johns' daughter.'

She was relieved when her tutor went on: 'Will you be examining the role of women in modern sects at all?'

'No.' Ah, just a little too quick, that answer. Dr Roe looked at her questioningly, but after a moment simply nodded. She had read that one, too.

Another silence slowly unfolded. Below, on Palace Green, Mara could hear people talking as they walked. It was so long since she had confided in anyone that she hardly recognized the feeling – an ache, or an impulse to stretch out a hand. She sat still. Her gaze wavered from Dr Roe's eyes and she found herself looking out of the window instead. A bright day. A seagull went gliding past.

'I think . . .' She cleared her throat. Something was pinching at it.

'I think it will help me make sense of . . . certain things. Of what's happened, I mean . . .' 'Certain things.' How stupid it sounded. Better to have said nothing at all. But a hand was gripping at her throat, and she could say no more.

'Good,' said Dr Roe at last.

I must beware of her silence, thought Mara. I of all people should know the power of the taciturn to make others blurt things out. She felt herself harden.

'It may be painful,' Dr Roe continued.

'I'll survive,' Mara said tightly. There was a strange expression on the other woman's face.

'Survive? That doesn't sound very positive.'

Believe me, it is. When you consider the alternative. Suddenly Mara thought, She really cares about me. Quick, say something.

'What do you want me to read?' Her lips felt stiff.

'Now then,' began her tutor. Mara studied her face as her eyes began searching along the shelves. It was a good face. Warm. You could draw it. 'Wesley's *Journal*?' The volumes were handed over. 'What about Quakerism? Do you know anything about the Quakers? Plenty about women there.' Another couple of books. 'And the Welsh Revival? Or is that too modern?' A further book. 'Are you Welsh? Johns is a Welsh name.' It was a question Mara never knew how to answer.

'My father's Welsh.'

'And your mother?'

'English.'

'You sound Welsh sometimes. Just a slight accent.'

Mara blushed. God, it was like having a stammer. You tried to train yourself out of it, but whenever you were tired or nervous or angry, there it was again. Mocked in Wales for sounding English, mocked in England for sounding Welsh.

'Well, carry on with the reading list I gave you.' Mara rose to leave. 'At this stage I think the best thing you can do is read as widely as possible. Don't worry too much yet about finding answers.'

'OK,' said Mara. The two of them stood looking out of the window. A large tree shed a handful of leaves, and people walked across the Green to the old library. Over to the left was the cathedral, with its great door and sanctuary knocker. Dr Roe's hand reached out and touched a bulb suspended in a hyacinth glass.

27

'I grow one every year,' she said. Mara looked at it. 'They never cease to amaze me,' went on her tutor. 'Each year they look so unpromising.' Was this a covert message? But her face showed nothing other than the memory of past hyacinths, the pale roots worming down into the water, then the tip of green beginning to point through the papery layers, reaching up – would it be pink or white? I'll buy one for myself, thought Mara.

'They always make me think of Sunday school,' said Dr Roe. 'The minister would show us one, and say how we could never guess from looking at it what it would be. An illustration of the resurrection, I imagine, though I can't really remember.'

Mara could see the pastor standing there with the bulb in his hand. She was there with all the other children in the chapel near her uncle's farm. A fringe of white hair curled around the man's bald head. She could even repeat what he was saying: 'And so, boys and girls, whenever you see an old dried-up bulb like this one here, I want you to remember the Lord Jesus . . .' She stopped, seeing the look of astonishment on Dr Roe's face. There was a giggle inside her trying to sneak out.

The other woman laughed. 'Surely you didn't suffer from a Chapel upbringing as well!'

'Not really. I stayed with my uncle's family sometimes. In the summer holidays. I went to Sunday school there.' Her throat was closing up again. She felt her hand behind her back playing with the end of her plait, twisting it round and round so that it snaked between her fingers.

'In Wales?'

Mara nodded.

'You took me right back to my childhood,' said Dr Roe. 'If only you knew how many things were supposed to remind me of the Lord Jesus. Pepper pots, weather vanes, soap bubbles . . .'

'Shoes with re-inforced metal toes,' said Mara. It was out before she could stop it.

'Exactly. And I cannot remember in one single case,' said Dr Roe, '*why* they were supposed to remind me of Jesus.'

The two of them looked at one another helplessly, then Mara heard herself giggle. She put her hands to her mouth. Dr Roe joined in. Eventually they lapsed into silence again.

'Would you like some coffee?'

'No thanks.' Mara's refusal was instinctive. She groped around for an explanation. 'I've already arranged to have coffee with friends.'

'With friends.' She really had friends?

'In Jesus?' asked Dr Roe.

'Yes.'

'Good. I'm glad you've found some kindred spirits. Have you met any of the students from Coverdale Hall yet?'

'Not really.' She began to collect her books together. Dr Roe helped her.

'Well, I hope you do. I tutor some of them. I enjoy it. Much though I enjoy teaching undergraduates, too, of course.' This was said with a smile. Was she being ironic about undergraduates? Or was there some specific pleasure involved in teaching these Coverdale students? A sly thought flashed across Mara's mind.

'I've met John Whitaker,' she said. She was intending to test Dr Roe's reaction, but to her consternation a strange feeling stirred in her as she said his name. Dr Roe was watching her instead. I'm blushing, she thought in amazement.

'Ah, Johnny,' said Dr Roe with another smile. 'And have you met Rupert, too?'

'No.' It sounded like a lie. She cast about desperately for something to say. 'I've met James Mowbray. The tutor.' Worse and worse. Now it sounded as though she was trying to cover something up. The silence leered at her.

'Good – I was meaning to suggest you contact James. He'll be an interesting person for you to talk to. You're familiar with his work on mysticism?' Mara's hands were shuffling about in her books. Stop it! They froze.

'We must arrange another time to meet,' said Dr Roe. She suggested a date. They both consulted their diaries. The weeks ahead were blank in Mara's.

'Fine,' Mara said, writing blindly.

'Great. Thank you for coming.'

Mara made for the door.

'Happy reading. Give my love to the boys.'

Mara's hand scrabbled at the knob.

'Just pull.' The door jerked open.

'Goodbye!' called Dr Roe.

'Bye,' muttered Mara, and closed the door. She stood for a moment in the corridor trying to order her thoughts. All this fumbling and blushing is a conditioned reflex, like Pavlov's slavering hounds. And to what? she sneered at herself. To broad shoulders and smouldering brown eyes? She reached the top of the stairwell, but, looking down, stopped. Shit. There in the doorway below, with his back to her, stood John Whitaker. He was talking to someone. Was he about to leave? Go, go! But then, impatient with herself, she began to run down. Her face bore its most contemptuous expression. She was almost past him when he turned abruptly, knocking into her, making her drop her pile of books. She bent swiftly to gather the volumes, her face burning.

'Whitaker!' said a scandalized voice. 'You might help!' and another pair of hands joined her in picking up the books. She glanced up. This must be Rupert. Blond and handsome as a *Boy's Own* hero.

'I apologize for my friend. He has no manners.' With a furious glance Mara seized the books, stood up and strode off. From behind her she heard a laugh.

'Don't worry, Anderson. Neither has she.'

Outside the air was cold on her cheeks. His laugh and voice still sounded in her mind. A northern accent. Pavlov's dogs quivered and leapt as she tried to silence them. This, no doubt, was what people called 'falling in love'. It was as random as being hit by a bus, or falling down a manhole on a dark night, but the mind began at once to find special meanings: Anyone could have fallen down that hole, but it was *I, I* who was walking along the street at that moment. Except in this case she had already heard the falling cries of Maddy and May. 'One of those smouldering animal types . . . We lust, my dear, we lust . . .' She stood still in the street and cast her mind into the future. She felt like someone with a long journey to make and began to walk again. There was no room in her world for men.

'Mara!' called a voice. She looked all around. 'Mara!' it came again, and looking up she saw Maddy and May waving from a window. 'Come on up,' they called.

Oh, God, I don't know if I can stand it. But she had chosen this, letting them into her room the previous day. She sighed and made her way to a door. They're so draining, she thought, climbing the stairs. It was like being mobbed by a thousand butterflies, or listening to a treeful of parrots outsquawking one another. She followed the sounds of laughter until she reached the room.

'We weren't sure you were coming,' said May. It was a typical student room: colourful posters, empty wine bottles, clutter. The smell of drying laundry filled the air from the clothes draped over the radiators. May began to make the coffee.

'We are here,' said Maddy, 'to strike a blow for feminism. Have a Jaffa cake. The thing I like about Jaffa cakes is that you can eat all the chocolate off, then the spongey bit, and leave the orange jelly draped over your finger.'

Mara declined the offer.

'We're conducting an experiment,' explained May. 'We're trying to find out what happens when women shout and whistle at men, rather than vice versa. Behavioural science. There should be quite a stream of them going past when the twelve o'clock lectures end.'

'Show the bastards what it feels like,' said Maddy. 'And possibly strike up an acquaintance with the better-looking ones.'

May handed Mara a mug of coffee. She took it and felt herself drifting away out through the open window and along the street, then up and over the rooftops. Her eye met the impassive stare of a pigeon as it swept past.

'What should we shout, I wonder?' asked May.

'A short roar of approval should be enough to start with,' Maddy said, experimenting.

'We're hoping you can whistle, Mara,' said May.

Mara shrugged dismissively, wheeling round until the river lay below.

'Shame,' said Maddy. 'We could do with a real building-site-type wolf-whistle. What do builders shout?'

They thought for a moment.

'Cheer up, love, it might never happen,' suggested Mara, pausing in her flight for a moment. She had been pursued by this call for years.

'A *little* tame, I fear,' said Maddy. 'Don't worry – I'll think of something when the time comes.'

'But that's precisely what does worry me,' said May.

The three of them sat drinking coffee. I am nothing but a point in the blue, no City, no people, only the air singing on all sides. In another world Maddy and May talked of this and that – concerts, essay crises, men, the approaching college ball – pausing when they heard footsteps and conversation in the street below.

A voice floated up, calling back Mara's attention: 'The upsurge in British chess over the last few years has been a-*ston*ishing.' The words hung like a speech bubble in the room. May and Maddy laughed in delight, and the sound brought Mara spiralling back down into the room again.

31

'What a useful phrase,' said Maddy. 'We must remember it for those awkward moments when conversation fails us.' She went across to the window and looked out. May joined her.

'Thick and fast they came at last,' said May, and from where she was sitting on the bed Mara could hear the sound of more people approaching. Maddy and May leant out of the window, then began calling out coarse compliments to the men passing below. Mara reflected that the people who said vicarage children were always the worst were probably right. Sometimes equivalent replies were hurled back, but generally there was only surprised laughter. This, thought Mara, trying not to smile, is incredibly childish. At last curiosity drew her to the window. 'Thank you, ladies!' called someone. It was as she had imagined. The victims did not wear that look of wincing anticipation or studied nonchalance seen on the faces of women who have to walk past workmen.

'I can't believe it. They're lapping it up!' said Maddy. It's because we pose no threat, thought Mara.

'Look! Here comes Rupert,' exclaimed May. Maddy craned her neck further out while Mara drew back.

'And Johnny Whitaker,' said Maddy. 'We discovered his name, by the way. Could you ever *truly* admire a man called Johnny?' The footsteps drew nearer. 'Contraceptives spring unfortunately to mind at the mention of the name.'

'Or fortunately,' whispered May. 'If you see what I mean.'

'Ah, yes. Take me, take me, Johnny! – talking of which, would you mind putting this on? A timely reminder in the heat of the moment.'

'Ssh!' said May.

By now the men were passing beneath them. An impulse seized Mara. Infected by the puerile atmosphere, she put her fingers in her mouth and let out an ear-splitting whistle. Maddy and May leapt, then squealed with laughter. Both men stepped out into the street and looked up. Mara stood out of sight in the shadows.

'Was that for him, or for me?' That was Johnny speaking. Mara's heart raced.

'Stop playing to the gallery, Whitaker.' Rupert. Just a hint of polite Edinburgh in his accent. She had not noticed it earlier.

'I'm not sure,' said Maddy. 'Well, fish them out, boys, and let's have a look.'

'Maddy!' May was shocked.

There was a laugh from below, then, '*Whitaker!*' Maddy and May shrieked, and the footsteps disappeared off down the street.

'I thought for a minute he was going to!' giggled Maddy. 'He was undoing his belt.'

'Maddy, you're awful!' said May in delight.

In the distance they just caught Rupert's voice saying, 'You're a disgrace, Whitaker.'

There was a long silence.

'The upsurge of British chess,' said Maddy at last, 'has been a-*ston*-ishing.'

'Over the last few years,' agreed May, and the two of them went into whoops. Mara felt herself starting to join in, sitting on the desk swinging her legs.

'Just a minute,' said May, 'you told us you couldn't whistle!' Mara said nothing, just sat where she was on the desk smiling.

'Show me!' pleaded Maddy. 'I've always wanted to be able to wolf-whistle.'

Mara was still refusing to explain some minutes later when there was a knock at the door. Maddy went across to open it, then retreated with a scream.

'Get the knickers off the radiator! It's Johnny Whitaker.'

He came half in, and leant against the edge of the door, hand resting on the top. He looked from one to the other. Mara stopped her legs from swinging. The smile left her face. Then he shook his head and laughed.

'What are you like?' he asked. What was the accent, Mara wondered, waiting for him to speak again. North-east?

Maddy and May looked at one another, baffled. 'What are we *like*?' repeated Maddy. 'Are you asking for a list of synonyms, or was that merely idiomatic?'

'Give me a dictionary, and I'll tell you.'

Mara looked at him sharply. This drew his attention and she turned casually away again. You're only acting the ignoramus, she thought.

'I could never marry a man who didn't know what an idiom was,' said Maddy. 'Could you, May?'

'I might have an affair with one,' said May after a moment's consideration.

'Sorry, girls – can't help you. I'm celibate.'

33

Mara stared. You're joking. He had *legover* practically tattooed across his chest.

'Oh, no!' said Maddy and May together.

'Oh, yes.'

There was a pause. He's serious, thought Mara in amazement, flicking her eyes away as she sensed he was about to look at her.

'Celibate? Why? Not permanently, surely?' asked May.

'Not now you've met us,' said Maddy.

But he would only smile.

'Isn't that rather like losing your driving licence and then being given a new Porsche?' persisted Maddy.

'Well,' he said, 'or a new JCB.' For an instant Maddy was open-mouthed in disbelief at being outdone by a man who didn't know what a synonym was. But the moment passed.

'*Whitaker!*' she rapped out in fine Andersonian manner.

Johnny laughed and asked her name.

'I'm Maddy, this is May, and this is Mara.'

'Maddy and May. Mara I've already met.'

The other two rounded on Mara accusingly.

So what? said her expression.

'We met before term started,' said Johnny. 'Then I ran into her in the Divinity School this morning.'

Mara looked at her watch, and this – as she had hoped – prompted May to say, 'Lunch.'

Maddy turned to Johnny. 'So glad you could call,' she said graciously.

'It's a pleasure to know you,' he replied in kind.

'It's a pleasure to be known,' she said. 'Even if not in the biblical sense.'

'Though that, too, no doubt . . .' May let the sentence trail like a discarded silk stocking.

'We may never know,' he said affably.

Mara found herself wondering why he allowed himself to be the target for this kind of witticism. Was he enjoying it? She picked up her books, and they all began to leave the room. 'Come and see us again,' the others were saying. 'And bring Rupert.' I'm not free any more, she thought, I am bound up in Maddy and May, and they will bring me in contact with others whether I like it or not.

Mara was out running a mile or so from the City, following the path as it wound through the woods. She was trying to regain her sense of perspective, her broad horizon. People were crowding too close and she could not focus on them with the cool detachment she usually enjoyed. Voices still clamoured in her mind, memories jostling as she ran, like a pocketful of pebbles. Rupert's face as she grabbed her books from him, and then Johnny saying, 'Sorry, girls – I'm celibate.' Well, that solved that problem. Not that it had ever been a problem. She thrust the thought of him to one side.

Occasionally she met other runners coming the other way, but mostly she was alone, hearing only the sound of her feet through the fallen leaves, or on the path, her breath coming and going – three paces in, three paces out, in, out, in, out. A blackbird started up out of the undergrowth pinking angrily. On and on she ran to see where the path went. *Rejoicing as a strong man to run a race.* She laughed in the silent wood. A Bible verse for every occasion. I must know thousands.

She was in her stride now, running easily. The path now led her up a steep incline, and she ran on without slackening her speed. It hurts, she thought, as each breath became shorter. Why do I do this? 'Pace yourselves, girls!' called the voice of her PE mistress. Cross country. Thirty girls setting off, winter-white legs, navy knife-pleated skirts. I was always first, she thought, panting. And I was always sick afterwards. Halfway. 'Dewi, Dewi, wait for me!' That's where I learnt to run. Chasing after my cousin. Three-quarters. I'm slowing. He was four years older than me and I loved him fiercely. But he didn't want a six-year-old girl with him. His friends jeered. 'You can play with us if you can keep up.' And off they went on their bikes. With me – pant, pant – running behind. A mile, two miles. Maybe three. Tears streaming down my face. Sometimes I never caught them. Sometimes they simply set off again. The top. She stumbled on.

The woods opened out into a field and there in the distance was the City with the cathedral standing guard over it. The sight of it made her stop. Her breath came in huge gasps. Even up here I can hear the bells. They chimed, remote and quiet in the distance. Three o'clock. A slight wind touched her burning face. Two crows were walking in the field and the sun shone off them as though their feathers were made of black glass. She tried to see Dewi's face. All she saw was his photograph. Where is he now? Not a month went past without her asking that, or dreaming that she had found him at last. She began to run again. His bones might lie in some shallow grave, for all she knew, with crows walking back and forth over his head. The family view was that he had probably gone to Australia. He had never written. But he wouldn't. Mara brought out another picture: Dewi on a sheep station. She had drawn it to comfort herself. But her memories were worn to threads. He was gone. Why can't I accept that? Why must there be an explanation for everything?

She crossed over a road and ran down to the old bridge across the river. When she reached the parapet, she stopped and looked over. A glassy cathedral hung upside down in the water, then fell into a million dancing shards as a boat passed. Slowly it gathered itself again. Walking now to catch her breath, she set off up the road to the college.

As she rounded the corner, she saw Dr Mowbray disappearing into Coverdale Hall and the sight jolted a missing memory into place. 'Does your father still have his legendary violent temper?' How could she have forgotten that? It was so extraordinary. Did that mean he had not always been as he was now – cold, reserved? She heard his biting voice telling her 'Control your temper' when she was in some childish rage. But 'he was always so passionate about everything'. This would require a lot of thought. She began walking and, as though it were an important form that must be filled in carefully, she set the idea to one side in some safe place or other and forgot it again.

CHAPTER 4

It was Saturday morning. Behind her open curtains Mara was already at her desk working. Another bad night. As she made herself some coffee, she felt as tired as if she had not slept at all. Her face stared at her from the kettle. The curved steel distorted her reflection. Staring eyes, pale hollowed-out face, black brows and hair. She moved her head until her reflection seemed to be all eyes. Her father's eyes. That was what everyone said: 'She has her father's eyes.' But Mara had always wanted blue eyes, like Hester; to be pretty, like Hester. 'They don't look very alike, for twins,' was the other thing people said. Mara had known how to interpret that from the age of about two and a half. She moved again and her face returned to normal. Just tired, with dark circles under the eyes.

All around the City leaves broke from the trees and fell. Crews moved on the river, and in the marketplace stalls went up one by one. Here and there curtains in college windows opened to reveal pale faces wincing in the sun, wishing they had not drunk so much the previous night. Across the street the Canon – back from mattins – filled his kettle. Toast was cooking in the basements where the college had its kitchens, and the smell crept up in the autumn air until it began to steal into the room where Mara was working. Breakfast, she thought, and left her books.

As she climbed the stairs again some time later, she met the polecat going down. He gave her a look of glassy-eyed contempt, which she returned with a sneer. They said nothing as they passed one another. The wall between their rooms was thin, and from time to time she had heard him swearing articulately and profanely against his background of high-brow church music. He had not deigned to speak to her since that horrible drunken encounter in the corridor. For days she had feared some kind of repetition, or of running into the group of gropers again, but nothing had happened. Gradually her anxiety faded and she began to observe the polecat more closely. He was the first attractive man she had met who did not make it his business to charm the birds off the trees. She returned to her desk, but as she reached for her book, a thought crossed her mind. Her hand hovered

37

over the page. His look – was it his natural expression, or was he imitating her? She ran the scene again mentally, and, at the moment of their passing one another, thought she saw a glint of amusement on his face.

She was still at her desk some two hours later when there came loud rapping on her door. She went and let Maddy and May in.

'We've come to ask you if you want to come on a bar crawl with us tonight,' said Maddy. 'We intend to persuade Wupert and St John the Divine to join us.' Here Maddy swooned on to Mara's bed.

'They won't come,' said May, trying on Mara's hat and looking at herself in the mirror. It was clear from her tone that this was an old argument. 'They'll have sermons to prepare, or something.' She waltzed over to the window.

'Well, I, for one, rate my charms higher than the attractions of sermon writing,' said Maddy. 'Just think how starved they are of female company.'

'There are women in Coverdale Hall,' said May.

'Yes, but what *sort* of women? Ask yourself. Have you ever met a woman training for the ministry who didn't look like a warden in a Nazi concentration camp? They all have moustaches and no dress sense. And they all have some unfortunate characteristic entirely of their own. My father had a deaconess once who used to clear her throat like this' – a demonstration – 'like a seagull swallowing a marble. And they are *all* dull. Dull, dull, dull.'

'So are nine-tenths of the men,' said May, as she tipped the hat forward over her eyes.

Mara felt a knot of cold hatred for Maddy, who at that moment turned to look at her. Maddy seemed to read the expression, for at once her tone became placating: 'I know, but one expects it of men, somehow. We should make every allowance for women clergy, I suppose. They only have men as role models, the poor things. No wonder they're boring.'

Mara looked away, out of the window, but Maddy went on: 'Oh dear – what dreadful things I say! It's because I think and speak simultaneously. Most people have a mental sieve to filter out the unspeakable from the speakable, but I was born without one. The obstetrician who delivered me said it was the worst case he'd ever known.'

Something in her tone made Mara turn back and look at her again. Maddy's face seemed as if it might at any moment tremble, and Mara realized in amazement that despite her crowing self-confidence, Maddy longed desperately for approval. With one cold look she had punctured Maddy as surely as if she had stabbed her with a needle. There was a silence, and in the end Mara tried a tentative smile. It was answered at once with a relieved grin. Maddy began talking again about her plans for the evening, although some of her usual boisterousness had gone.

'And so you'll come, then, Mara?' asked Maddy.

Mara shook her head. At once she read Maddy's thought balloon: *She doesn't really like me.*

'Please,' persisted Maddy, 'you've got to come. Our names sound so good together – Maddy and Mara and May. Like something out of Enid Blyton.'

'"A Night on the Tiles with the Three M's",' suggested May.

'"The Three M's and the Amazing Piss-up",' said Maddy.

'What about your surnames?' asked Mara, who could not be bothered to think of a title. 'I don't fit in there.'

'Ah, yes,' said May, 'but what about your nickname?' She tossed the hat with a spinning motion on to the chest of drawers. Mara gave her a look.

'Rupert and Johnny call you Mara Sweetie,' said Maddy.

They were watching for her reaction. She raised a disbelieving eyebrow. There could be few epithets she was less likely to attract.

'I'm still not coming,' she said. At length she managed to convince them, and they left her to her work, with instructions that she must join them if she changed her mind.

After they had gone Mara read for another half-hour about the lives of various women fanatics of previous generations. Fragments of Maddy's and May's conversation kept intruding. *'Rupert and Johnny call you Mara Sweetie.'* She had to admit to a pathetic flutter at the thought, and repeated her vow that she would never descend to Maddy's and May's level. They were pursuing the two men blatantly and relentlessly. Mara frequently caught snatches of facetious banter between the four of them and, knowing she would be unable to join in, she had tried to remain aloof. On one occasion she walked into Maddy's and May's room before she realized the men were there too. Rupert rose to his feet instantly. Johnny remained sprawled in a chair until a hiss from Rupert appeared to rouse him. He got up with a grin.

'Sorry. He's training me up to be middle class.'

'It's not a class issue, Whitaker,' snapped Rupert. 'It's a question of common courtesy.'

Mara withdrew at once.

'Don't worry,' she heard May saying as she hurried back down the stairs. 'She's always like that.' Mara paused to see if there would be a response.

'Actually, she's really a serial killer,' Maddy's voice said. 'But they've got it controlled by drugs. The college is helping rehabilitate her.' There was general laughter and Mara slipped away.

She sat and rattled her pencil against her desk edge, still thinking about Rupert and Johnny. What had drawn two such very different men to the same vocation at the same time? Why were they friends?

Maybe they needed one another. Certainly Rupert, left to his own devices, would soon become insufferably pompous. A perfect cleric, in fact. Whereas Johnny – she stopped, realizing she was getting dangerously close to daydreaming about the pair of them. Mara Sweetie, Mara Sweetie. She shook her head briskly and bent over her book again.

When the clock struck eleven, she picked up her hat and cloak and went out. She made her way down the cobbled street past the windows and doorways of Coverdale Hall, conscientiously not glancing in. When she reached the old bridge, she turned right and began to walk along the path beside the river, which led to the town centre, where she had some shopping to do. The wooded bank rose steeply, and from above the topmost branches the cathedral towers looked down. Leaves fell in ones and twos as she passed, and the air was tinged with the smell of smoke and decay.

Before long she came to the weir and stood watching the river folding over the ledge and falling into the white water below. Branches and tree trunks were caught here, carried downstream in some storm. Above the weir the water was calm, reflecting the arch of the bridge into a full circle in the river. You could almost walk on it, thought Mara. The sky and the clouds would lie under your feet as you went by. Jemima Wilkinson had claimed she could walk on water. Mara had just been reading about her. She had gathered a circle of devotees around her in the eighteenth century, and at some stage had promised to demonstrate her high calling by a miracle. One night they gathered at the lake's edge. 'There she goes,' the disciples would cry, watching the pale figure crossing the lake. 'Praises be to the Most High! This is the One of whom the Scriptures prophesied – the woman clothed with the sun with the moon under her feet!' But it had not been like that. Jemima had brought them to the water's edge and asked if they believed she had the power to walk on water. 'Yes, yes!' they chorused. 'In that case,' she replied, 'your faith has no need of a demonstration.' Mara smiled.

A real fanatic would have plunged into the inky waters and drowned, believing to the last watery gasp that God would intervene and fulfil his promise. Such people were the Chosen Ones, raised up by God to perform mighty acts, to proclaim mysteries, to gather the one true Church before the close of the age. Reason and common sense could gain no purchase on their minds. Mara knew this from bitter experience, from hours of arguing with her sister and trying to persuade her to leave the sect. A waste of breath. No matter how strange the thing which God commanded, he was to be obeyed. Who could question his wisdom? It was unsearchable. 'As the heavens are higher than the earth, so much higher are my ways than your ways, and my thoughts than your thoughts,' saith the Lord. In fact, the more bizarre the command, the better, for this proved that it was God speaking.

Maybe fanaticism was like being desperately in love. The sense of being special, chosen, the moving of mountains for the beloved. By now Mara had reached the steps which led up to the next bridge. She began to climb and, as if by word association, she found herself thinking of Johnny again. He would make a highly successful prophet, drawing off a group of bewitched women. She could picture them following him through the streets of the City, squeaking with excitement, like the rats scampering after the Pied Piper. Then she shook her head, realizing that she was trying in some way to protect herself by ridiculing him. She had been aware of this before, knowing that her expression whenever she happened to pass him in the street or in a corridor was one of aloof contempt. His expression was harder to analyse, and she was not entirely satisfied with it. It seemed bland and courteous, but sometimes she suspected that he had only just removed the smile from his face.

The marketplace was busy. She passed the stalls selling fruit and flowers, cheap clothing, toys and shoes. The far end was overshadowed by a church. Young people lounged around the monument that stood in the paved area, and pigeons dabbed this way and that in the sunshine, hoping for crusts.

Mara was watching idly when her attention was caught by the

sight of a girl standing alone in the middle of the square. She had long fair hair partly covered by a headscarf and her head was bowed as though she were studying the ground in front of her. Then she looked up. Her lips began to move. From where she was standing Mara could not hear what she was saying, but she saw how the people passing glanced and paused, then walked on again. Some of the youths under the monument called out. To be speaking to no one – the girl must be unbalanced. There were looks of embarrassment on the faces of the passers-by. Perhaps someone would come and take her kindly by the arm and lead her off.

Mara was about to turn away when she noticed that the girl was holding a black book. A Bible. She was preaching. For an instant the marketplace stood still as if it were carved in crystal, then a sound of hissing filled Mara's head and she turned and ran. Off up another street she went, passing through the crowds of shoppers, back towards the college. As she climbed the steps to her room she remembered what she had gone out to buy. A hyacinth bulb. She could almost have wept.

No one could fault Mara's determination. These words had appeared in one of her school reports; implying, of course, that practically everything else about her could be faulted. After lunch she had read doggedly about medieval mysticism until well into the evening, forgetting to go for tea as she strove to stifle the fears of the morning. By the time the clock was striking half past seven she felt secure enough to put down her book.

She yawned and stretched, and tentatively let her mind return to the image of the girl in the marketplace. It had been like one of those occasions when a smell – flowering currant, creosote in the sunshine – rockets you straight back to childhood. The sight of a girl preaching in a marketplace had been like a box of snakes bursting open. All those feelings of suffocation, of loathing, of rage, had come writhing out of her memory, and for a moment she might have gone back three years and been standing once again in the Church of the Revelation, with the praying hands reaching to touch her and cast out the demons of pride and rebellion. Those hands. Clutching, pressing. She had never been able to bear being held and restrained. 'We command the spirit of pride to come out of Mara in Jesus' name!' shouted a voice in her memory. And she had wept, trying desperately to believe it was true. Here at last was the reason for all her unhappiness. She could be exorcized and free. The hands pressed. The voices claimed the victory.

Mara spat at their memory and reached for her book and pencil. Rapidly a snake formed on the page, then another. As she drew, she became absorbed in the pattern of twisting forms as they wove themselves into a circle. When the drawing was complete, she found she was quite pleased with it. It was rather beautiful, in fact; like a crown. She flipped back in the book to look at the circle she had drawn earlier, with the Joker and the morris men. The two pictures seemed to belong together. Maybe this is what I am trying to do, she thought, to 'make sense of certain things', as she had mumbled to Dr Roe.

The thought of Dr Roe prompted another memory: 'A good face. You could draw it.' On a fresh page her pencil made a couple of sketching motions without touching the paper. She hadn't attempted a portrait for years. Caricatures were easy. She could do half a dozen now without hesitating – the polecat holding up *The Times*, Maddy and May bawling obscenities out of the window. Or Rupert, in an illustration from a boys' adventure story. The caption: *Rupert helped the strange young woman pick up her books.* Or Johnny piping through the streets followed by rat-women. If it could be done out of a sense of mischief, like Maddy's impersonations, then she might let her pencil scribble freely. But my talent springs from cruelty, she thought. She flung the book aside and realized she was impatient for some activity. Maybe she should have gone out with Maddy and May. Well, she decided, picking up her purse and leaving the room, I'll go and have a drink and see if they roll up.

She made her way down the cellar steps to the bar. It was still almost empty. The room would fill up as the evening wore on, but at that moment there was only a small group of Coverdale students sitting around a table in the corner. Mara could hear them deep in discussion about the authority of Scripture as she ordered her drink. She paid the barman and went to sit down where she could see the whole room and both entrances. Her habitual expression of disdain settled on her features. The conversation on the other side of the room went on.

'The problem with him is that he doesn't expound the text,' said a voice bossily. Mara glanced across, thinking for a moment that it was Rupert speaking. It was another of his kind. Coverdale seemed to be full of them, all wearing waxed jackets and springing to their brogued feet when a woman entered the room. Good families, good schools and – above all – good, sound evangelical principles. They had the Gospel sewn up: God's Creation, Man's Sin, God's Remedy, Man's Response. Women were gallantly sheltered under the generic umbrella. Mara smiled guiltily, remembering her condemnation of Maddy and her dull deaconesses. I'm no better than she is. Theological colleges obviously attracted recognizable types. And Johnny Whitaker was Coverdale's token rebel. She had been amused the previous day to hear someone saying, 'I've locked my keys in my boot. Has anyone seen Whitaker?'

She turned her thoughts away from him with an effort, and began listening to the Coverdale students. They were now talking about parishes. Final-year students, obviously. The infamous Curacy File had appeared in the college library and she had seen several different people leafing through it and making notes in their attempt to find a suitable (or at least bearable) parish to serve their title in.

'I'm off to Leeds this weekend,' someone was saying. 'It sounds a bit charismatic, but I'll have to look at it.'

'Hasn't Simon already been there?'

'Yes, but he turned it down,' said the bossy one. 'His wife didn't like the kitchen.' Good God, thought Mara. Get your priorities sorted out. Foxes have holes, the birds of the air have nests, but *Simon's wife doesn't like the kitchen.*

'Oh, that's not fair, Hugh!' protested one of the others.

'I'm looking at a parish in Sunderland,' said another gloomily. 'But I'm not sure I want to be that far north. All my family's in Hertfordshire and London.' The rest murmured sympathetically. 'Can one live without culture for three years? That's the question.'

'That's the cost of ministry, brother,' replied Hugh.

'Says the man who's going to Kensington.'

They were treating it light-heartedly, but Mara wondered whether a real fear of the north lay behind their laughter. She had seen a map of the country on one of the Coverdale noticeboards, with little pins showing where last year's leavers were serving. Most of them were south of Birmingham.

'Rupert's sorted out, I hear.' Mara grinned into her drink. An apt summing-up. Rupert was more sorted out than anyone she had ever met. His mission was to sort out everyone else, too.

'The old boy network,' said the Sunderland man cynically.

'Nonsense!' chorused the rest of the group, and dissolved into

44

laughter. Clearly a recognized Anderson catch-phrase. The talk broke up into several separate conversations and Mara stopped trying to follow it. She began to conjure up her inner moorland world.

Her attention was called back by the sound of feet coming down the steps. Johnny Whitaker entered the bar. Mara felt herself blushing.

'Ha'away, John!' called the other Coverdale students. He raised a hand. Mara had noticed that he was always greeted by this cry. Being mimicked still reduced her to psychotic rage, but he never seemed to care. He was the target of a great deal of undergraduate wit, which he always bore good-naturedly.

She noted with satisfaction that he had obviously resisted the gauntlet Maddy and May had thrown down to his celibacy. He was standing at the bar with his back to her, chatting to the barman. Suddenly she found herself thinking, I'd draw you in a hard hat halfway up some scaffolding. Why? she wondered, frowning. The image had been so crisp, she felt that she must have heard something to make her think that. Maddy saying he looked like a workman? Maybe – ah! she pounced on the thought. She had seen a builders' sign. Something Whitaker and Sons. That was it. Her face cleared. Then to her dismay she saw that a mirror ran the full length of the wall behind the bar. He had been watching her all the time. She looked away, feeling her colour rising again. He had caught her without her sarcastic mask on, half in and half out of her invisible cloak. She studied the table where her glass stood. He was paying for his drink and walking across the room. He would go past her and join the other Coverdale students and talk God with them. She sat watching the scratches in the varnish and saw – oh no – his drink join hers on the table. He sat beside her. She looked up, snapping her sneer into place.

'You all right?' Did she look ill, or something?

'Yes.' Her tone was aggressive.

He smiled at her. 'Just another little idiom,' he said. 'It's my way of saying "How *are* you?"' It could have been Rupert's voice. He was a better mimic than Maddy, even.

She looked down into her drink and muttered, 'I'm OK.'

'Where are your friends tonight?' Hah. The cowards hadn't even asked him.

'Out.' There was silence. He drank from his pint.

'Out?' The conversation at the other table went on. His easy manner was beginning to make her feel clumsy rather than aloof. Better to appear friendly and at ease. But how? She had never been able to make idle small talk.

'They're out in the town somewhere.'

'Out in the town somewhere?'

She glanced at him. Was he mocking her? Well, sod you, she thought, and picked up her drink. I'm sure you'd rather they were here, but I've spent too much of my life saying where my beautiful twin is. I'm not going to tell you where my wonderful friends are.

He seemed unabashed. 'How's the work going, sweetie?'

She rounded on him, eyes narrowed.

He struck his forehead. 'Sorry. That's meant to be patronizing, isn't it? I'm in trouble the whole time in Coverdale for doing that. How's the work going, Mara?'

'Fine,' she said, wondering if he could really be as ingenuous as he seemed.

'What are you studying, exactly?'

'Women and religious fanaticism.' This fell by chance into a general silence, and took on a pompous ring. The attention of the whole bar seemed focused on her words.

'Go on,' he prompted. She glanced at him cautiously and looked away again. There was nothing in his tone or his expression to indicate that this was not genuine interest. Her hand found the end of her plait.

'Well, I'm looking at the part played by women in fanatical religious sects.' I've just said the same thing in different words, she thought in despair. She forced her mind into the words she needed, picking up tiny beads with gloves on the wrong hands. 'I'm looking at the difference between being devout and being a fanatic. It's a fine line. And at what draws women to that kind of religion.' She looked into his face, expecting to catch his eyes roaming around for someone more interesting to talk to. They were fixed on hers. She felt a shock, as though she had peered through a dark window only to see someone staring out at her. Her hand began to twist her hair.

'Why women?'

'Because there are so many of them in that kind of sect.'

'But there are more women than men in ordinary churches,' he said. 'Are women just more religious than men?'

She shrugged and waited for him to answer his own question. Most men did, telling her what she meant, what she was trying to say. But he was looking at her steadily. What's the matter with you? she asked herself. There is such a thing as simple friendliness, even if you never practise it yourself.

'It's a question of power,' she said eventually. 'In a sect like that you can be a prophet, a leader. The mother of God even. The dispossessed are bound to be attracted. Women, the poor, social outcasts – suddenly they can be significant.' And hesitantly she began to explain what she was studying, checking his face at every sentence for signs of mockery and boredom. She saw none, and gradually she began to unbend, until his promptings were hardly needed to keep her speaking. At length she had nothing more to add.

'Another drink, flower? Sorry – Mara.'

She nodded, and he crossed to the bar. She watched him as he stood waiting to be served, and he caught her eye in the mirror and winked. This time she smiled back, not asking herself why terms of endearment were so much more acceptable in his beautiful north-eastern accent than in received pronunciation.

He returned to the table and sat down. They both drank and then sat for a moment in silence. Mara was beginning to wonder what they might talk about next – perhaps she could ask him what he had done before starting at Coverdale Hall? – when Rupert arrived. He bought himself a drink and joined them, looking at Johnny inquiringly for an introduction.

'This is Mara.' There was something in his smile as he spoke which brought her suspicion bounding back. 'And this is my good friend Rupert Anderson.'

Rupert stretched out his hand to shake hers, but she merely made a slight gesture with the glass she was holding. He withdrew his hand. The caption read: *She was the rudest young woman Rupert had ever met.* There was a taut silence, while Rupert's good manners adjusted themselves.

'Is Mara a Welsh name?' he asked.

She glanced at him contemptuously.

'"Call me Mara, for the Almighty has dealt bitterly with me,"' said Johnny. Mara jumped, surprised he knew the words. 'It's in the Bible, man.' Rupert gave him a long hard look.

'Is he making that up?' he asked Mara. She said nothing.

'Mara's doing some research on women and religious fanaticism,' said Johnny. She caught a look going between them which she had not been intended to see. The bastards are both laughing at me.

'Not women,' protested Rupert. 'Why is everyone studying women at the moment? What about men? You're not a feminist, are you?' This was asked with mock alarm, mitigated, Mara was supposed to think, by his smile.

'Yes.'

'You are?'

She stared at him offensively, knowing he was trying to charm her into being as pleasant as a young woman talking to two good-looking men ought to be. 'But why? I have never been able to understand it. What makes an intelligent, and, if I may say so, attractive young woman like yourself become a feminist?'

'Pricks like you, mostly,' she replied.

For a moment it seemed as though he had not heard her properly. He turned to Johnny in disbelief, then back to her again. *Rupert had never been so insulted in his life.*

'But – look, I'm sorry, you're going to have to explain that remark.' He was no longer smiling.

She shrugged.

'No, no. Come along, I'm afraid that's not good enough. If you're going to dish out insults like that, I think I'm entitled to an explanation.' Perhaps he had been a teacher? She drank some of her drink. 'Well?'

'How much feminist literature have you actually read?' she asked.

'I think I have a fair grasp of feminist principles,' he said after a slight pause.

'Yes?'

'Yes. Stop laughing, Whitaker,' and he began with great confidence to outline what he thought they were. No, not a teacher: a barrister. She watched him dispassionately as his arguments got flimsier. He stopped before he was really floundering and held up his hands in surrender. 'All right. Tell me about feminism,' he said with his charming smile once more in place.

'Read about it.' She stood up, thanked Johnny for the drink, and walked off. Being an unpleasant young woman, however, she did not leave the bar completely, but waited at the top of the stairs to hear what they would say.

Rupert's voice carried up to her with wonderful clarity: 'Good God. What a dreadful girl! That was like being savaged by a clam.'

They both began to laugh.

'Serves you right,' came Johnny's voice.

'What did I do? I have never in my life – I suppose she was eating out of your hand before I arrived?'

'Of course. You think I'm a rookie, or something?'

Mara's face burned. Then she jumped as someone opened the door to come down the steps.

'Whitaker, you're *supposed* to be an ordinand,' she heard Rupert say as she stepped out into the corridor. 'You can't seduce every lame duck you come across just because it's a challenge.'

'Seduce? Me?' More laughter, then the door swung shut on the students going down to the bar.

For a moment she was unable to move, then she walked to a door which led out on to the terrace behind the college. She stepped out into the night and stood motionless. The stars looked down, remote and unfeeling, from above the rooftops.

CHAPTER 5

Several days later Mara was searching along the shelves in the basement of the library on Palace Green. The librarian had given her a key and allowed her to wander freely among the outsize and old books. The room was completely silent, apart from the buzzing of a strip light. She was all alone. You could go mad down here. Maybe she would pull a volume off a shelf and see a manic eye gleaming through on the other side.

Her eyes wandered along the book spines, and she craned her neck this way and that. If she ruled the world, then a law would be passed which compelled publishers to print all book titles one way: either up or down the spine. She reached an old folio volume, and intrigued, pulled it from the shelf. *The Memorable Works of a Son of Thunder and Consolation.* It appeared to be the collected writings of an early Quaker. She opened it at random, and read:

This is the day of thy visitation, O Nation, wherein the Lord speaks to thee by the mouth of his servants in word and writing . . . The Lord will overturn, overturn the nation, and will create new heavens and new earth . . . and by his sword will the Lord plead with all flesh, and the slain of him will be many . . . the fire is kindled and the sword is drawn . . .

She closed the volume, and hugged it. Here was raw fanaticism, the fiery vision of the end of the age. *The fire is kindled and the sword is drawn.* The writer was long dead, buried perhaps in some steep Quaker burial ground under the bowing grass. She looked at the crumbling calfskin binding and the browned pages. What would the writer have felt if he could have known that some three hundred years later she would be there studying his tracts as part of a research project? She tried to cast her mind forward three centuries and imagine students examining the delicate leaves of ancient twentieth-century works. But we will probably have blown ourselves out of existence by then, she thought. It struck her suddenly that this idea was not too distant from the early Quaker vision. Perhaps each generation believed in a catastrophic end. She saw a section of her thesis unfolding: *This phenomenon may account in part for the recurring appeal of the Book of Revelation in the lives of religious sects . . .*

She went down the lane beside the Divinity School and turned along the road back to college. A pigeon hobbled along a low wall. Mara stopped to watch its progress. The pigeon stopped too and seemed to mistrust her, for it took off and disappeared on to a roof. An unpleasant memory stirred as she began walking again. *Lame duck.* Her eyes narrowed. To be regarded as strange, or nasty even, was one thing. But to be dismissed as a lame duck . . . She had gone back to this conversation repeatedly. It was not Rupert's words that really tormented her though, for who gave a fish's tit what Rupert Anderson thought or said? But Johnny Whitaker. That smug bastard. He'd been listening to her with such seeming attention while all the time thinking, A sad little person, but I'll soon have her eating out of my hand. Hah!

Her mind was buzzing so angrily as she walked that she was not aware that someone was falling into step beside her until she heard a voice saying, 'Psst!'

She turned. It was Rupert, and he received the full blast of her ill humour. He seemed not to notice, and held open his overcoat as though he were offering her stolen watches or dirty postcards. In the inside pocket she saw a well-known feminist text. For an instant her scowl wavered, but she clamped it firmly back in place and turned away.

'Would you like to come for a walk?' She looked at him in surprise, and he made a walking motion with his fingers in the air, as if to clarify the suggestion. 'Down to the river?'

She was so taken aback that she nodded. They continued down the road in silence. After about twenty yards Mara began to wonder whether he wanted to say something, or whether they would prom-enade solemnly to the bridge and back without uttering a word. She pictured him giving her a slight formal bow and retreating into Coverdale Hall. The caption: *Rupert remained unerringly polite, despite the girl's rudeness.* But at this point he spoke.

'Tell me, why are you so silent?' She flicked him a glance, but said nothing. 'Some people say you're shy, but I doubt that.' She still made no reply. 'I've come to the conclusion that you do it deliber-ately. It's a pose.' They walked on. 'You want people to look at you and ask, "Who is that beautiful, silent woman? Why is she so angry? Why is she so mysterious?"'

'Wrong,' she said. But her mind winced.

'Then why?'

'Conscientious objection.'

'To what? To speaking? Nonsense.' His self-assurance irritated her.

'Language distorts things.'

'That depends on your view of the function of language,' he said. By now they were nearing the bridge. 'If you assume that its primary purpose is to express truth, then I take your point. But it isn't. Its job is communication, the establishing of relationships. If I say to you, "Lovely weather," who cares what the weather is actually like? It's not intended as a statement of fact. I'm trying to establish contact with you. Human beings are social creatures, you know.'

She burned against him, too outraged for a moment to respond. But . . . but . . . stuttered her mind. Don't preach sociolinguistics to me, dickbrain. For all his fine words about *communication* he was using language to express truth. *His* truth, the truth that he was a man and therefore right, and that she was only a woman and by definition speaking nonsense. This was her main objection to language: that it was a means of domination, a tool in the hands of the privileged. But suddenly her indignation eluded her. Perhaps they were both speaking different types of nonsense? *Rupert enjoyed a good argument.* She felt a fleeting impulse to hit him with the book she was holding, to do physically what he was doing verbally.

Instead she said: 'I'd rather be left alone.' They stopped in the middle of the bridge. He looked as stunned as if she actually had hit him, and when he made no answer, her words began to sound brutal to her. She rested the heavy book on the parapet. A college crew went under the bridge. Well, it's true, she thought.

'I'm sure there are times when we'd all rather be left alone,' he said in the end. 'But that's not an option for a Christian.'

'I'm not a Christian,' she said. In some alleyway of her mind she heard St Peter's cock crowing. The cathedral clock struck one. She looked at Rupert. He was leaning back against the bridge looking up at the sky. At last he turned to her again.

'Look, Mara . . .' he began, then broke off. He passed his hand over his face, then seemed to study the ground intently, apparently at a loss for words. She watched him with interest, wondering what he could be about to say. 'I don't think this has ever happened to me before. I can't remember being disliked on sight like this.' He spoke, heedless of the fact that she might mock. 'I can see that I'm offending you at every turn, and I don't know what to do. If you'd really rather I left you alone, then I will.'

In a flash of self-knowledge Mara realized that for some perverse reason she had been punishing him because she was attracted to his friend.

How could she make amends? Quickly. He was about to execute his slight, formal bow and vanish.

'I don't want you to leave me alone,' she blurted out. Her ungracious tone was so much at odds with her words that he stood irresolute. Either this package was a birthday present, he seemed to be thinking, or it was a letter bomb. A mistake at this point might cost him an arm.

'Well, OK,' he said cautiously. 'If you're sure you don't mind having a prick like me for a friend.'

She scowled. 'Look, I'm sorry I said that.' Well, the tone left room for improvement, but it was an apology.

He took another tentative step. 'Well, I'm told I asked for it.' This was magnanimous, and on impulse Mara put out her hand. For a moment he seemed not to understand, then he shook hands at arm's length with a flashing smile, as though he were a lion-tamer fending her off with a chair. The thought brought a smile to her lips. His own smile relaxed into something more natural.

'You know, if you did that more often, people wouldn't be scared of you, Mara.' Exactly, she thought.

They began to walk slowly back towards the college. Mara started to feel that some of the responsibility for making conversation now fell to her. This was one of the uncomfortable implications of friendship. 'The upsurge of British chess over the last few years has been astonishing.' In the end she remembered the question she had almost asked Johnny.

'What were you doing before you started your training for the ministry?'

'I worked for a law firm in London.'

Coverdale Hall was in sight now. A few more sentences would see them safely there.

'Doing what?'

'I was a solicitor.'

Not a barrister, then. I was close, though. She bent her head forwards over the book to hide her smile, but not quickly enough.

'And what's so funny about that?'

'Nothing.' She managed to look serious. 'I'm sure you were very good at it.' They were standing in front of the main entrance to Coverdale Hall. *Rupert gave the girl an old-fashioned look.* Then he said goodbye, and with his hint of a bow, disappeared into the building. Mara walked on without troubling to hide her amusement.

When she arrived in Jesus College for lunch a few moments later, she found a parcel from her mother waiting for her. It sat beside her on the bench with the large book throughout the meal, and she wondered what it contained. It was not her birthday until May. At least there would be a letter, she hoped. Her mother was an entertaining correspondent.

As soon as she was in her room she began pulling the paper apart. Although she had formed no idea at all of what might be in it, she was nevertheless surprised to find a strange black dress and a pair of old shoes. What was her mother up to now? There was a letter several pages long, which Mara settled down to read. As she read, she was aware of smiling and even murmuring comments out loud. It was as though her mother were in the room. She was one of the few people Mara loved without reservation. This did not blind her, however, and many of her smiles were at her mother's continual, neat papering over of cracks. So large and so numerous were the cracks in the Johns family that Mara felt that by now the house must be made entirely of paper. Such well co-ordinated William Morris paper, of course, but one good stormy blast would blow it away altogether.

The shoes and dress, she learnt, had belonged to Mara's Great Aunt Daphne, her mother's father's sister. 'Why Grandma kept them all these years is beyond me,' wrote her mother. 'I suppose the world is divided into two types of people: the snails and the squirrels. The snails carry their all with them, while the squirrels hoard. Grandma is the worst hoarder I've come across. You can't imagine the amount of *things* she has managed to collect over the years . . .'

Grandma, she discovered, had suffered another stroke and was no longer capable of looking after herself, having set fire to the kitchen curtains one morning by accident. She had been moved to a private nursing home. Her large house was to be sold, and Mara's mother was now sorting through the *things*, trying to decide what to do with them all. It was typical of the family that Mara had been told nothing of this. 'We didn't want to worry you, darling. There was nothing you could have done. Besides, Grandma is very cheerful. She has decided that she is staying in a rather nice hotel, where she is taking a residential course in paper flower making. They do craft activities in the afternoons, sometimes, and we think that's where she has got the idea from. The matron is very nice . . .' Grandma could transform the grimmest of realities into something cheerful. Her strokes had not changed her, so much as distilled her character. In the end they would be left with quintessence of Grandma.

The dress had probably only been worn a few times by Great Aunt Daphne when she was a debutante in the 1920s. 'You can see from the label that it was made by one of the *better* London dressmakers. Georgette, and very good quality, of course. I thought you might enjoy wearing it, and I think it will fit you. Your wonderful *gamine* figure is perfect for those 1920s styles.' Mara grinned at this deft little piece of papering. In other words, Well, *you* won't have to bandage up your bosoms like they did in those days, dearie. Mara shook out the dress and held it to herself. Maybe it would fit. She kicked off her boots and slipped her feet into the bobbin-heeled shoes. They felt all right. She did a few charleston steps, but then felt a pang for poor Aunt Daphne. Tall and scrawny, like me. 'She was quite an accomplished Latin scholar,' papered her mother. Aunt Daphne had never married, and had been unable to avoid a life of looking after her irascible donnish father. Keeping his home, tolerating his whims, editing his notes. No escape on those black georgette wings into a good marriage. Unless, thought Mara suddenly, she had chosen her lot with care. Maybe she had thought it better to tolerate the demands of a dwindling father than the growing calls on her time of a husband and children. Once he was dead, her life was her own. She could behave as she chose in that rambling house, with no one to please but herself. Daphne – turned into a laurel by her father to escape the attentions of a lustful Apollo, and living defiantly on to be a tough old shrub that nobody could budge. The dress seemed more appealing in this light.

She put down the dress and took off the shoes. The next part of the letter described another cache of clothes discovered in a trunk in the attic. 'They belonged to your Aunt Judith.' This had been Mara's mother's older sister – something of a romantic figure, flying her aeroplane gallantly across the skies of the Home Counties until some terrible accident had cut her life short. 'If you have a penchant for wearing clothes from the 50s, here is your chance. I'm sure they will fit you, and it seems a shame to throw them out. I won't give anything away, until you've seen it. Judith was rather like you.' Mara paused for a moment. A vague sense of family history hung in the room, like the smell of an old chest opened after years of being undisturbed. She saw herself fleetingly as one of a long line of tall, thin, difficult women, and wondered how much of her behaviour was predetermined by them.

The rest of the letter was chit-chat about the parish, and a request for Mara to phone home occasionally. 'Daddy is out so much at the moment now he's rural dean. There's an interregnum at St Peter's, meetings every Monday and Wednesday, and now on Friday evenings as well.' This was another papered crack. If Mara phoned on those evenings, there would be no risk of having to talk to him. The letter ended with the hope that she would spend Christmas at home, and possibly go out with them to celebrate their twenty-second wedding anniversary. Mara grinned at this uncharacteristic error. Her mother had lost count, for this would have made her four months pregnant when she walked down the aisle. And her a Bishop's daughter! An image of the wedding came before her eyes, on one side the rows of unsmiling Welsh peasant faces, and on the other the large hats and charming politeness of her mother's family. The occasion would have been dreadful enough without episcopal shot-guns.

'And if you have a special friend you would like to invite too, then that would be lovely.' Mara tutted despairingly. Hope springs eternal in a mother's breast. After childhood parties mother would always ask: 'What did you have to eat?' Now it was: 'Did you meet anyone *nice*?' Mara supposed she would know her mother had finally abandoned hope when the wheel turned full circle and she asked about food again. They would talk companionably about salmon patties and asparagus tips long after men were forgotten. 'And Daddy sends you his love,' concluded the letter. Daddy did no such thing, of course, any more than she sent him hers, but her mother went on mediating these non-existent messages between the two of them in the immaculate paper house. She put the letter aside and turned to her books.

The days passed and she continued to read early Quaker tracts until their thunderous prose began to ring in her ears as she tried to sleep at nights. It was a far cry from the carefully structured arguments of modern scholarship. They preferred the blunderbuss approach. Any available material was stuffed randomly into the tract and then discharged in the general direction of the enemy. Like a theological version of the marital row. And another thing! Your doctrine of the atonement sucks! So much for the gentle, pacific Quakers.

George Fox strode through her mind barefoot, crying, *Woe to the bloody city of Lichfield!* James Nayler rode into Bristol in the rain, mounted on an ass as his followers cried thrice holy. Blasphemer! Flogged through the streets, branded, tongue bored through. His persecutors had turned him into a clearer symbol of Christ than his followers could ever have done. His fate troubled her. She felt he had been manipulated by a group of fanatics who were all driven by the wild forces let loose in times of eschatological fervour. A group of men as well as women, she noticed, although the books seemed to speak only of 'hysterical women'. She read and reread the texts, trying to understand what had happened. And then another figure began to haunt her – Martha Simmonds, long dead and forgotten, except for the part she played in Nayler's fall. Mara saw her at first as a victim of the patriarchal times, a strong, charismatic woman whom the Quakers felt they had to suppress. But gradually another image superseded this. Mara began to picture her with long hair like that girl in the marketplace, always ready to wash her master's feet. Not a victim: a calculating, manipulative woman. A woman who must have all eyes on her, who must have all the glory, under the guise of giving the glory to God. Mara recognized the type even across the centuries.

At last she reached the point where she could not force herself to read another word of Quakerly rant. She left her room to go and read the papers before lunch, but when she reached the common room it was already noisy and crowded. So she set off for Coverdale common room instead. A small voice inside her chanted, We know what you're doing! as she hurried through the college. It's just that it's always more peaceful there, she said. No farting undergraduates.

The room was empty. She leafed through the papers and found the *Guardian*. Then her eye fell on a book which said *Coverdale Quotes* on the cover. This should be interesting, she thought with a smile. It was full of several years' worth of witty and unfortunate sayings. Most of them were clearly amusing only when you knew the people who said them. She turned to the most recent pages and hunted for names she knew. Hugh: *I'm sorry, but I make no apology for this.* Rupert: *I know we all have to learn from one another, but I'm right.* Mara laughed out loud. Suddenly her own name leapt off the page: *If the good Lord hadn't intended us to fornicate, why did he create girls like*

Mara Johns? Johnny. Her face burned. What was that supposed to mean? It seemed to be in response to another student telling him that if the good Lord had intended us to smoke, he would have given us chimneys on the top of our heads. Did he mean she was an easy lay? But before she could decide, she heard his laugh in the corridor. She put the book down and hid behind her paper, seething. A child's voice carried across to her:

'Read a story.'

'Don't pester him, Michael,' came another voice. The mother.

'I want a story,' insisted the child.

'OK. Ha'away in.' Feet pattered to the door, then hesitated.

'There's a lady in there.'

'Ssh. That's not a lady,' whispered Johnny. 'That's a woman.'

Bastard. Mara stood up abruptly and threw the paper back on the table.

He gave her a cheerful grin. 'Are you off, pet? – Sorry! Mara.'

She walked out, leaving him with the child still demanding a story.

Later that afternoon Mara made her way to Maddy's and May's room. As she climbed the stairs she heard a laugh. Johnny was there. She paused, wondering whether to come back later. No. Sod him. I want to see my friends. She took another step and heard an unfamiliar female voice. It was speaking insistently as she approached the door. She entered the room. It was the girl from the marketplace. Too late to retreat. Maddy called her in as though her appearance was a welcome diversion.

'Come in, come in. Let me introduce you to everyone. This is Johnny Whitaker,' she said. 'Only you know him already; although not, as we established earlier, in the biblical sense. Or do you? He hasn't mentioned it. Perhaps he is too much the gentleman?' Doubt showed on every feature. 'We'll have to rely on you for details, in that case.'

While this banter went on Mara was aware of the strange girl. Was it her own morbid curiosity that made her want to look at her, or did the girl have some drawing power? Their eyes met. Mutual assessment. Instant loathing.

'And this is Joanna.'

The girl said hello, but Mara crossed the room without replying, and sat on May's desk.

'And that was Mara,' said Maddy. 'Don't take it personally. She's visiting us from a different planet, where politeness is seen as a sign of weakness.' Mara's lips twitched at this description of herself, and then she caught sight of Johnny grinning too from where he was sitting on the other desk across the room. At once all amusement left her face and she stared at him coldly.

'Well . . .' began Maddy, but for once she was talked down.

'The thing with theology,' said Joanna, 'is that it's taught without faith.' Mara felt a surge of contempt rising up inside her. 'The lecturers don't believe that the Bible is the Word of God.' This conversation must have been going on before I arrived, Mara thought. The girl's glance went darting and flickering from one to another. Her every gesture seemed designed to draw attention to herself. She continued earnestly: 'When one of them says something which contradicts the Bible, I simply put down my pen, stop writing, and fold my arms.'

Suddenly it became clear. The display was aimed solely at Johnny. Mara searched each face for reactions. Maddy seemed sullen. May, on the other hand, was hugely amused. It was she who broke the silence.

'Why are you doing theology, then?' Her face was perfectly serious, but Mara suspected she was attempting to draw the girl into further absurdities. The girl's face took on the look of a hidden and inward smile, as if she were secretly with child by the Holy Ghost. Before she could answer, however, Johnny broke in.

'Well, you'll not get a degree if you take that attitude.' If anyone else had said this, the girl would no doubt have replied (raising her eyes heavenwards), "So be it, if that is God's will," but Mara was not surprised to see her accepting Johnny's words submissively. She sat looking up at him, as if posing for a pre-Raphaelite picture of Mary of Bethany at the feet of Christ. Mara felt a sudden rush of understanding for Martha. No wonder she had stormed in and asked Jesus to tell her sister to help her with the serving. The surprise was rather that she had not hit Mary round the head with the kneading trough. On Johnny's other side May rested her chin on her hand and looked up at him, too. The two women were now mirror images of each other, but Johnny was too intent on what he was saying to notice what May was doing.

'It's one thing to disagree with the scholars,' Johnny was saying, 'but it's another to dismiss their ideas out of hand.'

'I just find it all so *confusing*,' said the girl. And she actually batted her eyelashes. Mara saw May mentally clapping her hands with delight. Johnny appeared to soften. God – he's not going to be taken in by this, thought Mara in disgust.

'Well, that's a different matter,' he said with a smile. 'It will seem confusing at first. Maybe the real question you want to be asking yourself is whether the Bible can still be the Word of God without being literally true in every detail. I think it can.'

This was the longest and most serious speech Mara had heard him make. The four of them sat in silence listening to his words, as though they were another pre-Raphaelite tableau of first-century Palestine. The scene was undermined by May's look of rapt adoration, which Mara was convinced Johnny had now seen but was ignoring.

'But it's so difficult,' she protested. Save me, Johnny! 'If you can't rely on every detail in the Bible, then it might all be untrue.'

Johnny shook his head, turning so that he was facing Joanna more fully, and unable to see May, who was shaking her head in sympathy. 'It might feel like that,' he said, 'but I'd say my faith is stronger now, rather than weaker, after a degree in theology.' May nodded.

'You've studied theology?' asked the girl.

'Oh, yes,' said Maddy, wresting the scene back to herself. 'They occasionally allow people with regional accents to read for degrees here. In his case it's because he's training to be a priest.'

'God's Man for Our Time,' said May.

'He's celibate, of course,' said Maddy. 'But you will have realized that. Unless you thought he always sat that way.' Johnny had a look of amused resignation on his face, and much though Maddy's behaviour irritated Mara, she preferred it to Joanna's brand of sanctified vamping. Maddy was opening her mouth for another speech, but Joanna was not to be upstaged without a struggle.

'So you're going into the ministry?' He nodded, and her face seemed to glow. 'That's amazing. That's really amazing. While I was reading my Bible this morning, Father told me I was going to meet someone today who had a special calling.'

Father! Mara squirmed.

'Do you have a Special Calling, Johnny?' asked May gravely.

'No. I just like the dressing-up,' he replied.

Mara watched the girl's face to see how she would react to this flippancy, but the secret glowing look was still in place. Father had obviously told her that Johnny was that special man. Yes, thought Mara. This is exactly how I picture Martha Simmonds weaving her

60

poisonous web round James Nayler. Her scalp prickled. There had been a girl just like her in the sect. Leah. A coy, manipulative trouble-maker. Always worming her way to the centre of every group, latching on to the most powerful and interesting people. Hester had never been able to see this. Nothing Mara said convinced her that Leah was evil. It sickened Mara to see her sister turned into a tireless campaigner for Leah's rights.

'It's just that . . . well, I've got a calling, too,' Joanna was saying. We're supposed to gasp and ask for more, thought Mara.

'Well,' said Maddy, clearly determined that nobody should oblige, 'you'd better pull your finger out and start working on your degree, then.'

'Said the pot to the kettle,' put in May.

'It's the Greek, really,' said Joanna, ignoring them. 'I don't always understand it.' This was aimed at Johnny and he was forced to look serious again.

'Look, I'll tell you what, pet,' he said, 'if you really are having difficulties with Greek –'

No! thought Mara in alarm. Don't do it! Johnny looked her way and stopped in mid-sentence. He stared at her in surprise. The girl turned to see what he was looking at, and instantly Mara's face became expressionless.

'If it's the Greek that's worrying you, why not ask the tutor to go over it with you?' said Johnny. 'They sometimes put on extra classes in the department. You'll probably find you aren't the only one struggling.'

Joanna shot Mara a swift malevolent look that was covered instantly by a smile. 'Maybe you're right,' she said with downcast eyes to Johnny.

'Of course he is,' murmured May, but this, apparently, was going too far. Johnny rounded on her.

'You watch it, young lady.' There was a tense silence, and although he had not raised his voice, Mara remembered one of her earliest impressions of him from their meeting in Dr Mowbray's study: that he had a quick temper. This was a mere spark, but enough to alarm Maddy. Mara saw her anxious look. It seemed odd that Maddy should be so nervous of anger, when so much of her behaviour seemed deliberately to provoke it.

'Sorry,' said May unrepentantly. She and Johnny eyed one another.

'What about tea?' asked Maddy, bursting in on the silence she was unable to bear. 'That universal remedy to all wrongs, that *panacea*. A Greek word,' she said, turning to Joanna, 'meaning "universal remedy to all wrongs". Who'd like some?'

'Please,' said Johnny.

Mara's attention had been diverted, so she had not seen how the staring match had ended. May was looking nonchalant – but was she blushing? Something had passed between the two. She looked at Joanna.

'So you've done Greek?' Joanna asked Johnny. Yes, she had seen something she did not like (a blown kiss?), and was now bending his attention back to herself, thought Mara.

'For his sins,' said Maddy, not allowing this to happen. 'And what a lot of Greek he has done. Tea, Joanna? Mara?'

Mara declined, and stood up to leave. As she was crossing the room, she saw Johnny give her a meaning look. I want a word with you, it said. She ignored him, and left. If it was that important, he could come and find her later.

As she climbed the stairs back to her room, she began to doubt her own assessment of Joanna. Perhaps she was so jaundiced by her previous encounters with the charismatic Christians of the sect that she automatically tarred them all with the same brush. The girl might simply be unfortunate, not sinister. A fellow lame duck. She tried to remind herself that fundamentalists were not a subhuman life form. Plenty of students were unsettled by the implications of their academic studies. And plenty more were attracted to attractive men. She went over to her window and looked out, thinking she would never know objectively what the girl was like. Maybe all she could see in Joanna was her own projected fears. The night was dark. It was Hallowe'en, and the lit-up windows across the river gleamed like jack-o'-lantern eyes.

CHAPTER 6

The days of early November passed by. Most of the leaves were gone from the trees. Big black crows like tattered clergymen congregated in the empty branches, and the students went about in overcoats they had borrowed from their fathers. Some of the coats had walked around the City twenty-five years earlier when they were new and smart. Now the voice of fashion had resurrected them to walk along the same streets again.

Mara was wearing her grandfather's long black cloak. The wind blew and the cloak swirled, slowing her progress. As a child she had held the sides of her coat out like wings on days like these, half believing the wind would pick her up and whirl her away. In her mind's eye she had learnt to walk along above the rooftops, seeing the world spread out on all sides. I'm losing the knack, she thought. An empty can went clattering down the street. Other people tie me down. But it won't be much work to cut myself free and dance off across the sky. I'm only here for a year, after all. I will keep all these people in my memory like a trunk full of *things* in the attic. A sudden gust of wind whisked her hat away, and she chased it as it rolled along the gutter. It came to rest outside the door under Maddy's and May's window as though it was *meant to be*. She had been intending for several days to visit her friends.

She entered the room. There were books lying open, but she had found Maddy and May at that awkward time of a student's day when it was too late to get in a really good afternoon's work, but not late enough to abandon all pretence of working altogether. Her arrival solved the dilemma.

'Time for tea!' May went to fill the kettle. Maddy rolled over on the bed with a yawn among musical scores and sheets of manuscript paper. Mara sat down, craning her neck to read the title of the book which Maddy had just let slide on to the floor. *Stormy Summer* by Margaux Spreadeagle. She gazed at Maddy in disdain.

'Oh, get that bloody superior expression off your face,' said Maddy, looking, Mara thought, like someone on a diet caught in the act of eating a whole pound of Belgian chocolates. 'I suppose you've never read a single romance in your life.' This was a clever move, Mara realized. Either she was the pot calling the kettle black, or she was a mass of prejudice and ignorance. She picked up the book.

'*His dark eyes blazed*,' she read aloud. May came back into the room and stood with the kettle, staring at her. '"*You damned little bitch*," *he bit out.* "*You want me as much as I want you! Don't think you can get away with this!*" *He strode from the room, leaving her white and trembling on the bed. As the door slammed, the realization swept over her.* "*My God! I don't hate this man – I love him!*"'

She looked from Maddy to May in disbelief, and they crowed with laughter. 'What *is* this crap?' and she flung it aside.

'She doesn't understand,' said Maddy in throbbing tones. 'She has never been left white and trembling on the bed with the realization, "My God! I love this man!"' Maddy retrieved the book and began reading again with such feeling that Mara was torn between disgust and amusement.

'It's a different *Weltanschauung*, you see,' explained Maddy, reaching for the mug May was handing her, 'but one entirely compatible with a feminist outlook. The men are masterful, overbearing and loose-limbed, yes, I know,' she said as Mara was about to break in, 'but they *invariably* end up marrying the heroine, which – let me finish – in terms of the genre, is a triumph of the female world view. He is tamed and subdued by the love of a good woman. Harmony and fruition prevail – like in *All's Well That Ends Well*. And you have to admit,' concluded Maddy, 'that that is the most compelling and tightly reasoned justification for reading crap that you have ever heard.'

'I intend to do my dissertation on that very subject,' said May from where she was standing at the mirror experimenting with various lipsticks. '"Beauty and the Beast: Fairy Tale Motifs in Popular Romantic Fiction, with Special Reference to Margaux Spreadeagle's *Stormy Summer*". What do you think of this?' She turned to them with a vivid, coral-coloured mouth.

'Ghastly,' said Maddy. May wiped it off and reached for another tube.

'"Vermilion Flare,"' she read. 'It sounds like the title of another romance.' She tried it, and turned to them again.

'An improvement,' said Maddy. 'It'll go better with your dress, too.' Preparations for the approaching college ball, Mara realized.

'Are you going to the ball, Mara?' asked May, blotting lipstick kisses on to a tissue.

Mara shook her head.

'Oh, but you must, you must!' they protested.

'Who with?'

This was supposed to be unanswerable, but they both replied promptly, 'The polecat?'

Mara had a vision of herself and the polecat locked in an endless snarling waltz, and laughed.

'Did I hear a strange sound?' asked Maddy.

'An unfamiliar sound!' said May.

Yes, ha ha, thought Mara, returning to her usual sour expression. She told them that she had agreed to wash up instead. There were plenty of jobs with a modest amount of pay at the college ball, and taking one of these was the honourable refuge of the overdrawn or the under-confident. Or the celibate. She had seen Johnny's name on the list of workers.

'Cinderella,' sneered Maddy.

'"Vermilion Flare: The Cinderella Myth in Post-War Light Romance",' said May.

'Why don't you ask Rupert to take you?' persisted Maddy. '*He* likes you.' There was a pause. With two seconds' thought she might have phrased this more delicately, her expression said. 'He likes you, *even if nobody else does*,' read the subtext. Mara suppressed a smile.

'But he's got a partner already,' said May. 'He's taking someone called Cordelia Chauffeured-Bentley, and a party of Somebody Someone-Somethings he was at Oxford with.' She started to apply eye-shadow.

'Could you marry a man with a double-barrelled name?' asked Maddy.

'It is our destiny,' replied May. Mara stopped listening to them as they began to talk about their own partners for the ball. Her mind was full of dancing and the black georgette dress. She heard the music and saw the swirling beads and the nodding of tall feathers. Aunt Daphne danced by herself to her own tune, while the other girls hovered white and trembling under the moon in male embraces. Off across the chiffon clouds went Aunt Judith's plane as the lights of the great house twinkled below; and there, dancing from star to star, went Great Aunt Jessie, who could see angels.

'She isn't listening to a word we're saying,' came Maddy's voice.

Mara turned to them indifferently. May had just finished her work at the mirror.

'Who am I?' She faced them. The eye-liner made her eyes appear enormous, and she cast her gaze heavenwards, taking up a swooning pose.

'Theresa of Avila?' suggested Mara. May laughed, and picked up a tea-towel and tied it over her hair. Martha Simmonds. Joanna.

Maddy snorted in recognition. 'Lucretia the poison woman. God, I hate that girl.'

'Well, we all know why that is,' said May.

'Because she's a tape-worm,' said Maddy.

'Because you can't hog the stage when she's in the room,' said May.

'I wouldn't *demean* myself by trying. "Johnny, let me worship you. Let me suck the sweat out of your second-best jockstrap!"'

'You thought that one up in advance,' accused May.

'She's a fool,' said Maddy, ignoring this. 'The one thing you must never, *ever* do is treat men like Johnny with respect. They get cocky. Except he was all cock to begin with.'

'In your fevered imagination,' said May.

'I've got eyes,' said Maddy. 'Unless that's a pair of socks down his underpants, of course. I'll have to ask him.'

Mara laughed.

'There's that funny noise again,' said May.

'Yes, and another thing,' said Maddy, rounding on Mara. 'You can bloody well stop signing Joanna into meals as your guest! We always end up having to look after her.'

Mara sat in silent fury. She had done no such thing. Had Joanna forged her signature?

'Mara denies all knowledge,' said Maddy. 'In which case St Theresa has signed herself in *illegally*. Outrage!'

'The Lord told me to,' said May, folding her hands and looking pious. Then, whisking off the tea-towel, she became herself again. 'You'll have to have a word with Mr Nasty Pasty,' she said. 'He controls the meal lists with a fist of iron.' This must be the catering manager and head chef.

'*Nigel,*' said Maddy scornfully. 'He always reminds me of a profes- sional snooker player – the cockney accent, the hair slightly too long, the pasty, pale complexion. I bet he even has a snooker table down in the bowels of the earth in his Salmonella Emporium.'

'She's scared of him,' explained May, wiping off the make-up. 'He caught her eating a lunch she hadn't signed in for.'

Mara stood up to leave, forgetting as usual to say thank you, or goodbye.

'Goodbye, Mara,' said Maddy with emphasis. 'No, no – it was our pleasure.'

'Yes,' said May. '*Please* don't mention it.'

And so she did not, but gave an idle wave as she left to return to her room. Her anger had been dissipated by their chatter.

She was still working that evening, but when she heard the clock chime nine, she paused and listened to the rain against the window. She reached for her black book to do some drawing. In her mind's eye she saw Aunt Judith's plane, and her pencil touched the paper. Then it suddenly seemed to her that the book was too small. She took two sheets of unlined file paper and sellotaped them together. Her pencil hesitated. She felt like a child turned loose in a field when it had been used to a narrow garden. The rain pattered on the glass again, and she began to draw.

This is Aunt Judith in her plane. She died years before I was born. I don't think I've even seen a picture of her. Then her mother's letter came back: *Aunt Judith was rather like you.* And so it could have been her own face behind the goggles, and her own black hair streaming out in the wind. The little bi-plane was high above the clouds, heading for realms unknown. Mara paused. The picture looked like an illustration for a story. *Aunt Judith*, she wrote underneath in gothic script. She enclosed the letters in a scrolled ribbon, and now she was reminded of stained-glass windows; of Gabriel with Latin words unfurling from his lips in a kind of medieval speech bubble, and the Virgin with a polite frown, casting in her mind what manner of salutation this should be. Mara's pencil began moving again. Another ribbon rolled out, this time from the back of the plane, as though Aunt Judith were towing a motto across the sky. What should it say? With a smile Mara filled in the words of the Miller of Dee: *I care for nobody, no, not I, if nobody cares for me.* And now the picture was complete. Or was it? As she looked at it, Mara began to sense that this was only a part of a larger picture.

After a moment's thought she tore another sheet out of the pad and joined it to the other two. On the new page she drew a cloud filled with Latin – phrases, words, tense endings, quotations – and on it sat Great Aunt Daphne. Her long thin legs dangled over the cloud's edge, and she had a sarcastic expression on her face. And not far away from her, stepping from star to star, as though they were stones in the local stream, went Great Aunt Jessie. In her hand she held her ear trumpet. What were the angels saying today? *You can eavesdrop, child, if you are very careful.* Mara heard the whispering voice in her memory. She said that to me, but I was too small to hold the trumpet for myself, so I never heard them. All around Aunt Jessie wound the words of her favourite hymn on ribbons: *Angels to beckon me nearer my God to thee. Nearer to thee, nearer to thee.*

And, now, thought Mara, let there be angels. She attached more sheets of paper and filled the sky with angels. Some passed by in dark glasses carrying briefcases. Others sat on a circle of stars drinking tea and discussing in Latin whether they believed in Bultmann. Others were gathering up and towing away the ribbons of prayer which had floated up through the clouds. Some prayers were long and ornate, some simply said *Help*. At the top of the picture the archangel Michael was rolling up his collect and tucking it under his arm. A phrase billowed out under one wing as though the wind had caught the words.

She sat for a moment and looked at what she had drawn. Then she folded it hurriedly and put it in her desk drawer, as though it were a secret which nobody must see. The idea of it had crept along her veins like strong wine. I won't sleep tonight for the planning of it, she thought; and although it was late she changed into her tracksuit and went out for a run. Her mind was buzzing with bi-planes and angels. Maybe the night air and the exercise would quieten them.

The wind was still throwing handfuls of rain as she set out running along the street. The wet cobbles gleamed in the streetlights, and she could hear the trees around the cathedral sighing and creaking. The great walls and towers rose up ashen in the floodlights, and at the sight of them she slowed to a walk. All the windows were dark.

She stood looking up at the towers in the white light, until she heard footsteps coming along the street. She had turned and was about to break into a run, when her name was called. Her heart leapt. It was Johnny. He came up to her.

'I've been meaning to talk to you.' His accent seemed more marked, as though the northern night air had drawn it out. 'The other day – what was that look for?'

'What look?' But she knew already what he meant. He was

standing in the shadow and she could not see his expression. The wind blew around them.

'The other day in Maddy's and May's room, when young Joanna was complaining about her Greek, you gave me a look.'

'Oh, then.' But the time she had gained had not shown her how to answer. He was waiting. The truth would have to do. 'I thought you were about to offer her some personal tuition.'

'Would that have been wrong?' She sensed an undercurrent of anger. He had not spoken to her like this before. If she could see him properly she might judge his mood better.

'Well, it's up to you.' The rain was cold on her face.

'I know that. I want to know why you think I shouldn't.'

'I suppose I wasn't sure you knew what you would be letting yourself in for.' She found herself unable to go on. It would be like trying to convince Hester about Leah. He wouldn't believe her.

'Well, Mara,' he began. His voice sounded a little softer. 'I want you to know I respect your judgement.' She stiffened. 'And I take what you think seriously . . .' The patronizing 'but' was coming. But I'm going to ignore your advice. But I think you're wrong.

'Oh, forget it,' she said rudely and turned to walk off. Immediately he seized her arm and spun her round.

'Don't you do that to me.' She stood still in shock. 'Who the hell do you think you are? You treat people as though they weren't worth *that*.' He snapped his fingers in her face. It was like a knife thrust. But now a faint light was on him, and she saw his anger pass as swiftly as it had appeared.

'By, you sail close to the wind, pet. Someone's going to murder you one of these days.' He let go of her arm. 'Anyway, I was going to say, I'm glad you warned me.' His tone was almost good-humoured now. They began to make their way slowly back along the street. She watched the light moving over the cobbles as they walked. 'She came to my room the next day and started to tell me all her problems. I thought I'd never get rid of her. I was thinking, Is it just me, or is this girl odd? I kept wanting to say, "Just a second, that can't be right", but the more she went on talking, the more I started to think it must be me. Weird. Mind you' – he turned to her – 'she probably *is* having trouble with the Greek.'

'I doubt it.'

'We can't all be born scholars, Mara.'

'Yes, but she must have done languages at school, and New

69

Testament Greek isn't that hard. It's a question of application, not brain-power.' But he was shaking his head. Finally she burst out, 'Look, I had to teach myself Greek.' There was a grin on his face, and she blushed with rage at herself. She had meant to say 'I managed to teach myself', or something, to imply that if that was the case, then surely Joanna could master it with proper lessons. But instead it had come out like a complaint. No nice young man offered to help *me*. And now he thought she was jealous. I'm not, she thought. It's just that he's too unsuspecting. I just couldn't bear to see him in her clutches!

And that, she had to admit, sounded exactly like jealousy.

They stopped by the main entrance to Jesus College. He seemed to be lingering. Was he expecting her to ask him in? But before she could decide whether she wanted to, a horrible thought struck her. Maybe he saw her as another difficult female latching on to him to pour out her troubles. She imagined him laughing with Rupert: 'I thought I'd never get away!'

'Good night,' she said, and climbed the steps.

'Good night, sweetie.' She heard the amusement in his voice, and turned back, her hand on the door. 'If you're ever having trouble with your work, don't hesitate to ask. Rupert and I would be glad to help.' For a fraction of a second she felt a great Swansea fishwife elbowing her way to the front of her mind to bawl a stream of obscenities at him. But she closed the door on his laughter and went back to her room.

It seemed narrow and quiet after the night outside. She had forgotten about her run. Should she go back out? After a moment's thought she decided against it and picked up a volume of early Quaker tracts. Surely their violent message would drive all other thoughts from her mind. She started to read. Page after page of faded ink on brown paper. The woes and warnings seemed dull. Other people's visions. The great and terrible day of the Lord held nothing but a mild and dusty academic charm. Where had all the fire gone?

From the other side of the wall she heard the rustling of paper and an impatient sigh. The polecat was still studying. Ferreting away in his obscure Elizabethan poetry, or whatever he was researching. Was it Shakespeare, even? She dimly remembered May telling her. Maybe he was a fellow insomniac? She turned back to her book, but not before she heard Johnny's voice: '*You treat people as though they weren't worth that.*'

70

At last she became absorbed in what she was reading. Outside the wind blustered, whirling away the sound of the bells as they chimed the passing quarters. Mara's fingers loosened her damp hair from its plait, shaking it out so that it could dry. Her eyes did not waver from the page, and as she read, her hair gradually found its way back into its natural curls, curls she would comb out with contempt the following morning. *Hailstones, vials, plagues, thunders, woes, judgments, are come amongst you.* She turned a page, and a strand of hair fell forwards and tickled her neck. As she brushed it aside, her fingers touched something. She glanced down. A spider.

With a scream she leapt from her chair and tore off her tracksuit top, flinging it away. Her hair snaked around her shoulders. Spiders everywhere. Every shadow moved and scuttled. The polecat was in the room.

'What's wrong?'

'A spider!' She pointed to the tracksuit on the floor. He bent and lifted it. The spider raced out. With a darting movement he had it in his hand and crossed to the open window. He turned and took a step towards her. It was her cousin Dewi coming to throw the spider in her face. She started back in terror. And then it was only the polecat walking across the room, showing her both his hands, empty, palms towards her.

'It's all right. It's gone. I threw it out of the window.'

After a long, long moment she felt the fear begin to loose its grip. She sat huddled on the desk with the polecat watching her.

'Whisky?' he asked.

She nodded. Anything. He went to his room. She hugged her bare arms around her. The wind came gusting in, and she was cold sitting in her running vest. She looked at her tracksuit top on the floor and her skin crawled. Voices began speaking in her mind. Well, you made a fool of yourself there, didn't you? . . . Still afraid after all these years? . . . Now he has a hold over you . . . It'll be all over college in the morning. Mara Johns is scared of spiders!

She heard him coming back, and there was a murmured conversation at the door. The field mice. I've probably woken half the bloody college. Then the polecat was beside her with two glasses and a bottle. He poured them each a stiff whisky. They drank. She knew he was watching her and that she was defenceless against his mockery. He sat beside her on the desk.

'God, you're a strange woman. I can't make you out. You aren't scared of me, but you're frightened of spiders.'

She said nothing, trying to gather her defences around her again. They held one another's gaze like hardened poker players. Then a strand of her hair fell forwards and she jumped, brushing it wildly aside.

'It's all right. Relax.' He reached out a hand and touched her hair. She sat still, cursing herself.

'You have curly hair.' His voice was amused, as though he had discovered she kept sentimental pictures of puppy dogs on her walls. She twitched her hair out of his fingers and twisted it away from him over her other shoulder. His eyes became fixed on her upper arm.

'And you have a tattoo.' Well, well, said his tone. So much for the puppy dogs.

She watched his face as he reached out a finger and traced the shape of the dragon. His grey eyes were half veiled, glinting under dark lashes and she realized with a shiver just how attractive he was. A series of new thoughts and conjectures seemed to be occurring to him as well. He might be a scholar making an important discovery – perhaps stumbling upon an unknown erotic poem by some dour puritan. Then suddenly his expression changed. He reached out, took her right arm and turned it over. She tried to pull back, but it was too late. The scar lay exposed, running from wrist to elbow along the vein.

'What happened here?'

'I cut myself.' The phrase see-sawed in the silence between two meanings.

'Hmm. Most people go cross-wise.' He ran a finger down the scar. 'How old were you?'

'Fourteen.'

He looked up. There was no trace of shock or disapproval in his face. 'I take it someone found you.'

'My father.'

'Careless. Or was that part of the plan?'

'No.'

'Was it his razor?' Her face burnt. 'A nice touch. I bet that taught him a lesson. Why didn't you finish the job later?'

'I changed my mind.'

His eyes were on her and, unable to bear his dispassionate gaze, she drained her glass and handed it back to him. The abruptness of the gesture seemed like a dismissal, and with a shrug he rose to leave. Her conscience twitched, and she remembered the sound of fingers being snapped in her face. Hurriedly, she stood up as well. The polecat glanced round as he reached the door.

'Look – thank you,' she said.

He gave her a quizzical look, as though he had encountered the phrase before but could not for the moment remember in what context. The door swung shut.

She sat for some time on the desk. From next door came the sounds of the polecat going to bed. Then came silence, apart from the swirling winter wind. I should have been nicer to him. I should be nicer to everyone. That's the whisky talking, she thought with a sneer. Her head swam as she moved from the desk and slowly got ready for bed.

The darkness filled with faces and voices, and she slid into a restless sleep. Her mother was there, talking about her tattoo, asking 'Why, darling, why did you have it done? You know you won't be able to get rid of it.'

'She's eighteen,' said her father. 'She can do as she pleases.' What did he care?

Dewi stood looking at her. 'Why do you have to copy everything I do, you stupid cow? Why do you have to be like me?' The dragon on his arm twisted as though it were alive, and she screamed. He laughed – or maybe it was the polecat? 'Why can't you be more like your sister?' But Hester wasn't there. Where had she gone? She ran to look for her, but tripped and fell. Johnny stood and stared at her.

'You treat people like dirt,' he said. High above her flew the angels. Their eyes were fierce and wild. They called to each other across the empty sky.

She woke in the early morning light. Her face was wet with tears and her head throbbed. The wind blew the curtain. From down below on the river came the desolate cry of gulls, driven inland by the storm.

CHAPTER 7

One by one the students woke in Jesus College, and remembered: tonight. Tonight is the night. Ball gowns hung in their polythene wrappings, fold upon fold of velvet or taffeta, gleaming secretly like gems by candlelight. The staff in the basement kitchens were at work, making the breakfast among the preparations for the ball. On go the eggs, in goes the toast; and as soon as possible, a hundred of these to slice, two hundred of those to marinate. The cathedral clock chimed the hours away – eight, nine, ten. Groups of students began decorating the halls and corridors, while others remained at their desks seeming to work. Eyes stole to the waiting folds of satin, or to where dress suits hung stiffly, like the ghosts of waiters or ushers haunting the doorway. Soon . . .

The clock struck midday and Mara was climbing the stairs in the Divinity School to see Dr Roe. She was glad to get away from the festoons and spangles and rustles of anticipation which filled the college. Maddy and May had talked of little but the ball for days. Dr Roe's study was a haven. Mara sat. Her tutor looked at her expectantly.

'I got your note,' said Mara in the end.

'Good. I was wondering if everything was all right. If you'd been ill.'

'No.'

'It's just that I was expecting you last Thursday.' Mara looked surprised. 'Well, according to my diary. I had a feeling we arranged it last time we met.'

'No,' said Mara again. She looked in her diary anyway, although she knew it was blank; and there against last Thursday were the words: 'Dr Roe. 11 a.m.' She stared. If it had not been her own handwriting, she would have sworn someone else must have written it. Panic surged up inside her. She felt her hand smoothing her hair and fumbling for the end of her plait.

'You're right,' she said. 'I must have forgotten. Sorry.' Was her voice sounding strange?

'Don't worry. It happens to all of us,' said Dr Roe. Maybe it did. Just a piece of absent-mindedness. Nothing to worry about. They began to talk about Mara's work, and she found herself gradually relaxing. The discussion turned to the idea of the end of the world.

'Do you think that groups with a highly developed eschatology tend to have a liberal attitude towards women?' asked Dr Roe.

'Not all of them.' A voice began speaking in her memory: '*Let your women learn in silence with all obedience. That's what the Word of God says, brothers and sisters. And any woman striving for more than her God-given place is guilty of disobedience. Yes! of rebellion against God. And there are some here in this room tonight who are not content with the place God has given them.*'

'Ah. You're thinking of the Anabaptists of Münster, perhaps?'

'Well . . .' began Mara cautiously, unable for the moment to remember anything about the Anabaptists of anywhere. 'I was thinking more of various modern churches. You know, breakaway groups. House churches.'

'And they believe the Second Coming is imminent? What do they teach about women?'

'Well, I heard of one which taught that women should be silent and obedient. And grow their hair long and keep their heads covered in worship. As a sign that they are under male authority.' Which is why I cut all my hair off that night I walked out of the church. *Shaved* it off, as the deputy headmistress put it. She had been suspended from school until it grew back, although they couldn't come up with a single good reason why. Her mother had been in tears. 'Darling, why? All your beautiful hair.' Mara called her attention back, seeing that her tutor was watching her closely.

'Why do some millenarian groups treat women as equals while others don't?' asked Dr Roe.

'Different attitudes to the Bible?'

'Good. Go on.' Dr Roe looked animated, but Mara could think of nothing to add.

Finally the other woman said, 'This strikes me as important. I think you ought to concentrate your work here for a couple of months. Try to explore the relationship between the Scriptures, the millennium and the role of women.' This sounded at once like the title of a thesis. They arranged another time to meet, and Mara wrote it in her diary, adding a full stop, as though pinning the information firmly in place. She looked up at Dr Roe.

'I'll try to remember.'

Dr Roe was looking worried. 'You aren't working too hard, are you?'

'No.' This was not precisely a lie, since 'too hard' was purely subjective.

'How many hours would you say you're doing a day? Approximately.'

Mara considered. 'About seven or eight.' This was a lie; but students usually lied in answer to this question. The difference in my case is that I do more, rather than less than I claim, she thought.

'Well, take it easy,' said Dr Roe as Mara rose to leave. 'I hope you have other things to do besides working. Are you going to the ball?' Mara could have screamed. Though I take the wings of the morning and dwell in the uttermost parts of the sea, even there will this question pursue me!

'No,' she said. 'I'm not.'

As she walked down the stairs, she felt the need to insult someone roundly and gratuitously. It's because I've been trying to be *nice* to people. And all because of Johnny Whitaker. It angered her to have to admit this. She still wanted to go and seize him by the arm as he had seized her, and say, Listen – there are good reasons why I behave as I do. Being nasty to people isn't just a hobby of mine. But she had to acknowledge that there was justice in his accusation. Her behaviour must look like arrogant contempt of others. But it's my armour. This was the kind of thing she heard herself explaining to Johnny – except she never would, of course. I will never be like Joanna, telling him all my problems. Something about him drew out confidences from others. Those dark eyes. There would be an upsurge of interest in going to confession wherever he served as priest. But she was being nasty again. She was out of the Divinity School now, walking back to college. She looked along the street and saw, coming towards her, someone else she must be nice to: Rupert. He greeted her.

'Hello,' she replied, and added with some effort, 'How are you?' Instantly she regretted it. A look of grave concern came over his face as though he were about to feel her brow. Why did people make it so difficult for someone to change? In a burst of irritation she said, 'That was just an example of phatic speech.' He looked blank. 'Intended to establish social contact, not convey facts.' He coloured slightly.

'Somebody told me you read English at Cambridge,' he said. She

76

inclined her head. 'And that you got a First.' She looked away. 'Why did you let me lecture you on the function of language? You might have stopped me.'

'How?' Impossible not to say it.

'Mara, talking to you is always a chastening experience. Do you see it as your mission to cut me down to size?'

It was her turn to flush. 'No.'

'Well, that's certainly how it feels, sweetie.'

This time she bit back her reply. He had made her feel so much in the wrong that she could not even protest at being called sweetie. All she could do was scowl.

'Going to the ball?' he asked cheerfully.

'No. I'm washing up.'

'Well, that won't take all night, will it? The last sitting is at ten-thirty. You'll be finished not long after eleven.' She stared. 'You're allowed to join in when you've finished your work. Didn't you know?'

The black georgette dress . . .

'Come on,' he urged. 'You'll enjoy it. I've got a group of friends coming. Why don't you join us?' The Someone-Somethings.

'I don't know,' she said in a bored voice. 'I might.'

He clearly took this to mean yes. 'Good. Wonderful. Johnny's joining us too, when he's finished in the dining-room. See you later, then.' And with a smile from him and a mutter from her, they parted. Johnny would be there . . .

She had walked about fifty yards down the road when she thought, Just a *minute*! What about *you* trying to cut *me* down to size? You're always criticizing me. She wheeled round, but he was out of sight. If I'm arrogant, so are you, Anderson. It's just that you're charming with it. But then her conviction wavered. What if he were right? She looked up at the sky despairingly.

The college was turning into a baroque heaven, with billows of pink muslin shrouding the ceilings, and cherubs clustered in little groups. Someone had obviously had difficulty with the cherubs. They looked thin and awkward, like the infant Christ in medieval triptychs. If I had a pen handy I could offer to fatten them up. But then everyone would know she could draw. She passed along corridors decorated with moon, stars and comets, until she reached her stair. On impulse she looked in at the main dining-hall. Lunchtime had suspended its transformation into Mount Olympus. Olive trees grew from the walls and vine tendrils were making their way across the ceiling. Reclining deities looked down disdainfully over their goblets of nectar at the students eating fish and chips.

Mara was wondering whether to have lunch earlier for a change, when she noticed Joanna. She turned to leave, but as she did so, a thought struck her. She walked across to where the meals lists were pinned, and sure enough, there was Joanna's name, 'Guest of Mara Johns'. For one horrible moment Mara wondered whether this was something else she had written, then forgotten about, but the handwriting was not hers. She looked up, and from the other side of the room saw Joanna watching her. Right, she thought in cold fury, and strode off to find Mr Nasty Pasty in his Salmonella Emporium.

As she went down the steps to Nigel's office she heard shouting. What bloody idiot had done something or other, something about the smoked salmon, and he had better things to do with his time than chasing round after people who were doing bugger all. As Mara entered, Nigel's first words to her were incorporated seamlessly into the tail end of his diatribe . . .

'. . . and if you've come here with some stupid complaint about the food you can piss off now.'

Aha! Here at last was an opportunity for unmitigated nastiness. The fishwife in Mara's mind folded her slabby arms, narrowed her eyes and prepared for battle. She sat casually on the edge of Nigel's desk. The two members of staff that he had been shouting at stood like statues.

'Have I caught you at a difficult moment, or are you always a complete shit?' she asked. She had an impression of two white faces with open mouths. The silence lasted several seconds. It was like watching a hand grenade spinning silently on the spot where it had landed. At last Nigel spoke.

'Yes, I'd heard you were a cheeky bitch.' He looked at her. There was to be no explosion. The fishwife departed like Satan in the wilderness until an opportune time. 'Well, what is it?'

She swung her foot idly backwards and forwards. 'Actually, I was going to ask you a favour.'

A gleam appeared in his eye. 'You think I'm going to do you a favour?'

She continued to swing her foot. 'Oh, no. Not now I've met you.' Mara saw the two staff members behind him trying not to smirk.

Nigel seemed to sense this, for he rounded on them suddenly, and said, 'God almighty, don't just stand there! Go and *try* to sort it out. I'll deal with the salmon later.' They disappeared.

'Now, then. What's this favour?' He tilted his chair and looked at her with a faint leer. 'Go on. I might just surprise you.'

'Someone keeps signing herself in for meals as my guest without my permission.'

'Well, what do you expect me to do about it? I can't spend my whole time checking the guest lists for every bloody meal.' He slammed all four legs of the chair back on the floor.

'So you're saying anyone can walk into college and sign themselves in for meals, and there's nothing you can do about it?'

He tilted the chair back again. 'Who is she, then?'

'Joanna Something –'

Mara was going to describe her, when he interrupted. 'Long, fairish hair, wears a scarf thing on her head? I know who you mean. What's she done to you? Stolen your man?'

Mara was completely wrong-footed by this: 'What man?'

'What man, she asks. Johnny Whitaker. Very popular man, our John.' He waited for a response, and when none came, added a further goad: 'I hear you've got a thing about him.'

'God, yes. I'd like to keep him in my room tied to a chair.'

'I bet you would.' He swayed on his chair with a lewd buttock-grabbing look on his face. 'Into bondage, are you?'

How come I'm having this conversation with this revolting man? Her anger against Joanna seemed remote. It had no connection with Nigel lurching about on his throne in this priapic underworld where all the college gossip seemed to trickle down and mingle with the fatty steam. She stared at her swinging foot.

Nigel brought the front legs of his chair down to rest again. 'Well, I'll have a little word with her. If you're very nice to me.'

'Thanks,' she said dully, and rose to leave.

He stood as well. 'What's wrong?' He put an arm around her shoulder and looked into her face. She shrank back; but this sudden switch from smut to compassion overbalanced her.

'I'm OK.'

He gave her shoulder a little squeeze. 'If you ask me, you've got nothing to worry about.' She tried to draw away. What was he talking about? He pulled her closer, and said, almost nose to nose, 'Seriously. I know his taste in women. She doesn't stand a chance.' He released her, laughing as she struggled to say something.

'See you tonight. Washing up?' And it seemed she was dismissed. You should have left it to me, said the fishwife.

When Mara got back to the dining hall Joanna had left. Different groups of students were sitting talking under the trailing vines. Mara collected her meal and ate her chips with Athena looming over her right shoulder and Aphrodite over her left.

The afternoon slipped away and darkness began to creep over the City, mild, with a hint of coming rain. Up on the windy station above the town students were waiting for trains from the south. They wandered nervously up and down the platforms. Had they been wise to invite that woman, this man, as a partner? Down in the streets below others sat in hairdressers' and barbers' as the night pressed in on the warm salon windows. Would the wind undo all the good work? What if this last-minute haircut was a disaster? And back in the college complex negotiations went on over bathroom rights. From steamy doorways came the smells of honeysuckle and passion-fruit. Watery footprints, powdery footprints.

Mara decided after a fierce inner debate that she would not join Rupert and the Someone-Somethings at the ball. Not if Johnny would be there. If people were talking already, this would make them talk all the more. 'I hear you've got a thing about him.' Good God. Who'd been saying that? Nobody could know. Unless – had he realized? She blushed in mortification at the thought that it might have been Johnny himself, talking to Nigel the way she supposed men did over a pint. She had seen them in the bar together. Well, the black dress would hang undisturbed in the back of the wardrobe. She turned to her books, but her thoughts were interrupted repeatedly. But if you could go – in another life, in another world – who would you go with? The voice nagged away as she worked.

The Scriptures, the millennium and the role of women, she thought, gritting her teeth. She made notes to herself about the Second Coming. What difference did it make to believe the Parousia was imminent? Was this conviction a mental assent to a calculated date? Or was it essentially an experience? And if it was an experience, did it lead to new ways of interpreting the Bible? Or did the method of biblical interpretation determine the nature of the experience? But as she thought about these things, they ceased to be academic questions jotted in her spiky handwriting. She was seventeen and back in the stifling room above the village library.

A summer evening. The windows were all open, but no breeze seemed to be able to find its way in. She was sitting beside Hester. There he was, the leader, whose name she still could not bring herself to form. She heard his voice.

'I have crucified the flesh with its passion and desires, says St Paul. And this is what we must do, brothers and sisters. We must crucify the flesh. God is calling you to nail your pride to the Cross. To nail your intellect to the Cross. He has many blessings he's just waiting to pour down upon us – eye hath not seen nor ear heard, nor hath it entered into the heart of man what God has in store for those who love him and are called according to his purposes, says the Word. But he's not going to give us these blessings unless we humble ourselves before him, brothers and sisters. Unless we let him sit in judgement on us, rather than sitting in judgement on him – questioning his will and his word in our boastful human pride . . .'

And suddenly she had thought, If this is the will of God, I want nothing more to do with it. The atmosphere seemed to crush her and at last, unable to bear another moment, she had walked out, shaking off Hester's hand and refusing to look into her hurt eyes.

The fields were beginning to turn as she hurried the two miles home. Out here the wind was stirring and she paused to watch it pass in silvery waves across the barley. All she could hear was a lark high overhead and the whispering field. For a moment she was at peace. Later she regretted leaving so quietly. Why had she not shouted – prophesied – 'If this is your God, I don't believe in him!'

The hair on her scalp was crawling at the memory. Why was I taken in even for a moment? What *is* the abiding attraction of revivalism? Mara thought of the countless surges of enthusiasm down the Christian centuries, wave after wave breaking across the Church. And each time it seemed new. This time it's the real thing, the converts always thought. And that *was* how it had seemed. The Church of the Revelation offered everything that was lacking in the empty High Church rituals she had grown up with. Spontaneity, lay ministry and, above all, real tangible proof of God's presence: speaking in tongues, prophecy. And healing. Not just those unprovable God-healed-my-bad-back miracles, but at least one miracle that defied even her hardened scepticism. That girl with a bad leg from her class at school. Beverley. She had always been excused PE and was often away from school for long periods having yet another operation to correct her limp. And then one night she had stood up in the meeting and danced. Healed. Doctors had been baffled. The local paper had done an article on it, with a photograph of Beverley posing awkwardly with a hockey-stick. *'Now I can join in at games like the other girls,' says sixteen-year-old Beverley.* Where is she now? wondered Mara. Had she ever made sense of that miracle? Would it shield her from loss of faith, or would it still bind her to the sect long after she had begun to doubt?

No wonder I believed, thought Mara. Nothing like that ever happened in my father's church. She pictured him, a distant robed figure way up at the high altar, his back to the congregation as he elevated the host. Suddenly it struck her that she had joined the sect to punish him for all the times he had turned his back on her. It had made no difference, though. She knew he was opposed to everything the Church of the Revelation practised and preached, and yet he had never remonstrated with her. Was it out of love that he had left her the freedom to choose? She would have felt more loved if he had raged and forbidden her.

But she caught her mind back from these speculations. She was not intending to include modern examples in her thesis. It was to be a historical study. Any insights she gained would be in the realm of the intellect, not the emotions; and this was the proper sphere of under-standing. Perhaps later she might be able to apply her discoveries to her experience and impose some order on the chaos of feelings. Her eyes began to stray to her black book, and then to the drawer where her angel picture lay folded. She had not added to it since that first night. Why not? Because it was associated in her memory with Johnny Whitaker's accusations. Having identified this as the reason, she jerked the drawer open, took out the picture and unfolded it.

Angels and mad aunts. She began by drawing clouds in the spaces between her earlier pictures. On one particularly menacing cloud she drew her mother and grandmother. They were attaching a silver lining to the cloud as though they were hanging Sanderson curtains in a vicarage sitting-room. Above them hovered the words of Julian of Norwich: *All will be well, and all will be well, and all manner of thing will be well.* Despite so much evidence to the contrary. Despite the fact that this world is a place where the innocent are deceived and the good die unhappily. And she folded away the picture abruptly, wrapping up the image which had slid into her mind – Hester in the rocking chair, her hands cradling her stomach, rocking, rocking for hour after endless hour.

Music started up in the dining-room two floors below. It was so loud that Mara could feel as much as hear it as the bass notes shook the foundations of the building. The ball had begun. Voices came up from the terrace, and Mara went to her window and looked out. The first couples were wandering on the lawn with their cocktails. The white of dress shirts gleamed, changing colour in the flashing lights. Her ears caught another sound: even above the immense noise came the sound of the bells, aloof, as though they came from another world far beyond all this. Seven-thirty. It was time to go down to the kitchens.

The grand staircase seemed to be reliving some of its past. Surely it was made to be glided down in silk or taffeta. Mara felt like a servant trapped upstairs long after she should have been sweating in the kitchens. The corridors were growing crowded, and yet the atmosphere still seemed tense. Perfumes and aftershaves filled the air. People were too clear-eyed and sober. The bared shoulders and elbows looked awkward. But the first drinks would take the edge off things, and then the college would be a magical place full of sparkling lights and beautiful people. Mara slipped through the door and down the steps to the kitchen.

Over by the sinks stood the other student who would be washing up. As she approached, Mara saw him pulling on a pair of rubber gloves and flexing his fingers as though he were a battlefield surgeon about to saw off a leg. Almost at once a parade of dirty crockery descended to them on trolleys to be sorted and fed through the machines, casualties of the warfare of feasting – sherry glasses, side plates, dinner plates, dessert bowls. The air was filled with clanking and swooshing, while from overhead came the sounds of music and footsteps as the unseen couples surged along corridors. Mara could see the tops of the chefs' tall hats as they passed backwards and forwards shoving large trays into ovens and hauling them out. The waste disposal unit gargled like a fat idol bellowing for more as the scraps tumbled down its metal throat. The work seemed endless – plunging cutlery into steaming sinks, stacking dirty plates on racks, unloading clean dishes. Just as Mara was wondering how much more there could possibly be, a lull came. They were between sittings.

Mara leant against the sink while the other student talked. He seemed to regard her as a neutral presence, an honorary male, perhaps? At any rate, he appeared to need no help from her in keeping the conversation running smoothly. She looked round the

83

corner and saw the two field mice folding paper napkins into fans and putting them into wine glasses.

A shout heralded the arrival of the next lot of dishes. The machines swished and steamed, and the young man talked on above the din. He was the one who had bellowed like a gorilla one breakfast, Mara remembered suddenly.

In the second lull Nigel brought them a bottle of wine. Condensation formed on the glasses as he poured. He handed them each a glass.

'Don't say I never give you anything,' he said to Mara. Strands of her hair were escaping and corkscrewing up into curls in the steam. She pulled at one to straighten it. The wine was blissfully cold.

'Look at her,' said Nigel suddenly to the gorilla. 'I'll never understand women. The ones with straight hair spend a fortune having it permed, and the ones with curly hair try to straighten it.' The gorilla focused on her with intelligent interest. 'Why don't you wear it loose?' persisted Nigel. He turned to the gorilla. 'Don't you think she'd look better with her hair loose?'

The gorilla considered the idea with surprise, as though he had been called upon to judge the merits of a length of slub silk. 'Yes. Much better.'

The arrival of the last lot of dishes prevented Mara from replying. She scraped platefuls of leftovers into the bawling metal god and continued the argument in her mind. I tie my hair back because I don't want to conform to some male ideal of femininity. Then why do you grow it long? Because it's cheaper and simpler than getting it cut every couple of months. She stared at the swirling prawns and melon. There was something else at work in her mind, she had to admit. Part of her was proud of her hair, that it grew so long and extravagantly. She kept it bound up, her secret, like the strength of Samson. Or was it really the hair of Rapunzel, which one day would bring the prince climbing up to her chamber?

At last it was all over. The chefs had gone and the machines dwindled into silence. From above came the music, shrieks and thumping feet. Mara and the gorilla looked at one another in the quiet kitchen and smiled.

'I wonder if we can go?' he asked. To the ball, the ball! whispered a voice in Mara's head. But she remembered that she was not intending to join in. Nigel appeared.

84

'Oh, I see. Stopped work already, have we?' He scanned the room for some incomplete task, an unwiped surface, a stray fork.

'We've finished,' pointed out the gorilla.

For a moment it seemed that Nigel would be forced to agree; but then he said, 'What about the floor?' Dismay on the gorilla's face. 'Oh, it's all right. I'll do it. Go on. Bugger off. Enjoy yourselves.' Nigel dismissed them like a bad-tempered fairy godmother worn out by a thousand ungrateful Cinderellas. 'Go and buy her a drink,' Nigel told the gorilla.

'Um ...' The gorilla had clearly visualized a better way of spending the evening.

'Ignore him,' said Mara, and the gorilla flashed her a smile and disappeared.

'Got other plans, have we?' asked Nigel with a knowing look and, finding this did not bring a response, added, 'He was upstairs in Coverdale dining-hall last time I saw him. He's finished work, so this could be your lucky night.' Mara simply turned and walked out, leaving Nigel to push the mop wearily about the floor.

Back in her room Mara stood and stared at the books and papers on her desk. The music below pounded on. It would be impossible to concentrate. Or to sleep. No wonder the polecat had disappeared to Oxford for the weekend. She might just as well go to the ball. Stuff the lot of them. They can think what they like. She would just wander about and watch people, then slip away again. Her pulse quickened as she went to the wardrobe and drew out the black dress. She would try it, and if it looked stupid, well, she had lost nothing. She had never intended to join in, anyway.

But as she slid the dress on she knew. It was perfect. Was this how Aunt Daphne had looked? Her reflection stared back at her and she watched her hands unravelling the long plait as though it were some other woman's hands and hair a long time ago. She shook her head and the curls writhed out. I look like Medusa. Or a dead woman. I'm too pale. She coloured her lips and outlined her eyes; she pulled on a pair of long black gloves, gave herself one last look in the mirror and left the room. The thought of Jezebel filled her mind, painting her eyelids and calling from her high window. One final revelling in her power before the eunuchs came and cast her out, down to the stones below.

CHAPTER 8

Mara was sitting in a stone archway in the cathedral cloisters listening to the rain. It was a week before Christmas and the City was almost empty of students.

She hugged her cloak more tightly round her and nodded her head to shake a drop of rain off the brim of her hat, as one or other of the mad aunts might have done when it had belonged to her.

Maddy's voice came drifting into her mind: 'I'm not a pillar of the Church. I see myself as a flying buttress: lending valuable support, but from the *outside*.' The whole episode played itself again in Mara's mind. They had been sitting in Rupert's room one afternoon towards the end of term. She remembered thinking how nice it must be for Maddy to feel excused from the obligation of going to church by one clever metaphor. It was probably a quotation from somewhere, but Maddy would never admit this. Rupert had been intensely irritated. The word 'nonsense' buzzed like an angry bee about him, but he was thwarted by the neatness of the image. Or was he trying to locate the quotation? It had been Johnny who had answered, blowing smoke from his cigarette up to the ceiling.

'The flying buttresses in the cathedral here are on the inside.' There was an interesting pause. Were they? Was he making it up, or did he really know?

'Flying buttresses are always on the outside, you ignorant northern fool,' said Maddy, 'as anyone who knows the first thing about building would be able to tell you.' And for some reason both Johnny and Rupert had found this amusing. Maddy registered surprise – it had not been one of her wittier offerings – then annoyance, when she realized they were laughing at her. 'And in any case, the cathedral doesn't have flying buttresses,' she added with the calm authority of a guide-book.

'What – no flying buttresses?' asked Johnny. Maddy eyed him with sudden caution. Could a man who didn't know what an idiom was be *au fait* with church architecture? He continued to smoke.

'What?' demanded Maddy. 'What, what?'

'Interesting.'

'Why? In what way?'

At last she extracted an answer.

'I was just wondering what stopped the outward pressure of the vaults.'

'Oh,' said Maddy airily, 'the whole structure is held together by some mystical spiritual process known only to the godhead.'

'Is that right, pet?'

And Maddy, seeming to sense she had been outdone, changed to another tactic: 'Why do you call me "pet" the whole time? It's so patronizing.'

'Because I think you're an animal.'

Mara smiled. The rain continued to fall. The City was becoming a castle in a folk tale. When I leave, a hedge of dense thorns will spring up all around it, till only the topmost stones of the cathedral tower remain visible. And inside the people I know will remain for ever as they are now, unchanging, bright. She knew she was missing her friends. That very evening they would all be meeting up at Rupert's party, and she would not be there. He had invited her, but she had chosen to stay behind, studying. She watched the rain, regretting her choice. Biblical fancy dress – what would I have gone as? Jael, with her tent-peg. Or Judith, if we're including the Apocrypha. Come in, my Lord. Have a drink. Why not put your feet up? Chop, chop. The archetypal castrating heroine.

She cast her mind back over the term. The City and its people already seemed to be part of the distant past, as though she were an old woman looking back on them. But as she thought about this, she realized that it was only now that she was alone and her friends had gone home that they appeared in her memory with this clarity. While she was with them, there were always blurrings. How could she know what they were really like? It was as though she were painting pictures and saying, 'They are like this.'

Was there a slight tenderness creeping into the brushwork? At any rate, she would keep the portraits when she left. They would not be worth exhibiting, but they were too interesting to throw out. She would come across them when she was sixty, perhaps. Oh yes. Rupert something or other. Anderson. Well, well. I remember him. And Johnny Whitaker. Yes. I wonder what they're doing now?

But what kind of picture would she paint of Johnny? He, of all her new friends, was the one she was least able to understand. She heard

Rupert's voice in her mind: 'The trouble with you, Whitaker, is that you're constitutionally unable to be serious. You undermine any sensible conversation in two seconds flat simply by opening your mouth.' Yes, it was his sense of humour that made him so difficult to pin down. It kept people at arm's length, while creating the impression of intimacy. She cast her mind back to that same afternoon in Rupert's room, remembering the leap in her pulse when Maddy asked Johnny and Rupert one of the things she had been longing to know herself.

'So why are you here, then? I mean, tell us your conversion story, boys.'

'Yes,' joined in May. 'When did you ask the Lord Jesus into your heart and life? Tell us, and we'll give you marks out of ten.'

'For drama and lurid details,' said Maddy.

'And uplifting gospel content, of course,' added May.

Rupert's story had been pretty much as Mara had expected it to be. As the son of a clergyman, he had grown up in the Christian faith. School chapel each week, hearty Christian camps in the holidays. He had gone 'off the rails a bit' at Oxford.

'How? How? What did you do?' Maddy and May had demanded immediately.

'Oh, the usual things,' was all Rupert could be made to say. In any case, he had been brought back into the fold during the Christian Union mission in his final year, and, after a few years working as a solicitor in London, he had started his training at Coverdale.

'You're so boring, Rupert,' said Maddy. 'I mean, that's hardly the Damascus road, is it?'

'I think we'll give him four out of ten,' agreed May.

Johnny, by contrast, had been converted by a vision on the way home from the pub one night. After a lifetime of doing – sidelong glance at Rupert – 'the usual things'.

'What things?' demanded Maddy and May.

'Well, you know. Getting drunk, screwing around, nicking cars.' Their eyes grew rounder with each admission. 'GBH, armed robbery, the usual things.'

'You lying git!' said Maddy, realizing belatedly that he was laughing at them.

'What did you do, seriously?'

'I never did anything seriously in my life.'

They persisted, but he would not part with any lurid details, leaving them wondering whether he had done any of the things he claimed.

'What sort of vision did you see?' asked May in the end.

'Well, it all began when the vicar came over to me in the pool room. He started to tell me this story about a man with two sons. The older one was a model son, the younger was a rebel.'

'What – the prodigal son?' said Maddy, as though she was being short-changed.

Johnny laughed. 'Aye, but I didn't know that at the time. I thought, some bastard's been talking about me. Or else my dad's put him up to it.'

'Were you a rebel, then?' asked May.

'What precise form did your rebellion take?' persisted Maddy. But he would only grin at them.

Full marks to both of them for not glamorizing their sinful past, thought Mara. She had heard too many testimonies which dwelt pruriently on the pre-conversion life. Salvation always seemed dull by comparison.

'Anyway, the younger son got half his dad's money and blew the lot, ended up down and out, then decided to go home and ask his dad for a job. "And what do you think his father did?" he asks me.'

Mara remembered the curious effect Johnny's account had had on her. It was almost as though she, too, were hearing the old story for the first time. She wondered if he would preach like this when he was ordained. His congregation would be tricked for once out of making mental shopping lists, or wondering whether they had left the iron on.

'So I said, the father comes out of the house and says, "Oh, it's you, is it? Well, you can bugger off. You've wasted my money, you've upset your mother, now piss off and don't show your face round here again."'

They had all laughed at this. But wasn't that what it ought to have been like? Mara wondered. The real outrage in the parable was the fact of the father's forgiveness. No wonder the older son had been so angry. That was the problem of knowing the Bible so well. It lost its power to shock.

'Go on,' prompted Maddy.

'And the vicar says, no, his dad sees him coming and runs out to meet him. He forgives him, gives him a big hug and throws a party for him. "Does he, bollocks," I said.'

A protest from Rupert.

'First official warning, Mr Whitaker,' said Maddy, like a Wimbledon umpire. 'We're penalizing you one point for bad language.'

'But that was before I was converted,' explained Johnny.

'So you wouldn't use that kind of language *now*?' said May.

'Certainly not,' he replied in a prim Anderson manner. 'But the vicar says, yes, that *is* what he does, because that's what God's like. No matter where you've been, no matter what you've done, he's waiting for you to come home.'

There had been a pause. The words echoed in a hollow place inside Mara's mind.

'And?' said May.

'Then some of my mates came in and started taking the piss. You know – "Our John's seen the light", all that stuff. So I said, "Listen, I don't need God, or you or anyone else telling me what to do. I can run my own life." Well, the vicar gave up and went home and I had a few more pints before closing time. On the way home I saw a vision.'

'I think the technical term is DT's,' said Maddy, getting on top of the situation again.

Johnny laughed. 'I don't know what it was. All I know is I turned the corner and there was this bloody great angel blocking the path.'

'*Angel*?' Maddy and May snorted with laughter, then fell silent, not knowing what to make of it. They sat watching him uncertainly to see if he was serious. Mara glanced at Rupert. He looked as though he had heard the story before.

'Well, go on. What did it say?' asked Maddy. '"Hail, thou that art highly favoured"?' May giggled.

'No. He said, "Don't mess with me, you arrogant little sod."'

'You liar,' said Maddy. 'Angels don't speak like that.'

'How do you know?'

'I just do. They come wafting along in their tinsel-trimmed nighties and say, "Fear not." It says so in the Bible, only you wouldn't know that, of course.'

'Being an ignorant northern fool,' added May.

The rain pattered overhead. Maddy and May had awarded him nine out of ten for dramatic content, then disqualified him on the grounds that it was a pack of lies. But it had rung true for Mara. It seemed to her that this was exactly how an angel might speak. Terrifying warriors, not effete pre-Raphaelite musicians. The bells chimed eleven. She roused herself and left the cloisters as she heard the sound of voices and feet approaching.

Mara was at her desk staring blankly at the wall. The room was silent. Only the ticking of the radiator kept her company. Even the polecat had gone home. She sighed and looked at the notes in front of her. Had she grown so accustomed to being with other people that she no longer really relished her own company? She cast her mind back to the day before term had begun, and saw herself looking down on the tops of people's heads and vowing to remain alone. At the age of six she had taken hold of the realization that she had no friends and transformed it into a fierce resolve never to have any. The transformation had been so powerful that this was the first time she could remember wondering whether somewhere inside her there was a six-year-old crying out for a friend. Her cousin Dewi had become her imaginary companion. He was so constant and loyal a champion that the real Dewi could only disappoint her, and finally vanish from her life without a word. I must be careful, she thought, binding up my happiness in other people. She opened her desk drawer and took out two photographs.

The first was a snapshot of her and Rupert at the ball. He was standing behind her with his arms wrapped round her waist, and he was laughing. Her hand was halfway to her mouth to cover her smile. Rupert had given her the photograph and told her to contemplate it every morning before breakfast. One of those impossible things: Mara Johns smiling. She studied her face. My mouth is too wide, she thought. The teeth were no longer crooked and the ugly metal brace had gone, but she still cringed at the mocking names of childhood echoing in her memory. Bugs Bunny. Dracula. Her teeth were too big and had crowded her narrow jaw. Well, they were straight now, at least, although that gap between the front teeth was very noticeable. But other than that, the smile wasn't too bad. Rupert and Johnny had taken to greeting her rare smiles by reeling back in a parody of stunned bliss, as though someone had let off a blunderbuss full of rose petals in their faces.

She leant the photograph against a pile of books. It had begun to seem like a still from a film: a young woman puts on an old black dress and is transported magically into another world for an evening. She walks and dances among ghosts and bright images until at last the pale light of morning gleams over the rooftops. Up the stairs she goes, back to her room. She takes off the dress and sinks into sleep. When she wakes, the spell is broken. Lying on her desk are two photographs: all that remains of her night of bliss.

Well, it had been more ordinary than that. She ran the film again and saw herself walking down the stairs . . .

Why am I doing this? I should never have worn a dress like this, showing off an expanse of scrawny chest and long skinny arms. And my tattoo shows. She regretted having it done, just as her mother had said she would, but she was too stubborn to admit it. Fortunately, the scar on her wrist was covered by her long black gloves. What shall I do with my hands? A drink. She pushed her way past people towards the bar. There in the distance she glimpsed Johnny Whitaker coming in the opposite direction. Her heart pounded. They drew close. 'Hello,' she said. He flicked her a glance. 'Hello.' Then he continued on his way without a pause. Disappointment ran cold over her.

She went out into the night. A star gleamed in a gap between the clouds and then was gone. Behind her the music pounded. The whole thing had been a mistake. Why had he looked at her like that? A casual glance, then on with whatever he was doing. He had been looking for someone else. And then, at that point of misery, Mara experienced the sudden shift of perspective which made her think, so what? We are so obsessed with people and things. For a moment she had glimpsed another world where it was the space between things which was real. The realm of angels. Objects were gaps, pools of mere nothingness. She saw the angels passing to and fro across the breadth of the universe, transparent, incorporeal, going about their business. All their works were righteous, and yet true compassion was impossible to them, for what did they know about suffering? She looked up and saw the same star coming and going behind the ragged clouds. *That which hath been is now, and that which is to be hath already been. Vanity of vanities.* She turned and began to make her way back to the college.

'Mara, Mara!' It was Rupert with the Someone-Somethings. Were they the ones he had gone off the rails with at Oxford? At his elbow was an attractive woman, cool and blonde in the dim light of the quad. Cordelia Chauffeured-Bentley. Rupert called her again and beckoned, and she went to join them. This was his sister, Rachel – 'Hello' – Mara traced a fleeting resemblance – and her fiancé Marcus; and these were several Oxford friends – 'Hello, hi' – whose names vanished into the night as Mara failed to commit them to memory. She was too busy watching them. And this was Cordelia Shefford-Bentley. Rupert had his eyes on Mara, and she was obliged to turn her amusement into a friendly smile. They all smiled back, drawing in closer than she liked. 'What a wonderful dress! We've heard so much about you! Doesn't she have wonderful hair! Aren't you studying women prophets or something? It sounds terribly interesting!'

They came from another land, from her mother's country. They would always bring wine and flowers. They would never forget the thank-you note. I'm only a half-caste. Could I join in if I tried? How *won*derful to meet you all! No. But she could at least be pleasant, and not go scything off through them with knives sticking out of her wheels like Boadicea's chariot. 'You must stay with us,' they were urging her. 'Don't be silly! Of course you must.'

'Please please please,' begged Rupert. She felt his arms go round her waist. A flash went off in the night. The moment of the photograph. 'Good God, you've got a tattoo.'

'Don't be rude, Rupert,' said his sister. 'I think it's rather beautiful.' They all peered and agreed. Really rather beautiful. This was how her mother had consoled herself. At least it wasn't vulgar.

'Are you coming with us or not?' persisted Rupert.

'Oh, all right.' An ungracious grinding of gears.

'You can share him with me,' said the silvery Cordelia. 'You'll have to divide yourself between us, Rupert. Shall you mind that?'

'Of course he won't. Come on, let's go and see this cabaret.'

Rupert hung back. 'Do you visualize that division as vertical or horizontal?' he said to Mara with a sort of laboured pedantry which made her wonder.

'Horizontal,' she replied, glimpsing the conversation's next turn.

'And which half would you prefer?' He looked into her eyes. 'Above or below the waist?'

'Below. Definitely.'

The Someone-Somethings laughed. Rupert was thumped on the back. The group began moving again. Rupert waved them off.

'We'll catch you up.' They glided away with laughter trailing behind them. Rupert turned back to Mara again. 'What lies behind your preference for my lower half, might I inquire?' Again that pernickety tone. It occurred to Mara with a flicker of amusement that he might be drunk, drunk in that kind of lucid, coherent way which continues to expound Heidegger whilst sliding slowly down the wall into oblivion.

'The fact that you wouldn't be able to boss me around.'

'Thank you. *Thank you*, Mara.' Well, she thought, you ought to be grateful. I waited till the others had gone before saying it. He took her in his arms. 'And what about my sexual prowess?' His face was inches from hers.

'I can't say I've ever thought about it.'

'I'm painfully aware of that.' He was definitely drunk. The fumes on his breath touched her face. 'You think my testosterone has been mystically transubstantiated into holy water. The moment the episcopal hands are laid on – *bang!* – the male member drops off.'

She stared at him in amazement. *Easy does it, Rupert, old thing!* said the caption.

'You're so pure you believe that we priests are like the angels in heaven: they neither marry nor whatever the hell the other thing is.'

'"Nor are they given in marriage." And you're not a priest yet.'

'Was that an invitation?'

Her denial was swallowed up by his mouth. She felt his tongue and his teeth, and his hands – *steady on, old chap!* - had they not been the hands of a Bishop's son, could almost have been described as groping her. She felt them kneading her skinny backside and pressing her hard into his groin. Bloody hell. The ordaining Bishop would have his work cut out. And rather belatedly she thought to struggle free. He released her. They stood looking at one another. Now what happens? she wondered. Was he about to apologize? *'I've been behaving like a dashed brute,' Rupert blurted.* Or: *'I've wanted to do that ever since I first saw you!'*

'You're supposed to slap my face,' he reminded her.

'I'm wearing gloves. It'll have to be an upper cut instead.'

'I'll risk it.' He tried to kiss her again, but she squirmed away.

Mara smiled at the photograph. She was still surprised how arousing those few seconds had been. Having tried sex once at fifteen and decided it was horrible, and then again at eighteen to check she had been right, this short grapple with Rupert had been a revelation. Even now when she chanced upon the memory unexpectedly, she felt that losing-your-footing-on-a-rockface sensation in the pit of her stomach. Nothing would come of it, of course. Except that she felt she actually liked Rupert, now she had seen him briefly off the rails with his halo crooked. He had appeared in her room the following day making strangely disjointed conversation. It was some time before she realized with a burst of inward amusement that he was angling for information about the previous night.

'I'm surprised you have the nerve to face me,' she said, assuming a look of cold outrage.

'Mea culpa.' He smote his breast. 'The fact is, Mara, I only have a very hazy recollection of last night. Charming, but hazy.'

'And you're worried about a paternity suit?'

He laughed, then was very still for a moment as he caught sight of her face. This had been too much for her. Her hand went to her mouth and covered her smile.

'Don't do that to me, you dreadful woman.' Then there had been a pause. Embarrassment crept up on them and their eyes wandered around the room. 'Look, anyway, I'm sorry if I . . . if you . . .' She looked at him and saw him run his hand through his hair. 'I wouldn't like you to think . . .' His awkwardness infected her and she looked away again. What could she say to reassure him that couldn't be construed as further invitation? Her hand was fiddling with her plait as they stood looking anywhere but at one another.

'Don't worry,' she muttered.

'Right. Well . . . Thanks.'

She glanced at him and saw his relief. There was another pause. They were still stranded in the middle of a swamp of embarrassment.

He recovered before she did, taking her hand and asking gravely, 'How was it for you?' She glared at him. Don't push your luck, Anderson. 'The earth moved?'

'Sorry, Rupert. I'm afraid you score negative on the Richter scale.'

'Thank you, darling. It's reassuring to know that whatever the situation, I can count on you to say the most wounding thing imaginable.' But he gave her hand a friendly squeeze and left.

She saw now that this exchange had restored their relationship to its original footing. He need not fear she had been swept away by his prowess. She need not fear he would lunge at her in deserted corridors.

The second photograph was of her and Johnny. She leant it against the books beside the snapshot. The two could not have been more different. They could have been of events over half a century apart, for the second was a portrait in sepia. There had been a photographer posing couples against a background of folding screen and parlour palms. 'Come on,' she remembered Johnny saying. She pulled back, not wanting a formal photograph which might whisper 'Couple.' But she had given way suddenly at the thought that her relúctance might arouse his suspicions.

She gazed at the result. It was unnerving. She studied the patterned screen, the palm in its brass pot, herself sitting stiffly in the chair with Johnny behind, his hand resting on the chair back like a Victorian patriarch. Had they agreed beforehand not to smile? She thought they had. At any rate, her rigid stare had the authentic look of family portraits of the last century. Johnny's attempt at a straight face was less convincing. She looked at it closely. This was the expression she had never trusted, that having-just-smiled or just-about-to-smile look. How false photography could be. It posed as reality. This is how it *was* at that particular moment – she sat like this, he stood like that. The facts were indisputable.

But it had all seemed so different. The two realities could scarcely be reconciled. Some time after she had joined Rupert and the Someone-Somethings the world had taken on that charming, but hazy quality characteristic of a couple of cocktails on an empty stomach. Her recollections from then on were no longer like watching a film. No. When she thought back to those patchy memories, she was not watching herself. She was a single point of awareness, concentrating in an unsteady world like a ship's steward with a tray of drinks in a storm.

She was outside again and Johnny was there.

'I saw you earlier,' she said.

'I know. I didn't recognize you. I passed you and thought, 'There's someone I know but don't recognize because she's dressed up.''

She turned her head slowly away to hide her joy. Her brain seemed to swim round, lagging half a second behind. He had not been ignoring her, then. She tilted her head back and gazed at the sky. The clouds raced on and on, lit up by a hidden moon. Her hair slid over her shoulders and brushed her back, warm as a shawl. She felt his finger touch her upper arm. The tattoo. He laughed.

'What are you like?'

'You've got one,' she accused drunkenly. 'But I suppose that's different.'

He laughed at her again and rested his hand on her bare shoulder.

She looked back up at the sky. If she stood still, he would keep his hand there. The music went on behind them.

'You know,' she said, 'if you look at one star long enough without blinking, it seems to spin.' I noticed this as a child, lying out on the hillside up above my uncle's farm.

'It's a well-known optical illusion,' he said. Was it? But it had been her secret discovery. 'You know what causes it?' She stared, and he took her hands with a smile. 'In my case, about six pints of beer. Ha'away, let's dance.' They began to move to the music.

He doesn't believe me. 'Try it,' she said, but he only laughed at her. 'It's possible to be drunk and right.' But her words seemed to be wading through deep water.

'Ah, but the difficulty is convincing people,' he answered. And they spun slowly like the stars, with her watching his face, while behind him passed trees and buildings and lights, trees, buildings, lights, until they were the only beings in the whole world, with the universe wheeling round them.

Mara paused and drummed her fingers on the desk. She was having trouble with the chronology. There were several other memories, but they were like a handful of holiday snaps that had got out of order, shuffled together in a drawer instead of pasted in the album. Only one stood out like an unmistakable landmark. She felt her scalp crawl at the thought, and she was standing again in the hallway under the skinny cherubs seeing Joanna coming. She was wearing a long blue 'Queen of Heaven' type dress, hair flowing and tears on her face, crying, 'Johnny, Johnny, I've got to talk to you!' and Mara turned and walked away. Snakes hissed and coiled in her head as she went. I will not stay and fight over him. Out under the night sky again, and there was the fishwife still biding her time, magnificent arms gleaming in the moonlight. You're so bleeding lah-di-dah, she said, walking off like that; while somewhere else there was a six-year-old weeping for a friend, any friend. She hugged her arms round herself as she stood on the edge of the light looking blindly across the dark hollow of the night.

'You're bloody useless, you are,' said a voice behind her. Johnny. She did not turn. 'You're supposed to protect me.' The words stung. So that's why he wanted my company.

'I imagine you can take care of yourself.' She continued to stare into the emptiness. His lips were at her ear.

'Mmm. I'd much rather you took care of me, though.' This

97

brought her head round fast. The crude tone had been unmistakable; and yet as she looked at him . . . Of course she was mistaken. He was not Nigel, after all.

'Well, you managed to escape.'

'Eventually. Why me, O Lord?' He made a despairing gesture.

'Because you're so good with us lame ducks.' She bit her lip. It was as though the phrase had been lying there in the undergrowth, tense and sprung, waiting for an unwary foot.

'Lame duck? Who said that?' The words had obviously jolted his memory. 'Did someone call you that, or is that how you see yourself?'

She stood cursing herself and hoped he would not remember and realize she had been eavesdropping. She waited for him to laugh. He laughed.

'So you think I'm practising my pastoral skills on you?' She made no reply. 'You seem to have a very low opinion of yourself. Unless' – he put a finger under her chin and tilted her face up till he was staring down into her eyes – 'you have a very high opinion of me. Which would be a big mistake, sweetie.' She jerked away in scorn. 'Come on,' he said, 'I'll buy you another drink, and you can tell me about the stars.'

They're all picking on me! wailed a little voice inside her. She snuffed it out in disgust. I sound like Joanna, she thought, as she let him lead her away.

That's why I dislike her so much, Mara realized as she stared at the photograph. She uses tactics I don't allow myself to use. I could cry and say 'Johnny, Johnny, help me', except that I never would. The people we hate most are always shadows of our worst selves. She put the photographs back in the drawer and tried once again to concentrate on her work. The others would all be at Rupert's party by now. Rain pattered on the window and she sighed.

CHAPTER 9

There was a promise of snow in the air. Mara turned her back on the station lights and began to walk the two miles through the dark to her parents' house. From overhead came the small shiftings and whisperings of the trees that lined the road. The world was holding its breath for the coming snow and for Christmas.

Christmas. Red and gold. Green and white. The holly with its berries in the vicarage garden. White candles in the dark church, and the gold of chocolate pennies or angels' wings. With each homeward step a childlike excitement mounted in her, as though she believed it could all be as it once had been. Sitting in bed hugging her knees, Hester in the other bed, her eyes shining as their mother read them *The Tailor of Gloucester*. The little mice sewing away at Christmas as the tailor lay ill. And in the church tomorrow night the congregation gathering for midnight Mass. She saw the dark-robed figures in the chancel silhouetted against the glowing reredos, moving silently, their hands raised as they lit the candles one by one in the candelabra overhead. One flame and another and another, black figures on gold. And in the vestry her father would be standing in his robes glancing into the mirror, the light sliding over his white cope and the secret gold of the lining gleaming and vanishing as he moved. She had not been home for Christmas for three years, but she knew that the next few days would be full of the old hostilities. They ran like cracks from foundation to rooftop, and her mother with all her skill would never paper over them. There would be silences like loaded weapons or words like biting steel. And worst of all, Hester's absence, which no one would mention.

I can't do this, she thought. I can't bear it. She dropped her bag and pressed her hands over her mouth to stop herself crying out loud. I should have stayed at college. The City loomed in her mind as she had seen it from the departing train, with its buildings rising up out of the freezing fog. The whole of the north had been clenched in a bitter frost, and the fog had worsened until she could see nothing from the window. The train could have been travelling down an endless white tunnel. She stood now under the trees. The branches stirred a little and she remembered the coming snow. Then some words appeared in her mind like a framed sampler. *Try To Be Nice*. Her mother's motto. It had hung invisibly on every wall of her childhood, and she had tried. She had been nice enough to burst a blood vessel, only nobody had ever noticed. Hester's niceness eclipsed hers, just as her prettiness had done, and in the end Mara had been driven to nastiness just so that she would not vanish altogether. But Hester would not be home this Christmas. Is that what I'm trying to do – take Hester's place? The thought stifled her. It would be like wearing Hester's clothes – too small, too short. A scream welled up in her. It was pointless. Her father's study door would remain closed against her. I've never been able to please him. I've tried and tried. I was never able to displease him, either. He didn't care enough. He's never cared about me. It was always Hester. She pressed her hands against her mouth so hard she began to taste blood. Then first flakes began to fall. Well, I'm here now. No point going back. Why not *try to be nice*? She picked up her bag and began to walk again as the snow floated down.

The vicarage was empty. Mara had been picturing her mother's greeting – the smile, and 'Darling you're home! You should have phoned. We'd have collected you from the station.' After a moment's thought she was glad to have the house to herself. It gave her a chance to make it her own again. She put a kettle on the Aga and stood warming herself. Tomorrow the smells of Christmas would fill the kitchen. Even now everything would be standing ready in the larder. She went to look, as she had always done as a child.

There was the turkey defrosting on the large willow-pattern platter. Two pheasants hung from a hook. The Bart had been, then. The traditional gift of dead wildlife from gentry to clergy. The shelves held rows of bottled fruit and jars of jam. Things to give away. Did the postman ever eat those apricots in brandy? Did the dustman mutter 'More bloody marmalade' as he trudged down the path? 'Why don't they just give money?' And on the floor stood the ranks of bottles which people had given to her father. Port, ginger wine, whisky, brandy. Why? Some received wisdom that all clergy from fat prelate down to humble priest are wine-bibbers and gluttons? But her father seldom drank. Maybe there were pewfuls of Johns ancestors forbidding it. He gave the bottles to rural deans and archdeacons when he was invited out to dinner. And they in turn probably gave them to deans or bishops. She saw the bottles slowly ascending the Church hierarchy until at last they found their way to the Archbishop of Canterbury.

There on the fridge was the Christmas cake, already iced and decorated. It stood like a little snowy landscape – house, trees, a robin (bigger than the house) and Santa Claus stuck on to his sleigh with a blob of icing. The sleigh was being pulled by an odd assortment of reindeer of different sizes and colours. They formed a chain which ran halfway round the cake. Mara smiled. This was how she and Hester had always done it, taking turns, adding one decoration at a time. Her mother had done the same as though it were a sacred family tradition.

The kettle began to boil and Mara turned and left the shadowy pantry. She stood with her coffee thinking about the cake. Snow was brushing the vicarage windows now. It must be getting quite deep. She put down her empty mug and went to the sitting-room, where the French windows opened on to the garden. She unlocked them and stepped out.

Behind her the brightly lit room shone out on to the lawn. She stood in a doorway of light with her face upturned. All around the snow sifted down, filling the spiky holly leaves, muffling the whole world. The flakes burnt as they melted on her cheeks and lips. Another shadow joined hers in the snow. She turned. It was her father. He must have been in his study all the time. They stood together in the silence watching each other. I will talk to him. I will really try. But she could find no starting place.

After a while he spoke: 'Did you have a good term?'

'Yes.' How short her answer sounded, as though in her anxiety she had snipped it off. 'Yes,' she tried again. 'It was OK.'

'Good.' They might have been speaking into nothing at all. The world and its sounds lay deep in snow.

'Well, it's a beautiful city.' He spoke formally, as though she were a parishioner.

'Oh, yes,' she agreed.

'And your course is going well?'

'Yes. I think.'

'And you get on well with your tutor?'

'Yes, thank you.' Silence. The sky shed its snow. How could she talk to him now, after more than ten years of hiding from him everything she thought or felt?

Suddenly she said: 'I'll miss my friends.' There was no mistaking the significance of this simple statement.

'Fellow students, are they?'

'Yes.'

'That's good.'

'Some are undergraduates.'

'Mmm.'

'And some are training for the ministry.'

'At Coverdale?'

'Yes.'

Silence closed round them again. Then from behind them in the house came the sound of the front door opening.

'I'm back, Morgan!' Her mother came into the room and caught sight of Mara. 'Darling! How long have you been here?' They came in from the snow, and Mara went to hug her mother.

'You smell of oranges,' Mara said.

'I know. We've been making Christingles for the crib service. The vestry is awash with orange juice. Have you eaten? I'll make you an omelette, and you can tell me all about your term. Have you had a wonderful time?' Mara's father left without saying anything. He doesn't want me here. She felt that old hollow desolation, like homesickness, except that she was at home. She followed her mother to the kitchen, but as she went, a thought struck her: That's what I do. I walk out without saying anything. 'Goodbye, Mara,' her friends would chorus pointedly. And what if her father had been thinking, She doesn't want me here now her mother's home?

Mara watched her mother as she cooked. She was so young-looking that people often mistook them for sisters. She had married early, and in some ways she seemed not to have grown up. Her policy was that life should be fun. No matter how grim one's existence was, fun would be had. Mara felt old and crabby by comparison. Her mother talked as she chopped the onions and mushrooms. Her conversation was like her letters, and required about as much response. This is why we are friends, thought Mara. Our relationship relies on her saying a lot, and my replying occasionally; the conversational equivalent of a postcard. This shed light on her friendship with Maddy and May. Mara ate while her mother talked about Grandma Flowers.

'She's as cheerful as ever, but she gets so confused. Oh, I meant to say she's coming for Christmas lunch. I'm picking her up before church. She's worked out that she's in a nursing home now, and not a hotel, so in some ways she's improved, I suppose. They've been trying to assess the extent of the damage done by her last stroke. And they ask questions to see if she's going senile – what year is this? who's on the throne? and so on. She knows all that, but she's no idea why they're asking. She said to me the other day, "That young Doctor – such a pleasant young man – but do you know, he *did not know* the name of the prime minister!" And the psychiatric nurse has been checking for aphasia by showing her everyday objects and asking what they are. But she – the nurse – is Indian, and Grandma thinks she's forgotten the English for "teaspoon".'

Mara finished eating. She pictured Grandma helping the medical staff with their basic English vocabulary.

'She said to me, "It's perfectly all right, you know. They know the names of all the medicines." I shouldn't laugh. It's all been rather difficult, though. At least the house has been cleared.' And just for a moment Mara thought her mother seemed old. One day I will be looking after her and saying, 'It's all rather difficult.'

There was a silence, and then Mara said, 'I wore the black dress.' Her mother's face lit up.

'Wonderful! It fits you? When? Where? You went to a party?'

'The college ball.'

'Darling – you said you were washing up! Oh, you joined in afterwards? Did you have a marvellous time? Who was your partner?'

'I just joined a group of friends.'

'Well, I hope you've got a photograph, so I can see what you looked like.'

'Somewhere,' said Mara vaguely.

'Well, find it, darling!' And Mara went straight to the pocket of the bag where she knew she had put the photographs, and handed them over with a smile.

'Darling, who *are* they?' She watched her mother's eyes flicking from one to the other, overwhelmed by this embarrassment of male splendour. Mara suppressed the urge to say, 'I've no idea – I just stopped the two best-looking men I could find and asked them to pose with me.'

'Well?' Her mother looked up. 'The dress looks wonderful,' she added a shade too late.

'They're both students at Coverdale.'

Her mother nodded brightly. Nothing wrong with marrying a parson. 'What are their names?'

'The fair one's Rupert Anderson.'

'Anderson. Not Gordon and Jean Anderson's son?' she asked, as Mara had known she would. She nodded. 'They were good friends of ours when your father was training. Gordon was curate at the university church. My, my. What a good-looking youth. Still, his father's terribly attractive. And who's this?'

'Johnny Whitaker.'

Her mother was stumped. He was nobody's son that she knew of. She had noticed the slight blush, however, and knew which one to praise. 'What extraordinarily handsome friends you seem to have. I think I prefer the dark one. He looks like a rogue. Is he a bit of a rough diamond?'

Honestly, mother. And this is Mara's fiancé – something of a rough diamond, but we're terribly fond of him. 'Well . . . I suppose . . .' began Mara.

'Oh, *wonderful*. I do like unsuitable men. It's the raggle-taggle gypsies syndrome, I suppose. Oh, what care I for a goose feather bed, with the sheets turned down so bravely-o,' sang her mother.

'When I can sleep on the cold hard ground, along with the raggle-taggle gypsies-o,' thought Mara, her eyebrows rising in astonishment.

'Your father was *deeply* unsuitable, of course. Which is why I ran off with him. You look shocked, darling!'

'No, no.' Yes.

Mara had never before delved into the mystery of her parents' attraction to one another. A startling answer to this unasked question now suggested itself. She straightened her knife and fork on the plate. Good God – didn't they know that the only function of parental sex is procreation? This recalled something Mara had been meaning to say, knowing it would amuse her mother.

'Do you realize that you wrote in your last letter that this will be your twenty-second wedding anniversary?'

'Well?'

'Well, I'm twenty-two in May.' She looked at her mother, waiting for the penny to drop.

Her mother looked back at her with a smile, as though she were standing in front of another slot machine waiting for a different coin. Then the truth burst in. Mara's mouth fell open.

'I thought you knew,' said her mother. 'It's not supposed to be a secret.' Mara smoothed her hand over her hair, unable to meet her mother's gaze. 'I'm sorry, darling. I honestly thought you knew.' No you didn't. You never told me. 'We weren't trying to keep it from you.' Mara could think of nothing to say. At this point her father entered the kitchen. Mara blushed. There was silence. He looked from one to the other.

'Mara's just discovered the disgraceful circumstances of our marriage.'

'Has she, indeed?' His tone was cold, but Mara glanced at him in time to see a smile flash and vanish. In her mind she saw the wedding again – rows of dour Johns faces on one side, and the gracious smiles of the Flowers family on the other.

'Was it terrible?' she asked.

'I think we rather enjoyed it,' replied her mother.

'The *wedding*, I meant.'

'So did I.'

Her father appeared unconcerned. He had wandered to the table and was looking at the two photographs. In Mara's eyes they, too, had become tainted with the embarrassment of the moment. If only she could whisk them away. Her father pointed at one of them.

'That's the Anderson boy. You know, Jean and Gordon Anderson's son,' said her mother. 'The other one's called Johnny Whitaker. They're both training at Coverdale.' She never forgot a name. When she got to heaven she would be able to introduce the entire glorious company of the elect to one another without turning a hair. You must meet Basil the Great. Basil, darling, do you know C.S. Lewis? Clive, this is Basil.

Mara watched her father pick up the other photograph. Her whole body tensed. Why do I still care so much for his approval? She tried to appear nonchalant. At last he looked up.

'Are his attentions honourable?'

'He's celibate.'

Their gaze met for a second; two pairs of ice-grey eyes glancing off one another like steel blades. Mara looked at her mother, who was studying the picture of Rupert with renewed interest.

'Celibate, is he?' said her father, putting down the photograph. He had a Marines-telling expression on his face.

Mara flushed with anger. He thinks I'm a little innocent.

'Shall we open a bottle of something?' asked her mother.

'Not for me,' said her father, snuffing out the celebratory impulse.

They remained in silence like actors on a stage who had forgotten their exit lines. Then Mara rose abruptly, unable to bear it for another minute. Her father reached out and picked up the picture of her and Rupert. She stopped.

'I'd like to keep this. If I may.' He sounded like a police detective appropriating a piece of evidence to use against her.

'What for?'

He laid it down again. 'Not if you want it.'

She pushed it towards him. 'Have it.'

For a moment it looked as if this would become a battle: shoving the thing backwards and forwards. Then he picked it up again.

'Thank you.' He left the kitchen, and a moment later she heard the study door close. The other photograph lay on the table.

'It's like all those ancient family portraits,' said her mother. 'It really ought to go in a heavy silver frame, of course.'

Mara held up the silver glass ball before hanging it on the tree. She saw her face swimming in it, and the room behind her. I might be trapped in it for a thousand years like a ghost in a bottle. I look like someone else. Her hair was loose over her shoulders, and she was wearing a red dress. She fixed the ball on a branch, dislodging a sprinkling of pine needles. The ball bobbed and came to rest. Mara smoothed her dress. It was from Grandma's attic hoard. Maybe Aunt Judith had worn it one Christmas, looking at her reflection in silver spoons and candlesticks. I think I like it, she thought. When did I last wear bright colours?

Her mother was thrilled. 'It looks *wonderful*. That colour, like those beautiful dark peonies – perfect for your complexion. But you must wear your hair down with that shawl collar.'

Her face stared at her now from a green ball. She remembered how she and Hester used to make goldfish faces in it. A record of Christmas carols was playing as it had always done. '*In the bleak midwinter, long ago . . .*'. The decorations were as old as she was. She lifted them one by one from their paper nests and arranged them on the branches. Christmas, Christmas, whispered the paper and the faint sound of pine needles dropping. '*Noël, noël,*' sang the choir. Spices drifted in from the kitchen – mulled wine and mince pies for the callers at the vicarage.

The fire snapped on the hearth, and Mara turned to look at it. It flickered and spat again. The log basket was nearly empty. It had become the focus of a family waiting game. Who was going to chop the wood? Mara's mother was waiting for some nice strong parishioner to call in so she could enlist his help because the vicar had a bad back. Her father was waiting for her mother to pop out on some errand, so that he could chop it himself. And Mara, who was quite capable of chopping wood, was waiting till they were both busy so that she could sneak out like the son they never had to the wood pile. *'Peace on earth and mercy mild . . .'*

The doorbell rang and Mara's father emerged swiftly from his study to intercept any potential choppers. Mara continued to decorate the tree. There was a conversation in the hallway as she stood with a red ball contemplating the gaps. *Hester should be here to tell me where it should go.* She shut the thought out and leant forward to fasten the bauble on the nearest branch.

'A visitor for you.' Mara continued to look at the tree, not realizing her father was addressing her. There was a laugh. She whirled round.

'Johnny!' *Joy to the world!* 'What are you doing here?' He was walking towards her, and she, not knowing what she was doing, went to meet him, smiling as though he had come back from the dead.

'I happened to be passing.' He kissed her cheek.

'Passing?' *No one passes this village.*

'On my way north from Rupert's party.' *Don't go getting ideas. You're nobody special,* said his expression. Her joy was doused like a light. She stood turning the glass ball round and round in her fingers. Her face burnt, and suddenly she became aware of her father again. An exchange of glances like sniper fire had gone between him and Johnny, which she had all but missed.

'How are you, flower?'

'All right.' She made an awkward gesture. 'I was just doing the tree.'

'Carry on.' He went over to the hearth where her father was standing – stiffly because of his back – and leant against the mantelpiece. Mara hung the ball on the tree. It was the last one. Only the star now. She reached to fasten it on the top then stepped back to admire her work.

'Beautiful,' said her father a little austerely.

'Yes,' agreed Johnny. Mara turned and smiled at him. 'I could stand here all evening watching, in fact.' She eyed him suspiciously and he laughed. Even her father's lips twitched. But at this point her mother entered the room.

'Hello, do we have a visitor?' Her eyes lit up with recognition. 'It's Johnny, isn't it?'

Johnny smiled as they shook hands. My God, he's flirting with my mother. And she's flirting back. *We won't go until we've got some, so bring some out here!* Mara turned back to the tree in amazement and began to fiddle with the decorations, listening as her mother began some expert delving. You've been visiting Rupert? How are the Andersons? And you're on your way home now? Where's home? You're spending Christmas with your family? Mara listened as her mother extracted more information from him in two minutes than she had gained in a term. And what were you doing before you went to Coverdale? The family firm? Building contractors? That'll be useful if the church roof falls in. Mara gazed at her reflection in a blue bauble. I'm trapped in a tiny glass world as a punishment.

'I hope you can stay for the inevitable mince pie,' her mother was saying as she went to put the kettle on. He already seemed more her mother's friend than her own. Mara, this is Johnny. He used to work for the family building firm before he started at Coverdale. And suddenly Mara remembered the flying buttresses. No wonder he knew about the outward pressure of the vaults. Allinson, Whitaker & Sons. I wonder? She turned to look at him. Before she could find anything to say, her mother reappeared.

'Can I ask you a huge favour?' Of course she could. 'We're in need of a strong man to wield an axe – Morgan's hurt his back and we're out of wood. Could you?' Of course he could. She's annexing him to her kingdom.

In a burst of anger Mara said, 'It's all right – I'll do it later.'

'You won't,' said her father. Out came the family knives.

But Johnny was picking up the log basket and asking, 'Where's the wood, then?'

'Mara will show you,' answered her mother. Tra-la! a man to chop the wood. A fine young man. Mara marched out, her face like a clenched fist.

'There's the wood, and there's the axe,' she snapped into the freezing night.

Johnny picked up a log. 'What are you so mad about?'

'I can chop wood, you know.'

'So what?' He was eyeing the spot where the blade would strike. He raised the axe. 'Maybe he doesn't want his daughter chopping wood for him.' The blow fell, splitting the log cleanly.

Mara watched the two pieces fall into the snow. She could have cried. He doesn't want me at all. I'd be hacking away with a blunt axe with the tears rolling down my cheeks, and he'd just turn away and close the study door. Johnny threw the pieces into the basket. The axe fell again. You're so bloody good at it, she thought bitterly.

'I wouldn't,' he said.

'Wouldn't what?'

'Want you chopping wood for me.' He balanced a log. 'Know why?' Down came the blade.

'Because you're a patronizing northern male bastard.' She listened in wonder to her voice.

Johnny lowered the axe slowly and took a step towards her. 'What did you say?'

She stared unflinching, and saw the fishwife raise her pint and salute her. Why have I never done that to him before?

Suddenly he laughed. 'I thought I'd been getting off lightly all these weeks.' He began chopping again.

Mara watched as the chips flew and the basket filled up. What a masterful display you're missing, Mother.

He glanced up and saw her watching. 'Like a turn?'

'No, thank you.' He knew she had been impressed.

'The dismembered body of a man in his twenties was found on Christmas eve in a vicarage garden,' she imagined the news saying. 'He was the victim of a frenzied attack. A young woman is helping police with their inquiries.'

He finished work, and they stood looking at each other, till at last he shook his head as though he had warned her a thousand times, and she simply wouldn't be told. How quiet the village was. I used to imagine Bethlehem was like this, she thought. *Above thy deep and dreamless sleep the silent stars go by.* I could stand here till the Second Coming looking at him. Think of something to say. Quickly.

'Is it your family firm that's working on the cathedral?'

He grinned. 'That's the Allinsons. They're the masons. The class. We're just common brickies. Partners since the thirties when my grandfather got up Hilda Allinson's skirt.'

'Was she your grandmother?'

'No. She was the wife of old George Allinson, esquire, of Allinson

Grange. A respectable married lady. Until young William Whitaker came along with his eye to the main chance. Not quite so respectable after that, or so I've been told. Did wonders for the family business.'

'What did old George say?'

'Nothing. Hilda had him wrapped round her little finger.'

A costume drama unreeled in Mara's head: thirties drawing-room, rough hands climbing silk stockings, gasps and grunts among the antimacassars. A flash young brickie with Johnny's face. She felt herself starting to blush and groped around for something to say.

'Why wouldn't you want me chopping wood?'

'Why?' he smiled as he picked up the log basket. They began to walk back towards the house. 'Because you're a stroppy stuck-up Welsh bitch.' And you'll never know what I was going to say, said the expression on his face as they walked into the kitchen.

They sat drinking tea with the fire crackling happily. Mara's mother handed round the mince pies. Does anyone actually like the things? Mara wondered. So much pastry, so little fruit. A parable of life. The angel of the Lord stands by to make sure we don't just lift the lid, eat the fruit and discard the case. Or raid the mincemeat jar with a spoon. We must all wade through our predestined quota of pastry.

'How do you find Coverdale Hall?'

Mara froze. Her father was taking over the job of delving. She looked across at her mother as Johnny made some noncommittal reply.

'Did you fit in well?'

'No,' said Johnny cheerfully.

'I imagine yours is the only regional accent in the place.'

'There's one Scot, and a Londoner.'

'And are you mocked?'

'Am I?'

They both laughed and Mara realized that they were comparing experiences. She heard Dr Mowbray's voice again: '*Morgan-baiting was something of a college sport.*'

'It's the informal side of the training,' Johnny said. 'Knocking the working-class edges off me.'

'You'll let that happen?'

'Not while I've breath in my body. Mind you, I've had to learn a new language. They couldn't understand me when I arrived at Coverdale.'

'And now they can't understand you back home,' said Mara's father.

Johnny laughed. '"By, listen to our John. He's gone posh."'

'But it's a middle-class profession. You can't escape that.'

'I know. It's a disaster,' replied Johnny. 'I mean, you walk into church and someone puts a one-thousand-page service book into your hand. The person up the front has an educated southern accent. What kind of message does that give off? I'll tell you what kind: "Unless you're a middle-class professional, forget it. It's not your church."'

'Ah, but it's bound to happen, isn't it?' said her father. 'Christianity is a religion of the book. Its ministers have to be literate. And education goes hand in hand with power in our society.'

Mara sat tense, waiting to hear if Johnny could answer this. She desperately wanted him to acquit himself well in front of her father.

'Oh, *man*! What's this? Some kind of theology of despair? You know, that's what really pisses me off most. Sorry.' Her mother made a broad-minded gesture. 'Hearing a priest say there's nothing we can do about it, I mean,' Johnny added.

'That's not what I said,' replied Mara's father. Mara gripped her teacup. 'I'm talking about a tendency inherent in Christianity to ally itself to wealth and status. I'm all in favour of subverting that.'

She felt herself breathe again. He wasn't angry.

'Good. So am I.' Johnny laughed. 'Making church less like court would be a start. You know – the hushed atmosphere, the weird language, the funny clothes. And worst of all, not having a clue what's going on, but knowing you're in big trouble. Just like being up in front of the magistrate.'

At this her father laughed too. Mara saw her mother frown. The poor boy. We must cherish him. He's got a chequered past.

'Well,' said her father. 'Don't let them grind you down.' He sounded wistful. Mara wondered if he was looking round the William Morris sitting room and asking himself how he had been so smoothed and tamed.

There was a tea-drinking pause. Mara's mother's eyes had been following the conversation like a tennis umpire.

'It must be interesting to be part of an undergraduate college. Theological colleges can be rather intense and inward-looking.'

'It gives a different perspective, I suppose.'

'It has its disadvantages too, I should think. Undergraduate pranks, and so on.'

'Yes – and the likes of your daughter giving us a hard time.'

Mara looked up, startled, and Johnny patted her knee kindly.

'My rooms at Cambridge looked out over one of the women's colleges,' said her father unexpectedly. Mara saw her mother smile. 'Where a lot of dedicated sunbathing seemed to take place.'

Mara sat stunned between two unthinkable thoughts: the idea of her father lusting out of his college windows at the sunbathing undergraduates; and the idea that it was this kind of 'hard time' that Johnny meant she was causing.

'And how do you find the academic side of things?'

'A struggle. I sweat blood over the Greek. Unlike Mara here, who taught herself.' She cringed at the memory of Joanna and the whole embarrassing episode.

'Darling,' exclaimed her mother. 'You didn't tell us! When?'

'Over the summer,' muttered Mara into her tea cup. 'It was nothing.'

'There you are,' said Johnny. 'It was nothing.'

'She's always been a bit like that,' her father said.

It was as if he were apologizing for her. Tears were starting in her eyes. Johnny stretched.

'I'd better be on my way.'

'"For you have promises to keep,"' said Mara's mother. '"And miles to go before you sleep."' Johnny stood up, and Mara rose swiftly too, for fear her mother would embarrass her with further wild quotations. She stood miserably amongst the goodbyes, Christmas greetings and exhortations to drive carefully because of the ice. There was one last delay as Johnny was compelled to sign the visitors' book, and then at last they were outside in the cold. Their feet crunched on the frozen snow.

'He thinks the world of you, you know,' said Johnny as he unlocked the car.

'He might say it, then,' she burst out, too unhappy to pretend she did not understand. *'She's always been a bit like that.'*

Johnny laughed. 'He's proud of you.'

'He's not.'

'Ha'away. You're perverse. You misinterpret everything. Just imagine,' he went on in the tone adults use when telling children about Santa Claus, 'that there were people in the world who actually liked you.'

'And do you like me?' Say it, then. Say it. He leant down and kissed her cheek again.

'Me? No.' He climbed into his car with a grin and started the engine. She saw his arm raised through the open window as he turned at the gate and drove off. *Trahe me post te.* The exhaust swirled around her then melted away. She turned and looked at the house. It was like a Christmas card, with the snow on the roof, the windows lit up and the candle burning steadily in the porch. Her father sat in his study. She watched him as he read and made notes. *'He was always so passionate about everything.'* She saw him as he might have been at theological college, sitting at his desk, lonely and mocked; too young to be tied to a wife and two crying babies; raging at his loss of freedom and at his tormentors and their calm superior world. Was that how it had been? In the porch the candle flame guttered in some unseen draught. Mara began to walk back towards the house. The flame steadied itself and burnt on in the uncomprehending dark.

CHAPTER 10

When Mara woke, she could not tell at first where she was. I'm at home and it's Christmas, she realized. She thought about her parents: her mother sunbathing, and her father looking down out of his window and seeing her, like King David seeing Bathsheba as he walked on his roof late one afternoon. We must have been conceived in August, Hester and I, over the long vacation. Had she gone to the farm with him? Or had he visited the palace? And what had they thought at the palace when the dreadful news broke? What wedding plans were set swiftly, smoothly into motion? Small reception. Large bouquet. Our son-in-law Morgan. 'Something of a rough diamond, but we're terribly fond of him.' Twenty-two years ago. What a Christmas that must have been.

Mara heard her mother's footsteps coming along the corridor, and sat up in bed. The door opened, and her mother came in with a cup of tea.

'Happy Christmas, darling. I'm just off to fetch Grandma. Everything's ready for lunch, so stay in bed as long as you like.'

Mara listened to the footsteps going down the stairs and a moment later heard the car starting up. She sat drinking the tea. Just a minute, she thought suddenly, I haven't opened my stocking. I must be getting old. She drew it crackling towards her and began to pull things out. A sugar mouse, tangerine, shiny new penny, a paperback novel, a small present. She felt it through the paper to see if she could guess what it was. Flat, rectangular, heavy. The photo frame. She tore off the wrapping. I knew it. Her mother had gone out yesterday to buy it for her. It was beautiful: silver, probably Victorian. She's even polished it up. Mara sighed. To please her mother she must now put the photo of her and Johnny in it, and this would change the picture from a spur-of-the-moment joke into a significant event. From now on it would seem to say 'Engagement Photograph', and she would have to leave it behind when she went back to college. She lay down again, thinking how sad it was that a beautiful present given with care and love should spoil the receiver's pleasure. She would no longer be able to come upon the photo accidentally in her desk drawer among her bank statements and letters. Her mother had deprived her of this picture as surely as her father had the other.

'I'd better warn you – she's worse.' Mara's mother was putting on her gloves before leaving for church. The organ was just audible in the hallway where they were standing. 'She seems to be inhabiting a noun-free world. I'm afraid you'll be in for a guessing game. She usually knows what she's trying to say, but the words simply won't come. Or the wrong ones pop out.' She looked at Mara anxiously. 'Will you be all right?'

She looks like Hester when she says that, Mara thought. 'I'll be fine.' Like Hester trying to protect me from the other children. They were always nicer to me when she was there.

Her mother hovered uncertainly.

'It's only an hour,' said Mara in exasperation. And she's still my grandmother. She watched her mother leave, then went through to the sitting-room where Grandma was dozing in an armchair. She had a blanket round her shoulders and her handbag was by her feet with its handle standing up stiffly as if it would at any moment be grasped and carried off on some errand or visit. The face was frail and hollowed out. But at that moment she woke, and Mara sat swiftly beside her as she was struggling to get up.

'Happy Christmas, Grandma.'

'Happy Christmas, my dear.' Mara kissed the hollow cheek. 'You look charming in that – that – oh, you know, that –' She was pointing to Mara's clothes.

'This dress?'

'Exactly. That press. Dress. You look lovely, my dear. I seem to remember your –' Mara watched her hunting for the word. 'Oh, dear.' Grandma laughed.

She thinks it's funny, thought Mara suddenly, a wonderful joke at her expense that she of all people should be unable to speak.

'Your –' she began again. 'She had a – like that.'

Ah. 'Aunt Judith?'

'Exactly. Judith. My niece.' Daughter, thought Mara, but let it pass. 'She had a bed dress like that.'

Mara smiled at her. 'It's the same one. Mother found it in your attic.'

'Well! Fancy that!' Then Grandma had a sudden idea. Mara saw it appear, and wondered how long it would be before they could clothe it in words between them. 'I've just had a – When I'm gone I should like you to have my – my – the, you know, the –' She tutted in frustration. 'Silly old –'

'Give me a clue,' suggested Mara, and Grandma clapped her hands together in delight.

'This is like –'

'Charades.'

'Exactly. Now, I should like you to have my –' She made a motion to her neck.

'Throat cut?'

'No, no. You're as bad as your – no.' She gestured again.

'Pearls?' This was clearly closer. 'Jewellery of some sort?' Grandma was nodding and pointing to the dress. 'Something that goes with this? This colour?'

'Yes!'

'Garnets?'

Bingo.

'Barnets. I'd like you to have them, my dear.'

Mara thanked her and kissed her again. When would I ever wear garnets?

'Now,' said Grandma in a different tone. Hah, thought Mara. I can guess what this is. 'Your mother tells me you've got a –' You're on your own here, Grandma. They eyed one another. She knows I know. Oh, the power of words. 'She says you've got a –'

'A what?' A sunny disposition? A lead-crystal whisky decanter with six matching tumblers? A Kalashnikov? She watched Grandma trying to think of a way of miming her meaning without reference to the male member. She gestured.

'Muscles?'

'No. You're being difficult.' Another gesture.

'A moustache? A beard.'

'No. You know perfectly well what I – MAN!' cried Grandma triumphantly. 'Now I want to hear all about him.' Not a chance, Grandma. 'Your mother says he –' She pointed to the wood basket. Chop, chop.

'Yes. He did.'

'Tomorrow,' said Grandma with satisfaction. What about tomorrow?

'Yesterday, do you mean?'

'Why, yes,' answered Grandma, as though this was what she had said. 'And she says he's extremely –'

Mara smiled. No need of a word here. 'He certainly is extremely.'

Grandma patted her hand. 'Well, I hope you'll be very happy.' You'll pay for this, Mother. 'You know, I wish you –'

Mara looked into her eyes. Ah, if she had the words, she would give me an old woman's wisdom. She would say what only a grandmother can say, because it would be flung back at a mere mother. Mara watched her looking into her store. Everything was still there, only all the labels had vanished. 'I wish you could be happy. I often think – Hester, you know. So hard. But you, my dear, you're a –' Fists.

'Fighter.'

'Yes. You must never give up.' She patted Mara's hand again, and Mara felt that some kind of promise was required of her.

'I won't.'

'That's right. Things always get beggar, my dear.'

'I'm sure they do,' said Mara, struggling not to smile. There was a silence, and in the distance she could hear the organ playing. 'O, come all ye faithful . . .' The church would be full of the annually faithful, in their thicket of new pullovers and Christmas jewellery. Children would be clutching toys, so full of held-in excitement that the toys themselves must cry out in sudden squeaks and whirrings during the interminable prayers.

'Well,' said Grandma. 'I'm sure there's, you know, to be done in the, the – I'll just go and –'

Mara stopped her. 'You just sit there. It's all done.' She needs to be doing something for someone. All her life she's done things for people.

'She doesn't trust me,' said Grandma.

How easy it would be to slip into those soothing little falsehoods: Nonsense, Grandma. She just wants you to relax.

'No. She doesn't.' Grandma was not taken aback. 'I set fire to the –' she went on, pointing to the curtains.

'I know.'

Grandma sighed. 'I'll never be normal again, you know.'

This was too much for Mara. She got quickly to her feet. 'I'll go and make us some tea.'

'Thank you, darling. That'll be lovely.'

Mara stood in the kitchen waiting for the kettle to boil. In the church another carol was playing. *It came upon the midnight clear.* The words formed in her mind as she stared out of the window: *And ever o'er its Babel sounds the blessed angels sing.* The blessed angels sang on incomprehensibly in their noun-free, pain-free realm. The kettle boiled and Mara made the tea. She left it brewing and went to see if Grandma was still sitting obediently where she had left her. She saw from the door that the chair was empty. The old –

'Grandma!'

Grandma lay stretched on the carpet, her open eyes staring at the ceiling. Mara stood still. The fire crackled. The clock ticked. On the chair the blanket was curved like an empty shell where Grandma's shoulders had rested. The bag stood on the floor with its handle still waiting to be grasped. All that went before led up to this, and all that comes after grows out of it. I should go and feel her pulse or listen to her chest. But she continued to stand. It's nothing. Let her go. They'll be back from church soon. She stood waiting and waiting, and yet each time she looked at the clock its hands had not moved.

At last she roused herself. Doctor. I should phone a doctor. Some impersonal managing force took over in her. It walked her into the study and dialled and spoke, as though she were nothing but a piece of machinery operated by an unseen hand. The doctor was on his way, said the voice. She sat at her father's desk to wait. I shouldn't be here, she thought. It was a private room. There were things to learn from it which should remain hidden. It was like watching a sleeping face with all its hopes and sorrows laid bare. She got up to leave, but as she did so, she glimpsed the photograph of her and Rupert. It was tucked into the corner of a picture frame. She stood transfixed. He just wanted a photo of me to keep. And unable to bear the thought, she left the room and closed the door.

The doorbell rang. She jumped, then went to answer it. There stood their family GP, the one who used to come out to see her and Hester when they were ill as children. She let him in. He was as brusque as ever.

'Not much of a Christmas for you, eh? Bad luck. Where is she? Through here?' He strode into the sitting-room with his bag. Mara watched as he bent down and felt for a pulse. He listened for a moment with his stethoscope and shone a light into her eyes. He closed the lids and stood up.

'She's dead. Heart attack, probably, but I'm not her doctor so I can't write a death certificate. There'll have to be an inquest. Don't worry – it's routine. I'll set things in motion. Parents at church, I suppose? May I use the phone?'

She pointed to the study door. The doctor disappeared. She heard him talking. Grandma lay as still as ever, seeming to sleep now her eyes were closed. The doctor emerged.

'The police are on their way. Don't look shocked – they're the coroner's representatives. They'll contact the undertakers who'll take her to hospital. May take a while as it's Christmas day.' He paused and looked at his watch. 'Can't stay, I'm afraid. Sick child to visit.' She remembered his cold stethoscope on her own chest. 'Do you want me to fetch someone to sit with you?'

'No.'

'No. Will you be all right?'

'Yes.' She was watching the fire flickering.

'Look at me, Mara.'

She turned and stared at him. Those eyebrows. They had always fascinated her. Did he comb them downwards into a fringe, or did they grow that way?

'You're sure you'll be all right until your mother gets in?'

She saw what he was thinking and turned her back on him. Damn you for knowing so much about me.

'Answer me, Mara.' He took her arm and shook it.

She rounded on him, face white with rage. 'I'm still here, aren't I? I'd have done it by now, if I was going to.'

His expression changed. 'Yes, you probably would.' There was a silence. 'I'm glad you haven't.'

He was still holding her arm. Slowly he turned it over. There lay the scar, like a white snake along her arm. In the church the last carol began to play. He was the only one I didn't fool, she thought. He knew I was going to try again, and had me sectioned. I hated him for it so much I never gave him the satisfaction of telling him I'd changed my mind. They stood a moment longer.

'It's faded,' she said.

'They do. In time.' He tightened his grip for a second, then was gone.

Mara went through to the kitchen like a sleepwalker. The vegetables were standing ready, and the Christmas pudding was rattling in its pan on the Aga. There was the teapot. She reached out and touched it. Still hot. Suddenly a wave of panic mounted in her. She fought it blindly. She was an old woman. She died peacefully. There's nothing I could have done. She hugged her arms round herself, seeing the eyes staring at the ceiling. Her teeth began to chatter. What if she went next door and Grandma rose up to meet her, with those eyes staring, and her hands reaching out, reaching out to clutch at her? Even if she closed the door the hands might come scrabbling at the other side. Oh, come home. Come home, Mother. I should have let the doctor fetch someone. At last the organ began to play again. The service was over. Slowly the terror subsided, and she was left standing in the kitchen listening to the pudding as it rattled cheerfully. Her mother would be another quarter of an hour or so, greeting people and talking. Then she would come home. Then the police would arrive. Then her father, back from doing sick communions. Then the undertakers, maybe. And then they'd be a houseful for Christmas after all.

Mara made herself go through once more to the sitting-room and look at Grandma. She slept on peacefully, gone to her long home. I just went out to make some tea, and now she's dead. I shouldn't have teased her. I should have told her about Johnny. It would have made her happy. Why wouldn't Mother come home? I have no one. No one to talk to, no friends. I could phone Johnny. His number will be in the visitors' book. But she knew she would not. She might burst into tears at the sound of his voice, and he'd have to wait and say reassuring things: 'I'm still here. It's all right.' Like a Samaritan. They were probably taught that kind of thing at Coverdale. She hardened her heart against the thought and went to wait in the porch to see who would arrive first.

The next hour was one of the strangest she could remember. A police car drew up just as her mother was approaching the vicarage, and they entered the house together. Her mother was 'coping marvellously'. She was competent with the policeman and solicitous of Mara. The kettle went on again and the sound of the policeman's radio crackled a sort of counterpoint to the pudding on the stove. At least she stopped short of offering me brandy, Mara thought. It's as though she were ministering to the bereaved instead of being the chief mourner herself.

Then her father arrived home with the undertaker. They too had met in the drive. The undertaker was young, and he was so obsequiously condoling, so undertakerly in his manner, that he seemed like a caricature of himself. Mara could see her father eyeing him with growing distaste. He must know him professionally. But now the vicar himself was one of the bereaved. They were all drinking tea, and a wild laugh rose up in Mara. We're a stage version of an Agatha

Christie: the vicar (dour and silent), his wife (coping marvellously), his daughter (rather difficult), the policeman (bluff and honest), the undertaker (oily). Poor old Grandma had got the short straw and was playing the corpse. Seized by another mad urge to laugh, Mara rose abruptly and went out of the house.

She stood in the bright sunlight. The snow shone all around, making her blink. Wave upon wave of suppressed laughter shook her. If they were looking out of the window, they would see her shaking shoulders and think, Poor child. Such a shock for her, alone in the house like that. She tried to control herself for fear her mother would come out to her, hug her and say something like 'Don't be too sad, darling. She had a good life.' And sure enough, the door opened behind her and she heard footsteps crunching across the snow. Shit. She braced herself for the maternal bosom, but the hug never came. She turned. It was her father. He had a strange guarded expression on his face, and he was carrying a glass of sherry which he handed to her.

He cleared his throat. 'Your mother's invited them for lunch.'

Mara glanced at his face. He's trying not to laugh, too. There was a dangerous pause as they stood biting their lips and pretending to look at the snowy garden. They must find something to say, or they would end up weeping and clutching themselves out there in the snow.

'Good service?' she gasped.

'Yes.'

Another whooping silence. Mara dug her shoe into the snow. They were standing where Johnny had chopped logs the previous evening. Chips of wood lay under their feet, scattered around like crusts for the birds. She kicked at a fragment. The laughter was subsiding.

'Good worker, isn't he?' said her father. And all at once she was desperate to know what he thought of Johnny. Did he like him?

'Yes.' Her eagerness made her tone curt. Had she made him drop the subject? She drank some sherry. It was ice-cold.

Her father's foot started to nudge a chip of wood forward. 'Mind you, I don't think much of his navigational skills if he was passing here on his way from Rupert's.'

Mara looked up in surprise, then found herself picturing a road map of the country. Aha. She turned away to hide her smile.

'He's fond of you.'

'He's celibate,' she muttered.

'So you said.' He began shifting another chip.

She knew if she asked he would say more, but she couldn't bring herself to speak. After another moment he went silently back into the house. 'He thinks the world of you.' That was what Johnny had said. Just as her father had said, 'He's fond of you.' What sort of person must I be that people have to tell me things like this? Perverse, misinterpreting everything. She thought of what lay waiting in the house: festive meal with policeman, corpse and undertaker. She felt as though she would never want to laugh again.

The meal was swift as both visitors were in a hurry. It was too long for Mara, and when the phone rang, it was she who left the table to answer it, glad of a chance to escape.

'Happy Christmas, Mara.' It was a voice she did not recognize.

'Happy Christmas,' she replied guardedly. Parishioner? Relative? Someone who knew her. She waited for the voice to say more, hoping she would not have to ask who it was. She could hear another family Christmas in the background.

'You all right, sweetie?' My God. Johnny. She half dropped the receiver.

'Fine,' she said in spite of herself.

'Having a good time?' Someone else was speaking at his end. 'Who's that you're phoning?' she heard. There was an exchange muffled by a hand over the receiver.

'How's it going? – ha'away, bugger off, will you? – Sorry. Been as bad as you were expecting?'

'Worse.'

'Worse. What are you like, Mara? Why is it –'

There was a scuffle and another voice came on the line. 'Hello, Mara. You all right there, flower?' The voice might have been Johnny's, but the accent was stronger. 'I just wanted to say, happy Christmas, and you're too good for him, pet.' There was another scuffle. 'And now I'm handing you back.'

'Sorry. My brother. Worse in what way?' The sounds of laughter and conversation at his end made the vicarage seem colder than ever.

'Well, you know . . .'

'Yeah, families.'

'Sounds quiet. Just the three of you? No – your Grandma's with you, isn't she?'

'Well. Yes and no.' Say it, you fool. Her hands were sweating so that the receiver slipped again. She could hear his brother saying something and laughing.

'Ah,' said Johnny. 'Senile, is she?'

'Um. Dead, actually.'

There was a pause like a stopped heart.

'You're kidding. When? Today?' He must have put his hand over the receiver, but she still heard him saying, 'Piss off, Charlie – this is serious. Someone's died, man.' There was an abrupt silence. It was as if she had reached out and blighted their Christmas, too.

'I'm sorry, pet.' He was shocked. His accent was stronger now, making him sound like his brother. 'It happened today?'

'Yes.'

'I'm sorry,' he said again. There was a long silence. 'Do you want to talk about it?'

'No.' But nor did she want him to go. She had to say something, or he would hang up. 'I almost phoned you earlier.' Her throat was feeling tight.

'You did? You should've done. Have you got my number?'

'Yes.' She tried to swallow.

'When was this?'

'Earlier. Before my parents got back from church.' It felt as though there were hands round her neck gripping tighter and tighter.

'You mean –'

I only went out to make some tea. It was all going to rush out. She pressed her hand over her mouth.

'You were alone with her when she died?'

'Yes. Look, I'm going. I'll see you at college.' She hung up on his voice saying, 'No, wait, Mara.'

She ran up to her room and shut herself in. Back to college. Soon I'll be back. A day. Two days. I can't bear it here much longer. She would be travelling north again, feeling the weight slip from her with every vanishing mile, until at last she saw the City from the train windows and her heart rose up, lighter than air, to where the angels walked on the wind. She could survive another couple of days.

On the bed lay the novel her mother had given her. She sat and began to read. Outside the frost deepened. On and on she read, as though the novel were a fire to stave off the fear that stalked there.

Lent Term

CHAPTER II

The City was carved in ice. Not a breath of wind stirred, and the river between its banks was hard and still. It was Epiphany – time for the wise to come seeking. The streets seemed empty. People ventured out as little as possible. It was treacherous underfoot. Steep paths, icy cobbles. High up on the face of the cathedral all was quiet. There were no masons on the scaffolding, no plumbers on the roof. Icicles as thick as arms hung from gutters and gargoyles, and each night it froze deeper.

Mara was at her desk studying. Page after page passed before her eyes. Prophecies, delusions. She made notes and her mind struggled to form connections or find patterns in the material she read. All the while she was cold. From time to time she reached out and felt the radiator. Surely it wasn't working? And yet it was always hot under her touch. In the end she got up and put on another pullover. The cold seemed to have seeped into her marrow. She went back to work, huddled over a book, with her hands pulled up into her sleeves.

Afternoon drifted into evening. The bells chimed the quarters as they passed, like posts marking a road deep in snow. She had seen no one for days. Somewhere on the outskirts of her mind a childhood fear was creeping. What if the Second Coming had taken place, and she had been left behind? At last the fear emerged clearly enough for her to notice it, and she half-smiled at herself. Still worried about that? But she knew that in an unguarded moment it could rear up, bulging with horror to block out the sky, turn the moon to blood, and cast down the stars like figs in a winter gale. How often had she woken on her uncle's farm stunned with terror, sure that a trumpet blast had just torn the world in two? Christ had taken the elect and she'd been left behind. She would lie in the silence until some sound – an owl calling, a distant sheep – unlocked her joints, and she would sit up in bed to see if the cousins were still in the room. There was Faye, at the other end of the bed, and Elizabeth on the other side of the room, and little Morwenna – still all there sleeping peacefully. At least she wasn't the only one left. Then she would get up and pass softly from room to room to see if anyone was there. Her aunt and uncle – she could see their shapes under the quilt, Uncle Huw snoring; but were they saved? Maybe they'd been left too? It was not until she reached Aunt Jessie's room in the attic that she was sure the rapture had not taken place. There she lay, breathing like a child. The Lord would have taken Aunt Jessie for sure. She was looking forward to it, her robes ready, washed white in the blood of the Lamb, and everything. She would be taken up and meet him in the air. The ear trumpet stood like a monument in the moonlight as Aunt Jessie slept. Mara smiled at the memory. Tears of relief would steal down her cheeks as she crept back to bed. Come into my heart, Lord Jesus. This time I really mean it.

Strange that I never looked into Dewi's room, she thought suddenly. You'd have thought he'd be my touchstone. My saint. I'd have washed his feet with my tears and dried them with my hair, if he'd let me. She turned back to her book, but not before the fishwife had thrust her face up close and said, He was a worthless little shit. She put her hands over her ears. Worthless, he was. Mara read on resolutely until the fishwife retired muttering into her smoke-filled beery bar. Page after page. The clock struck eleven. She'd forgotten to eat anything. There would be nowhere open at this hour, and she had no food in her room. Well, tomorrow would do. Tired and hungry she went to bed and at length grew warm enough to fall asleep.

She woke hearing the bells strike two. The moon must be full, she thought. It was shining into her room through the open curtains, casting shadows across the floor. As she watched, the light seemed to intensify. Perhaps she was imagining it? She waited, and yes, sure enough, it was growing brighter all the time. She sat up. Not the moon, then. It was some kind of light down on the riverbank shining up at her room. Was the college to be floodlit like the cathedral from now on? This seemed so unlikely that she got up out of bed and went over to the window. The whole sky was white. Strange and beautiful. It must be some kind of atmospheric phenomenon. She tried to think what it might be. Something caused by the extreme cold? Phosphorescence? St Elmo's fire? Then, as she watched, the light began to gather itself. Slowly before her horrified eyes it drew itself in, forming itself, burning, burning. Her hands clawed the curtains shut and she stumbled back to bed, blocking her eyes, her ears with the covers. But she knew it was still there, fluttering at the glass.

She woke and turned on the light. Six o'clock. Dear Christ. She gripped her hair hard in her hands. That was the worst dream she'd ever had. She pressed her knuckles against her skull. Horrible. She'd been convinced she was awake. She had even heard the bells. Then she shook herself and got out of bed. The room was colder than ever. She could see her breath as she hurried to wash and pull on another of Grandma's hoarded dresses. It was made of wool, but even so it was scarcely warm enough. She put on a pullover too and realized she was hungry. It was still too early to go out and buy food, so she turned to her desk. As she did so, she stopped. There was something different about the room. Then she saw. *The curtains are shut.* I never shut them. Her hands gripped her hair again, and she felt her mind plunging out of control. I always leave them open. Well, I must have been walking in my sleep. She strode across to the curtains and yanked them open. A face stared in at her. She leapt back with a scream, then stood trembling and cursing herself. It was her own reflection in the window against the dark morning sky. Get a grip on yourself, woman. She'd work till nine and then go out and buy something to eat. She sat at her desk and read. The sky lightened outside. It was not until the bells were striking eleven that her hunger reminded her to go out.

She emerged through the heavy college door. Her movements were clumsy from the cold and the layers of clothes she was wearing. She pulled her hat down closer on to her head and wrapped her cloak around her. A taxi pulled up as she was edging cautiously down the steps, and the polecat climbed out. They exchanged disdainful glances, and Mara set off towards the town centre. The beginnings of a smile gleamed in her mind. At least she wouldn't be the only one in college now. There had been something cordial in those New Year sneers.

She walked on, picking her way carefully along the bits of pavement which had been salted or shovelled.

It was a dream, a dream born of hunger and cold. Of course it was. But she knew nothing would persuade her to leave the curtains open tonight. A dream, said her rational mind, and yet another part of her knew better. *A man of God came unto me, and his countenance was like the countenance of an angel of God, very terrible.* If hair could stand on end, then hers surely would have done. She remembered Johnny and the 'bloody great angel' blocking the path and calling him an arrogant little sod. Maybe that was what had prompted the dream. 'That was no dream,' whispered a voice. She sighed impatiently. My problem, she thought to herself, is that I hold two contradictory opinions simultaneously: a liberal demythologizing of the Bible coupled with a childlike belief in miracles. She bought bread and fruit and made her precarious way back to college. Her feet paused at the bottom step as though they were unwilling to carry her up to her room again. They were behaving like Balaam's ass, who saw the Angel of the Lord standing in the path with his sword drawn. Balaam cursed and beat the ass with a stick. Sensible man. She ran up the stairs, knowing she'd feel better when she'd eaten.

The afternoon slid past. The polecat was moving around his room, and the sound reassured her. She was no longer hungry, having eaten for the first time in a day and a half, and an atmosphere of normality was returning. The room remained persistently cold, however. She wrapped her cloak around her as she worked, but by nine it was becoming unbearable. She felt the radiator. It was cold. There must be air in it. Maybe the polecat had a radiator key? But she wasn't going to go and ask him.

She worked on until the clock struck ten, and then her resolve left her abruptly. She rose, left the room and knocked on the polecat's door. *Andrew Jacks*, said the name plate. He called her in. She entered, but before she could utter her request, a tide of warm air embraced her.

'You've got a heater!' she said, as though accusing him of cheating at Finals. So? said his expression. The cold brought on a momentary oblivion and she went across and knelt in front of the heater to warm her hands. The polecat was watching her with contempt. Her dignity was compromised, but she stared haughtily none the less.

'My radiator's cold.'

He raised an eyebrow. 'An apt metaphor.'

Her stare disintegrated into surprise. Was that a glint of humour? There was a reassessing pause.

Then he spoke again: 'Whisky?' She almost smiled.

'Yes.'

He got up from his chair, and while he was finding two glasses, she looked around. It was unnerving. The room was a mirror image of her own. Their two beds would be side by side, but for the wall. And he was clearly a man who liked his creature comforts. Framed pictures, not posters, all in fearsome good taste. A Paisley silk dressing-gown on the back of the door. He saw her looking and seemed to read her thoughts, for he showed her the whisky bottle with a sardonic flourish. Very expensive malt whisky, and a large bottle. He handed her a glass and poured.

'My father's a GP. He gets given things.' His tone was casual, but this was unmistakably a symbolic gesture: fifty warheads, say. There was a pause while Mara assessed whether it was worth entering a process of bilateral disarmament.

'So does mine. He's a clergyman.' Fifty warheads it is.

The polecat raised his glass. 'To our fathers. Damn them.'

They drank, waiting for the next round of negotiations.

The polecat stretched out a foot in an elegant brogue. 'I'm wearing a dead man's shoes.'

'I'm wearing a dead woman's dress.' She watched him and saw he was about to sabotage the talks.

'How appropriate. You look like a dead woman.' The fingers went back to the red buttons. She gave him her blank offensive stare.

'You've lost weight. You look like something by Munch.' That's probably true, she thought. *The Scream.*

The warheads swivelled this way and that, lining up on their targets.

'And you look like an Aubrey Beardsley.' She saw that one strike home.

'Petruchio back yet?' Boom! Massive escalation. She felt herself blushing. Little shit. 'He's got you well tamed, hasn't he? Good God – you practically behave like a real woman with our Johnny. You even smile.'

Yes, ha ha, she sneered.

'You never smile at me.'

'I don't find you amusing.'

The polecat lifted his glass and looked at the light shining through the whisky. He turned his cool gaze back on her. 'You don't find me six foot three and hung like a Minotaur, you mean.'

She ran her eyes over him insultingly. 'True.' But she had to admit to herself at last that she found him attractive. And amusing. Minotaur. Was that what he called him? The warmth of the fire had reached her at last and she took off her cloak. She took another mouthful of whisky and was looking around her again when she began to shiver. A sick dread rose in her. Balaam's bloody ass again. The drink slopped in her glass and the polecat reached and took it from her. She clamped her arms round herself to stop the trembling.

He watched her for what seemed like hours until the panic drained away again.

'I saw an angel last night.' The ass had spoken. Fool! She had thrown down every last defence, and could only wait helpless.

'Ordinary, or arch?' he asked, as though they were discussing the sighting of a woodpecker.

'I don't know.'

He handed back her glass. 'Wings?'

'Yes.'

'How many?'

'I don't know.'

'What did he want?'

'I don't know.'

'Did he speak?'

'I shut the curtain on it.'

He pursed his lips. 'Foolish.'

Suddenly she was annoyed and everything became normal again. 'It was a *dream*,' she said.

'Of course.'

There was a silence. I'm going to have to go, she thought. She finished her drink and began to gather up her cloak.

'You can take the heater,' said the polecat unexpectedly. She stared. Had she disarmed him totally with her kamikaze talk of angels? 'On certain conditions.' Yes. That was more like it. The spoils of war. She folded her arms.

'What conditions?' You think I'd sell myself for an electric heater?

'That you sit next to me in the dining-room.' She gawped. 'For a fortnight.' What! Why? 'Three meals a day.'

'All right,' she said.

There had to be some catch, but what on earth was it? She got to her feet. He rose too, unplugged the heater and followed her out. The air in her room felt icy. I'd probably sell myself for a pair of woolly bedsocks, she thought. He put the heater down. Was she going to have to say thank you? They stood eye to narrowed eye.

'What made you think I wanted your body?' he asked.

She stared contemptuously. 'The fact that you've got a prick.'

'*Jesus*,' he said with an offensive shudder. 'I can think of places I'd rather put it, darling.'

She flushed. He had beaten her comprehensively. She was losing her touch. He turned and started to leave.

'Thanks,' she said to his back.

He turned and regarded her as though she had offered to warm his slippers. 'Don't fawn.' The door swung shut.

Early January went past slowly, cold and grey, like a line of defeated soldiers. Mara's room became warm again. There had been some problem with the college heating system, a typed notice on the board said. The domestic bursar apologized to any students who had been inconvenienced. Mara returned the heater to the polecat, but the deal stood. She went down to the dining-hall three times a day with him. They seldom spoke, just sat beside one another in silence like an old married couple knit together by a million tiny hatreds and unable to break apart. Occasionally she sensed that he was watching her sidelong under his lashes. What did he want? Term arrived before the fortnight was over. People would talk. Was that what he wanted? Well, they would have something else to talk about in four days' time when she abruptly stopped sitting next to him. She wondered, as they went down for the first dinner of term, what stories would circulate. The noise seemed immense. Maddy and May called her over, but she shook her head and sat beside the polecat. She saw Maddy saying something to May, and knew they would tackle her later.

As she ate, Mara overheard various accounts of Christmas drunkenness and dissipation. The conversations went predictably to and fro. She looked down at the unappetizing stew in front of her, then put down her knife and fork and moved the plate away. Out of the corner of her eye she saw the polecat pause fractionally, then continue eating. Suddenly she knew. He wanted to make sure she was eating properly. *'You look like something by Munch.'* She sat wide-eyed with disbelief. Why would he care? Then another thought occurred to her: why had he never once mocked her about her fear of spiders? Or referred again to her wild talk of angels? A new category appeared in her mind: polecat, acts of kindness performed by. The whisky. The heater. Her mind prickled in outrage.

The plates were collected and dishes of crumble and custard were passed along the tables. Mara sat scowling, unable to decide whether she would have eaten any if it had not occurred to her that the polecat was watching over her diet. He placed a dish in front of her. She prodded it with her spoon. Rhubarb. I hate rhubarb. She pushed it away.

'Stop pouting,' said the polecat. She turned an icy stare on him.

'*Pouting?*' She had a mental image of herself grinding the dish in his face. At last – a *raison d'être* for rhubarb after all these years. Mara spent the rest of the meal watching the skin forming on the custard.

The meal was over. The polecat rose to leave and Mara went silently with him. What would he do if I ate nothing? she wondered. And how does he know I don't go back to my room and throw it all up again? They were approaching the foot of the stairs when Mara pictured herself making retching noises for him to hear through the wall. At that moment he glanced at her and caught her grinning. He turned away in disdain, but she saw his lips wavering into a smile as they began to climb the steps.

'Stop smirking,' she said; and they paused, looked at one another, and, at last, smiled together. Record the moment in tablets of stone, thought Mara. They continued to their rooms in silence. The smile had transformed him. She saw how very engaging he might be if he chose.

She settled down at her desk again and had just opened a book when she heard the sound of feet coming up the stairs. Two sets. Galumphing, and scampering. Maddy and May. The door burst open, and Maddy goose-stepped across to Mara, swung the Anglepoise lamp round and shone it into her eyes.

'Speak, fool!' she hissed. 'Did you think you could get away with it?'

Mara made no reply.

'You deny it, *ja?*'

Mara sat in silence.

'Then you admit it!'

Maddy's face was quivering with mock rage. She was going to be one of the rare prima donnas with acting skills that equalled her voice. When Mara still said nothing, Maddy thrust her face up close and bawled out a stream of German. 'You understand that?'

'Yes,' said Mara with a smile. A list of prepositions taking the dative. She could remember learning it herself. 'How was your Christmas?'

'I'm asking the questions!' roared Maddy. 'But actually, it was wonderful,' she said, reverting to her normal tone. 'You should have come to Rupert's party, by the way. It was truly Bacchanalian. Or am I getting my mythologies muddled? What would a party with a biblical theme be?'

'Gomorrean?' suggested May.

'Hell,' said Mara.

'Oh, just because you weren't there, you old cow. Anyway, it was wonderful. *Divine.* Rupert went as a World War One flying ace.' Maddy was waiting for Mara to guess.

'Pilate?'

'The polecat went as the Camp of the Children of Israel,' said May.

The polecat went? Mara hadn't realized he knew Rupert that well. 'What about you?' said Mara aloud, seeing that Maddy was bursting to tell her. 'The Scarlet Whore of Babylon?' She half-expected to be hit for this.

'Actually, I did,' said Maddy, watching Mara suspiciously.

May, who by now had wandered across to the mirror and was trying on Mara's collection of hats, said dreamily, 'I went as Delilah.' She hummed a little tune to herself and turned this way and that, looking at her reflection.

I bet I know what she's so smug about, thought Mara.

'And quite coincidentally,' said Maddy, not entirely managing a careless note, 'Johnny Whitaker went as Samson.'

'I had no idea he would,' said May airily. It would have been an easy guess, though. He would hardly have gone as the boy Samuel.

'Did you make him sleep upon your knees?' asked Mara. They looked at her open-mouthed. 'As the Good Book says,' she added, smiling at their shocked faces. They glanced at one another uncertainly. Tut, tut. Vicars' daughters, and they don't know their Bibles. Then she realized that her scripture knowledge had been learned at a Welsh Chapel Sunday school. Or during those forty-five-minute sermons, when she had been driven by sheer boredom to read great chunks of the Old Testament. Nobody could really tell her off, because it was the Word of God, after all. And very racy some of it was, too.

Suddenly Mara realized that something interesting had been said and she had missed it. Maddy and May were talking about mistletoe.

'I couldn't believe my luck,' said Maddy. 'I was bracing myself for a brotherly peck on the cheek, but my *God.* I thought I'd wee myself. What is the church *thinking* of, letting him loose in a parish?'

May giggled. 'I know. He ought to have an archiepiscopal health warning stamped on him.'

Rupert? Or Johnny, even? Surely not.

'But could you marry a man with tattoos and a lion skin?' asked Maddy.

They looked at one another and sighed simultaneously. 'Yes!'

It *had* been Johnny. Hah! Celibacy was clearly a flexible concept. He'd never kissed her. If she'd been there, would he have done? She consoled herself with the thought that Rupert had kissed her, and not Maddy and May, the night at the ball. Even if he had been drunk at the time.

'And Rupert,' said Maddy. 'What about Rupert, then? That boy's been misspending his youth as well, or I'm a Girl Guide. Did you see where he had his hands? All of a sudden, I'm in favour of polygamy.'

'Polyandry,' corrected Mara, pedantically.

'Oh, meow!' sang Maddy.

'Yes, you certainly should have come,' said May.

'What as?' asked Mara, atoning for her pettiness by offering herself as a target.

'The Witch of Endor?' suggested May. 'Lot's wife?'

'One of the seven thin cows of Pharaoh's dream?' suggested Maddy.

Even Mara had to laugh at that. May began twirling round the room in Mara's cape.

'Let's go out,' said Maddy suddenly. 'Oh, take that thing off, May. You look like you've got to be back in the dressing-up box by midnight.' She turned to Mara. 'No offence. Let's go out for a walk. It's a beautiful night.'

'It's cold,' said Mara.

'So what? The moon's out. Look.' Maddy went across to the window. Mara felt herself wanting to shout '*Don't!*' Maddy opened the curtains and she and May looked out.

'"With how sad steps, O Moon –"'

'Oh, do shut up!' howled Maddy.

'"– thou climbst the skies! How silently –"'

'"Say it's only a paper moon!"' boomed Maddy's magnificent contralto.

'"– and with how wan a face!"' bawled May.

'"Sailing over a cardboard sea!"'

The battle grew louder and louder, and there was a thumping on the wall from the polecat, and then a hammering on the door. Mara went to open it. Rupert. And Johnny. But her smile froze even as

Rupert was saying, 'Happy New Year, sweetie,' and leaning to kiss her cheek. Joanna was with them. Mara was hardly aware of Johnny asking her if she was all right. Joanna was upon her.

'Hello, Mara. What a wonderful room. You're so lucky.' Sparkle, sparkle. She was treating her like a bosom friend. Mara took a step back, but Joanna drew near again. Rupert was talking to Maddy and May, but Johnny leant against the wall watching Mara and Joanna. 'I hope I get a room like this when I'm in Jesus, but I'll have to take what I'm given, of course.'

Mara stood very still. What's this?

'Didn't I tell you I've applied to change colleges? I've finally admitted to the Lord that He's right, and I should have applied here in the first place. But I was rebelling.'

She looked coy. Mara heard snakes in her mind. They came writhing out until they stood in a deadly halo around her head. The girl chattered on about the Lord.

'He had to show me I was rebelling against Him. You'd have thought I'd have learnt by now, wouldn't you? Anyway, to cut a long story short, I'm changing colleges. The Lord's wanting me to work for him here.'

She was gazing up into Mara's face as though she were intent on seducing her. The snakes gave a warning rattle. Just *fuck* off.

'We were just going out,' said Mara distinctly. She went and took her cloak from May, who was still wearing it. 'It's a beautiful night. The moon is out, and we,' she pulled on her hat, 'are going for a nice walk.' They were all staring at her.

'Isn't it a bit cold?' asked Rupert.

'Yes,' said Maddy, apparently forgetting her earlier words. For a moment nobody moved.

Then Johnny spoke. 'Ha'away, you soft southerners. Since when has it been too cold to go out for a drink?'

At this, Maddy and May raced off for their coats. Mara could hear them receding into the distance as she went down the stairs with Rupert, Johnny and the girl. She tried to block out the sound of her chatter as they made their way through the college towards Coverdale Hall. Rupert and Johnny will go for their coats, she thought, and I'll be left with her.

But then she heard Joanna asking: 'Will I be cold, do you think?'

It was addressed to Johnny, but Rupert answered a little impatiently, 'Well, were you cold coming over here?'

'I was a bit . . .'

There was a short, stubborn silence, then Rupert, who had the disadvantage of being a gentleman, offered to lend her a pullover. The two set off together. Johnny disappeared to his own room, leaving Mara standing in the hallway.

If she gets a place here, I'll have to leave. She stared at the notices pinned on the board. I shouldn't let her have this hold on me. It's as though she's a catalyst. Seemingly harmless, but speeding up some terrible chemical process inside me. The notices lifted and fluttered as the door opened. Maddy and May came in, wrapped up against the cold.

'My God, you really hate that girl, don't you?' said Maddy. 'We're going for a *nice walk*. Sorry sorry sorry!' She put out crossed forefingers to ward off the flash of anger in Mara's eye. She still couldn't take being mimicked.

'Why do you hate her?' asked May. 'Apart from the fact that she talks about the Lord as if he was her boyfriend.'

The fishwife's head appeared at the window of her bar: 'She gets on my tit ends.'

'She does? How?' Maddy's eyes strayed over Mara's spare figure in wonderment.

'"With God all things are possible,"' quoted May.

'"Although for men it is impossible,"' continued Maddy, and they both began to giggle. Mara wondered afresh why she put up with them, but she had to admit that she no longer felt as though she was about to fly into a million pieces.

At last the others came back – Joanna looking elfin in Rupert's guernsey – and they all set off down the cobbled street which led to the bridge and the river. The moon followed them across the windows and above the rooftops. Maddy began singing again, '*Moonlight Becomes You.*' The song was punctuated by shrieks as she lost her footing. Joanna was squealing and clutching at Rupert's arm, no doubt because Johnny was falling back and waiting for Mara.

'St Agnes' Eve. Ah, bitter chill it was!' called May.

'Just shut up!' came Maddy's voice. 'Or I'll start singing again.'

'Spare us!' said Rupert in the distance.

Johnny drew near to Mara. She stared stubbornly at the icicles which hung like knives from the gutters. The others were drawing ahead.

'Are you all right?' he asked. 'I was worried about you after I phoned.' But not enough to call again. 'I'd've rung back, but you said you didn't want to talk.' She said nothing, struggling to control her rising temper.

'I want to see the river,' Maddy's voice floated back to them.

'How was the funeral?'

'I didn't go.'

He made as if to speak, then checked himself. People always disapproved if you didn't attend funerals. Not paying proper respect.

'You don't have to handle me with kid gloves.'

'Fair enough,' he said. Ahead of them Joanna slipped on the ice and wailed until Rupert helped her up. Mara made a scornful noise, and suddenly Johnny stopped.

'Look, we all know she's a pain in the arse, but so what? The rest of us manage to put up with it, so why can't you?'

She could see the moon reflected in an attic window behind him. It was full.

'Look at me!' He seized her shoulders, and she stood not daring to turn away from him. 'I hate it when you do that.' Then she saw the anger give way to something like disgust. He released her. 'You're not exactly the easiest person in the world yourself, Mara.'

'Stop picking on me!' she burst out.

He gestured in exasperation. 'What am I supposed to do? First of all I'm handling you with kid gloves, then I'm picking on you.' He walked off. *Women!* said the thought bubble trailing after him. After a moment Mara followed. Just because he kissed your friends, jeered the fishwife. Yes, but he shouldn't have. Either he's celibate, or he's not. He shouldn't fool around.

The others had made their way down to the bank. She watched Johnny join them.

'Do you suppose it's thick enough to walk on?' she heard Maddy asking.

'No!' said Rupert and Johnny in unison. They were standing under the trees. Each twig was white with frozen snow as though an untimely spring had set them all flowering in the moonlight. Mara stumbled down the bank to the others.

'Look, it's hard enough to stamp on,' Maddy was saying. Then there was a great shriek as her foot plunged through. Rupert shot out a hand and hauled her back on to the bank. Maddy stood howling and shaking her leg as the rest of them laughed.

'It's not funny! Ow, ow! It's cold. Shut up, you fat bastards!'

'The answer is, no, it's not thick enough to walk on,' said Rupert when he had enough breath to speak.

Mara wandered a little way upstream. Snow had fallen on the ice, and the river was a white road under the stars. Fast black water running underneath. She gazed at it. Surely it could bear her weight? It had been frozen for days. She stepped on it cautiously. The ice creaked but held. She took a few more steps. Her heart pounded. Walking on water. The others were still laughing on the bank as she moved silently across the ice.

'I'll have to go home and change,' wailed Maddy. 'I'll get frostbite and it'll turn to gangrene and my leg will have to be amputated. It's not funny, Whitaker!'

'Serves you right,' said Rupert.

Mara stood watching them.

'Where's Mara?' asked May suddenly.

'Here,' she said from the middle of the river. They all wheeled round.

'My God! Mara – come back! You'll fall through. You've seen it's not strong enough!' Rupert stood gesturing her back.

'It's always thicker in the middle,' she replied.

'I don't care. Come back now!'

'Please, Mara!' begged May.

They were all pleading at once.

'It's quite solid,' she reassured them. 'Look.' And she jumped up and down.

To her astonishment Maddy began to cry, and Rupert started to talk to her as though he were persuading her off the railings of the Golden Gate Bridge. Surely they could see the ice would have cracked by now if it was going to?

Johnny made a move towards her, but Rupert held him back.

'Don't, John. You'll both go through.' They all stood as if they were carved of ice themselves, and, seeing that they were genuinely frightened, Mara relented and turned to the bank again. She was about to walk back when Joanna began screaming hysterically. 'She's going to die! She'll fall through! She's going to die!' Rupert shook her, saying 'Shut up! Just shut up!' but the girl continued to scream. Mara turned, looked up the white river and changed her mind. She began to walk. No foot had ever trodden there. A mad glee seized her and she broke into a run. Their cries fell away behind her and she was running with the moonlight under her feet, and about her head a hundred thousand stars.

CHAPTER 12

It was mid-morning the following day when Mara unlocked her door. A note was pinned on it: *I want to talk to you. Rupert.* There was a sound. She jumped, but it was only the polecat.

'Where have you been?' he asked.

'In the library.'

'What, all night?' She put on her most offensive stare. 'Rupert and Johnny are after your blood. What have you done?'

'Walked on the ice,' she said, letting herself in. He followed her without waiting to be asked.

'Walked on the ice? You've got a death-wish, girl.' She gave him a sneering look and hung up her cloak and hat. 'Is that what you have in mind? Drowning? You've given up the idea of slow starvation?'

What was he driving at? Suddenly she knew. 'That's what you're supposed to ask, isn't it?' she said nastily. 'So that when they come up with the stretcher you can leap out of your room like a nice helpful little doctor's son and say, "She always said she'd take a hundred paracetamol."' She saw that she had succeeded in angering him at last.

'Christ, you're such a bitch!'

'Well, get out if you can't take it, you interfering little –'

She froze. Footsteps on the stairs. Rupert and Johnny. She looked at the door, then back at the polecat. His eyes were full of malicious anticipation. They had been about three seconds from face-slapping, but the fight vanished like a burst bubble.

'May I stay and watch?' The polecat asked.

Instantly Mara's heart hardened. She sat casually on the edge of the desk. 'Tell me if I flinch.' The footsteps were almost at the door.

'Flinch?' said the polecat. 'You don't know Rupert. You're going to be flayed alive.' He arranged himself in a chair. There was a knock.

'Come in,' she called.

In they came. One look at their faces told her that she had seriously underestimated what lay in store. Rupert bore down on her. Short of jumping out of the window, there was no escape.

Instead she took mental flight off, away, out on to the moorlands of her mind, trying to block out his savage words. Phrases kept roaring across the sky, deadly as fighter jets. '*Your constant attention-seeking . . .*', '*Your contempt of other people's feelings and opinions . . .*' The moorland was beginning to slip away. She would burst into tears. Her only hope was to anger him into losing control. Her stare changed from vacant, to bored, to insolent. She saw it beginning to take effect.

'You're not listening to a word I'm saying!'

She started to say, 'Sorry, what was that last bit?' when Johnny grabbed her and hauled her roughly to her feet. His face was white with fury. She cried out in fear.

'You might not care what happens to you,' he shouted, 'but I do.' He shook her till her head spun. Dimly she was aware of Rupert protesting. 'Don't you ever fuck me around like that again!' He let her go and she stumbled back against the desk. The door crashed shut. There was a stunned silence, then she heard Rupert asking if she was all right.

'Yes, thank you,' she answered coldly. But she was not. Johnny's anger had split open her defences like a shell, and all Rupert's corrosive words came pouring in. '*Selfish . . .*' '*Manipulative . . .*' '*Behaving like a spoilt princess . . .*'

'You're going to have to face up to the consequences of your behaviour, Mara.' He put a hand on her arm. His voice was gentle now. 'If you behave unreasonably, then I'm afraid that's how people are going to treat you.' It was a veiled apology for Johnny's violence.

She shook his hand off. 'I don't give a toss how you or anyone behaves.' She stared at him, and saw not anger but something else in his face.

'I think you've made that abundantly clear,' he said quietly. He went, closing the door behind him.

The moorland stood desolate, not a bird in the sky. Strange winds winnowed the hills. The aftermath of Armageddon. She turned to the polecat.

'Ow,' he said. He was looking at her in awe, as though she had just climbed out of a wrecked car and was lucky to be alive. 'Nice teamwork.' He rose to leave. 'Sweet of you to let me stay, Mara. It's so frustrating trying to listen through the wall.'

She was too sick at heart to make any reply. The bells chimed eleven, and she listened to them stupidly. Was that the time? Her books lay on the desk in front of her. She picked one up and started to read. '*Awake, all you that are asleep, and stand up to judgement; the angel of judgement is come, and the time of harvest draws near.*' The words passed before her eyes, but they were meaningless. She could still hear Rupert's voice and feel Johnny's hands gripping her arms.

The days passed. Outside the temperature rose. Great sheets of ice began to glide down the river, and snow slid from the rooftops in sudden rushes down on to the streets below. Every tree and gutter in the City seemed to be weeping. Then the rains began. The river rose up as if it were possessed, tearing at the banks as it carried down branches and trees. Mara stood watching from the old bridge. She had not seen Rupert or Johnny since they had walked out of her room. Maddy and May were ignoring her. News of the incident had spread through the college. Mara had been sent to Coventry. Well, she thought, I've spent most of my life there, so I shouldn't mind.

She stared at the brown water swirling beneath her. To have had friends and then to have lost them. Why did I let it happen? If Joanna hadn't screamed . . . If the polecat hadn't provoked me . . . The bells chimed one. She would have to brace herself and go back to college lunch with everyone glancing at her and thinking things. And whispering. They were all calling her 'Princess'. The polecat must have repeated what Rupert had said. She had pushed him too far. What else might he broadcast? She's scared of spiders . . . She thinks she sees angels . . . Everywhere she turned, she felt the words 'And serve her right' quivering in the air. Well, I'll get over it. She could almost think 'So what?' without some stinging phrase of Rupert's whipping through her mind. 'You think the rules don't apply to you.' She began to walk back to college, gathering her defences around her. Pray to St Bartholomew, the patron saint of the flayed alive. In her mind's eye a trail of bloody footprints followed her up the street.

Her face was a stony mask during lunch. Maddy and May sat on the other side of the hall. Nobody spoke to her. She left and climbed the stairs to her room. She was feeling for her keys when the polecat appeared.

'Coffee?' he said. This was the first concilliatory gesture anyone had made, but it brought out a perverse anger in her.

'Been punished enough, have I?'

'No one's punishing you.'

'No one's talking to me, either.'

'Well, you never talk to anyone.'

My fault, of course. She unlocked her door.

'Look, if you just unbent a little, Princess, it would be all right. Come and have coffee.'

This left her with no easy way of refusing. She could see that this new nickname was going to be like a ring in the nose of a fierce bull. Anyone who dared come near enough to grab it could force her to do anything. She followed him into his room and sat down. The smell of coffee filled the air. I bet he buys it in Fortnum and Mason's. Hand-roasted and ground by Guatemalan peasants. *What's so wonderful about you that you can afford to despise everyone else?* I'll never be free to think a single thought again. Her anger roused itself. The polecat was watching her.

'"Your face is as a book where men may read strange matters."'

Macbeth. How appropriate. Come in, Duncan. Sit yourself down. Everything all right? Sleep well.

The polecat handed her a cup of coffee. Her sense of general outrage sharpened and focused on him. 'Why is everyone calling me "Princess"?'

She saw a flicker of amusement. 'Who knows where these sobriquets originate? It's like speculating why everyone calls me "the polecat".'

'You can dish it out, but you can't take it.'

Then unexpectedly he smiled. 'Have you thought of apologizing?'

'What – to you?'

'Don't be ridiculous,' he said, as though he were above such things. 'To the others. To your erstwhile friends.'

She looked stubbornly down into her coffee. Apologies were the fines levied for social misdemeanours. Pay up, or we'll punish you in other ways. The idea that she might voluntarily apologize had not occurred to her. And yet she had done once already to Rupert, months ago, for calling him a prick. He had responded generously then. But she could not believe that this time so much damage could be undone by the word sorry.

'It ought to work,' said the polecat, as though he were suggesting a method of starting a car on a cold morning. 'It's the currency these Christians deal in, after all.'

She felt herself recoil from his cynicism. 'You think they're stupid?'

He considered. 'Well, I suppose it's a better system than escalating retaliation and reprisals. I just find the nicey-nicey atmosphere in this place so cloying.'

'Which is why you like me, I suppose.'

Don't presume, said his look. 'Why I sometimes enjoy your company, possibly.'

She looked at the rain running down his window. I don't have the energy to fight him any more.

'You're getting soft,' he said.

'I know.'

The polecat reached out and took her mug. 'Look, go and find them and say sorry, for Christ's sake.' She started to protest, but he held out a hand to help her out of her chair. 'Just do it.' He clicked his fingers. 'Come on. The longer you leave it the worse it'll get.'

He was right, damn him. She took his hand and let him pull her up.

'You're such a fool, Mara.'

'I know,' she said again. Then she caught sight of his expression. 'Piss off, you posturing little git,' she snarled and stomped out of the room.

As she walked through the college towards Coverdale Hall, she found herself thinking of a dozen things she really ought to do first. I never used to be such a coward. Her heart was pounding as she approached Rupert's door. I'll go from here to Johnny, then to Maddy and May. She paused before knocking. There was silence. Oh, let him be out! She tapped gently. The door opened. It was another Coverdale student. The room was full of people sitting with bowed heads. Oh, hell. I've interrupted a prayer meeting.

'I'll come back,' she whispered, and started to walk away.

'Mara.' She turned. It was Rupert. He came out into the corridor and shut the door behind him. For a moment they stood looking at one another. Her prepared words deserted her, but she would have to say something, now she was here.

'Sorry,' she blurted out. She felt the urge to rush away, but was held back by the thought that above all else, she must not behave like a spoilt princess.

'Thank you for coming, Mara.' He half smiled. 'I'd almost given up hope.' The idea that he'd been waiting for days for her to creep penitently back was too much.

'Well, you know where my room is. You could have come to me.' I'm doing it again. Her thought was mirrored in his face.

'Hardly. You told me you didn't give a toss.'

'I was upset.'

'You were upset?' She saw he was going to start all over again. 'I can't think why you should be. I don't suppose you heard one word in twenty.' She stared past him, saying nothing. 'Look – you're not paying attention now, either! What *is* the point?' They were trapped in an endless destructive cycle.

She made one last effort. 'Well, I'm sorry.'

He gave his slight bow. 'All right. Let's just forget it, Mara.' But she knew he was thinking, That's all very well.

What more do you want? she thought. Blood? She felt tears rising, and turned away. Walk slowly. Not like a spoilt princess. She heard him going back into his room.

Her resolution to go and apologize to Johnny wavered. Supposing he shouted and swore again? She stood dithering in the corridor. Besides, she didn't know where his room was. But this sounded so pathetic that she stepped forward purposefully. How difficult can it be to find a room, for God's sake? It was up in the attics, somewhere. She turned a corner and caught sight of a notice tacked to the wall. *Johnny Whitaker's room*, it said, with an arrow pointing to a doorway. Another hand had scrawled underneath *One at a time, please, girls*. He was always the butt of college humour. And he never seemed to mind. Maybe he would greet her with that same easy tolerance now. She went through the door and up a narrow, twisting set of stairs. Her fingernails were digging into her palms as she approached his room. He was definitely in. She could hear music, and a brief snatch of whistling.

'Come in!' he called before she could knock. He must have heard her footsteps. His was the only room on the corridor. She went in. He was at his desk.

'Just a second,' he said without turning round. She waited while he finished the sentence he was writing, trying to use the time to gather up the right words. He turned, and she saw surprise, followed by his characteristic look of suppressed amusement.

I hate them both, she thought. This is the last time I apologize to anyone.

'I came to say sorry,' she said tightly.

He laughed. 'I could tell from your face. Come here.' He put out a hand.

She hesitated, then thought, Princess Mara, and went across to where he was sitting. Before she could stop him, he had pulled her down on to his lap as though she were a tavern wench.

'You're completely mad, Mara, you know that? What made you do it?'

'I don't know,' she said witlessly, not knowing anything at all, in fact – whether to struggle up from such an undignified position, what to do with her arms and hands, where to look, or what to think. Or whether she liked it. He wrapped his arms round her and gave her a crushing hug.

'Well, I'm sorry, too.' He let her go, and she retreated nervously to another chair and sat back in it with her arms folded. He put on a serious expression and cleared his throat. 'I'm sorry for forgetting myself and my calling.' He sounded so exactly like Rupert that she was torn between laughing and bursting into tears. 'I'm sorry for losing my temper so appallingly. No, no' – he raised his hand to ward off a possible contradiction – 'I'm responsible for what I do in a fit of temper. I'm sorry for laying violent hands on you, a woman (however great the provocation), and for using that kind of language under any circumstances, let alone to a woman (however great the provocation). Oh yes – and for slamming the door.'

She sat with her hands over her mouth. He'd even got Rupert's mannerisms right. 'I think that just about covers it.'

'Did he say all that?'

'Did he? But you mustn't blame him, sweetie. He'll be OK when he's got a pulpit to preach from. Have you dared face him yet?'

She nodded.

'Good. He's been impossible to live with for days. So you're all friends again?' He saw her expression. 'You're not friends. What happened?'

'I said I was sorry, but –' She broke off.

'What, like this?' He scowled and snapped the word ungraciously.

'Don't mock me!'

But he was staring past her with a bored expression on his face. Her anger flipped over suddenly into amusement. No wonder it drives them wild. He grinned at her and lit a cigarette.

'What made you do it, then? Walk on the ice, I mean.'

What had? She thought back, and saw again the white road under the stars.

'I don't know. Because . . . because you can't normally stand in the middle of the river. It's a different point of view.' This was clearly making no sense at all to him. She tried again. 'Like hanging in the air, or something. Or being on a high building looking down. You see everything differently.'

He considered her words. 'Yes. I can understand that.' He drew on his cigarette. 'I've spent half my life messing about on scaffolding.' There was a silence. Maybe he was thinking back to when he looked down on everything, the town below him, the streets, the women passing. 'Have you ever been hang-gliding?' he continued. She shook her head. 'You'd enjoy it.'

She didn't quite dare say, 'Isn't it a bit dangerous?' She tried to imagine it – swimming in the air, looking down on the landscape as though it were the sea bed. 'I dream of it,' she said. 'Flying. Walking on the air. It must be the best feeling in the world.'

'Well . . . no.'

'You've been?'

'A couple of times. With my brother. He belongs to a club.'

'And you don't like it?'

'It's OK, but it's not the best feeling in the whole world.'

She pictured herself wheeling on the wind against the heavens. 'What could be better?'

He tapped the ash from his cigarette. 'Sex.'

She gawped, then felt a burst of impatience with him. 'Apart from that.'

'Sorry,' he said contritely. 'My second favourite thing in the whole world, you mean?' He sat thinking for a moment. 'Mmm. Still sex, I'm afraid.'

Give me a break! She blushed. 'I think it's overrated,' she said coldly. 'I'd rather smoke a cigarette. It's less trouble, and it generally lasts longer.'

He blew a cloud of smoke up to the ceiling and looked at her speculatively. 'Regular or kingsize?' She bit her lips to stop herself laughing. 'A word of advice, sweetie. I wouldn't go around saying things like that. It sounds like a challenge.'

'I'm not stupid,' she snapped. 'I know what men think: "Ah, well, that's because you haven't slept with me."'

'Exactly.'

'And I don't *go around* saying it. I just said it to you. You're celibate.' He was looking at her in undisguised wonder. 'You said you were!' she said in sudden alarm. Surely she hadn't imagined it!

'Yes, yes. You know, Mara, for an intelligent woman . . . Look, it's like being a reformed alcoholic.' She looked at him blankly. 'My name's Johnny Whitaker and I'm a womanizer. I haven't had sex for four years, three months and six days.' Why does he have to trivialize everything? He glanced at his watch. 'And two hours, forty minutes.' He went slowly cross-eyed, as if at the memory, and slumped back in his chair. 'Apart from once or twice,' he admitted, sitting up again. 'But that was an accident.'

'Surely it's just a question of willpower?' She saw another look of disbelieving wonder on his face. Well, isn't it? she thought angrily. He leant forward and put his half-smoked cigarette between her lips.

'You go away and smoke that, Princess.' He patted her cheek and pointed to the door. 'Out.'

She went, her face burning. His laughter followed her down the corridor. She stubbed out the cigarette in the bathroom and ran off down the stairs.

They've all gone mad. Everyone I know is acting out of character. The polecat's being nice, Rupert's being ungentlemanly, and Johnny Whitaker's started talking about sex. Unless that's what they've always been like, only I never realized. I need some fresh air.

It was still raining, but she went out of one of the back doors and on to the lawn. The air seemed mild and she walked to the terraced garden, which dropped steeply down to the river. She could see it racing far below. I shall have to go and find Maddy and May, she thought. But instead of going to their room she continued to stand watching the river. What would it be like to be part of it? To be plunged over the weirs and swept at last out to sea? Maybe I have got a death-wish. But I'm not actually trying to kill myself. I'd know what to do if I were, and this time I'd succeed. The razor blade held firmly, warm water flowing, and the blood dripping red, red, on the white enamel, then swirling away. I would have succeeded that time too, if my father hadn't happened to come back. Hammering at the bathroom door, then the wood splintering inwards as consciousness slipped.

A branch was carried dancing downstream as she watched. Maybe she had been cheating. Not fully committed to staying alive. She thought back to that moment of fierce decision: I choose to live. For many years it had been little more than a stubborn resolution to see the thing through, coupled with an intermittent curiosity to find out what would happen next. Nothing had mattered, really, but you may as well live as die. But now – it all seemed to matter so much.

Suddenly she saw what she had done. Life had taught her this – that no friend can be trusted. Whenever she had loved someone, she had lost them somehow. Enemies were more reliable. Her actions had been an unacknowledged attempt to escape before she was betrayed again. Yet there was another part of her that continued to believe and trust, and was trying to undo the damage. Why else had she stepped back from the brink and apologized? She stood a moment longer in the rain, then turned and made her way to Maddy's and May's room.

They were subdued and embarrassed when she apologized. May began to make tea and Maddy seemed unable to find a single thing to say. Mara would have given anything to hear their normal ludicrous banter.

At last Maddy said: 'Aren't you frozen? You're soaked through.' But then she appeared to be reminded of ice and drowning, and this avenue of conversation closed abruptly. Mara forced it open again, like the widow who must speak calmly about her dead husband to set her comforters at ease.

'I know. I was standing watching the river without my coat on.'

They were completely silenced, and then Maddy offered her a sweater. To her relief they began to regain some of their animation as they opened and shut drawers and discussed the merits of various pullovers. By the time they had fixed on a pale blue lambswool sweater of Maddy's, they were practically themselves again. May handed her a towel and Mara took off her wet blouse.

'Silk,' said Maddy accusingly, pointing to Mara's camisole. Another part of Grandma's hoard. 'Don't you ever wear a bra, then?'

'Do eunuchs wear jockstraps?' asked May. They were back on form.

Mara began drying herself.

'A tattoo,' said Maddy in astonishment, pointing. 'I suppose it's a man-eating dragon? When did you have that done?'

'When I was eighteen.'

'Maybe I'll get myself one,' said Maddy, peering at it. 'A nude man on my inner thigh, or something. I'll ask Johnny Whitaker to pose for me. Does it hurt?'

'Yes.'

'Then maybe I won't.' She was moving away again when something else caught her eye. 'What happened to your arms?'

Mara glanced down and saw the bruises. For a moment she could not think, then she realized. 'It was . . . I don't know. Nothing,' she stuttered. 'I bruise easily.'

'It looks like hand marks,' said May, coming over to look.

'So it does,' said Maddy. 'Some great virile male clutched her to his pectorals in a passionate grip.'

She was safe. She knew that they both thought the idea ludicrous.

'"I'll tame your proud beauty!" he muttered hoarsely,' began May.

'"Never!" she moaned breathlessly,' continued Maddy, 'repelled and yet strangely attracted to her would-be violator.'

'Feeling his proud manhood thrust against her, through the delicate silk dress, now roughly torn from her shoulders . . .'

Mara began to unravel her long plait and dry her hair, smiling as the story unfolded with orgiastic speed.

She reached for the sweater, but Maddy flourished it defiantly: '"You may force my body, but you will never conquer my heart!"' she bellowed. 'Except he does, of course, in the end.' She handed over the sweater.

Mara looked at it dubiously. 'Haven't you got anything darker?'

'Oh!' said Maddy in plummy tones. 'Her Royal Highness Princess Mara of Iceland would prefer something darker, would she?'

Mara snatched the sweater and pulled it on. The others stood back to survey the effect.

'I hate you,' said Maddy. 'It looks far better on you than it does on me. Why do you wear dark colours all the time? You look like the undertaker's daughter. I'd lend you a skirt too, only you're so thin –'

'*Painfully* thin,' interjected May. 'Skinny, even.'

'– that it would fall off you.'

They had forgotten about the bruises.

Mara climbed the stairs to her room several hours later. The dining-room had seemed a different place. She sat with Maddy and May, and the faces of those around her had looked benign, not hostile. The polecat came out of his room as she was unlocking her door. His eyes swept over her.

'Good God. Have you been having sex?'

'Get lost.'

He drew close, reached out a hand and took one of her curls.

'I did you a favour earlier,' he said, twining the curl in and out of his fingers. 'At least, I think I did.' She waited to see what he would say. 'It must be this colour. You look beautiful.' She stared. 'I was in the college office and a girl was asking for the spare key to your door.' She stood dumbstruck by both these statements. Beautiful? What girl? 'The porter was about to hand them over, but I intervened. She said she was your friend, and that it was all right – you'd given permission.' Joanna. 'I may possibly have been a little unkind,' said the polecat thoughtfully. 'At any rate, she left with a trembling lower lip.' It must have been her.

'Long fair hair?' My voice sounds strange.

The polecat inclined his head. 'I saw Nigel forcibly ejecting her from the dining-room the other day. At your request, he said. Anyway, there's now a little note in the porter's lodge to the effect that nobody is to be given your keys.'

She'll find a way. Thank God she wasn't waiting for me. Going through my things. Mara felt a scream welling up in her. Her attention was called back as she felt the polecat tugging gently on her hair.

'I take it I did the right thing.' He was watching her face.

'Yes,' she said absently. 'Yes.' Then suddenly she thought, Beautiful? and she looked at him in astonishment. Had he really said that? All at once she felt too shy to meet his gaze. He let go of her hair, and she turned away from him and opened her door. There on the carpet lay a note. She stooped and picked it up. It must have been pushed under the door. The handwriting was unfamiliar, but a sudden dread seized her. She opened it, saw the words *message* and *the Lord*, and her hands began to tremble. The polecat stepped forward.

'From her?' She nodded. He took the letter and tore it up. 'Forget it. You never even saw it.' He turned to go back to his room. She called him back.

'Andrew.' They both stood still in complete astonishment that she should have spoken his name. 'If she comes up here, and you see her, will you get rid of her?'

He raised an eyebrow. 'Is this the woman who can face Rupert Anderson without flinching?'

She tried to think of some sneering response, but in vain. In the end she shut the door on him to hide her mounting tears. Work. I must work. Her hands fumbled around on the desk among her books and notes. Oh, what am I going to do? What am I going to do? She opened a drawer. There lay the angel picture. She pulled it out and unfolded it. There were no men. Nothing but women and angels.

She took hold of her pencil and began to draw. Men in their buildings. Men in their churches. In charge. In control. They had their feet firmly on the ground, while high over their heads went the women and the angels, walking on the wings of the wind.

CHAPTER 13

'It's probably time you were thinking in terms of a piece of written work. Before Easter, if possible.' The tutorial was ending. 'Let's say, about ten thousand words.'

'OK,' said Mara. Dr Roe was beginning to elaborate when the phone rang. Mara let her mind drift away as the conversation went on. She looked across at the window. The hyacinth jar was empty now, the bloom faded and thrown away. I never did buy one of my own, she thought. Everything seemed muffled and strangely distant, as though she were viewing the world through a diver's helmet. The students in the corridors and streets might be shoals of fish, their mouths opening and shutting meaninglessly as they swam past. Dr Roe was replacing the receiver.

'Sorry about that. Now, this piece of written work.' They spoke about Mara's studies a while longer, then fixed another tutorial.

'Do you think it's been helping at all?' Mara looked blank. 'You mentioned last term that one of the reasons you wanted to study this subject was . . .' Dr Roe paused, perhaps having forgotten the awkward phrase Mara had blurted out. 'Make sense of certain things.' Had it helped?

'Not really,' she said. She had wanted it to be like the intense study of one tiny island – flora, fauna, climate, etc. – from which she could extrapolate knowledge about the whole chaotic archipelago of religious experience. But she had made Sinbad's mistake. The island was the back of a vast slumbering sea beast, and it was waking at last, disturbed by her minute proddings and skittering feet. Leviathan. *He maketh the deep to boil like a pot. Upon earth there is not his like, who is made without fear.* Mara realized that Dr Roe had asked her something and she had missed it.

'Sorry,' she said, and added wildly, 'I was thinking about Leviathan.'

'Ah, Hobbes. Yes, that might be an interesting angle. I'll be interested to see what you make of it.'

Damn. Now I'll have to read the bugger, she thought. 'You asked me something, I think,' said Mara, retreating hurriedly from the

155

treacherous sand bars of seventeenth-century philosophy.

'Yes, I was wondering whether you're free next Friday evening.' Oh no. 'I'm having a few friends round for supper, and wondered if you'd like to come?'

'Next Friday?' Mara pretended to think. 'What a shame' – she heard her mother's polite getting-out-of-invitations voice – 'I'm afraid I can't make that.'

'What a pity. Never mind.' The other woman smiled. 'Another time.'

She knows. Mara rose to leave, feeling callous, yet too listless, somehow, to make amends. They said goodbye, and Mara started down the stairs.

The air outside was cold and foggy. Above the rooftops the sun was a pale disk coming and going behind the dirty clouds. It was Lent, and the whole world seemed to be locked in penance. As she walked, Mara caught herself thinking, I wish it were all over. I wish it would pass. I wish I were dead and sleeping in my grave. Ahead of her was a group of students, dawdling and talking. Their laughter echoed in the street.

'I'm going to go and open all my Valentines, now,' said one. Of course. Valentine's Day. She'd always hated it. To those who have will more be given, she thought. People like me just have to pretend we don't care. She entered the college and went straight in to lunch without bothering to check her pigeon-hole.

She was joined at the table by Maddy and May.

'What a tiring morning,' said Maddy. 'I've only just this minute finished opening my Valentines. I've been saying for years now that I must hire a part-time secretary.'

'Did you get any, Mara?' asked May.

I bet they've sent me one, thought Mara suddenly. Just like my mother used to, in case I felt jealous of Hester. 'I haven't looked.'

'What! Unnatural woman!' cried Maddy. 'I'll go and check for you.' And off she went before Mara could say anything.

'We sent dozens,' said May. Mara made no reply. 'With sonnets and acrostics in. It took us hours.'

And I bet they're complaining about essay crises by the end of the week.

Maddy reappeared, brandishing a handful of envelopes. Mara prepared a bland expression.

'Four!' exclaimed Maddy. 'And a note from somebody.' She handed them over.

'Thanks,' said Mara, putting them down and picking up her fork again.

'Aren't you going to open them?' asked May in astonishment.

'I'm eating my lunch.' She continued calmly with her meal while they abused and cajoled her by turns. Even the magic word 'Princess' could not provoke her to open a single card, however. Their attack changed direction.

'I suppose you're not coming to the college Valentine party tonight, either,' accused Maddy.

'Right.'

'Oh, but you must, Mara,' begged May. 'We missed you at Rupert's Christmas party. You've got to come!'

'Why?' they asked. 'I hate sixties parties.'

'Mini-skirts. It's just a male fantasy.'

'Well, you don't have to wear one,' pointed out Maddy. 'You could wear hotpants instead.' They amused themselves for some time with similar suggestions, and in the end Mara left in disgust.

'You're such a prude,' was Maddy's parting shot.

It was not until she was climbing the stairs that Mara remembered. 'And a note from somebody . . .' Oh no. She fumbled through the envelopes until she found it. It was typed. She was so convinced that it was from Joanna that for a moment she could not make sense of its contents. At last it took on some coherence. *I should be grateful if you would come and see me.* The Principal. Why? Was this just a routine chatting to postgrads, or had some rumour reached him? She looked at the note again. Four-thirty on the fourteenth. But that's today. It was such short notice that she began to fear he really had heard something. 'Your friends are concerned about you,' the Principal might say. Well, she'd be able to fob him off. She'd lied through her teeth to any number of would-be counsellors in the past.

She climbed the last flight of stairs to her room and was feeling for her keys when she saw a bouquet of flowers propped up against her door. Red roses. Her hand flew to her mouth in alarm. They couldn't be for her! But the card bore her name. She caught them up and let herself swiftly into her room. Her heart was pounding. Who had done this? The handwriting would tell her nothing. They had been delivered by a florist. Suddenly she smiled in relief. Mother. Of course. Just the sort of thing she'd do to cheer her up. She opened the card. *For my Princess*. Oh, God. Rupert. Or Johnny. Or the polecat, even. She should have been pleased. Instead she felt like the victim of a practical joke. She stood holding them. What am I going to do? Put them in water, at least. She took them out of their cellophane. I don't even have a vase. I can't bear to ask the polecat. Maybe the field mice can lend me one? She went to see.

'We saw the bouquet,' said the smaller of the two as she handed Mara the vase.

'Yes,' said Mara. They smiled shyly at her, clearly hoping to be told more. 'Thanks for this.' She gestured awkwardly with the vase, and left them disappointed.

Mara arranged the roses perfunctorily and put them on the mantelpiece. Right. Work. She turned back to her desk. The cards. She felt an urge to throw them unopened into the bin, but found that even she was not that unnatural. She tore them open one after another, and couldn't guess who had sent a single one of them. It was worse than getting no cards at all. But she put them on the mantelpiece beside the roses before opening her books.

The bells chimed four-thirty and Mara made her way down the steps to the Principal's study. She knocked and he called her in.

'Thank you for coming,' he said. 'I like to see my postgrads every so often.' His urbane charm struck her afresh. A bishop in the making? Yes, the episcopal aura hovered over his head like a polite mauve halo. 'How's your research going?'

'Very well, thank you.'

'Now, remind me – this is a one-year MA course?' She nodded. 'Are you intending to upgrade it to a Ph.D?' No, she thought with sudden violence. Never. 'I only ask, because if you are, you need to plan ahead a little. The applications for scholarships have to be in by May the first.'

'I'll think about it.'

'Good. Talk it over with Dr Roe.' She nodded. There was a pause. Now he's going to ask the real questions. 'And you're enjoying college life?'

'Yes, thank you.'

'Good.' He was sitting watching her, his elbows on the arms of his chair, fingertips touching one another. A bishop's body language. 'Good,' he repeated. She met his gaze. They were both playing their cards so close to their chests that it was impossible to tell whether they were even playing the same game.

'You probably know that I'm your moral tutor. *Personal* tutor, as we say these days.'

'Thank you. I'll bear it in mind.'

'Or we could easily arrange for you to talk to someone else, if you'd prefer.'

'No.' He continued to sit watching her over his half-praying hands. 'Forgive me, but you seem to have been unhappy this term.'

She flushed. Impossible to deny the charge. She seized on the nearest thought: 'My grandmother died this Christmas.' The words felt like a betrayal.

'Ah, I'm sorry.' Would it satisfy him? 'Were you close?' She nodded. 'Was it sudden?'

'Heart attack.'

'I'm so sorry.' She had an image of Grandma lying on the sitting-room carpet, eyes staring at the ceiling. 'Is there anything else that's troubling you? Would it help to talk?'

'No,' she said suddenly. 'I want to sort it out by myself.'

'You're sure?' She was cornered, but was ready to fight for her right to be left alone. He inclined his head in deference to her choice. 'Well, I'm sure you have friends you can talk to, in any case.'

A picture of Rupert in mid-lecture came to mind. 'Hah. They talk to me, mostly.'

And the Principal smiled, as if Rupert had just appeared in his mind too. 'Yes. I'm sure you have no shortage of moral tutors.'

She almost smiled back. Never before had her morals been so thoroughly tutored.

'Well,' he said in a concluding sort of tone, 'I mustn't keep you. You'll let me know if there's anything I can do?'

She nodded and made for the door. Her hand was on the door knob when a thought flashed through her mind. She turned.

'There is something.' He waited. Oh, God. How can I put this without sounding petty and stupid? 'There's the girl . . . Joanna something.' Her hand groped behind her back for the end of her plait. 'She says she's applied to Jesus. From another college.' The Principal inclined his head. She really has! In her panic she plunged on: 'Well, if she comes here, I'm leaving.'

There was a terrible silence. If she could have grabbed the words back and devoured them she would have done. The Principal looked at her in silence.

'Can I ask why?' he said at last.

'Because . . . Because I think she's dangerous. Unbalanced.' She saw a look cross his face. Know thyself, it seemed to say. In desperation she took a step towards him. 'Please. No one believes me. She's deluded. I've met people like that before.'

There was another awful silence.

'I haven't offered her a place yet,' he said eventually. 'I'll certainly consider what you say.' No you won't. 'I'm intending to interview her next week.' She'll be polite and rational, and he'll ask himself, Which of these two young women seems the most sane to me? Which would I prefer to have in my college? There's no one to speak out for me. The others think I'm horrible to her. Unless . . .

'You could talk to Andrew,' she said.

'Andrew Jacks?' She nodded. 'Thank you.' He made a note. She waited miserably for him to dismiss her again. He rose.

'Don't worry unduly,' he said, crossing the room to open the door for her. 'I'll let you know my decision. Goodbye.'

She blundered off up the stairs again and sat down at once to work.

It was evening. The building shook with the first bars of party music. Mara sat at her desk staring fixedly at the page in front of her. She was beginning to wish she had not been so stubborn. The whole college would be there, both halls. She bent her mind forcibly back to her studies, but she had read only one paragraph when there was a knock at the door. Will they never give up?

'What?' she snarled.

The door opened and the polecat entered in tails. She looked him over disdainfully. Well, I suppose someone must have been wearing tails in the sixties.

'Aren't you coming?'

'No.'

He came over and leant against her desk. 'Why not?'

'I hate sixties parties.'

'Why, Princess?'

'The clothes.'

He swung his leg casually back and forwards, watching her face. The music boomed three floors below.

'I'll lend you my dinner suit.'

'No,' she said automatically. There was a pause. Or then again . . . She began to waver, and saw a sardonic smile appear on his lips.

Well, she'd never be able to work with all the noise, anyway. He vanished and returned almost at once with the suit. She took it from him and examined it.

'Bespoke,' she said.

'But not by me.'

'A dead man's suit?'

She looked at him. His eyes were gleaming in amusement. She waited for him to leave so that she could change, but he seemed not to notice. *Excuse* me, she thought as he leant back against the desk again. He caught her expression, and with a look of surprise, shrugged and left. She pulled the shirt on over her camisole, and fiddled clumsily with the cuff-links. The trousers were going to need – ah, braces. She fastened them inexpertly. Tricky business being a man. She found a belt of her own and fastened it round her waist for good measure. The jacket was too broad across the shoulders. She looked at herself in the mirror and felt in the pocket for the bow-tie. Damn, she thought as she drew it out. How on earth do you –

At that point the polecat returned. 'Let me.' He came up behind her. She looked in the mirror and saw his head beside hers, eyes concentrating on his fingers as they began to form the knot. She could feel his body against hers. Her heart began to race. Then he paused. He undid the knot again, and she watched in shock as his fingers began undoing the buttons of the shirt. She caught his hands, but he continued to the next button.

'Don't be stupid, Mara.' She stared at his reflection in amazement.

'What's wrong?' He had that classic male 'I don't know what you're talking about – nothing could be further from my mind' look. He pulled the shirt open so that the camisole showed, leaving the tie draped round the collar. 'Much better,' he commented. 'It looks too butch done up.'

She felt his hands undoing her plait, and she stood mute. I never know what he's playing at. Her curls slid free and he ran his hands through her hair. She watched his face, but could read nothing there. He just looked like an artist at work, a couturier or coiffeur creating a masterpiece. He turned her round to face him.

'You need a button-hole.' The roses, she thought, her eyes darting towards the mantelpiece.

He followed her glance. 'Oho.' She flushed. 'And who are they from?'

'I don't know,' she muttered.

He went across and broke one off. 'Watch their eyes,' He fixed the rose to her lapel. 'You'll know the right man by his reaction to this.' Did he already know? 'There.' He stepped back to admire his work. What's he playing at?

'Well? How do I look?'

His lips twitched. '"Tis with you e'en standing water, between man and boy."'

She saw her opportunity. 'Did you play Malvolio in a school production?'

He looked at her in distaste. 'I'm an English graduate. I *study* Shakespeare.'

Yes – themes of equivocation, or something. She began to move towards the door. They went down the stairs towards the music. The polecat linked his arm through hers.

'"What shall I call thee when thou art a man?"'

Ganymede. She bit back the answer. They would end up spending the night trying to catch one another out with fragments of Shakespeare. He tutted, and she felt a surge of anger, but kept her resolve.

'*As You Like It*,' he offered as a clue.

She rounded on him. 'I know where it's from,' she said violently. 'I'm not going to spend the whole bloody evening vying with you!'

'All right. All *right*. Christ.'

'It's not all right. You're always playing games.'

He grinned and started to whistle. After a moment she recognized the tune: *Gaudeamus igitur*.

She pulled her arm away. 'Sod off.'

The students in the hallway were starting to look at them. I'm going mad, she thought. Why am I picking a fight with him over a bloody quotation? A cold misery crept over her. What's the point of it all? At that moment the music stopped and a voice announced that food was now being served in Coverdale dining hall. A mass of students surged out of the room and moved in the direction of the food. The polecat linked arms with Mara again, and she let him lead her along with the crowd.

They entered the dining-room. Maddy and May were already there, standing talking to Rupert and Johnny. The polecat steered his way towards them.

'You said you weren't coming!' accused Maddy. 'And that's not

162

sixties.' She was wearing a short dress with violently swirling patterns and an astonishing bust-line like twin warheads pointing at the enemy.

'Ah, but she looks wonderful,' said Rupert. His eyes rested fleetingly on the rose, and Mara felt the polecat pinch her arm.

'I'm surprised you approve of cross-dressing,' said Maddy.

'She feels upstaged,' explained May.

'Lies!' cried an outraged Maddy.

May giggled. She had arranged her hair in a beehive style, and attached several large bumble bees to it. Both she and Maddy were wearing false eye-lashes like tarantula legs, which they now fluttered simultaneously at the men before going to collect a plateful of food. They have so much more fun than I do, thought Mara.

'Happy Valentine's Day, Mara,' said Rupert, leaning to kiss her cheek. 'Why is it that women in men's clothes look stunning, while men in drag look ridiculous?'

'Because society views women as inherently ridiculous,' said Mara. He raised his eyes heavenwards. *Rupert had forgotten that the girl was a castrating feminist bitch.*

'Is he being a prick again?' asked Johnny.

'Thank you, Whitaker. It was *supposed* to be a compliment,' said Rupert.

Johnny looked at Mara. 'Do I get a kiss, too?' he asked.

'Me first,' said the polecat.

Johnny laughed. 'No way, Andrew.'

Mara flushed. Neither of them kissed her. Rupert tutted in exasperation. She looked from one to the other, and wondered suddenly if she was missing something.

'What's this?' asked the polecat disdainfully, indicating the work clothes Johnny was wearing.

Johnny grinned. Mara couldn't read the messages which were passing back and forward.

'I tried to explain that DJ doesn't stand for donkey jacket,' said Rupert, 'but he wouldn't listen.'

Johnny gave a slight Andersonian bow, and the four of them followed Maddy and May to the food.

I shouldn't have come, thought Mara as they sat round a table. Maddy was entertaining them with a rendition of 'Help' in Covent Garden style between mouthfuls. The room was full of shrieking and laughter. A conga was forming noisily. It wove in and out of the tables, growing all the time. I'll find a moment to slip away, thought Mara.

'Eat,' said the polecat in her ear.

She had no fight left and began to eat.

'*Won't you ple-ee-ease help me!*' boomed Maddy marvellously above the noise.

At last they had finished eating, and at Johnny's suggestion they all headed for the college bar. People and noise everywhere. The conga caught them up in its coils as it wound along the corridors, down the steps and through the bar. They broke off and found a corner. The polecat brought Mara a drink. He drew up a stool behind her and sat close. She felt his arms go round her, and looked up at the mirror on the wall of the bar to see his head beside hers again. She drank, feeling her heart begin to pound. Why is he doing this? She watched the others to see if they had noticed.

Rupert was explaining something to May, who was undermining every word with flutters of her false eye-lashes. Mara could tell from his expression that he didn't mind. Maddy was singing again, and this time Johnny was joining in. He has a good voice, thought Mara in surprise. She had an image of him on a rooftop somewhere against the sky, whistling and singing in the wind. By now he had taken his jacket off and he looked more like a builder than ever. She watched the muscles moving in his arm as he raised his drink. If I had a pencil . . . He glanced across at her, and she looked away, back at the polecat in the mirror. He was watching Johnny with a brooding expression, and his fingers were playing with her hair as absently as though it were his own. We're quite alike, she thought. Similar height and build, similar colouring. Except he's better-looking. Same nasty disposition. Suddenly his eyes were on hers. She jumped slightly, and he looked at her questioningly.

'I was thinking how alike we are.'

'God, yes. Twin souls.' He laughed softly. She felt his lips at her ear. 'And I bet we're sitting here lusting after the same man.'

Her mind reeled back. Her lips moved, but she could find no words. *Nothing is, but what is not.* Her hand felt stupidly for her plait which wasn't there.

'Then you're gay.'

'Oh, come off it. You knew that, Mara.'

She shook her head.

He laughed. 'Well, you must be the only person in the whole university who didn't.'

She reached out blindly for her drink. No wonder. No wonder. *'What makes you think I wanted your body?'* His face as he said, *'Don't be stupid.'* And he wanted to kiss Johnny, not me.

'This isn't another game?' she asked. But she saw in his eyes that it was not. He began playing with her hair again, watching her, waiting for her to respond. Maybe I knew. Maybe I did. I'd never let another man do what he does. And a sigh escaped from her. Despair, or relief, she wasn't sure which. Say something, you fool. He'll think you disapprove.

'I'm useless at these things,' she blurted out. 'I never know what's going on.'

'I've noticed.' He leant forward and kissed her cheek. 'It's frightening. You need a guardian angel.' She flinched. 'At any rate, you need another drink.' He went to buy her one, leaving her stupefied. After a moment Mara realized that Rupert was speaking to her.

'Have you lost your twin?' She scrabbled wildly for a reply.

'He's at the bar,' said May, pointing.

He meant the polecat. Her hand shook as she picked up her drink.

'What's wrong?' asked Rupert. She said nothing. He pursed his lips in irritation. He had never quite got over his anger at her for walking on the ice. She stared at her drink.

'She thought you were talking about her sister,' explained May. 'She's got a twin sister called Hester.'

I've got to get out! But at once they were all crowding in with questions, leaving her no room. You've got a twin? Why didn't you tell us? Are you identical twins?

May began answering for her. 'They're not identical, are you, Mara? Hester's shorter, and – well, we love Mara dearly, of course, but Hester's . . . beautiful. In a more conventional way, I mean,' she added as Rupert protested.

'Why didn't you tell us?' demanded Maddy. Mara said nothing. Oh, get me out of here! 'I've always wanted to be a twin.' Rupert and Johnny crossed themselves simultaneously. 'Shut up, you bastards! I think it would be wonderful.'

'You should invite her up,' said May. 'What's she doing these days? Did she go to Cambridge, too?' The polecat returned and handed her a new glass.

'No.' Her throat was parched. The subject had come upon her too suddenly.

'Well, what does she do?' asked Rupert in irritation.

'Nothing.'

'Nothing? What do you mean, "nothing"? You mean she's unemployed?' Her mind was stuttering. Just give me time. 'Why do you always have to be so mysterious?' snapped Rupert.

Anger reared up, blotting everything out. 'Because it's none of your fucking business!' The bar grew strange before her eyes. Rupert opened his mouth to speak, but Johnny laid a hand on his arm. It was all happening in slow motion. Like a dream. They were all staring at her. She put her glass down with a clatter and plunged heedlessly out of the bar.

The night was foggy. Mara stood under a tree down on the steep terrace. The party went on overhead in the distance, song after song. Above it all the bells chimed. Quarter. Half. Three quarters. I'm losing myself. Like sand through a clenched fist. If only I could get a tight enough grip. Well, I'm not beaten yet. I'll go and explain. There's no problem. I was just taken by surprise, that's all. But she made no move. Her hand pulled and pulled at a strand of hair. Footsteps. The polecat. He drew close, took her hand.

'Is this to do with me?'

'No.' How clear her voice sounded. 'It's about my sister. I'm going to go and explain.'

'The party's over,' he said. 'They're all in Rupert's room. Why don't you come?'

She pulled away. 'I just need time.'

'You've been here nearly two hours.'

She tugged at her hair until she pulled a handful out.

'Don't, Mara.' He caught her hand again. 'Look, this is a spiritual thing, isn't it? You aren't an atheist, are you?' She shook her head. 'Then pray, for Christ's sake.'

'I can't,' she burst out.

'Why not?'

'You don't understand,' she shouted at him. 'I'm lost. I'm an apostate.'

'Then God will help you.'

'He can't.'

'If he's God, he can. By definition.'

'You don't believe in God.'

'True.'

'How can you live?' She tried to pull free, but he gripped her harder than ever. 'If there's no God, there's no point. No foundation for anything. No morals, no meaning, no hope. You've got nothing.'

'I know,' he said.

'Then how can you live? What can you do in a world like that?'

'What amuses me.'

'That's your creed?'

'Yes.'

'Then why do I matter to you?' The bells chimed in the silence.

'I don't know,' he said at last. 'That's the Joker in the pack, isn't it? – caring for people.' They stood in the fog and the branches dripped all around them. Softly she let the strand of hair fall. 'Come along,' he said, and led her back to the building.

All four of the others were in Rupert's room. They fell silent as she and the polecat entered. Maddy and May were sitting on the bed in their outrageous costumes. A strange calm came over Mara. She was an actor with an easy part. Rupert took a step towards her. She spoke her first line:

'I'm sorry I swore at you.'

'I'm sorry I provoked you. I don't want to force you to talk.'

'It's all right. I don't mind. It was just –'

Johnny took her hand suddenly. 'Don't do that, sweetheart.'

She looked and saw she had pulled more hair out. He let her go. She twisted the strand round her finger, tight, tighter. 'I don't mind telling you.' The hair cut into the flesh. 'My sister's dead. It's not supposed to be a secret.'

'No!' burst out May.

'What happened?' asked Rupert.

'She drowned.'

Behind her she felt the polecat gathering her hair in his hands, pulling it gently from her grip. May began to sob. Mara watched them all. Maddy was crying too. If it were on stage, it would be bad acting, but it was real. Real tears from under those ridiculous lashes.

'She drowned in Galilee.' Even her lines were ridiculous. She felt the polecat's hands sliding gently through her hair, over and over again.

Only Rupert seemed able to speak. 'What . . . Was she on holiday? I mean –'

'She lived there. On a community.'

'A kibbutz?'

'A Christian community. The Church of the Revelation.'

'Oh, God.' This was Johnny. She looked, but he had turned away.

'Not . . .' Rupert began. 'It's been in the papers. Is it the same group? There's some scandal.' She saw he was struggling. 'The leader's on trial.'

He's on trial. One day, when this is long past, I shall dance.

'I hope he burns,' she said.

'Oh no, Mara.' Rupert's face was white. 'Then she was one of them.'

'She can't be dead,' sobbed May. 'When did she die?'

'Last June.' I was sitting Finals.

'It was . . . Was it an accident?' asked Rupert.

'An open verdict.' No note. Nobody saw. Nothing. The polecat's hands were still moving through her hair.

'I can't bear it!' said Maddy. 'Why didn't you tell us?'

Great streaks of eye-liner had run down her face. What was there to tell? She was dead. Mara shrugged.

'Haven't you talked to anyone about it?' asked Rupert.

'I'm fine.' Why couldn't they see that? 'I'll be all right.'

'But you'll have to –'

'Don't, Rupert,' broke in Johnny.

There was a pause. A moment of calm. Of beauty, almost. Then the lights started. Her hands went to her head as her vision filled with jagged flickering.

'I've got a migraine,' she said. 'I'm going back to my room.'

She walked through the corridors, stumbling as her eyesight failed. The polecat took her arm, leading her up the stairs, opening her door for her. She knew what lay ahead. Pain and darkness. Her head was bursting with light, brighter than any refiner's fire. The angel of judgement. The end of the world.

CHAPTER 14

She was out running in the woods. Each step was harder than the last. What's wrong with me? Rain was falling. Her feet slid on the path. I'll never get up the hill. She forced herself on. I will do it. I will. Halfway. Her feet slipped and she fell. She struggled up from the mud. A man appeared at the top of the slope. He had white hair and a white face. She saw his hands move to his flies and she turned and slithered down the slope again. Run, run. Why would her legs not work? Her heart would burst. The trees twisted and bulged. There would be more men there, behind the bushes, round the corners, rearing up, undoing themselves. Sweat was stinging in her eyes. She was on the road again, feet pounding. Over the bridge. Up the cobbled street. College steps. Too soon. I shouldn't have gone out so soon after a migraine. Oh, God. She bent over, hands on knees, gasping for breath. I'm covered in mud. At last she straightened and went in through the door. Her legs shook under her as she climbed. Sleep. I'll shower and sleep till lunch. Last flight. One step at a time. She found her keys, fumbled with the lock and entered her room. She closed her eyes and leant against the wall in relief. After a long moment she opened them. Joanna was sitting on the bed, waiting for her.

'Get out!'

The cleaners – they'd let her in. The girl sat with her stupid secret smile on her face. Behold the handmaid of the Lord. She's been looking through my things.

'The Lord's wanting me to give you a message.'

'Tell him to fuck off.'

The girl twitched and opened and shut her mouth. 'You can't say that.'

'Get out.'

'You're rebelling against God. You've got a spirit of rebellion.' Her scalp crawled. A million snakes writhing. 'How often do you pray, Mara?'

'How often do you masturbate?' Red spots like slap-marks appeared on the girl's face.

'You've really got to get down and pray and repent, Mara. I'm not the one that's telling you that. It's the Lord. I'm saying what I'm told to say.' Go! Get out! Just get out! 'He's saying that he's been patient with you, but that his patience won't last for ever.' Oh, Christ, this stench of rotting piety. The Lord, the Lord, the Lord says! This is what drove me out. I lost him, I lost it all. It was smeared over, Christ smeared over with the cloying ointment of whores, with their tears, rubbed by sanctimonious whores; human filth and blood.

'I know you hate me,' said the girl, kindly, gently, 'but it's not me you're hating – it's Jesus. I understand, though. It's hard for you, Mara. I know it is. The Lord's shown me it's because you're jealous. You know that he's set aside a special man to work with me. God's doing a new thing. There have been prophecies and words of knowledge about it. He's shown me I need to be under the headship of the man he's chosen. I asked him for a sign, and he's given me one.'

'Just get out!'

'You see – you can't bear to hear it, Mara, because it's true. You know it's the truth. I'm going to pray that you'll be released.'

Strange syllables began to bubble from her lips. She came towards Mara with outstretched hands. Oh, God help me, help me. Mara retreated. Her face twitched. She was against the wall, groping for the door. Suddenly it opened. The polecat.

Joanna leapt in alarm as he came towards her. 'I was just –'

'Get the fuck out of here!' he spat. She scrabbled for her coat and fled from him. Mara stood rigid.

'Jesus Christ.' The polecat took her arm. 'What did she do? What happened?' He touched her lip. 'You're bleeding.' She rubbed the back of her hand over her mouth and saw a smear of blood.

'I think I must have bitten –'

Darkness.

A patch of carpet. She was sitting on the bed staring at the floor between her feet. The polecat was beside her, arm across her shoulders, hand keeping her head down. I must stop calling him that. Andrew. Andrew. She straightened up slowly.

'Better?'

She nodded. Her head throbbed.

'Where the hell have you been?'

'Out running.'

'God, you're such a stupid bitch. Have you eaten anything?' She set her face stubbornly. 'I'm calling a doctor. You're ill. I bet you're anaemic.'

'I'm not.' She pulled away from him. 'I don't need a doctor. Just leave me alone, will you?'

'All right.' He stood up. 'Listen to me: I can go out of here and call a doctor, or I can go and fetch Rupert and see if he can persuade you. Which would you prefer?'

'You shit.'

'Be nice to me, Princess,' he said. 'I know too much about you. If I go and talk to the right people, you'll be sectioned and put away so fast you won't know what's hit you.' Her blood ran cold. He'd do it. They'd believe him – he's a doctor's son. No. No. Not now. Not again. 'Right – am I going to make an appointment for you?'

'Yes,' she whispered, resolving to cancel it.

'Good.' He left the room.

She went to shower. Her face stared at her from the mirror; pale, wild, stained with dirt and blood. Her lip hurt where she had bitten it. No wonder the polecat was worried. *Andrew* was worried.

When he returned, she was dressed and unwinding the towel from her head.

'Tomorrow at ten,' he said, taking the towel and beginning to dry her hair for her. 'What did Joanna want?'

'A message from the Lord. I'm rebelling. She says. He says.'

'Forget it.'

'Yes.' I need to work. To drive all this from my mind. Andrew handed her the towel.

'You look terrible. Why don't you try to sleep?' No way.

'OK.'

His eyes were on her. She met his gaze obdurately. He went across to her desk and began to pick up her books and notes.

'What are you doing?' He walked towards the door. 'You can't do that. Give them back.' She clutched his arm and sobbed. 'Andrew. Please.'

'Don't beg.' He was gone.

She sat on the edge of the bed, head in hands. What am I going to do? She had other books, but he might hear her crossing the room to fetch them. He might even come to check what she was doing in five minutes' time, anyway. Well, I can sit here and think. He can't stop me. Women and marriage in seventeenth-century England. Marriage conduct guides: *If ever thou purpose to be a good wife, set down this with thyself: my husband is my better, my superior.* The role of women in the radical sects. George Fox: *You do not deserve to have wives, you speak so much against women.* But her mind kept stumbling back to the woods. That man. Just a sad old man. I shouldn't care. It's not as if I haven't seen it before. The man in my uncle's village. I was six that time. It shouldn't bother me, for God's sake. But to run from him and find her waiting. *As if a man did flee from a lion and a bear met him, or went into the house and leaned his hand on the wall, and a serpent bit him.* She began to shake as she sat, too afraid to sleep, too afraid to cross the room for a book. What could she do? Wait for it to pass, quarter by quarter.

An hour later there was a knock at the door. Her again! But the door opened and it was a woman Mara had never met before.

'Mara Johns?' She came in. 'I'm Dr Buchanan. What can I do for you?' But . . . but . . . He lied. The bastard lied. The doctor was pulling up a chair and sitting by the bed. Think. Quickly, quickly. What will he have told her?

'I've had a migraine. And . . .' Sweat was forming on her upper lip. She wiped it away with the back of her hand. 'I was wondering . . . I've been feeling a bit faint. I was wondering if I might be anaemic. Possibly.'

The doctor was running her eyes over her assessingly. 'It's possible. We'll do a blood test.' She was like a brisk version of Dr Roe. 'Been feeling tired?'

'Yes.'

'Sleeping well?'

'Yes. OK.' A lie.

'How much do you weigh?'

Another lie.

'Eating well?'

'Well, you know. College food.' Themes of equivocation. She thinks I'm anorexic.

'What are your periods like?'

I knew it. 'Same as ever.'

'What does that mean?' asked the doctor a little sharply.

'Well . . . OK. Irregular.'

'Hmm.' There was a long pause. She doesn't believe me. 'We don't seem to have any notes for you at the Practice.'

'Yes. Sorry. I haven't got round to registering.'

The doctor pursed her lips and Mara told her the address of her GP at home, knowing that her notes were still in Cambridge. With a bit of luck I'll have left here before they catch up with me. The doctor asked more questions, and Mara made a concerted effort, answer by answer, to build up an image of herself: highly strung, intelligent, academically ambitious, but fundamentally sensible.

'I expect I've just been overdoing it a bit.' She hit upon a promising seam of lies. 'I've got this paper to write before the end of term. It's sort of important. Change of status to Ph.D.' She watched with relief as the doctor began to categorize her: highly strung, over-ambitious, basically sensible. 'I'll clearly have to ease off a bit.'

'Yes. Take a break. Can you get away for a weekend?'

'That's an idea.' Thank God she hasn't got my notes in front of her.

'Well, let's do that blood test.' Mara offered her left arm. 'Have you got good veins? Good God. A doctor's dream,' she said cheerfully. The needle went in. Mara kept the other arm clamped to her side, as though the doctor's eyes might penetrate the sleeve and see the scar. 'There. Good. Press here.' The doctor closed her bag. 'I'll let you know if you are anaemic. Now – do you need any migraine tablets?' Mara shook her head. 'Well, try to rest. Make sure you're eating properly.' Momentary flicker of earlier impression. 'See if you can get away for a couple of days.'

'Thanks for coming. I feel a bit stupid.'

'Don't.' The doctor smiled. 'No trouble.' She left as smartly as she had come. Mara was on her feet the instant the door closed. Right. How dare you do that to me, you . . . But another wave of dizziness sent her stumbling back to the bed. As she waited for it to pass she saw Andrew's face saying, 'Be nice to me, Princess.' Anger was swallowed up in a tide of fear. *'You'll be sectioned so fast, you won't know what's hit you.'* Sedation. Soft-soled shoes squeaking in endless corridors. Voices asking, 'Would you like to talk about it? How do you feel about it? You're going to have to co-operate with us at some stage, Mara. Why not now?' She curled up on the bed.

Mara woke. It was dark. There was another knock at the door. What time was it? She groped for her bedside lamp and turned it on. Six-thirty. The door opened. It was Andrew with a tray of food, which he carried across to the desk.

'Compliments of the chef,' he said with a sardonic look on his face. 'Who says, and I quote, "She's to eat it all, and not go losing any more weight, or she'll be too skinny. I like a good handful to grab a hold of."' He crossed to the bed and sat down. 'A more compelling argument in favour of anorexia I find it hard to imagine.' This jolted her memory.

'You called the doctor out.'

'And I expect you lied to her comprehensively.' He was watching her face. 'Not clever, Mara. You're the most untalented liar I've ever come across.'

I'm convincing enough when my back's to the wall. 'I want my books back.'

'Tomorrow. Come on. Eat. We don't want to disappoint Nigel.' He put out a hand and she let him pull her up, for a nasty thought had leapt into her mind: she needed him to back her up if the Principal asked him about Joanna. She began to eat.

'Your friends want to know if you're receiving visitors.' Oh no. Crowding in with their compassion and questions. She forced down another mouthful. 'Well, what shall I tell them?'

'Tell them I'm not feeling . . . I'll see them tomorrow.' She looked up and saw pity in his eyes. Her face burned. 'Don't patronize me.' The look vanished, and he raised a cool eyebrow.

'You sound like Scarlett O'Hara. "Tomorrow is another day."'

She knew he was trying to help, to anger her back into her usual defiance, but it was hopeless. She continued to eat, hoping he wouldn't see the tears welling up in her eyes, hoping they wouldn't spill over.

'I'll tell them to bugger off,' he said, leaving as casually as ever, but she knew he had seen.

She pushed the plate away and went back across to the bed and sat down. The evening stretched out ahead of her, and beyond it the night. Then the next day, and the next. Outside the wind was beginning to rouse itself. She heard the rain against the window, and the sound of the bells pealing. It was Thursday. They always practised on Thursday. The peals seemed to come in bursts on the gusts of wind.

There was a knock at the door. It was Rupert. Andrew had not told him, then. He came in and sat beside her.

'I won't stay long. I just wanted to see if you were all right.'

'I'm fine.' The window rattled angrily.

'Mara, I know you don't want to talk, but don't you think –'

'I don't mind talking. I'll talk. What do you want to know?'

He ran his hand through his hair. She saw he was choosing his words with care. 'I'm just concerned that you – that – People need to grieve, Mara, and –'

'So you've done a course on bereavement counselling?' He winced as though she had scratched his face. 'I've read all that stuff. I know what they say.' She saw a burst of his old irritation.

'Then you know all about denial.'

'Denial?' She stared at him. 'I'm not denying anything. I'll tell you anything you like.'

'Yes, the facts. But what about what you feel? You never say a thing about what you feel.'

'Because I feel nothing. What's there to feel? She's dead.'

'Mara, for God's sake. She was your sister. Your twin. You must feel something!'

'I've nothing to feel with. My soul's been amputated.'

She saw his concern give way to anger. 'You're so self-dramatizing!'

Her own anger leapt up to meet his. 'And you – you tell me what to feel, how to behave the whole time! What are you – my fucking priest or something? My father? Why don't you just leave me alone? I never asked you to care about me.'

He grew pale. She had wounded him beyond anything she had intended. The sound of the bells swirled round the building on the wind.

'I'm sorry,' he said. 'I came wanting to help, but I can see I'm only –' He broke off. The wind rattled the glass. They stared at one another across a wilderness of misunderstanding, until he left without another word.

The night was full of wind and rain. Milk bottles went skittling down cobbled streets. Slates were whirled from rooftops. She slept fitfully. The whole City shook. The chimneys, the trees, the weirs were all roaring. The bells chimed two and she got up and pulled on her tracksuit again. I just need to clear my head. She crept down the stairs, hoping Andrew would not catch her. A good long run is all I need. She was out on the howling street, walking, running, walking again until the day began to break and she could see the black clouds hunting across the sky.

She climbed back up the college steps and opened the door.

'God knows,' said a voice in the hallway. 'She's not in her room.' It was Andrew talking to Rupert. She turned to creep away, but they caught her and held her arms, and she was screaming, cursing them, clawing at their hands. Then Johnny was there.

'Let her go.'

Dimly she heard them arguing.

'She needs help, for God's sake!'

'You're making it worse. Let her go!'

'Jesus Christ – look at her! She'll hurt herself.'

'Just let her go!'

She tore free and ran from the building.

These are the angel paths, the windy walk-ways. The air is bright with angels. Their faces are the faces of statues, their eyes like eagles' eyes fierce and just. They watch her as she passes among them high above the City. The wind blows free. Far below she sees herself running along the street, a tiny figure stumbling down towards the river, where the water races by. The angels look on. Poor child, she says of herself. She has too much to bear. The angels make no reply. Their keen eyes know each thought. It will pass, she tells them. The wind sings. She will be glad to know someone is watching over her.

The water raced by. At last she looked up at the bridge high above her. Someone was leaning there, watching. It was Johnny. She turned back to the river. When she looked round again, he was standing on the bank waiting.

'Don't touch me.' If he comes any closer, I'll – She watched him, tensed for his first move. But he was still. 'I'm not going back.'

'Let's go to the sea,' he said. His words made no sense. Then the truth dawned: it's a dream. She went with him to his car. I've had dreams like this before, she thought as the City dwindled behind them. She watched the miles glide past the window until they reached the coast.

'I'm not worried,' she said as she got out of the car, 'because I know it's all a dream.'

'Fair enough,' he said.

'I can wake myself up if I really want to.'

'Right,' he said, and she walked towards the beach.

The air was filled with booming as the waves crashed in. Foam lay high among the rocks as she passed. On and on came the waves. There was seaweed like ropes under her feet, and scattered crab claws. She looked out to sea and saw the sharp points of rock disappearing with each swell. She ran forward and the water raced to meet her. Another wave came in. The spray leapt up and struck her from head to foot. This is no dream. She was on her knees in the shingle as wave after wave crashed in. The grief she had carried for so many months was being born. She fought it off, but it seized hold, choking cries from her, again, again, until at last it emerged, bloody, raw, screaming. She turned and saw Johnny waiting in the rain.

'Why?' she shouted, struggling up. 'Why? You're going to be a priest. You're a man. You tell me why.' He said nothing. 'She was beautiful. I loved her, and she's dead. He did this to her. He was a man of God. He laid his hands on the sick and they were healed. She had his child and it died. It died because it was born with no brain. It wasn't even human. It's a joke, and she thought it would be healed. I hate you all, you men, you priests. You think you've got the truth, when it's nothing but lies. Think about this when you're at your altar dealing out God to the people – that when I said all this to you, you had no answer.'

He continued to stand in the rain, taking it all without a word. At last she turned from him and ran off along the beach. The waves come and went, came and went. She ran on with the water racing under her feet. Tears streamed down her face and the wind whipped her sobs away. I could have stopped it. I knew what he was, and I did nothing. If I had spoken out, she would be alive today. She stopped running and cried out in pain as though two great hands were wrenching her ribs apart and breaking her whole body open. Drag down the heavens. Fling the mountains into the sea. There was not enough hatred and rage in the whole universe for this. Not enough water in all the seas to wash it away. Further up the beach she saw the birds grouping, flying and regrouping on the sand. She heard their cries coming and going on the wind. What am I going to do? The City reared up in her mind, the cathedral like a black rock in a treacherous sea where ships went down and all were lost. I'm not going back. She turned and saw Johnny coming towards her. That's why he's here. To make me go back. They sent him after me. He drew close.

'I'm not going back.'

'All right.'

He waited. The sea birds called in the distance. It's a trick. They planned it beforehand. They knew I'd trust him. He took a step closer.

'Don't touch me!' she cried.

He stopped. 'What do you think I'm going to do?' he asked, taking another step towards her.

She leapt back. 'You're going to force me to go back!'

'Why don't you want to? What are you afraid of?'

'They'll have me put away.'

'Who will?'

'Andrew. Rupert. They think I'm mad. They'll tell the Principal. They'll call the doctor back and I'll be sectioned again.'

He was watching her, patient, careful, like a man trying to recapture a bird. He moved and she flinched back again.

'I'm not going. He said he'd do it. He said he'd get me sectioned again.'

'Well, that's putting it a bit strongly.'

'You're lying!'

'They just want you to agree to a few days in hospital.'

'No. It's the same thing! I'm not going!' He was coming towards her. She screamed. 'Don't make me!'

'I'm not going to. Now listen –'

'No!' It was a trap. The waves boomed on to the rocks. She turned to run and he caught hold of her. 'Get your hands off me!'

'Just listen, will you?' She was spitting and clawing in terror. 'If you run now, you'll have the police out looking for you.'

'I don't care. I'll hide.'

'They'll find you.'

'No!' He pinned her arms to her sides. She struggled but it was no use. 'Let me go! Please. I can't stand it. I'll kill myself. If you put me in hospital, I'll kill myself.' She was sobbing now.

'Listen,' he said, holding her fast as she fought against him. 'There's a retreat house a few miles north of here. Why don't you let me take you there? For a week or two?' She stopped trying to break free and looked up into his face. They watched each other. 'I know you think I'm trying to trick you. You think I'll drive you back to college instead.'

'You will.'

'Look, I'm not saying trust me, because I know you don't. I'm just saying this is your best option. If you don't want to go to hospital, you'll have to take the risk.'

The fight went out of her. 'You'll take me to this retreat house?' It was getting dark. She saw the gulls twisting on the wind over the sea.

'Yes.'

'You won't take me back to college?'

'No.'

She started to cry again. Slowly, slowly he relaxed his grip and cradled her head against his shoulder.

'It just hurts so much,' she sobbed.

'I know, sweetheart. I know.' He stroked her hair until her sobbing subsided. 'Come on. You're cold and wet. Let's go.' They walked into the wind and driving rain.

It seemed strangely quiet in the car as they set off. She felt stunned. Tears continued to slide down her face and drip on to her hands. Her grief seemed dull and ugly now, like street after street of derelict houses which she must walk through until at last she was free of it all.

'I haven't brought any clothes. I've got nothing with me.'

'Don't worry. I'll bring you some tomorrow.' Signs for the retreat house began to appear. Fear seeped in again. What would it be like? What if she couldn't sleep, or eat? What if they were right, after all?

'Do you think I'm mad?'

'Totally.' She glanced at him and he smiled.

They turned into a long wooded drive. It was nearly dark. The wind blustered about the car. Lights appeared through the trees ahead and as the car drew up she could just make out the dark shape of the house.

'What will they think?' she asked in panic.

'They're expecting you.' He turned off the engine. 'I phoned earlier and said you might be coming.' There was a pause, and she heard the rain spattering on the windows. When he's gone, I'll run. No one will find me. She sensed him watching her. After a while he spoke again. 'You said back there you'd kill yourself.'

'I won't.'

'Look at me.' She turned. His eyes were searching her face. 'Thinking of running away?'

She jumped. 'N-no.'

'No? Well, one thing's for sure – if you do run, you won't have to worry about killing yourself, Princess, because I'll find you and wring your fucking neck.' Her mouth dropped open in shock. He meant it. But then he smiled at her and put a hand on her arm. 'Don't mess it up, sweetie,' he said softly. 'Come on. You owe me this. I'm already going to be in deep shit as it is. Don't make things any worse for me.' She looked into his eyes and saw with sudden clarity the risk he was taking for her. If he had misjudged her state of mind and she killed herself . . .

'I won't mess it up,' she said.

'Good.' He opened the car door. 'Wait there a second. I'll see if I can find one of the brothers.'

He was gone. Monks. Why hadn't she guessed? She leant her head back in despair. She'd escaped from doctors only to run into the arms of the Church. She opened the car door stealthily and got out. Johnny was some way off, talking now to a robed figure. They were silhouetted in the light of the open door. She began to back along the drive. Don't look. Don't let him see me. Another step, another. She was nearly out of their sight. She turned. Run! But with the first pace she stumbled and fell. She scrambled to her feet and, looking up, saw a pale figure hanging in the gloom. Terror shot through her. Then she saw it was only a crucifix, life-size, and she had tripped on its step. Rain beat on the plaster body, dripping from the thorns round the bowed head, running down the bare legs. It's too cold to hang there naked, she thought; and to her amazement she found she was crying for pity. In the light of day it would be the kind of religious statue she despised, vulgar, sentimental; but now in the half-light she could think of nothing but how cold and lonely it looked. Words she knew she did not believe crept across her mind: *In this thy bitter passion, Good Shepherd, think on me.*

She turned and, with tears still falling, walked back towards the house.

CHAPTER 15

When the flood is past. She could not remember where the words came from. Not from the Bible. From a poem? *When the flood is past*. She was sitting watching the stream that ran deep in the valley beneath the retreat house. Everywhere there were signs of earlier flooding – broken trees, mud and grass choking the undergrowth, and rubbish hanging from twigs. She could see how high the waters had come. The river ran quietly now. How long have I been in this place? She thought it was about four or five days. The monks had left her more or less alone, letting her sleep and eat and wander as she chose, but she knew they were keeping an eye on her. It was very quiet under the dense pines. She might almost be on the sea bed. The branches creaked as the wind bent the treetops this way and that far overhead. Down at the roots all was still.

She sat watching the surface of the river, and the trees and sky which seemed to lie beneath it. Where there's life there's hope. That's what people will say, taking my arm kindly. What hope have I got? The belief that all this will pass. *The living know that they will die, but the dead know nothing*. Better to have died, then, and to know nothing. Hester is the fortunate one. Faithful unto death. She never had to live with this. She never knew it was all a lie.

She leant back against the tree trunk and closed her eyes. Tears crept down her cheeks and her mind drifted on the surface of sleep. The tree behind her back moved gently as the wind tugged at its top. Memories floated by. Her aunt's voice, speaking angrily: 'She can't cope! I have four children, and she can't cope with two. When they were babies, yes, all right. I can understand that. But now? Why do I have to take her child?' I am waiting terrified in the dark hallway. I know I shouldn't be listening. They are speaking Welsh, which they think I can't understand. 'You think I haven't got enough to do already without this? First your Aunt Jessie and now this? Supposing I couldn't cope either, all of a sudden?' At last Uncle Huw speaks: 'She's my brother's child, and she stays.' There will be no more words. Just the clashing of plates, the slamming of drawers, the sullen dripping of washing on the rack. I will be no trouble. Never asking for things, never wetting the bed. I must stay here because they don't want me at home.

It's the sound of the river. That's what's taking me back. I haven't really thought about all this for years. She tried to remember how often she had been sent to stay with her aunt and uncle. Three times? Four? Or was it more than that? She was no longer sure. She knew her father had taken her there when she was a baby, and she could remember another occasion when she had been about six. The other times blurred together. I used to hide between two rocks by the stream above the farm. The bracken made a roof and I would read in the greeny light, listening to the water. There were never enough books. *Black Beauty. Pilgrim's Progress. Inquire Within upon Everything.* I read them all. And when all else failed, there was the Bible.

> *The best book to read is the Bible.*
> *The best book to read is the Bible.*
> *If you read it every day, it will help you on your way.*
> *Oh, the best book to read is the Bible!*

We sang that in the chapel Sunday school. And another one: *Read your Bible, pray every day, if you want to grow.* And I did pray. Every day: 'Dear Lord, let Dewi be nice to me. Let him want to play with me. Don't let Aunt Susan be cross with me. Please don't let there be any spiders in my room. Please, please don't let the Second Coming happen before I'm ready.'

It's as though my time there was made up of fear and misery. Things must have improved, though, or I would never have chosen to spend my summer holidays there. My happiest memories are of August on the farm. Dewi was there, teaching me to wolf-whistle, to bowl, letting me drive the tractor sometimes. Once he gave me a penknife. Memories worn out long ago with overhandling. But now other less savoury things came floating by. Hide and seek with Dewi and his friends. They had a pact, running off so that she remained unfound hours later, still waiting, hoping. I'm seven years old, and I'm sitting in the barn in the dark. No, not the dark. I'm blindfolded and tied up. He will come and rescue me in the end. I've been here a long time. I'm weeping into my blindfold, because I know there are spiders in here. At last Uncle Huw finds me. 'How long have you been here?'

'I don't know.' He unties the knots.

'Who did this?'

'I don't know.' He is very angry.

'It was Dewi, wasn't it?'

'I don't know, I don't know.' I've been here so long I've wet myself, and I run off in shame and fear. When I see Dewi later, I can tell he has been crying. He has been beaten, and now he will punish me.

Elizabeth is the oldest. 'Why can't I have a room of my own? Why do I have to share with them? Faye's always poking into my things!' She bends down to dab nail varnish on to a hole in her tights so it won't run. Now she has a red blob on her leg that looks like blood. Three in the room, and four with me. Elizabeth hates it. She escapes into her magazines. One day there will be a dreamy guy for her. But how? No discos, no youth club, no parties, even. 'I hate this bleeding farm.' I have to share a bed with Faye. We sleep one at each end, and she kicks me in the night. 'I hate you. Everyone hates you. Dewi hates you. He told me he does. Nobody wants you here, so why don't you just go home so I can have my bed back?' Faye is my age. They tell her to look after me and that we should be friends, but she gives me Chinese burns to see if I will cry. 'You know why everyone hates you? Because you're ugly. You're so ugly that when you grow up, no one will ever want to marry you. Even your parents hate you. That's why you have to come and live with us. I heard them telling Dad.'

Sometimes Morwenna plays with me, but she's only a baby, and I get bored.

Aunt Jessie died when I was ten. Elizabeth got her room. The next summer Aunt Susan cleared the box room in the attic and I slept there instead. It was too small, really, you couldn't open the door properly because of the bed, but I loved it. I used to lie staring out at the hills through the little window. It was my heaven. A month of bliss every summer. Tagging along after Dewi. Helping with the baling. Building dens. Paddling in the stream. 'Well, she's no trouble,' said Aunt Susan once to a neighbour. Her lips were tight. She had no time for us girls. Dewi was the only one she loved.

The last week of school was always unbearable. Five days till I go to the farm. Four days. Three days. Flies droning in the classroom. Two days. One more day and I'll be there . . .

'Why were you crying last night?' Faye asks Aunt Susan this at breakfast. Aunt Susan says nothing and her face goes red. 'Why were you crying? You were moaning.' Aunt Susan reaches out suddenly and smacks Faye's face. Faye bursts into tears. 'Now what have I done? I was only asking!' Aunt Susan leaves the kitchen. 'It's not fair! What have I done?' I heard her too, and on other nights, and Uncle Huw grunting, once, like someone swearing. Dewi is eating his breakfast. He doesn't talk to us, because he is fourteen and a boy and we are only ten-year-old girls. But Faye keeps on saying 'It's not fair!' and in the end Dewi says, 'They were having it off, stupid.' Faye stops crying with shock.

'No they weren't!'

'You don't even know what that means,' says Dewi.

'Yes, I do! It's what they do to have babies. She says she doesn't want another baby.' Faye is right, but Dewi jeers at her.

'I suppose you think he's only fucked her four times.'

'You're not allowed to say that word! I'm going to tell! You know you're not allowed to say that word!' He says it again, then gets up and goes out laughing. Faye screams after him, 'Dewi, you're not allowed to say that word!'

The farm is a hateful place. One of the ponies has a great dangling thing and it tries to climb on the other ponies' backs. Sometimes there are dogs stuck together, quivering. Dewi has a magazine in his bedroom, hidden carefully, but Faye has found it. She shows it to me. He'll be in trouble, because the girls have no knickers on and they've got their legs open. One of them is squeezing her breasts as though she's holding them out for someone to take. She has a stupid smile. Faye hides the magazine under Dewi's mattress where Aunt Susan will be sure to find it when she makes the bed. She'll take it to Uncle Huw and he'll hit Dewi with his belt; but if I warn Dewi, Faye will pinch me, and she'll tell about the magazine, anyway. In the end I creep into his room and steal it. I take it out on to the hills, far away, to the place they called World's End, and then I burn it with my magnifying glass. I burn the stupid smiling girl first, burning out her smile with a point of sun. Nobody ever finds out.

She dreamt that she was awake. Hester was there, peering into the stream, and calling her. 'Mara, there are treasures in the stream.' She bent over to look, and sure enough, there were tiny bottles in bright colours, and gold and silver coins. 'They said you were dead, Hester.' Hester stared in astonishment. Then they both laughed and laughed at the very idea.

She woke to find herself sobbing. After a moment she leant

forwards and looked in the stream. No treasure. There were tiny fish darting about. As she watched them flicking to and fro a strange feeling crept over her. She was being watched. She turned. There was a man among the trees. She froze, but then he stepped forward, and she saw it was Johnny. He came and sat beside her.

'How are you doing, flower?' Her answer was choked by tears. He put his arm around her and she leant her head against his shoulder as though he were God and had all the answers. She was too weary to despise her weakness.

In the end she said: 'I dreamt she was here. Just now. I was asleep.'

'What was she doing?'

'Looking into the stream.' She started to tell him about it, but the sense of desolation broke over her afresh. Hester, Hester. She was gone. I'm alone. A mirror with no reflection. 'She was always *there*.' Johnny hugged her close. 'Even when we were apart.'

'Were you apart much?'

'Yes. Just after we were born. I was sent away. And sometimes while we were growing up, too.' She sensed his astonishment and could not bear to meet his eye.

'They sent you away as a baby? Why?' He pulled away slightly, trying to see her face. She looked down at the ground where the tree roots were showing like veins through the earth. 'Why?' he asked again.

'Because . . . There were reasons. My mother couldn't cope.'

'Couldn't cope? Is that a polite way of saying she cracked up?'

'No.' She heard the defensive tone. 'It was just difficult for her. With two of us. She was ill. She kept having to go into hospital.'

'Where did you stay?'

'With my uncle's family. In Wales.'

'Was that all right?'

She hesitated. She wanted to say 'I loved it!' but found she no longer could. 'Not really.'

'Why not?'

'They picked on me. My cousins. And my aunt didn't want me there.'

'Then why did your parents let you go there, if you were unhappy?'

'Because they had to. Don't keep asking me! My mother couldn't cope. That's all there is to it.'

She covered her face with her hands, seeing for the first time how the two lies had been balancing one another all these years: my mother couldn't cope, so I was sent to the farm; which was OK because I loved it there. But I didn't. I hated it. Why couldn't she cope? She pressed her knuckles into her forehead, trying to keep out the unbearable thought that was forming. *She didn't want me. My own mother didn't want me.* It's not true! It was my father who rejected me. Not her. Suddenly she saw that there were not only papered cracks, but whole rooms and wings bricked up and papered over, hidden so cunningly that she would never know they were there. Unless someone like Johnny came along on the outside and counted the windows and realized something was missing. Eventually she looked up again, watching the stream running over the stones.

'I don't want to think about it.' They sat for a moment in silence.

'Tell me about Hester, then.' Where could she begin? 'What was she like?'

'Not like me. She was . . . she was . . .'

'Not clever?'

'She was clever.' She was sounding defensive again. 'Well, not brilliant, maybe. She did well at school. Better than I did, in some ways.' Never asking *why*. What's the point of it? Always absorbing and accepting what was taught. 'She was beautiful.' His lips twitched and she saw how her words seemed to be begging for a compliment. 'She had dark hair. Like mine, only straight,' she hurried on. 'I always wanted straight hair. Mine never looked shiny. And her eyes were blue, not grey.' Something in her had clicked open and confidences came rushing out. 'People were always saying, "Well, you wouldn't think they were sisters even, let alone twins." She was much smaller than me. And she was always nice.'

He laughed. 'Even your worst enemy wouldn't say that about you, Mara.'

She was stung. Even at a time like this he was laughing at her.

'I meant it positively. She didn't have a mean streak in her. She wanted everyone to be happy.' But there was still a trace of amusement in his face. He got out a cigarette and lit it. 'I'm not saying she was perfect!'

'You're not? What were her faults, then?' He crumpled the empty packet and tossed it aside. She stared in faint shock at his action and he retrieved the packet with a grin. 'Could you imagine murdering anyone, Mara?'

'Yes,' she said after a moment's thought. 'Why?'

He nodded slightly, as if this answered some private debate he had been having with himself. 'So what were her faults?'

'What's murder got to do with anything?'

He blew a cloud of smoke away from her. 'You're middle-class.' He grinned again at her bewilderment. 'My definition: more likely to commit murder than drop litter. But carry on. Tell me about her faults.'

'Well . . .' What had she been going to say? He had made her lose a grip on her thoughts. 'She was too trusting.' There was a pause.

'That's it?'

She was beginning to feel like a fruit machine played by someone on a lucky streak. He was cranking her arm with questions and the words kept tumbling out.

'It's hard to live with someone who wants you to be happy the whole time. She was . . . There were some things you couldn't tell her, because she would always be trying to understand and make everything better. She was like my mother. It was easier to say nothing. She always believed people were what they said they were. You couldn't say . . . Oh, I don't know, something like, well, so-and-so's a poisonous trouble-maker, because she would just listen with big eyes, trying to work out what was making you say that. You know – is she upset? What has she got against her? How can I make her feel happier about her? All that stuff. She'd never think anyone might actually *be* a poisonous trouble-maker. Or if they were, it wasn't their fault. Nobody had ever really listened to them.' She stopped.

'We're talking about someone in particular here, aren't we?' he asked after a moment.

'Yes,' she whispered.

'Someone in that sect?'

'Yes.' Leah. Turning Hester into her lackey. Shackling Hester to her with the threat of suicide. 'Nobody else understands me, Hester.' And trying to convince her that I was a child of Satan.

'Are you going to tell me about it?'

'Oh, it was just this other girl. She latched on to Hester. They used to pray for me. That I would be delivered from demons.'

'Sounds like Joanna.' She said nothing. 'Wasn't your sister on your side?'

'Of course she was! We loved each other. It wasn't her fault. I told you she was too trusting.' I can't bear it. He's making me betray her. 'But she was good. Don't you laugh at me! You never knew her, so you can't judge. There really are people like that,' she sobbed.

He put his arm round her again. 'I know. But don't you sometimes hate them for it?'

She jerked away from him. 'I loved her!'

'Yes.'

But had she? Hadn't Hester always used up all the air and sunshine and left Mara with nothing to grow on? A pale lanky weed beside a beautiful flower.

'I did!' She cried huge gulping sobs. Her face felt bloated and ugly. She couldn't stop herself blurting out more: 'She didn't lose her temper like I did. I was always in trouble.' She sensed him trying not to laugh again.

'Sorry,' he said, catching sight of her expression. 'I'm not mocking you. It just reminds me of my brother and me. Strict demarcation. He was the good one. I was the bad lad. He left me with no option, you see.' He knows what it's like, she thought. Her tears gradually subsided. 'I suppose that makes him the bad one, now I'm going into the Church. Now I'm so superhumanly good.' He finished his cigarette and threw the end in the stream. Was that bitterness in his voice? She watched the cigarette-end float away, thinking how little she really knew about him or his family.

'Could you imagine murdering anyone?' she asked.

'No. Not in cold blood. Manslaughter, maybe. If I caught my wife in bed with another man, or something.'

'You don't have a wife.'

'True. Not any more.'

Her mouth dropped open. 'You mean . . .' She groped for words. 'What happened?'

'I caught her in bed with another man.' Her heart lurched. His tone was so casual. 'What's wrong? Ah.' He laughed. 'No – my brother and the pub darts team all pinned me down and sat on me while she climbed out of the back window. I never laid a hand on her.'

Her lips felt cold and stiff. 'Sorry.'

'Don't be. I was glad to see the back of her, to be honest.' There was a silence. She listened to the hissing of the wind through the pine branches, wondering, reassessing. 'So now you know. That's why I'm celibate, of course. If I remarried I couldn't be ordained.' He picked up the crumpled cigarette packet and began tossing it from hand to hand.

Of course. Why hadn't she thought of it? But celibacy? That seemed a bit extreme. She suspected a lot of clergy were less scrupulous.

'So you don't believe in sex outside marriage?'

'Oh, I *believe* in it,' he said. 'I just don't agree with it. Unless she's very attractive. Or I'm very drunk.' She despaired of getting a sensible answer out of him. 'Or *she's* very drunk, and I'm feeling sorry for myself. Or –'

'Look,' she broke in, 'I just meant the Church doesn't require you to be celibate, does it?'

'Ah, you mean, screw around all week, then preach about sin on Sundays? There's a thought.' He considered it, still flipping the cigarette packet to and fro. 'Yes, I rather like that.'

'You seem to think screwing around is the only alternative to celibacy!'

'Well, isn't it? Oh, I see – one of those "serious committed relationships" I keep hearing about.'

She snatched the cigarette packet from him. 'Will you stop doing that! Why do you have to be so flippant the whole time? You must have had at least one serious relationship.'

'Why must I?'

'Well, you've been married, for God's sake.' He raised an eyebrow, and suddenly she felt very naive. Her face burned. 'You must have been serious about her at the time,' she persisted.

'Must I?'

'Or why did you marry her?' He gave her a look, and she knew she should back off. She felt her fingers crushing the cigarette packet tightly. He picked up a handful of stones and began throwing them one by one into the stream.

'I married her because she told me she was pregnant,' he said without looking at her.

'But that's Victorian!' She saw him tense, and cursed herself. 'I mean, I'd never marry someone just because I was pregnant.'

'I'm sure you wouldn't, pet.' He continued flicking stones into the water. 'But to quote you, you can't judge, because you don't know my family. Or my town, for that matter.' He still had not looked at her.

'You mean, you'd have been ostracized?'

189

'Possibly,' he said, eyeing her cautiously. She had seen him do this to Maddy on more than one occasion: pretend not to understand polysyllabic words.

'Can't you be serious for one minute?' He grinned at her. 'And stop throwing stones!' she wanted to shout. 'So you've got a child?'

'No. She was lying.' He turned away again, and she watched his profile, trying to gauge how much more she dared ask.

'How long did the marriage last?'

'Before she ran off? About two months. Let's talk about something else, shall we?'

'You never loved her?' He said nothing, and although she knew she was pushing him too far, she could not stop herself. 'Why did you sleep with her, then?'

He rounded on her. 'Because she was my brother's girl. It was a little hobby of mine – trying to fuck any woman my brother fancied. Is that serious enough for you?'

She shrank back. 'But why?'

'Because I could. Because, my God, there was always one thing I was better at than him. You don't like that, do you? You'd rather I was perfect.'

'No.' She watched her fingers trembling as they tried to uncrumple the cigarette packet. There was a taut silence. Why did I do that? Make him say what he hates to admit, and what I hate to hear.

'Sorry,' he said shortly.

'It's OK.'

She felt herself wobbling on the brink of tears again. He sighed and she looked up to see him opening a new packet of cigarettes. He caught himself in the act of throwing the cellophane away, and glanced at her. She saw the glimmer of amusement with relief. He lit a cigarette and inhaled deeply. The trees creaked in the wind and he lay back, seeming to watch the branches moving against the sky.

'The Church says I'm fit to be ordained even though I'm divorced. I've been forgiven, you see. But not if I get married again.' She looked down at him. He seemed to find the whole thing amusing. 'And then when I'm priested, it's OK again. I can get married. But not in church, of course.' He was smoking calmly, watching the treetops. 'In theory, a bishop who was divorced and remarried could refuse to ordain me if I got married again. Good, isn't it? I like being an Anglican.'

'You're angry,' she said, suddenly realizing.

'All the time, Princess.'

'But you're always joking.'

'Just my way. You're always fighting.'

Maybe his way was better. She was tired of fighting.

'You could live in sin, of course,' she said, thinking aloud. 'If you were very discreet. The church would turn a blind eye.' The good old C of E. He sat up, and she saw too late what she had laid herself open to.

'Mm-mm-mm. Yes *please*.' His eyes seemed to linger on her lips. 'On second thoughts, discretion has never been my strong point. We'd better not risk it, Mara.' She turned away, her face on fire. 'I couldn't live a double life, flower,' he said. She looked back swiftly, but in another instant the flicker of seriousness was gone. 'Here.' He put his cigarette between her lips as he had done once before. 'Much safer than living in sin. You'll probably die of lung cancer, but at least you won't burn in hell.' She threw the cigarette into the stream. He laughed, lit another one and lay back again, shutting his eyes.

For the first time she was able to study his face properly. She let her eyes learn the way his hair grew from his forehead, the shape of his eyelids, the dark fringe of lashes, and the laughter lines still there although his face was relaxed. Her mind traced for itself the outline of his mouth, committing it to memory. Suddenly he spoke, and her eyes darted away guiltily.

'You know, if you subject a structure to enough pressure it'll give way at its weakest point.' She looked back, heart pounding, but his eyes were still closed. 'Obvious, I suppose. The same goes for people.' He put the cigarette to his lips. Was he trying to tell her something?

'What's your weak point, then?' she asked.

He opened an eye. 'You don't need me to tell you that, surely?' Was he talking about sex again? She blushed.

'No.'

'I thought not.'

He closed his eye and continued smoking. She watched him furtively, and then another thought struck her. What if he had been talking instead about his quick temper? She blushed again. After all, he had just told her he could imagine killing someone.

'I suppose I'm just trying to say I'm under a lot of pressure at the moment.' He had been talking about anger, then.

'Yes.'

'I try to keep a tight rein on myself, but ... Well, it's the old story. The spirit is willing, but the flesh is weak.' He grinned. 'Or vice versa, in my case.' Suddenly it sounded like sex again. He opened his eyes and looked at her, waiting for some response.

'All right,' she muttered. 'I know what you're saying.' She stared at the stream. But did she know? Was he warning her that one day, in a fit of self-pity, he might try to seduce her? Or that if she pushed him too far, he might throttle her and throw her body into the river? But having said she understood, she could not now ask for clarification. He reached out and put a hand briefly on her arm.

'Thanks,' he said, 'I'm just mad at the whole world at the minute.' She continued to stare miserably at the water. After a moment he stretched and stood up. 'I'm going to have to go. Walk back to the car with me?'

They climbed against the wind, making their way up the steep field above the woods. The house appeared over the brow of the hill. She didn't want him to go. Tears began welling up, but she clung to her last scrap of pride.

'Sorry I'm so wound up,' he said unexpectedly. 'I'm preaching in college chapel tonight, and I've got cold feet about my sermon.'

'What's it on?'

'Oh, Jeremiah sounding off about something.' He ran his hand over his face, then shook his head. 'It's all about doubt and vocation, which I can do without, quite frankly, at the moment.' He flung his arms wide. '"O Lord, thou hast deceived me and I was deceived. Thou art stronger than I and thou hast prevailed." As far as I can make out, it means, "God, you used me and dumped me. You're stronger than me, and you raped me." Not very Anglican.' She saw his flippant manner reasserting itself, and found she was laughing against her will as he unlocked the car. 'Have you thought how long you'll stay here?' She said nothing. 'Well, give me a ring when you want to come back, and I'll pick you up.' He gave her a quick hug. She willed her hands not to clutch at him.

'Thanks,' she said as he got into the car, and she cast about for one last thing to say to him. 'Did you get into trouble for bringing me here?'

He paused. 'With Rupert? There was a full and frank exchange of opinions.' She saw she would get no more out of him. 'Give me a ring, sometime. You're missed, sweetie.'

As he drove off, grief closed in on her again. His presence had been keeping it at bay, and now it flooded her, bringing with it a cold tide of guilt that she should have forgotten Hester even for a short while. She turned abruptly into the woods which surrounded the car park and stumbled through the undergrowth, half blinded by tears.

CHAPTER 16

Mara sat up in bed. Today was her last day. She was returning to college. Her mother, alerted by the Principal, was driving up to collect her. How can I face her? I must get up and go out, she decided. One last walk to try to prepare myself. She pushed the covers back.

It was a mild day. She went out of the house and made her way up the drive towards the road. The sound of a hymn being sung in the chapel floated out to her as she passed. It was a Lent hymn, and after a moment the familiar words went through her mind:

> Lord Jesus think on me,
> And purge away my sin.
> From earthborn passions set me free,
> And make me pure within.

Earthborn passions. Passionate lust or passionate anger. By thy cross and passion, good Lord, deliver us.

She reached the end of the drive and turned along the narrow country lane. The first signs of spring were visible in the hedgerows – coltsfoot, celandines – and she could hear the early lambs bleating in the distance. Her mind had gone back repeatedly to her conversation with Johnny by the river, worrying at it (sex? anger?) until she was no longer sure what he had actually said, let alone what he might have meant by it. Something caught her eye in the undergrowth. The first violet, she thought with pleasure, but when she stopped and peered more closely it was only an old scrap of chocolate wrapper. How could a man as good-looking as Johnny be attracted to her? Was it possible? Her heart was beginning to race at the thought, when the truth hit her like a glass of cold water in the face. The risk for him lay in her circumstances, not her attractiveness. He would be all too well aware of the potentially explosive situation they were in. Her grief, his kindness. Too many clergy had found themselves enmeshed like this: something that began as pastoral concern flaring up into fornication or adultery. She forced herself to examine her motives and found that they could not bear such scrutiny. Her mind squirmed.

She began to walk on again. I'm like Joanna, she thought with loathing. I'll have to keep him at arm's length from now on. Just when I was getting to know him at last. It's not fair. She felt a tear creeping down her cheek and she smeared it away angrily. Well, it's March now. By the middle of June it'll all be over. Three months, then I'll never have to see him again. I can survive till then. Some remote part of her exhaled as though with relief. Why do I find sex so disgusting?

Her two encounters so far had both conformed unhappily to the Hobbesian view of the life of man: nasty, brutish and short. The first time especially. Fifteen was too young. Despoiled. Deflowered. Good words for it.

Someone's party. She had tagged along with Hester, resolved to lose her virginity to find out what all the fuss was about. 'Why don't you and me go for a little drive, darling?' Car pulling into a dark lay-by, sticky vinyl seats, steamed-up windows. She was too terrified to say she'd changed her mind. 'What's the matter with you, for Christ's sake? Relax, darling.' Sweaty hands wrenched her open as though they were jointing a chicken, as he drove his thing into her. Mara's flesh recoiled from the memory.

The second time should have been better. A good-looking third year in her first week at Cambridge. An argument in the college bar about feminism. He had followed her back to her room spitting with rage. 'You know what you need, don't you?' And she had replied coolly, 'OK, then. Do it.'

They faced one another in silence.

'OK. Get on the bed.'

Mara was unsure, looking back, who had been calling whose bluff. She had disguised her fear as contempt, and this had completely unmanned him. He had scarcely managed three thrusts and an apology. They avoided one another for the rest of the year. What a pitiful tally. A crow cawed from a dead elm as though it were laughing at her. It would be different with Johnny, though, whined a voice. No it wouldn't, she said to it. I'd probably still panic and freeze up.

The road ahead curved along the side of a hill. She followed it, and as she rounded the bend, the whole landscape suddenly opened up in front of her. She stopped still in surprise, watching the sunlight and clouds chasing over the rolling hills. For one dizzy moment she could almost feel the earth whirling under her. *If only I could, now, fling the road away under my feet and hurl myself into the waiting sky.* She stood, head back, eyes closed. Some thought was coming upon her. She felt it gathering itself, and then it burst into her mind. *I want to paint this.*

She took a deep breath. *I remember this point. It was always like this – the moment of conception, when you believe this time you'll really achieve it – walk with the angels on the wings of the wind. But even as the brush touches the canvas, you have failed. The vision is dragged down by the oil in its feathers.* She wondered if it had been this – the repeated striving and failure – that had driven her to turn her back on painting.

Memories of school jostled in her head. She could almost smell the classrooms and feel the stifling boredom. Art lessons had been a liberation. In the sixth form she spent all her free time in the art room. She saw herself again, painting huge canvases while the Third Years pored over cheese-plant leaves or halves of red cabbage. Only the art teacher had any idea what she was trying to do. Everyone else thought it perverse that someone who could draw so well should want to paint abstracts.

Another memory. She was in the office of Mr Doncaster, the head of the sixth form. 'And you'll be applying to Art College, of course.' It had not even been a question. Mara had gone into the room uncertain, wanting to discuss the decision which was tearing her apart, but instead she heard herself say: 'I want to read English at Cambridge.'

A short, barking laugh from Mr Doncaster. Now at last came the teacher's chance for revenge. He had suffered too many years of mute insubordination from this difficult girl. 'I doubt you're really up to Cambridge. Your A-level predictions are nowhere near good enough. Go away and think about it again.' So she went away and applied directly to a Cambridge college and talked her way into a place. This had redounded to the greater glory of the Bulbourne High School for Girls, and she had never been forgiven for it.

The sound of a curlew rose up in the distance. She stood a moment longer watching the sunlight and the shadows chasing across the hills. *Maybe I made the wrong choice.* For the first time she let herself wonder whether the satisfaction of settling a score with a hated school was enough. Something in her said it was not. *Well, I can live* with the consequences of my wrong decisions. She set off again, climbing a stile and beginning to walk impatiently along a footpath. I still intend to have a successful academic career. I made that choice, and I'm not going back. I'd sooner drop litter. She cursed herself, seeing how her mind kept sneaking back to Johnny.

Back at the friary, the car park and entrance hall were full of people. She caught snatches of conversation as she made her way through a crowd which she realized must be a group of curates arriving for post-ordination training. I'm glad I'm leaving, she thought, running up the stairs and leaving the laughter and in-jokes behind her. There was something overpowering about large numbers of clergy in a confined space – like fifteen prima donnas in a stuck lift.

It did not take her long to pack and soon she was sitting on the edge of her narrow bed wondering when her mother would arrive. She felt as though she were waiting to go into an exam hall. Their next meeting would be crucial. It would decide whether they would go on with the polite lies and silences or at last let the truth in. It waited like a dark stranger in a dim hallway. What eyeless sockets lay concealed? What face half eaten away by disease? Better to throw the lights on and know the worst. After all, it might prove to be nothing but an old cassock hanging on a hatstand.

She got up and crossed to the window, too nervous to remain sitting any longer. The wind was stirring the branches of the chestnut trees which surrounded the house. I suppose I ought to go and say thank you to the monks. She was embarrassed at the thought. Who was in charge? The Abbot? the Father Superior? She'd heard the monks talking about someone called Tom as though he might be the head. My God, what about *paying*? How much do I owe them? She had no idea, and for a moment she was paralysed by the fear that she could not afford it; but then the mental picture of her mother's cheque book and fountain pen propelled her out of the door and down the stairs.

The main hallway was quiet. Mara was hovering there when one of the brothers appeared. Seeing her uncertainty, he stopped.

'You look lost. Can I help you?'

'Um . . . yes. Is Tom the –'

'Tom's the guardian, yes. Did you want a word with him?'

She nodded, and the monk set off down the corridor motioning her to follow. As she walked, she was aware of a nagging guilt that she had been so self-absorbed during the weeks she had spent in the friary. She was shown into a room where a grey-haired monk was sitting at a desk. He smiled at her and rose to his feet.

'Tom, Mara would like a chat with you.' With these words the first monk left. He knows my name, thought Mara as the door closed. Maybe they all know all about me. Tom gestured to a couple of armchairs and they both sat down. A mistake. She had only intended a brief conversation. A clock ticked on the mantelpiece. She cleared her throat.

'I really only came to say thank you for letting me stay here. I'm going back to college today.' She was trying to make her voice sound pleasant yet not confiding, but her tone was at odds with the old armchair. Its sagging springs and escaping horsehair seemed to say, 'Relax. Spill the beans.' She was sitting stiffly to combat this impulse. 'I think it's been a valuable time.' She heard her stilted words and saw Tom incline his head. He looked relaxed, and yet she could tell he was listening with his whole being, aware of every tone and gesture and hidden clue. His silence drove her into the classic error of blurting out more: 'I feel . . . fortified.' It sounded so odd that she clamped her mouth shut, resolved to say nothing else.

In the end he spoke: 'You're feeling fortified.'

It was a pleasant voice, and she would have liked it, had she not spotted that he was using that bloody non-directive counselling technique. It had always driven her mad to hear her own words batted straight back at her. She felt that look coming over her face.

'Yes,' she said perversely. 'I'm feeling fortified.'

If it had sounded peculiar the first time, now it seemed preposterous. They fell into silence again. The clock ticked. He was watching and waiting. The silence went on until she began to feel wild and strange. She had a sudden urge to bowl him a bouncer: I think I'm in love with you. Then she remembered why she was there. She cleared her throat again.

'The other thing is, I was wondering how much I owed you? What your rates are, I mean.'

He looked at her thoughtfully. 'Well, I wasn't thinking of charging you, exactly.' She blushed. 'How about a contribution? I can certainly let you know our rates. Anything you might like to give us towards that amount would be fine.'

'The problem is I don't actually have my cheque book with me, but if I could . . .' She fumbled to a stop. Money was almost as embarrassing as sex.

'Send us a cheque, then. No problem.'

Now was her chance to rise and leave with another polite thank you, but she continued to sit. Silence opened up between them again. She saw Tom's right hand move to the cross he wore round his neck. The fingers closed around it, and she knew that this was a mute prayer. Her eyes remained on his hand, waiting for it to move. With each tick of the clock the stillness in the room seemed to intensify. Outside a robin sang.

'Mara, what do you want?'

'Nothing!' The word shot frightened out of her.

'What do you want, Mara?'

Freedom. To be free of all this guilt and fear and shame. To be absolved.

The ticking of the clock grew louder and louder in her ears. She watched as slowly his fingers uncurled from the cross. He raised his hand and pronounced the absolution. The familiar words slid over one another like pebbles worn smooth by centuries of tides. She felt her lips whisper 'Amen' and her hand moving to cross herself before she could stop it. A great sigh left her, as though her soul had been dislocated for years and had at last been slipped back into joint. For a moment she sat still in wonder, then a sense of outrage seized her. How dare he do that without asking? He had tricked a response out of her, meaningless as a knee-jerk in a doctor's surgery.

She stood up angrily and turned to leave; but she had only taken two steps when she leapt back with a cry. Tom was beside her in an instant. The room seemed dim and she groped for his arm.

'Did you see that?' She could feel her brain gibbering.

'See what?' Her mind was still squeaking with terror when to her amazement she heard herself laugh. It seemed to come bubbling up from a forgotten spring. 'What did you see?' asked Tom. The laughter died back down again. Tick, tick, said the clock.

'An angel.'

They stood looking at one another.

'Do you want to tell me about it?'

She shook her head, and he continued to watch her. Was he afraid she was mad?

'I've seen it before,' she heard herself gabble, as though this would reassure him. For a moment the memory of it made her quiver. The terrible countenance, eyes burning with wrath and fierce joy. Very cautiously she turned her head round, but there was nothing there, just a shaft of sunlight coming through the narrow window. She turned back to face Tom again.

'I'll be all right,' she said.

His fingers were curled round the cross again, as though he were consulting God to see whether to believe her. Then he smiled and stretched out his hand. He seemed to be welcoming her back. Part of her rebelled, yet in spite of herself she reached out her hand. He grasped it.

'Angels should always be taken seriously, you know.' He was smiling as he spoke, but she could tell that this was a warning. She thanked him again and left.

Outside it could have been a new world. Everything was sharp and clear; the chestnut buds dancing against the sky, the crocuses shivering in the lawn. Mara wandered until she reached the crucifix where she tripped that first evening. She would see her mother arriving from there.

An angel.

An *angel*? Had she gone mad? A blackbird busied itself in the undergrowth near by, turning over the dead leaves. She'd never felt more sane. But that was what mad people always thought. Aunt Jessie had seen angels all the time, and was baffled when no one else could.

'Look, child, Mount Sion, the City of the living God!' she had said, pointing to the bare hill above the farm. 'You see them? An innumerable company of angels, as the Bible tells us, and the spirits of just men made perfect. Pastor Jenkins walking in sweet communion with the blessed angels. There, look! You see him?'

'No, Auntie Jessie.'

'Ah, they have eyes and see not.'

Sometimes Mara almost could see them out of the corner of her faithless eye in a dancing patch of sunlight, or a piece of floating thistledown. The farm became a holy place for her. Bethel. None other than the house of God, the gate of heaven.

As Mara looked at the sunlight on the bare branches, the same feeling she had known as a child came over her again. This world was no more than a thin membrane stretched out over eternity. At any moment it might peel back and the glory come blazing through. On days like this it seemed so near, the fabric pulled so fine that it was lit up from behind, beyond, and every shifting play of light, each moving leaf, might be the shadow of the just passing to and fro behind the veil among the angels.

'What did he want?' Andrew's voice spoke in her mind. She remembered his dispassionate interrogation: 'Wings? How many? What did he want? Did he say anything?' But it was useless. How could you analyse and quantify something like this? Words would not do. The angel had said nothing, but she knew there had been a message if only she could understand it. She sighed and tilted her head back, watching the leaping twigs and the clouds in flight on the west wind. She was still there, wondering, as her mother's car made its way down the drive.

They were driving south. The landscape slipped by, moorlands, dry-stone walls.

'Yes,' said her mother, continuing out loud what had been an internal conversation, as she often did, 'pub meals are so much more substantial in the north. And cheaper, of course. You're sure you had enough? You're still rather thin, darling.'

'Yes. What day is it?'

'Wednesday,' replied her mother, deflected from Mara's diet. 'Only two weeks till the end of term.' There was a silence, and Mara knew her mother was working round to a non-threatening way of asking if she would be spending the vacation at home. 'Look – a heron!'

'Careful!' said Mara, and her mother tweaked the wheel abruptly. The bird made its way on slow wing beats across a river. Maybe I will go home. 'I thought I might come home for Easter.'

'Oh, darling, that's wonderful!' Mara tried not to cringe away from her mother's enthusiasm. 'Why don't you invite some of your friends to stay as well? You know we've got masses of room.'

'I might.'

Her mother began humming. Maybe she was already planning lunch menus and mentally putting out guest towels and soap. The car wandered slightly towards the middle of the road. Her driving was a metaphor of her life. She approached it blithely, confident that it would all sort itself out if only everyone behaved with the decency she knew thay were capable of.

'I met quite a few of your friends yesterday,' her mother went on. 'I spent the night in college. It felt rather like being an undergraduate again. Maddy and May popped in. I saw Helen Poppett just the other day at a clergy wives' do, and she said that you and May were both in Jesus. Oh, and I saw Johnny, too.' Her mother knew better than to glance at this point. 'I didn't manage to track down Rupert, though. I'd like to meet him. I saw him baptized, you know. Winchester cathedral. Destined for greatness. He was out taking a Youth Group somewhere.' Mara watched the lambs on the hillside as her mother continued to talk. 'And I met Andrew, and Lucy and Carol, of course. They *are* nice, aren't they? They invited me in for tea.' Lucy and Carol? Mara racked her brains guiltily. The field mice? Her mother slowed for a wandering sheep. 'And I must say, I do like Andrew.' Andrew? *Like*? What's he been playing at, making himself agreeable to my mother? She felt a twist of jealousy. 'Completely insufferable, of course, but I've got a soft spot for him.' Ah, she's found a phrase to tame him. Just like she'd done for Johnny: 'a bit of a rough diamond'. Maybe I'll see him today . . . She jerked her mind back from the thought angrily. 'I hope you don't mind,' said her mother, 'but I've brightened your room up for you a bit. It seemed a bit bare and institutional.' Oh, God. She's William Morris-ed it.

'Thank you.'

They drove for a while in silence. Signs for the City began to appear. Twenty miles. I'm going to have to talk to her about my childhood. If I don't do it now, I never will. Her mother was humming again. Fifteen miles. Twelve. Speak. Say something. She looked down at her hands and tried to unlace the fingers. I can't talk to her. I can't do it.

'Anyway,' said her mother as though they had not just sat for fifteen minutes without a word, 'I hope you're feeling better now, darling.'

'Yes.' It was a whisper.

'If there's ever anything Daddy or I can do, you know you only have to ask.'

'Yes.' It was a gift, a shining arrow pointing out the way. 'Why was I sent away when I was a baby?' There. It was out, bald and ugly.

'Oh, but I thought you knew all about that, darling!' Mara gritted her teeth. Her mother was glancing at her, but Mara stared at the road ahead. There was a pause, then her mother said, 'I'm afraid I simply reached a point when I couldn't cope. Post-natal depression is terribly common, darling. Just one of those unfortunate things.' She pulled out sharply to overtake a tractor. 'It's not something we ever really talk about.'

Well, maybe you should have done. Maybe if you talked about these 'unfortunate things' I wouldn't be so fucked up now.

There was another pause. Eight miles. The cathedral would be in sight soon. Her mother was no longer glancing anxiously at her. Mara could see her hands gripping the steering-wheel tightly.

'If you think . . .' her mother began. 'If it would help you, darling, I could try to explain.' Mara glimpsed the terrible guilt through the cracked surface.

'No.' Why are you saying this, coward? 'It's fine. I'm fine. Really. It's nothing. I was just wondering, that's all.'

'Well, all right. If you're sure.'

'Yes.' Her mother began to brighten.

This is what we always do: collude, protect one another.

'It wasn't that we were trying to get rid of you. You know that.'

'Yes.'

'If we'd thought you were miserable with Huw and Susan that would've been different, of course.' They weren't looking at each other. Her mother's hands were still locked to the wheel. 'But you always said you loved it at the farm. You asked to go every summer. You were *wild* to go.' Mara heard the plea, but could not make herself speak. Her mother turned to her. Suddenly, the road ahead –

'Careful! That lorry!'

The car swerved and a horn blared.

'Goodness!' said her mother in relief. 'Where did he come from?' They rounded a corner rather fast. 'Look, there it is.'

The cathedral rose up in the distance and cast its long shadow over Mara's heart. Her body ached with dread. The car could have been a tumbril bearing her so steadily towards the City. Drive slowly, drive slowly. Every ghost and every fear she had ever fled would be lining the streets in silence to watch her ride by. 'Take me home, Mummy!' she wanted to cry. 'I don't want to go through with it!' But she knew if she ran now she would spend the rest of her life running – a coward, a fugitive from the relentless grace of God. With every second the cathedral grew, gliding on the countryside like a ship at sea as the car swept round the outskirts of the City.

CHAPTER 17

They met no one in the college entrance hall or on the stairs. Mara's mouth felt dry as she climbed, preparing her pleased reaction to the brightened-up room. My keys, she thought suddenly. Where are they? When did I last have them? She paused on the final flight of steps.

'I think Andrew's got your keys,' said her mother, seeming to guess what Mara was wondering. 'He said you dropped them, or something.' That was it. Yes. As I ran from the building all those weeks ago. She heard them falling again in her memory, clashing on the stone steps. He must have told her the whole story. Mara began to climb again, trying to block out the picture of herself as Andrew must have seen her last: screeching and clawing like a soul sliding into hell. Her knees were trembling as she reached his door. There was a note pinned on it. *Piss off*, it said in Andrew's immaculate script. His idea of a 'Do not disturb' sign. She knocked. The door opened and there he was, the same as ever.

'Can't you read?'

'Just give me the keys, you prick.'

'Darling!' protested her mother.

'I see you're feeling better,' said Andrew.

They watched one another for a moment, then he smiled and drew her into his arms. I've really missed him, she thought in amazement. 'Cashmere?' He stroked the arm of her pullover. Her mother had bought it as a cheering-up present. 'Unusual colour. It suits you.' The colour of dark red peonies. 'You still look like a suffragette on hunger strike, though.'

'Andrew!' Her mother was clearly going to spend the rest of the afternoon scandalized.

Andrew went to fetch the keys.

'May I watch?' he asked, handing them over. Mara's mother looked slightly flustered.

'Andrew helped me choose things for your room. I hope you don't mind, darling.'

Now this will be interesting, thought Mara as she unlocked her door. She stepped in.

'Oh!'

The room was transformed. Not a William Morris touch in sight; just plain, strong colours – dark green, wine-red, blue. The white walls which before had seemed so stark, now looked cool and clear. Mara's eye travelled swiftly round. Plants, flowers, a rug with colours like jewels, and on the window-sill a red glass bowl lit up by the afternoon sun. The whole room sang with light and colour. She turned and saw Andrew link his arm through her mother's. The two of them stood watching her.

'She likes it,' said Andrew.

'Oh, do you really, darling?' Her mother was less sure.

'I love it.'

Mara's eyes swept round once more, then she glanced back at Andrew. He raised an eyebrow. There's some trick. Some clever joke of his that I've missed. She looked round again, this time more carefully. There was an old bent-wood hatstand with all her hats hanging on it. She smiled. This was her mother's touch. She went across and hung up the cloak she was holding.

'What's this?' She pointed to one of the plants.

'It's a pineapple plant,' said her mother. 'Isn't it pretty?' Mara reached out a finger to touch a beautiful serrated spike. 'Careful – it's extremely sharp.' A metaphor in a pot? Mara shot Andrew another glance. His eyes glinted maliciously. Very clever. But there was something else. She could see he was still waiting. The room reminded her obscurely of the Pre-Raphaelite Brotherhood, painting away, working their gem-like colours into a wet white canvas. She stood wondering, but after a moment noticed her mother glancing at the wall behind her. Mara turned and saw the mirror. She laughed out loud.

'I like it!'

'Well . . . Good.'

Her mother's face looked doubtful, and Mara could see she was wondering how anyone could genuinely like such a florid Victorian monstrosity, with its gilt cherubs, swags and scrolls. Mara walked across to it and touched the glass with a fingertip. She watched her mother and Andrew in the mirror as they turned to one another with a smile. I told you so, said Andrew's look, and her mother shrugged in happy defeat. Mara pictured them in some junk shop, Andrew insisting that the mirror be bought and her mother in agonies, torn between good taste and good manners. As she watched them, she began to sense a quotation hovering. She could hear its insistent rhythm: *te-tum te-tum te-tum*. What was it?

'Why don't I put the kettle on?' asked her mother. 'I've brought you various goodies.'

'Thank you.'

Her mother began to busy herself. Mara watched her reflection. She was still so beautiful. No grey in the smooth black hair. She looked up at Mara's face in the mirror and they smiled at each other.

'I'll just go and get the milk from the fridge.' Her mother left the room and Mara rested her elbows on the mantelpiece and frowned into the mirror. Aha – te-tum te-tum te-tum te-tee. *The Lady of Shalott* . . . Of course. She looked at Andrew's reflection. Was that his nickname for her? Weaving away at her web in her solitary room, watching the world in a mirror. Andrew came and stood behind her, leaning his chin on her shoulder. She scowled at him.

'What, Princess?' His arms were resting on hers as they studied one another in the mirror.

'Shouldn't it be cracked from side to side?'

'Clever woman,' he said with a smile. 'You know your Tennyson.'

'You're such a bastard.' She could hear her mother's footsteps coming back along the corridor.

He bent his head and kissed the side of her neck softly. 'I missed you.' He moved away as her mother came back into the room, but Mara continued to stand with her arms on the mantelpiece, watching the two of them with the teapot and cups. She could still feel the place where his lips had touched her.

Mara's mother began telling Andrew about some china she had discovered in Grandma's hoard. On the chest of drawers stood a large expensive-looking plant in a terracotta pot. There was an envelope leaning against it which Mara had not noticed before. She opened it and drew out a card. 'Welcome back,' she read, 'hope you're feeling better. From the JCR.' She stared in disbelief. She hardly deserved one small cactus even. However much money had they spent? She couldn't believe they'd done this. Unless Andrew had gone round asking for donations. That might well have sent a spasm of terrified generosity through the college. Like giving the Mafia a flag day. But for all her sarcasm she could feel tears pricking her eyes.

★

Her mother had gone. Mara stood alone on the college steps, feeling like an abandoned child. She had wanted to plead with her mother to stay, and she knew she longed to be pleaded with, and yet neither of them said anything. At last Mara turned and went back through the door up to her room.

Andrew was sitting on her desk, swinging a foot idly. There was silence, then the familiar sound of the cathedral bells chiming four o'clock. Mara sighed and wandered restlessly to the window and looked down to the river far below. *Flowing down to Camelot.* She dashed the quotation from her mind in exasperation. You horrible man, she thought, looking at Andrew. He smiled at her. He's even done the washing-up, she thought, seeing the cups and saucers stacked neatly on the desk. Maybe everything would be all right. She felt herself begin to relax when the memory of Joanna burst into her mind. A cold hand seemed to grab her throat.

'Calm down.' Andrew was there taking her hands. 'Breathe slowly. Come on: slowly, or you'll pass out again.'

'Did Joanna come back?'

'No. And she won't, either.'

'You don't know that!'

'Oh, I do.' He was smiling again. 'I went and found her in her college and we had a little chat. She's agreed not to pester you again.' But God told her to.

'What did you do to her?'

'Oh, nothing much. Bared my fangs a little.'

'But what if she gets a place here?'

'I've talked to the Principal. He won't offer her a place.' Thank God! 'Look, if the worst comes to the worst, you can take out an injunction against her, Mara. I think you'll find I've saved you the trouble, however.'

'But you're competing with God! She won't do what you say.'

'Trust me.'

'You're not omnipotent, Andrew.'

'You try crossing me sometime, Princess. You've no idea how unpleasant I can be when the whim takes me.' She felt her jaw tighten. 'I am going to make you sort your life out, Princess.'

'I can sort my own life out.'

'Manifestly untrue. Come here.' He patted the desk and she went and sat beside him putting on her blank, offensive stare. He smirked. 'You're going to hate me.'

'No I'm not.'

'Yes you are. I've decided to be your self-appointed moral tutor cum therapist.' She felt a blaze of anger, but the smile on his lips told her that this was what he intended. She stamped the rage out. 'You need me, little one. You spend your whole life blocking out and losing the things you don't want to face.' Her stare was back in place.

'Fine.'

'OK.' He looked a little cheated. Good.

'So what will you do now?' he said.

'Oh, I don't know.' She stared at the piles of notes and papers. 'Sort my desk out, I suppose.' An expression flickered across his face. He's been going through my things! Of course he had. He'd had her keys, hadn't he? For a moment she almost lost her grip. He was smirking at her again as she struggled. 'Find anything interesting, did you?' she managed at last.

'Oh, yes. I didn't know you could draw, by the way.' Her face burned. He'd found the black book. Her only consolation was that she didn't keep a journal. 'I particularly liked the angel picture.' Her hand flew to her mouth. He opened her desk drawer and pulled it out. As she looked at it, she saw that it might as well have been a journal: her father in his study with a 'Do not disturb' sign; Rupert in his pulpit saying, *The trouble with you, Mara*; Johnny the Pied Piper followed by rat women. It revealed more than she dared to think. Andrew looked up from the picture.

'But where am I?'

'Nowhere. You don't feature in my world.'

He laughed. 'I said you'd hate me.'

She seized a pencil and began to draw him, camp and decorative as an Aubrey Beardsley, lounging on a cloud with a whisky glass. Up among the women.

'I hope I'm not an honorary woman.'

She added a pair of wings. 'An honorary angel.' She looked up, and saw that for once he did not know how to respond. All she needed now was an apposite quotation. Shakespeare? No, something he won't be able to locate. *Whatsoever thy hand findeth to do, do it with thy might*, she wrote, *for there is no work, nor device, nor knowledge, nor wisdom in the grave, whither thou goest.* Wasn't that his philosophy? She straightened up and looked him in the face.

'Ecclesiastes,' he said.

'Clever man. You know your Bible.'

He gave her a contemptuous look. 'Don't you know a fallen choirboy when you see one?'

She folded up the picture and put it back in the drawer. 'I'm going out.'

'Where?'

'To find Rupert.' She saw him register this with surprise. 'Was that on your little list of things to nag me about?' He looked at her with distaste. A thought struck her. 'Do you happen to know whether . . . whether he and Johnny . . . well . . . argued? About me, I mean?'

'The clash of the Titans,' he answered. 'Want to hear about it?'

'No.' Curious though she was, she couldn't bear to listen to his malicious paraphrase.

'Rupert blames himself for your misfortune, you realize.' '*I blame myself for this,*' *the anguished Rupert cried.*

'Why?'

'God knows. You were clearly a basket case long before he met you.' With these words he left the room.

She listened to him moving about next door. A moment or so later she heard his door open and close, then the sound of his footsteps going off along the corridor and down the stairs. Thank God. She sat at her desk. I won't go and see Rupert quite yet, she thought. I need a minute to compose myself. She was still raw from Andrew's treatment of her. If she went now she knew she would only burst into tears. Why had he taken it upon himself to sort her life out? I suppose he thinks it's for my good. She felt another surge of rage, knowing she was powerless to stop him. She put her head in her hands, foreseeing months of him relentlessly laying bare her weaknesses. Perhaps if she could guess what he was intending to tackle her about, if she made a list of the things which she was avoiding . . . She had an appealing vision of herself answering Andrew's inquisition in a cool negligent tone. 'Oh, that. I've thought about that, done that.' The urge to piss someone else off was not the most noble reason in the world for soul-searching, but it would have to do.

The bells chimed reassuringly. At least she had dared to come back. After a while she began to hear a voice murmuring in her memory. His voice. The leader of the Church of the Revelation. What was his name? She had refused to say or even think it for so many years that now she could no longer remember. His face was erased, too. But she could still hear the cadences of his voice, and at last, as she waited, she heard the words:

'There's a lot of talk about the role of women in our society today. And there's a lot of talk about the role of women in the old denominations. But God has called us out of the old ways, brothers and sisters. He's doing a new thing. He's laying bare his mighty arm afresh in our generation, sending forth his mighty Word, sharper than any two-edged sword, piercing even unto the dividing asunder of soul and spirit, and of the joints and marrow. And this is why I say there's a lot of talk about the role of women in the old denominations and in our society. A lot of talk, but not much obedience. Not much obedience to the sovereign will of God. Because the Word of God makes God's will about men and women very plain to us, brothers and sisters. "Wives, submit yourselves unto your own husbands, as unto the Lord. For the husband is the head of the wife, even as Christ is head of the Church." This is what the Bible says. There are some who would say that this is out of date. Well, it is – and I praise God for that. It's nearly two thousand years out of date, but it's still the Word and will of God, who is the same yesterday, and today and for ever. Hallelujah!'

In her memory Mara heard all the congregation calling out, 'Hallelujah! Thank you Jesus!' She could see Hester's rapt expression, her eyes shining as she listened. What's wrong with me? she thought. Am I the only one here who wants to shout *no*? A band of tension gripped her forehead, pressing tighter, tighter, as if her head were in a vice. Why couldn't she believe like Hester did? Behind her she could hear a woman start to sob. 'Pray for our sister, there,' said the leader. 'Those around lay hands on her and pray for her. The Lord's touching her heart now and doing a lovely work of healing.' Mara could not bring herself to turn. She could hear people all around murmuring, praying in tongues. What if they were praying for her? Maybe they could all see her sinful rebellion. Maybe she needed their prayers. Why is my heart so hard? The leader began again. His voice was gentle now.

'I know this is a hard teaching for some of you.' Mara flinched. He seemed to be looking at her. 'The Lord's saying that there's one young woman here tonight who has been listening to the whispering voice of the tempter as he speaks through the mouth of the media, through the mouth of feminist literature. The Devil's been telling you that the Bible is wrong, that it puts women down. But I want to say to you that this is a lie!' Mara jumped as he shouted the word. How could he know what she was thinking? The voice grew soft again, as though she were the only other person in the room. 'But the Lord knows your heart, my sister. He knows how your earnest desire is to serve him, and he'll honour that. God longs to raise women up, not put them down. Submission isn't slavery – it's a joy, a privilege.'

Mara brought her fists down suddenly on the desk, making the cups and saucers rattle. How did I stand it? The intolerable pressure of trying to believe a lie – feeling the plates of your mind grating against one another, glimpsing the molten wrath through the cracks, building up, building up, until one day, boom! Your landscape is obliterated. Shock waves travel halfway round the earth. 'Cognitive dissonance' was what the experts called it. Krakatoa in your skull.

If I hadn't believed it all so fiercely in the first place it would never have come to this. But how could you be lukewarm? Either it was true and the Kingdom of God was breaking in, or it was nothing but lies, filth and manipulation. There was no neutral ground with miracles, no way of saying 'how fascinating' over your sherry glass if someone had been healed. And people had been healed. She had seen, and sceptic though she was, there had been no denying it. And to this day, she could make no sense of it. If it meant anything at all, it must mean everything: the end of the age, the Coming of Christ. She sighed. And the wreck of a faith like this was great indeed.

A polite inherited Anglicanism would never go down like that. It would simply be de-commissioned and left to rust in a quiet dock. She put her head in her hands again.

She set off at last for Rupert's room. She was passing the dining-room when Nigel emerged from the doorway of the servery as though he had been lying in wait.

'Well, well. Look who's back,' he said with a friendly leer. The corridor was too narrow for Mara to back off and she felt herself being clutched round the waist. 'And how are you, my beautiful?'

'All right.' The words just managed to escape between her tight lips. His face was eighteen inches too close.

'Have a nice time with the monks, did you?'

His innuendo stuck to her like flypaper, giving her an uncharacteristic urge to reply in kind: 'Chance would be a fine thing!' Instead she answered, 'Yes, thank you.'

His hand strayed from her waist to the small of her back and lingered there. 'Smack him round the head,' commanded the fishwife, as Nigel ran his eyes over her.

'Still a bit thin, aren't you?'

'I'm all right.'

'I'll say you're all right.' He waggled his eyebrows salaciously. Mara stepped away in disgust. 'Hang on – I haven't finished with you yet.' He clutched her again. 'Now, just you make sure you come in for every meal like a good girl. I want to see a clean plate, or I won't let you out of the dining-room. I'm serious.' He wagged a finger.

'Yes. Fine.'

'Good girl. You could do with a bit more flesh on you.'

She tried to slip away, but he was too quick, giving her buttock a valedictory squeeze. The fishwife was on him in a trice: 'You do that once more, and you can kiss your nuts goodbye,' she snarled. Mara saw a flicker of nervousness in Nigel's grin. Hah.

'Ooh. She's turning nasty.' He turned and disappeared along the corridor towards his salmonella emporium.

Mara made her way towards Coverdale Hall. The fishwife cracked her mighty knuckles with satisfaction. But what if Nigel was just trying to be kind, and was hampered by only having one method of relating to women? Perhaps he had been taught it at catering school. Today's lecture: Bum-Squeezing in the Walk-in Fridge.

She climbed the main stairs of Coverdale Hall and knocked on Rupert's door. He called her in.

'Mara!'

He crossed the room in two quick strides and took her in his arms. She moved slightly, but he held her all the tighter. It occurred to her with a sudden cold shock that he might be in tears. His face was buried in her neck, and she raised a tentative hand to his hair.

'Rupert?'

At last he released her. There were tears in his eye-lashes. But he's never like this, she thought in dismay. She watched as he struggled to regain control, running his hand through his hair and attempting to speak.

'You're back.' His voice sounded hoarse.

'Well . . . yes.' Don't let me laugh. She bit her lip.

Too late: he had seen. A much more characteristic expression crossed his face. 'Yes. Obviously.' He was almost himself again. 'And as disrespectful as ever.'

'Sorry.'

There was a silence. Rupert glanced at his watch. Had he been about to go out?

'Coffee?' he asked a little wildly. She shook her head. He picked up a file and put it down again, then straightened the biros on the desk. 'I've got a five o'clock lecture, I'm afraid.'

'I won't stay, then.'

'No. Yes, I mean. Please stay. I'm not going yet.'

'OK.'

'Good. Thanks.'

There was another silence, then they both began to speak simultaneously. They stopped, and laughed slightly.

'Go on.'

'No, you,' he said.

'I was only going to say I feel much better.' Outside the cathedral bells began to chime for evensong. Quarter to five. He wouldn't have to leave for another ten minutes. She began blurting again: 'Look, sorry I was so awful.'

'Awful? You weren't awful. I was the one who was awful.' They could certainly fill ten minutes out-apologizing one another.

'No, you weren't. You were trying to help.'

'*Trying*, yes.'

But here they floundered. The bells chimed on and on.

'Hadn't you better go?' she asked, unable to stand it.

He glanced at his watch again. 'Not for five minutes.'

She saw him run his hand through his hair again, and realized a very serious apology was imminent.

'Mara, you're being very generous.' She looked away in embarrassment. 'You're not saying anything, but I know you've put up with a lot from me. Acting as though I was God. Trying to sort your life out for you.' Suddenly she knew she was hearing Johnny's words. This was what they had argued about. 'I know I made everything worse for you at a time when –'

'It's OK, Rupert,' she broke in. 'Let's just forget about it.'

'I can't just forget about it, Mara.' '*I shall never forgive myself as long as I live*,' cried Rupert. 'I was so convinced I was right, that –'

'Rupert –'

'– that I knew what was the best for you –'

213

'Rupert!' She stamped her foot and he stopped in astonishment. 'Will you do something for me?'

'Of course.' The slight bow.

'Will you just *shut up*?'

'But . . .' He summed up the look on her face. 'Of course.' He shut his lips and stood as though the rest of the apology were buzzing around inside his mouth like a trapped fly. She could not help smiling at him.

'Mara,' he said, putting his hand dramatically on his heart, 'for a smile like that I'd walk barefoot from here to John O'Groat's.'

She blushed, and in her surprise answered randomly: 'How far is John O'Groat's from here?' as though assessing the scope of the gesture. Query: how many miles more significant would the statement have been had he uttered it in South Kensington? He gave her a withering look and began to collect up his pen and paper. As she watched, she thought she could see faint lines on the back of his hand. Like scratch marks. She started guiltily.

'What's wrong?'

She pointed. 'I did that, didn't I?'

He followed her gaze. 'This? It's nothing. Don't worry.'

How can he say I wasn't awful? He stood there smiling at her, and she could feel tears of mortification in her eyes.

'Mara, I thought we were forgetting about it.'

She nodded. He drew close and laid a finger on her cheek. She felt her breath shorten as he bent his head. At that moment the door burst open unceremoniously. Rupert sprang back.

'You might knock, Whitaker!' he said.

Mara whirled round, her face scarlet. Johnny stood there laughing.

'She's back! Ha'away, give us a hug, then.' She went and was crushed briefly in his arms. 'You all right, flower?' He let her go swiftly. 'Are we skipping the lecture?'

'No, we are not.' *Rupert was nettled by the sudden interruption.* 'Come along, Mara.' He held the door open for her.

The three of them walked along the corridor towards the stairs. Mara could feel herself becoming more embarrassed with each step. She scraped around desperately for something to say. 'How did your sermon go?' It sounded absurdly bland and vicar's daughter-ish.

'Don't ask,' said Johnny shortly.

'It was excellent,' insisted Rupert. His tone seemed to defy a host of absent detractors. Whatever had happened? She glanced from one to the other as they reached the foot of the stairs.

Rupert changed the subject with the ease which came from generations of good breeding. 'Shall we see you in the bar tonight, Mara?'

'Possibly.'

'Possibly?' Rupert smiled at her.

They reached Coverdale lecture hall. Johnny went in without a word. Mara stared at his taut profile in dismay as he passed her. What did I do? She turned to Rupert, but he shook his head faintly, as if indicating he would explain later.

'Tonight, then? About nine?' he said.

'OK.' With a smile he followed Johnny into the lecture hall. Mara stood for a moment in the corridor bewildered. What could possibly have happened?

The sky was a mass of cloud, apart from a strip of watery light low across the horizon where the sun was sinking. Mara sat at her window watching. There was music in her mind: a tune for Johnny (a familiar ostinato of lust) and now a tune for Rupert (a sudden passionate trumpet cadenza). She laughed. I'm feeling breathless. What had come over him? Tears in his eyes, hand on his heart. He had never been like it before. Her conviction wavered slightly at the memory of the drunken clinch at the college ball. And the Valentine roses. Was he . . .? Could he be . . .? She leant her chin on her hand and gazed at the fading band of gold above the rooftops. And if he is, what do I think about that?

She sat in the gathering darkness wondering. The evening star appeared between the clouds, then vanished, like a lighthouse on a distant coast. Her mind found its way wearily back to Hester. She closed her eyes and wept. At length she grew silent. She knew that the tide of grief had passed its highest point, but its ebb would be bitter, and long, long. Far above her the star winked its message across the lonely strand of the sky.

CHAPTER 18

Mara woke in panic fighting for breath. She was back at her parents' house for the vacation. The vicarage was quiet. She felt as though a great weight was pressing on her chest. She sat up and turned on her bedside light. Keep calm. Breathe. In. Out. Oh, why hadn't she gone to the doctor with this cold? She couldn't get enough air. In. Out. It was three in the morning. Wasn't steam supposed to help? She got out of bed, pulled on her dressing-gown and went downstairs.

She stood in the kitchen waiting for the kettle to boil. Just don't panic. In. Out. In. Out. She had been coughing badly for over a week. The clock ticked. The kettle began to murmur on the Aga. Good Friday. Or Saturday by now, she supposed. The darkest night of the year. She went to the pantry and found a lemon and sliced it up. Lemon, honey and whisky. Grandma had always sworn by it. Mara moved quietly, knowing if her mother came down and heard her terrible laboured breathing she would call the doctor out. The kettle boiled.

She sat at the kitchen table breathing in the steam from the mug. Her chest eased a fraction. The whisky bottle stood on the table in front of her, a Christmas gift from a parishioner. Each breath became easier and she began to relax. Her mind drifted until she was back in the college bar with Andrew. He was quizzing her about her relationship with her father. Johnny was in the bar too, but sitting with the group of students Mara had overheard discussing curacies back in October. She had since learnt that this was Johnny's 'Coverdale Group'. All the ordinands belonged to one, and they were supposed to set their own agenda and meeting place. Mara suspected it was largely Johnny's influence which led to this particular group meeting in the bar, where the social and the theological seemed to melt fuzzily into one another.

'So basically,' said Andrew, 'everything you do is an unacknowledged attempt to win your father's approval, isn't it?' She opened her mouth to deny this, but he raised a hand. 'Just a minute.' He was listening to the conversation on the other side of the bar. After a moment Mara realized they were discussing homosexuality and the

Church. She found herself listening in mounting dismay. Nothing was said that she hadn't heard a dozen times before – hating the sin but loving the sinner – but she was hearing it with new ears now Andrew was beside her. Oh, God. They don't realize he can hear them. In desperation she began to talk about her father, but Andrew hushed her again. She sat in agonized silence.

'Let's go and join them,' he said. There was a look in his eye which made her hang back.

'Don't . . .'

'Don't what? Make a scene? God, you're so suburban.' He picked up his drink and crossed to the other side of the bar. Mara dithered, not knowing whether to join them or run for her life.

Johnny looked round and saw Andrew. 'Sit down. We've just been talking about your sort.' There was a rigid silence as the rest of the group took this in.

'I heard.'

Andrew sat beside Johnny. Mara perched on the edge of a stool, wishing she'd escaped earlier. The other members of the group were shifting as nervously as she was.

'So what did you decide?' asked Andrew. He scanned round. They avoided his gaze. Johnny was grinning broadly. 'Well, come along boys. What will you say when someone like me shows up at your altar rails?' Silence. One of the group rose and left, murmuring some kind of excuse. 'Think. What did our Lord have to say about homosexuality?' persisted Andrew, assuming the manner of a tutor addressing thick undergraduates. Mara could see that they were riled, but that nobody was prepared to take him on. His nastiness on the debating floor was legendary.

'Nothing,' admitted the man who didn't want to go to Sunderland.

'Exactly. Bugger all,' said Andrew. 'Doesn't it worry you that you're building a complex ethical structure to deal with something that Christ never mentioned once?'

'Yes, but Paul mentions it,' said the bossy one who reminded Mara of Rupert. What was his name? Hugh. 'You're driving a wedge between Paul and Christ. You can't do that. You can't pick and choose texts as it suits you.'

'All right. What does Christ have to say about divorce, then? Several rather specific things, I seem to remember. Like remarriage counting as adultery. And how does that square with Church practice?

I think we're in danger of picking and choosing our texts a little here, too, aren't we?'

'Look, you're being incredibly patronizing,' protested Hugh. 'We all know you can run rings round us academically, but give us some credit. We're trying to do justice to what the Bible says, at the same time as working out a sympathetic pastoral response to –'

'To the *problem of homosexuality*? What *problem*? You mean you have a problem with it?'

'Yes. There *is* a problem with it if you take the Bible seriously.' Help me someone, said Hugh's expression.

'You're on your own here, Hugh,' said Johnny.

'Well, I shouldn't be!' snapped Hugh. 'I'd like to hear you say one sensible thing on this subject. Just one. On *any* subject, for that matter. See if you can.' Mara stared at him, astonished. This sounded like about three years of pent-up aggression.

'Why not?' agreed Andrew. 'Why don't you guide us through this thorny issue, Whitaker?'

'Well, Andrew,' said Johnny formally. 'I think we decided that God doesn't blame you for being homosexual. We couldn't agree on whether it's nature or nurture, I'm afraid; but whatever the cause, God still loves you. God really loves you, but you must never, *never* have sex.' Mara saw Hugh colour angrily at this parody.

Andrew laughed. 'It's all right for you, you bastard,' he said. 'Your preferences are catered for.'

'No they're not,' said Johnny. 'My preference is for screwing all the women in the world. We all have to exercise some restraint.'

'Yes, but you can walk down the aisle with the woman you love, and the church will bless your union. What does the church offer me?'

'Well, Hugh here thinks we can all pray that God will heal you of your perversion,' said Johnny, brutally paraphrasing the earlier discussion. Hugh coloured even more deeply. Mara found herself thinking that even if Hugh had dug himself this hole, there was no need for Johnny to push him into it so callously. 'Would you like to be prayed for, brother?'

'Mmm. Just man to man in private, you mean?' asked Andrew.

'Want me to lay hands on you, too?' asked Johnny.

'You're profane, Whitaker!' Hugh stood up suddenly. 'I don't have to stay and listen to this.'

'Fine.' Johnny shrugged and lit a cigarette.

'No it's not *fine*. I find you totally offensive. Your language, your sense of humour, your attitude –'

'Yeah, yeah. And your attitude to Andrew isn't offensive?'

'I'm not listening to this,' repeated Hugh and walked out.

Mara sighed and stirred the pieces of lemon. Although Johnny had been defending Andrew, this incident had left her thinking less well of him. She couldn't put her finger on it, but there was something nasty underlying his flippant manner. And it had not been just that one occasion, either. She had watched and noticed that he was drinking and smoking more heavily. His language had worsened too. It was as though he had suddenly tired of being the good-natured college buffoon, but that the college was not ready to offer him any other role. Hugh's reaction was typical of the mounting hostility to the new Johnny. Once she rounded a corner in Coverdale and caught the tail-end of a conversation: Johnny saying to Rupert, 'I don't know if I can take much more of this.' She had drawn back, knowing she was not meant to hear. 'He's struggling with his sense of vocation,' was how Rupert explained it.

The story of the Jeremiah sermon did not remain a mystery for long. Mara heard reports of it from all sides, and began to regret she had not been there herself. Whenever she thought about the sermon, she could only see and hear it through Maddy, whose account had been the most vivid and amusing:

'And you won't believe it, but *Nigel* was there,' Maddy had told her. 'In fact, most of the domestic staff were there. And practically all the college. Maybe someone should do some research into the role of sex appeal in church growth. 'But the best joke of all was that Johnny's *brother* was there. He has a *brother*, can you believe it? There is a God. One man like that could be accident, but two . . .'

'. . . looks like carelessness,' said May.

'Anyway, he arrived just before the service started with four of Johnny's old workmates. Without telling him. Did you know he used to be a builder? You could have knocked me over with a piece of scaffolding. In they all trooped – hard hats, tattoos, dirty overalls – all cramming themselves into the last empty row, so when Johnny came in from the vestry there they were, broad shoulders bursting out of the tiny pew, grinning and winking at him.'

Mara pictured the scene, Johnny frozen in the middle of the aisle, staring at the sniggering builders, his new life confronting his old. What would have passed through his mind?

'You could see the chaplain shifting nervously in his stall wondering if he was going to have to throw them out, and them never quite behaving badly enough to justify it, just dropping hymn books and snorting in the prayers, that kind of thing.' Maddy became the twitching chaplain and the builders by turn. 'When Johnny stood up to preach they applauded, then it went deathly quiet. He started to read a sermon on Jeremiah. The chaplain stopped sweating, and I thought, that's it, the fun's over. But after about a minute Johnny stopped, and said "Does anyone want to hear this?" Of course, they said no to a man. The chaplain tottered to his feet and hovered, wringing his hands, but before he could say anything, Johnny tore up his sermon and said, "I'll tell you a story, then."'

What had followed, as far as Mara could piece together from the various accounts, was a lively (if scurrilous) re-enactment of the parable of the Prodigal Son. The congregation, according to Maddy, had not laughed so much since Grandma's proverbial tussle with the mangle. So what was the big problem, then? But here Maddy and May could shed no light. Something had happened in Coverdale Hall afterwards, they thought.

Rupert had been her source for the rest of the story. She had met him in the bar, as she had arranged, on her first night back at college. She had arrived first and sat with her glass locked into her hand with embarrassment. Thank goodness they had such promising subject matter to discuss. He appeared, and she had tried not to watch his lips as he spoke, or to think how very, very nearly they had kissed her only hours before. He seemed to have forgotten, and she gradually composed herself.

'The real trouble started in the sermon class after chapel,' Rupert was saying. 'That's when we always meet to discuss the sermon.'

'Who's "we"?'

'The staff and students. And it would have been all right if he'd managed to keep his temper.'

'Why, what were people saying?'

'Well, that we were supposed to be in the middle of a sermon series on Jeremiah; that it wasn't a sermon, as such, more of a stand-up comedy routine; and that some of his conclusions were theologically dodgy.' She glanced at Rupert, and saw him struggling not to smile. 'And finally, that nowhere in the Bible does the Prodigal say,

"Bugger this – I'm off home."'' Mara bit her lips. If only I'd been there.

'But you thought it was excellent?'

'Yes. Most of us did. It's just one section of the college who find him a bit hard to take. I tried to make him see that, but it was too late.' He closed his eyes for one despairing moment at the memory. 'Well, the staff encourage frankness, I suppose. Nominally.' He paused and drank. She stole a glance at him, and he caught her eye and smiled again. 'The only good thing was the look on everyone's face. I thought about you. You'd have enjoyed it.' Mara blushed in surprise that she had been in his mind at a moment like that. How much of his time did he spend thinking, Mara would like this, or, She would find that funny?

'What did he say?'

'His main point – this is a summary – was that given the number of people in the chapel that night who never normally go near a church, a nice polite middle-class exposition of Jeremiah wasn't appropriate.'

'Well, he's probably right.'

'Of course he's right. But nine-tenths of the room were too offended by his language to hear his argument. Idiot. He completely sabotaged his own cause by losing his temper and walking out.' Slamming the door, thought Mara. Was this how her father had been at theological college, boiling over in sermon class – 'That sermon cost me blood!' – and storming out?

'How will he survive in a polite middle-class profession?' she wondered out loud, remembering her father's words at Christmas.

'He wants to be an industrial chaplain.' Did he? Yes, that made sense.

'But he'll have to do a curacy.'

'Yes. If he can survive three years of parish ministry, he'll be all right.'

'Will he?'

'Survive? God alone knows. Not unless he learns to control his temper. He's got a good bishop, though.'

At this point they caught sight of Johnny coming towards them through the bar. Rupert turned the subject smoothly and began talking about the parish he would be serving in himself. Johnny bought a drink and sat down. He listened to Rupert, but his eyes were fixed on Mara. She felt herself blushing.

'Talking about me, were you?' said Johnny. Rupert made a movement of protest. 'Have you heard enough, or do you want my version as well, Princess?' Mara opened her mouth uncertainly. She could smell anger in the air like an approaching thunderstorm. But suddenly he grinned. 'I tell you, it was like being a lion in a den of Daniels.' They laughed and then Johnny himself changed the subject. It was never broached again.

Why was he behaving like this, though? Surely there were more mature ways of sorting out your vocation? She grinned suddenly. Says you, Mara. Her own behaviour over the past months had hardly been a pattern of maturity. There had been times when he had seemed like his old self, though. Down in the bar again on the last evening of term.

'I could never marry a man with a weak chin,' Maddy was saying. 'I couldn't even have an affair with one.'

'And I couldn't marry a man with a glottal stop,' May replied.

'That rules you out, Whitaker, I fear,' said Andrew, condescending for once to join the trivial banter. Johnny was wearing a look of guarded ignorance.

'I *certainly* couldn't marry a man who didn't know what a glottal stop was,' said Maddy, taken in, as ever, by Johnny's expression.

'Or an idiom,' he said with a smile. Maddy stared at him suspiciously.

'What about you, Mara?' said Rupert, turning to her unexpectedly. She felt herself blushing slightly. 'What kind of man couldn't you marry?'

'A clergyman.'

As she sat in the quiet kitchen at home she felt again the nasty jar which this reply had given to the conversation. She had spoilt the flippant mood by answering seriously. It had been Andrew who had broken the silence.

'A clergyman? Thy exquisite reason?'

'Because I'd want my husband to be married to me, not to God and twelve thousand bloody parishioners.'

There was another jagged pause, then Johnny whistled. 'That one came from the heart.' He laughed and the tension broke.

'I could marry a clergyman if he was well endowed,' said Maddy. 'In every sense of the word, of course.'

Rupert was angry. 'I totally disagree.' Mara saw his heightened colour. 'You can't say that. We have emerged from the dark ages,

Mara, even in the church. Any clergyman worth his salt would put his wife and family before his ministry these days.' Mara said nothing, and her silence seemed to provoke him further. 'If I married, then my first calling would be to be a husband, not a priest.'

Rupert had followed her back to her room later. 'I'm sorry I was so short with you back there,' he said.

'That's OK.' He kissed her cheek.

'I hate being at odds with you, sweetie.' Stop bossing me around then, she thought. 'Look, let me take you out for a drink in the vacation sometime.'

'Thanks.'

'I'll be at my parents'. Why don't you come over?'

'OK.'

That was how it had begun. But the casual suggestion of a visit to the pub had somehow grown into a full-blown invitation to stay at the palace. He'd almost tricked her into accepting.

She winced. No getting out of it now. What shall I wear? she wondered. What shall I take? What shall I say? And above all, *why* has he asked me? Did he take women home all the time, or were the Right Reverend and Mrs Gordon Anderson bracing themselves for a possible daughter-in-law?

It had all become so complicated. She stared down into her mug, watching the pieces of lemon rotating gently. She had always seen Rupert as someone who had got everything sewn up. He would marry some charming girl from the right background (Cordelia Chauffeured-Bentley?) and have a quiverful of children all with good strong biblical names (Hannah, Rebekkah, Barnabas, Joshua). And one day he would probably be a bishop like his father. Which meant that she must be imagining his attraction to her. Rupert would never *dream* of presenting his mama with a girl who had a tattoo and used the F-word. Unless he was hoping he could mould her into a good clergy wife. Good Lord, deliver us! On the other hand, it might be her ineligibility that attracted him. She might be an outward expression of all the rebellion and violence that he repressed in himself. Perhaps this explained his unlikely friendship with Johnny.

Johnny. Johnny. The kitchen was warm, and Mara began to grow drowsy from the whisky. I'm letting my guard slip, thinking about him. But she lay back in the feeling, sunbathing in it as though she were on a hillside under an August sky. She knew the ground beneath her was as dry as tinder. One spark of passion and the whole lot would go up. And here I am playing with matches, she thought, letting her mind stray over the contours of his face as he lay in her memory under the swaying pine trees at the friary. She could hear the wind, see his dark hair, his eye-lashes, trace the outline of his lips . . .

There was a sudden clatter and she jumped awake. She had knocked the mug over, spilling what was left of her drink. She stood up and found a cloth. I'll make another and take it back to bed with me. She was filling the kettle when she heard footsteps overhead. Damn. I've woken them. The steps came swiftly downstairs and her father appeared at the door, his face white.

'What's happening? Are you all right?' His eyes looked wild. He had clearly woken suddenly and horribly.

'Sorry. I'm getting a drink.' She put the kettle on the ring. 'Did you think I was a burglar?' His eyes fell on the knife she had used to chop the lemon. Its blade was short and wicked.

'I don't know what I thought.' His eyes slid away again.

A bout of coughing seized her. She fought for breath, seeing him standing helpless. He made a move as if to help her.

'I'll be OK,' she gasped.

'You need a doctor.'

'Tomorrow.' The fit passed. 'I'm going to make another drink and go back to bed.'

He nodded. She made herself pick up the knife calmly and slice some more lemon. She could feel his eyes on her. Was he forcing himself not to flinch? She added some honey and whisky to the mug. They stood waiting for the kettle to boil.

Seven years ago. Easter Sunday. They should all have been out of the house for a good hour and a half. And yet he had come back and found her. Why? She could hear his voice, his fists pounding on the bathroom door. 'Mara. Are you all right in there? Open this door. Mara. Mara!' and the sound of the wood splintering as she slid unconscious.

The kettle boiled. She turned to the Aga, but as she did so, another bit of memory clicked into place. She seemed to be watching it in slow motion with a strange ringing sound in her ears. The door crashed open and he was staggering in, his hands reaching out. She could see the naked shock on his face. He was speaking, saying something in Welsh. She watched his mouth shaping the words. The last thing she saw before she blacked out was him bending over her.

He was still in his vestments. White and gold for Easter. For resurrection.

'Shall I do that?' he asked.

She roused herself. 'No. It's OK, thanks.' Her hand was trembling as she poured the water. 'Would you like something, too?' He shook his head. He looked old and weary. She saw for the first time what she had done to him, and she had no words, no way of making amends. 'Sorry if I disturbed you.' She went upstairs, leaving him still standing in his dressing-gown in the empty kitchen.

The morning was mild. Mara was sitting at the kitchen table again, reading the paper. Her mother was round at the church helping with the Easter lilies. Mara pictured her amongst the oasis and chicken-wire. No. I could never marry a clergyman. Her mother was well-liked in the parish, but how could the army of flower arrangers wield their flails of scorn with true vigour if the vicar's wife was there? This was why Mara's mother attended all the countless flower festivals, meetings, bazaars and fêtes. It also robbed people of the opportunity to observe that it was a pity Mrs Johns didn't show her face at parish events. I couldn't do it, thought Mara. As a child she could remember overhearing people grumbling about her father. 'You-know-who wants to change the time of the Friday Mass,' one would say. 'Does he, indeed. I hope you told him he can't.' Mara's face would burn with rage, but there was nothing she could do. If she was rude, they would use that against her father, too. 'It's a pity he doesn't control his daughters.'

Now she heard his footsteps in the hallway. She buried herself in the crossword, embarrassed by their encounter last night. She thought he would go straight to his study and continue his sermon preparation, but he came into the kitchen.

'I'll run you to the doctor's in a moment.' She looked up. He was taking his cassock off. 'There's a surgery this morning.'

'Actually, I'm feeling much better.' She saw him thinking, Nevertheless.

'I'm heading that way, anyway,' he said.

'Don't worry,' she replied, not looking up from the crossword. 'I'm feeling fine this morning.' There was a pause, then the newspaper was ripped suddenly from her hands.

'Get off your arse and into that car *now*!' he roared. Her mouth dropped open. 'Just do as you're bloody well told for once in your life, girl!' She was too shocked to move. He reached out and jerked her to her feet.

'You're hurting my arm!' she squeaked, but he propelled her to the front door with no more compassion than if she had been a difficult ewe on the farm. The door slammed behind them.

'Get in the car.'

Her own anger caught up belatedly with his. 'Don't you tell me what to do!'

But at this his temper went up another six gears. 'Don't you answer me back like that!' For a moment she thought he was actually going to hit her. 'No daughter of mine is going to behave as you do in my house! You hear me?' A kind of glee rushed up inside her, and she opened her mouth to yell back. He was too fast for her. 'I've had enough of your selfish histrionics. You think no one suffers but yourself. What about your mother?'

'Oh, that's right! Bring her into it!' But her words were flung aside.

'How do you think she feels? How do you think I feel? What do you think it's like to have a daughter who's a cold-hearted, selfish bitch? When did you last give a thought to anyone but yourself?' His words stung like slaps in the face. She was starting to cry. 'Now get in that car.'

'I can't,' she shouted. 'It's locked, you ignorant Welsh peasant!'

There was a sudden dreadful calm. His face changed. Mara whipped round to see what he was looking at. There standing in the drive were three of the flower arrangers, open-mouthed, secateurs in hand. They had come to cut some forsythia from the vicarage garden as they did every year.

'Excuse us, ladies,' said her father, unlocking the door. Mara got into the car and they drove off in an angry shower of gravel, leaving the three women still frozen in a shocked tableau on the drive.

She sat with her arms folded across her chest, rigid with hurt and rage. Neither of them said a word. He was driving too fast. The car pulled up outside the surgery.

'I'll wait out here,' said her father.

'Don't bother!' She slammed the door.

The waiting-room was stuffy and she grew angrier with every dragging minute. Phrases she might have used on him came tumbling into her mind. Counter-accusations, searing insults. She stared at a rack of pamphlets in front of her. *Thrush. Everything you need to know*. She could feel angry tears welling up again. He had never, ever raised his voice at her before. And yet it all seemed so familiar. Even the 'No Daughter of Mine' speech. Suddenly she remembered. Of course – Uncle Huw. She could see him again in the farm kitchen, tendons standing out in his neck as he roared at Dewi or Elizabeth: 'This is my house, and by God, you'll do as I tell you!' So that was it. The legendary Johns temper. And strangely enough, she felt more her father's daughter now than she had ever done before.

'Mara Johns,' called the receptionist. She rose and walked to the doctor's room. It was her own family GP behind the desk. Damn.

'What can I do for you?' He peered at her through his preposterous eyebrows. If only it had been one of the other doctors.

'I've got a cough.'

He asked her one or two brusque questions, then reached for his stethoscope. 'I'll have a quick listen,' he said. She felt the cold metal on her back. 'Breathe in and out slowly.' She did her best, feeling a fit of coughing threatening. 'How long has it been like this?'

She shrugged. 'Not long.' She began to cough. Bad timing.

He listened. 'Hah.' He began to write a prescription. 'I'm putting you on antibiotics. Another time don't leave it this long or you'll end up in hospital.' He fixed his wily eyes on her like a ferret peering out of a hedge. 'We've had a request for your notes from your new practice. What are you playing at? You know your notes are in Cambridge.'

'I must have forgotten.' She did not even bother to make it sound convincing.

'Hah,' he said again. She put out a hand for the prescription, but he ignored her.

'Do you need advice about contraception?'

'What?' She gawped. 'No, I do not.'

'Don't get on your high horse,' he said blandly. 'I always ask my young women patients that. You'd be surprised how many girls sit there trying to pluck up courage to ask me.'

'Well, I wasn't. And I'm quite capable of buying my own, thanks.' She would have given anything to look as cool as she sounded.

'Free from the Family Planning Clinic,' he said.

'Actually, I'm not –' She felt the absurd phrase 'sexually active' about to fall from her lips. 'I don't actually *need* anything.' She was blushing in full glory now.

'Well, don't go leaving it to chance, young lady.' He handed her the prescription. 'Any idea how many pregnancies are actually planned? Less than half. Happy Easter.' She went out with her ears still burning.

Mara left the surgery and crossed the road to the chemist to collect her prescription. As she returned with the tablets, she saw her father coming out of a florist's with a large bouquet of roses. An Easter gift for her mother? She felt slightly awkward at this insight into their relationship. Still making romantic gestures after all these years? Or was it simply habit? She waited till he was safely in the car, then crossed and let herself into the passenger's side. He glanced briefly at the chemist's bag she was holding and started the car.

They drove without speaking, both staring stubbornly ahead. This felt familiar as well. She remembered the long silent feuds at the farm. Most families specialized either in short sharp rows to clear the air, or week-long smouldering silences. Her uncle's family was equally at home with both. It provided a stark contrast to her mother's family, where people were calm, rational and urbane, and there was no bawling and blaming. No wonder I'm so screwed up, she thought, with a dual heritage like mine. She stole a glance at her father's scowling profile, and to her surprise he pulled over abruptly and stopped the car.

She tensed herself for another diatribe, but all he said was, 'I'm going to have to ask you to drive. I can't see properly.' She went cold. Words like 'brain tumour', 'stroke', bubbled up into her mind.

'Why? What's happened?'

'Migraine,' he said, getting out of the car.

They swapped sides.

Mara started the engine.

'I get them, too.'

'You do?'

She felt his surprise. God, how much more do we have in common that we don't know about? She drove the last couple of miles home.

'What do you usually do?' she asked as they pulled up at the vicarage.

'I try to ignore it.'

He's worse than I am. They went into the house and he put the roses on the kitchen table. She stood irresolute. The silence had been broken without the fight being alluded to.

'Can I get you anything?' she asked, feeling a little shy.

'A cup of tea.' He sat down and closed his eyes. She put the kettle on, wondering whether he really wanted tea, or was only trying not to crush her. He had his back to her, and she watched him, and could see the tension visible in every muscle of his neck and shoulders. 'You should go and lie down,' she wanted to say, but surely this would make him snub her. If they were different people, she might have given him a shoulder massage to unknot the tension and soothe it away. But they never touched one another. She could reach out her hand now and lay it on his shoulder. But she pictured him jumping in surprise, or turning round to see what she wanted.

The kettle boiled and she made the tea. When she turned back, he had his head in his hands. She put the mug gently on the table beside him. He looked up, and for a second she thought he was going to take her hand.

'Thanks.' She was standing near enough for him to reach out if he wanted to, but he made no move.

'Can I do anything else?' she asked.

He drew the cup towards him. 'No. Thanks.'

There was a silence. Mara could hear someone practising the organ in the church. Her father stood up and made as if to move. Then he stopped.

'You could talk to your mother,' he said abruptly.

'*Talk*? I do talk to her!'

'She says she's tried, but you just cut her off.'

'But . . .' That's not fair! She's the one who won't talk. Was this how she saw it? He turned to leave. 'I'll try,' she blurted out to his back.

'Thank you.'

She listened to his footsteps going back to his study, feeling like a wounded child. Why does he have to be so hard? Why won't he touch my hand, even? Because he's like you, said a voice in her head, he thinks you'd only snub him.

It was not until the evening that Mara found the opportunity and the courage to do as she had promised. Her mother was rolling out marzipan on the kitchen table for the simnel cake. She looked up and smiled, but Mara thought she could detect a nervous cheerfulness in her manner.

'You know, it bothers me each year. How *do* you divide a lump of marzipan into eleven equal pieces?' She laid the circle of marzipan on the cake and began to press it down. 'I always end up with one apostle bigger than the others.'

'Well, why don't you divide it into twelve and then just eat Judas?' Her mother put on an expression of mock horror. 'Or you could make him into a cross for the middle,' added Mara piously.

'You do it.' Her mother handed her the remaining marzipan and Mara divided it up. There was a silence as they made the eleven apostolic blobs. Mara rolled out Judas and began to make him into an ornate Celtic cross. She sensed that her mother was about to *talk* and resolved not to cut her off again.

'I hear you and daddy had words.'

'Did he tell you that?'

'He mentioned it.' Her mother was fixing a blob into place with a dab of apricot jam. 'But I overheard Mavis Malaprop muttering to the others in the baptistry this morning.' She giggled at the memory. Mavis's words were treasured up to become part of vicarage folklore. 'She said, "There's been a fricassee at the vicarage."' The two of them had to stop work for a moment while they recovered from their laughter. 'What were you arguing about?'

'Oh, nothing, really. I didn't want to go to the doctor's,' said Mara.

'Oh, darling!' said her mother a little crossly. 'You really must get something for that cough.'

'It's all right. I went. He gave me some antibiotics.'

'Good.'

'He also gave me a little lecture on birth control.'

'And did you *want* a little lecture?'

'No. But he seemed to think I was sitting there trying to pluck up courage to ask him.'

'Well, you might have been, I suppose.' Mara had only told her this as an amusing anecdote, and was frustrated that her mother was taking it seriously.

'Well, as I've no intention of sleeping with anyone at the moment . . .'

'Intentions,' said her mother, 'are a notoriously unreliable form of contraception.'

Mara bent over her marzipan cross in embarrassment, realizing her mother was referring to her own experience. But wasn't this an opportunity to *talk*? 'What did Grandma and Grandpa say when you told them you were pregnant?' she asked, continuing to embellish the cross with close concentration.

'Mummy was wonderful. She went with me to tell Daddy. He just said "Ah". I can remember the silence, the old clock ticking majestically. At last he said, "And have I met my future son-in-law?" The terrible thing was I had this overwhelming urge to laugh.' So that's where I get it from. Mara pictured the scene. The Bishop in his study, the disgraced daughter biting her lips. Mother being wonderful.

'So there was no question of your not marrying him?'

'Oh, no. But then, I wanted to. Passionately.' Mara felt herself blushing. 'He was so different from all the other young men one met. They were all so . . . I suppose I went up to Cambridge wanting to escape. I loved my parents dearly and I know I probably made them rather unhappy. But home was . . . stifling.' By now they were both fiddling industriously with the marzipan. 'Things don't always turn out as you imagine, I suppose.' They lapsed back into silence.

'What will you wear to Rupert's?' asked her mother. Mara glared at her, the train of thought being all too apparent. Her mother laughed. 'Apropos of nothing.'

'I haven't decided. Look,' she said, showing her mother the finished cross to distract her.

'Darling, it's wonderful! You're so clever.' Mara watched her transfer it carefully into the middle of the apostles, then put the cake into the Aga to brown. 'Now, how about some coffee?' She put the kettle on. They sat at the table.

'I was only nineteen when you were born,' said her mother.

Nineteen! Don't cut her off. Say something. 'It must have been . . . difficult.'

'Yes. I never finished my degree. Morgan was sitting his Finals when you were born. Then he taught Classics for a couple of years at a boys' school. It was all rather . . . Money and so on. He wouldn't take anything from Mummy and Daddy, of course. After that he started his training for the ministry. I wasn't much help to him, really.' There was a long silence. Her mother went bravely on. 'I had post-natal depression, you see.'

Mara forced herself to follow. 'Yes. You said.'

'Well, to start with it was post-natal psychosis, actually.' Terror sang through Mara's veins. 'It's a chemical thing. Hormones, I think. It's just one of those things that sometimes happens. You had to be taken away. For your own sake. Your father took you to Huw and Susan.'

I don't want to know. But her lips spoke anyway: 'Why? What about Hester? Where was she?'

'With me, in hospital. The psychiatric ward.'

'Why couldn't I go with you?' Who was asking these questions?

'I was ill, darling. I got terribly confused. I thought you were someone else's baby.'

You rejected me! Say it. Just say it! And all my life since then you've been trying to make it up to me. But you never will. Nothing you do will ever make up for that. She looked up and saw her mother biting back the tears. For a moment she felt the words would burst out of her, but then the rage passed.

'I seem to have survived,' she heard herself say.

Her mother wiped her eyes. 'Oh, darling. I'm sorry.'

I'm the only daughter she has now. The thought of Hester rose up like another unscalable peak. Had they climbed this high only to gain a view of further ridges stretching out beyond one another into infinity? Mara reached out and took her mother's hand.

'We'll probably be all right.' They dried their eyes. 'Although I don't think that cake will be.'

Her mother leapt up and rescued it. 'I forgot the coffee, too,' she said. They sat drinking and chatting in the warm kitchen. As they talked, Mara could sense they were skirting round the foothills, sizing up the task which lay ahead. They were still sitting there an hour later when her father came into the kitchen in his cassock.

'I'm going over to the church now,' he said.

Her mother stood up. 'I didn't notice the time,' she said. 'We've been talking and doing the cake.'

Mara felt her father glance at her, and cringed in case he said something approving; but when he merely looked at the cake, she felt a surge of hurt disappointment. *Nothing I do is ever good enough for him.*

'Mara made the cross,' said her mother. Her father nodded.

'Very good.'

'You don't even like marzipan,' Mara burst out. *I'm behaving like a five-year-old,* she thought.

He stared at her. 'My appreciation is aesthetic, not culinary.' There was a pause. He sounded like Andrew.

'I'll go and get my coat,' said her mother. 'Why don't you come with us, Mara? You always used to love the Easter vigil.'

Mara looked away in embarrassment. 'No thanks,' she muttered. 'I'll stay here.' Her mother disappeared, but her father remained in the kitchen. Was he going to say something? Perhaps he thought she was cutting her mother off again. She looked at him defiantly, and found she couldn't read his expression. Maybe he was about to bawl, 'Get off your arse and into that church!'

Suddenly his lips twitched. '"Ignorant Welsh peasant"?' he said, as though her words had only just at that moment filtered through into his consciousness. He shook his head and left the room, but she thought she saw him smiling as he went.

They had gone. Mara picked up the cake and took it through to the pantry. On the shelf there was a bowl of dyed eggs for the Sunday school children. On impulse Mara picked out a pale blue one and took it back to the kitchen. She found a black pen and began to decorate it. Her parents' initials began to form on the egg's smooth surface. It's years since I did anything like this for them.

The service would be well under way by now. She pictured the dark church, and the one point of light – the paschal candle. Then the time would come for the reredos to be opened. A sudden blaze of gold. *He is risen!* All the lights coming on together. She continued to draw the intertwined letters, thinking of the two different families which had combined to make her what she was. The minutes slid by. Hester and I used to sit at this table every Easter doing this. She was so lost in her work that at one point she looked up to admire Hester's egg, and saw only the empty chair.

In the church the service was ending. She heard the organ playing the Easter hymn:

> *The strife is o'er, the battle done.*
> *Now is the victor's triumph won.*
> *O let the song of praise be sung.*
>
> *Alleluia!*

She bent her head again and continued drawing through her tears.

CHAPTER 19

This joyful Eastertide, away with sin and sorrow, sang Mara's mind. It had been raining, but now the sun had tempted her out to wander along the footpaths around the village. The middle of Easter week. A warm wind was blowing and she felt as though her soul was coming out of hibernation. In her mind she was high above the fields, striding across the blue heavens in her seven-league boots. *Hester and I used to climb the highest hills on stormy days and leap into the gusts of wind.* She felt so close now that Mara could almost have reached out and held her hand.

She paused for a moment. *Isn't this what we always called the Primrose Path?* She looked about her, and sure enough, there were the pale clusters of primroses along the hedge. She gathered some for her mother, as she and Hester had always done, and continued along the path. It led to the bottom corner of the churchyard. How many years was it since she had gone in there? Three? Nearly four? She had never visited Hester's grave. Perhaps today was the day? There was the old iron gate. It squealed as she opened it and entered. It had all seemed like a joke at the time – gathering together, weeping, putting a cold body in a box into the earth. Mara had not gone to the funeral. Despite her mother's bitten-back tears. What was the point?

She walked between the rows of graves. Her eyes sped swiftly from one to the next until her sister's name leapt out. The letters were still too new and sharp. Hester Johns. Her dates. The words of Julian of Norwich: *All will be well, and all will be well, and all manner of thing will be well.* The sunlight was shining on the wet grass and on the trees and hedges. The wind stirred. It might be a stranger's grave, and yet it was Hester's body lying down there under the turf. Mara let her eyes roam over the gravestones all around. What would this quiet scene be like on judgement day? She saw it busy, like a Stanley Spencer resurrection, with people clambering stiffly from their graves as though the long sleep of death had been a nodding off in a suburban lounge.

She sat down and leant her back against Hester's stone, closing her eyes. The sun warmed her face. *The trumpet will sound and the dead will be raised*. We shall be changed. All around the graves will split open with a sound like rifle shots, like kernels bursting, unable to hold in the new life any longer. Sown in dishonour and weakness, raised in glory and power. Sometimes she caught glimpses of it, seeing the knots and tangles on the back of the tapestry and making a wild guess about the other side. Impossible to convey, though. Heaven always lost something in translation.

If only Hester were here. Oh, Hester. Why did you have to go and drown? The tears began to run down her cheeks. Ten years from now she knew she would no longer feel like this. The white stone would be mildewed, the letters a little blurred. If only it were all over. But there was only one way out: on through the middle, one foot in front of the other until at last it was all behind her.

She opened her eyes and jumped to see a clergyman standing a few yards away from her. Some kind of aggressive explanation rose to her lips, but she saw that he had not yet noticed her, but was staring intently at some point over to her right. She sat very still watching him. He was oddly dressed. Almost theatrically. How many clergymen still wore frock coats, for goodness' sake? He must be one of those tiresome poseurs who joined the Church because they liked the dressing up. But he hardly looked the type. His face seemed gentle and serious. He was about forty, dark hair just turning grey, not particularly tall. Her father would probably know who he was. What was he staring at? She was about to turn when he roused himself and walked smoothly on between the gravestones. He disappeared from her view behind one of the ancient yew trees.

Mara stood up and stretched. Rising up from the grave, she thought. She looked back at the headstone one last time. All will be well. She knew her mother believed this devoutly. On impulse Mara bent and laid the primroses on the ground. Her mother would see them and guess that she had been at long last to see the grave, and her optimism would be rewarded. Maybe all would be well. She would certainly be glad that Mara was unbending. The thought almost prompted her to pick the flowers up and toss them away. Why is it always ten times harder to do what you want to do, when you know other people are wanting you to do it? She headed back to the vicarage.

The kettle boiled and Mara made two cups of coffee. Her mother was out, but her father usually emerged from his study at about this time. When he did not appear, she began to wonder whether she should take it to him. She remembered her mother's injunction: 'Never disturb Daddy when he's in his study.' Oh, for God's sake, she thought, putting the mugs on a tray. She went to his door and knocked. He called her in. She had not set foot in the room since Christmas day when she had rung the doctor.

'Coffee,' she said, putting the mug on the desk. The egg she had decorated was sitting beside his glass paperweight. He sat back a little and looked across at her expectantly. Was he waiting for her to go?

'Have a seat,' he said. She sat down suddenly in astonishment, almost as though he had pushed her into the chair. They drank their coffee in silence.

'Who's the nineteenth-century clergyman prowling round the graveyard?' she asked, for something to say. He stared at her in complete amazement. She blushed, realizing what he must be thinking. 'I went to see Hester's grave,' she muttered. Now he could tell mother. The parental cup runneth over. He nodded, as though he were thinking of something else.

'So you've seen old Simeon?'

'Simeon?'

'Simeon West. Yes. Well, well.' He shook his head. 'Did he frighten you?'

An escaped lunatic? That might explain the clothes. 'He didn't see me.'

'What was he doing?'

'Well, staring at something. Then he walked off.' Her father was nodding as though this was what he had expected. 'He seemed a bit strange, but not *frightening*.'

'I know, but some people just find the idea frightening. He was incumbent here in the 1820s.'

Her mouth fell open. 'You mean – you're joking!' I've seen a ghost, and I didn't even realize. She heard herself giggle. Her father was twisting his coffee mug round on the desk trying not to smile. 'Shouldn't you exorcize him or something?'

'Tidy him up? He seems pretty harmless.'

'I thought you didn't believe in ghosts.'

'I don't. I think he's a sort of memory attached to the place.'

'What sort of a memory? How can you *see* a memory you don't have?'

He shrugged. 'Do you have a better explanation?'

'Have you seen him, then?'

'Once or twice. Usually round this time of year.'

She watched as he began to leaf through a pile of papers on his desk. He pulled something out and passed it to her. It was a homemade Easter card.

'This is very good,' she said in surprise. It was an angel, drawn, as far as she could tell, with a wax candle. A landscape of fields and hills had been painted over the top in water-colours, so that the angel seemed to be transparent, hovering in the foreground. 'Did one of the Sunday school do it for you?'

'Open it.'

She did. *To Daddy with love from Mara.* She stared in disbelief.

'When did I do that?'

'When you were about seven or eight.'

And he'd kept it all those years. He reached out and took it back, and she knew that the moment had come to ask him what she had always wanted to know. Quickly. If she stopped to think, her courage would fail.

'You remember the time I tried to kill myself?'

'Yes, Mara.'

Her face burned. 'Yes. Well, what made you come back?'

He began twisting the mug round again, carefully, as though the action required his full attention. 'I suddenly knew something was wrong. Terribly wrong.' He cleared his throat. 'I left the curate in charge and ran back.' She saw him picking up his skirts, stumbling through the churchyard with terror in his eyes, stole flapping wildly.

'I'm glad you did.' It had taken her seven years to say it.

'Hah.' He smiled suddenly. 'You were hopping mad at the time.'

She smiled back, and suddenly they were struck by shyness and drinking their coffee again.

Her father was the first to break the silence. 'What was so terrible – why – what made you do it? I never understood.'

She saw her fingers smoothing the plush of the armchair neatly all in the same direction. He deserved a real answer. She forced her mind back through the years.

'Nothing had any point. It was all empty.'

'But why?'

'I don't know.' Try. There must have been something. 'I suppose I couldn't stand it when Dewi disappeared. Not knowing if he was dead, even.' She rubbed the plush back the wrong way, and began to draw stripes across it. 'I suppose he was my hero. And school was awful. Nobody liked me. I always felt that you . . . that everyone . . . that Hester was the favourite one. I tried to make a list of reasons for living. Only I couldn't think of any.' She sensed him twitch as if in pain. There was a long silence. *I'm sorry. I'm sorry.* Her finger trembled as it drew.

'Hester wasn't the favourite one, you know.' She ducked her head. *We love you both just as much as the other.* Her parents had always said that, but she had never been fooled. He cleared his throat and said something in Welsh, then broke off, seeing her expression. 'Sorry. I was saying I didn't know you'd taken it so hard. About Dewi, I mean. If it's any comfort, he's alive still. He rang here a couple of months after he disappeared.'

Her heart leapt. 'Where is he?'

'He wouldn't say. Afraid I'd tell his father. He just wanted his mother to know he wasn't dead.' Was that some kind of relief? It had all gone on so long she could no longer feel anything. 'I always thought Huw was too harsh on that boy,' her father said. 'Trying to make him something he wasn't. It's not as if it's a matter of choice, that kind of thing. That's where Huw and I differ. I swore I would never treat you the way my father treated us. Someone somewhere has to break the pattern.'

Her hand paused in its movement. So this was what lay behind his cold self-control. He had vowed she would not suffer as he had done. But he had made her suffer in another way. They were too alike, and in rejecting so much of himself he had ended by seeming to reject her. 'You tried too hard,' she wanted to say.

'The trouble with being a parent,' he said, 'is that you only get one go at it. If you get it wrong, then that's it. No second chances.'

'And with being a daughter.'

'True.'

We used to speak Welsh together. Until the time he said it wasn't fair on Hester because she couldn't understand. They finished their coffee. *That's why I've forgotten it all. To spite him.* She looked up and caught his eye flicking away from the clock on the wall behind her. He wanted to return to his books.

'I'll let you get on,' she said. *I sound like a parishioner.* She put the mugs back on the tray and headed for the door. She turned back and saw him already opening a book.

'I normally take sugar in my coffee, by the way,' he said without looking up.

'Then why didn't you say so? You've got a tongue in your head.'

She saw him grinning as he bent over his book again. And that, she thought, closing the door, would do very well as a family motto: *Why didn't you say so?* She saw it under a coat of arms. Two mules pulling stubbornly in opposite directions. *Cur ita non dixisti?*

Mara was sitting on a bench in the vicarage garden enjoying the late afternoon sun. The image of old Simeon gliding between the graves filled her mind. Maybe she had been hallucinating? Or else she could have drifted asleep and dreamt the whole thing. A dream fuelled by forgotten anecdotes of the local ghost. Unless he really was a lost soul in need of his namesake's *nunc dimittis*. She shivered. Better to agree with her father. Old Simeon had done this so often in his lifetime – walked in the graveyard; paused, lost in thought; moved on – that he had worn a groove in the history of the place. Maybe in centuries to come people would see a tall girl sitting weeping on a bench near where a vicarage once stood. She wiped her tears away.

In a moment she would have to go back indoors and see if her mother needed any help. Her parents were going away that evening on holiday, and her mother was in the throes of her pre-holiday ritual. Her guiding principle was: maximum pleasure for others at maximum inconvenience to herself. Ironing, packing, baking, stocking the freezer. She didn't trust Mara not to live off whisky and Bath Olivers while they were away. Footsteps came up behind her and Mara sighed. And now she'll be bringing me a cup of tea. But before she could turn round she felt a hand on her shoulder and someone's lips at her ear:

'I bet you thought you were safe, Princess.'

Andrew! She was on her feet, unable to keep a stupid broad smile off her face.

'What are you doing here?'

'I've come to spoil your vacation.' If she had been a hugging sort of person – she folded her arms self-consciously.

'Your mother's making tea and suggests in the meantime you show me the church.'

Mara scowled. She had not set foot there for years, as her mother well knew. 'You don't want to see the church.'

'Of course I do. Come on.' He clicked his fingers at her as though she was a dog being taken for a walk. 'It's got some of the finest medieval wall paintings in the country.'

He set off. Was he serious? Well, she supposed someone as fearsomely cultured as he is would be interested in churches. He waited for her to catch up and linked his arm through hers. She was smiling again.

'Pleased to see me?' Andrew asked.

'No.'

'Don't be. I intend to make you cry.' But he was smiling too.

'How long can you stay?'

'Well, I have to be in Oxford tonight.' That would take him less than half an hour. He'd be here for a while then. Good.

'What's happening in Oxford?' she asked to cover up her pleasure.

'Oh, nothing. I've been offered a research fellowship.' Oh, nothing. As if it were a second-hand briefcase.

'Clever boy.' He shot her a nasty look.

'I can't decide whether to accept it.' They went through the lichgate. 'The question is, can I stand being in the same university as my brother?'

'You've got a brother?' Hearing how absurdly suspicious her tone sounded she added hurriedly, 'I mean, you've never mentioned it.'

'God, you're so solipsistic. It's theoretically possible for things to exist without your having any knowledge of them, Mara.'

They stood a moment in the church porch. Fair enough. But she still couldn't imagine him as part of a family. She reached out and opened the door. The familiar church smell greeted her – polish, age, the smell of the spring flowers. They went inside. It was so completely unchanged that the experience was banal. It might have been only days, not years, since she had last been there. She watched Andrew's profile as he tilted his head back to look at the wall paintings. The angel of judgement with his long trumpet. Gabriel appearing to the virgin. She wondered what Andrew's brother was like. After a while he called her over in the slightly hushed tone people use in churches.

'Look at this.' He was pointing to one of the ancient pillars. 'This is a pre-Christian symbol.' The hare. She'd forgotten all about it. She went and looked at the small blurred carving, remembering how she used to touch it, as though it possessed some secret power. 'The hare was a sacred beast in pagan Britain. Boudicca used to keep one up her skirts and release it before a battle.'

Why can't he say 'Boadicea' like normal people? 'Oh, stop showing off.'

His laugh echoed in the empty church. 'Just warming up for when I see Alex.'

'Your brother?'

'If I have one.'

'Is he older than you?' He nodded. 'What's he like?'

'He's a theologian.'

'But what's he *like*?' she persisted, trying belatedly to build up a context for Andrew.

'Like? Well, our house-master at school described him as an arrogant young bastard with the moral outlook of a tom-cat.'

'Well, yes.' He's your brother, after all.

He caught her expression. 'You cheeky bitch.' They walked up the aisle together towards the chancel. 'He's the sort of person who got articles published while he was still an undergraduate.'

'And you didn't?' There was a pause. He pursed his lips. Aha. The brogue was on the other foot for once.

'He's read everything. He's heard of everything. He's good at everything. In fact, if he had a nice disposition as well, he'd be bloody insufferable.' She bit her lips. 'I hope you're not laughing at me, Princess.'

'Of course not, Andrew.'

They reached the chancel steps and to Mara's amazement he genuflected. The action must have been instinctive since she could see he was not conscious of it. She turned away to hide her surprise, and walked up towards the altar and looked at the reredos. How many hours had she spent in the past looking at it? There were the three bored angels, each holding a scroll with *Sanctus* written on it. They looked like stranded hitchhikers with signs saying, *Heaven, please.* Her attention was called back by the sound of the organ being switched on. She turned and saw Andrew sitting at it, pulling various stops out.

'You can't,' she said and knew at once that she should have kept quiet.

His eyes mocked her. 'Can't I? Watch me.'

He played a few bars of chopsticks very badly. She went across to him in alarm, knowing her father was probably lurking about somewhere, and would be annoyed to find someone vamping on the precious organ.

'Don't, Andrew. You can't just fool around on it. It's supposed to be a very good instrument.'

241

'And is it?' He fumbled out another couple of bars, grinning at her anguished face.

'Well, I don't know. Everyone says so.' The lack of good organists was a sore trial to her father.

'Can't you tell? Good God. Are you completely culturally illiterate? Listen.' He leant forward and pulled some more stops out, and before she could say anything, he broke into Bach's toccata and fugue in D minor.

Mara stood dumbfounded for a moment, then began to laugh. She walked back to the middle of the chancel, exulting in the sound. The old church probably hadn't heard anything like it for decades. She watched him play, and saw a focused intensity – a passion, almost – that she would never have guessed at. Perhaps he had loved the Church, its rituals, its music, its life, and somehow he had lost it all? A fallen choirboy, he had said. The piece ended on a glorious crescendo, loud enough to blast the gilt angels out of their apathy. Gradually the last echoes died away and there was silence again. Mara looked across and saw Andrew sitting with his head bowed. For a long time neither of them spoke. Outside a blackbird was singing in the graveyard. Then she heard Andrew say bitterly, 'Shit.' She slipped away into the vestry, leaving him alone. After a moment she heard him turn the organ off and follow her. She looked round and saw his usual sardonic expression.

'"Farewell, remorse, all good to me is lost. Evil be thou my good."' Macbeth? No. Milton? She knew he had seen her uncertainty. 'Book Four, *Paradise Lost*.' She watched him wander over to the vestments cupboard and look inside. 'But of course, you recognized it.'

He was going to be worse than ever now, to punish her for seeing his weakness. She bit back the urge to say 'Don't' as he tried on a stray biretta. He went across to the piano still wearing it and played a casual riff. A malicious look crossed his face. The tune sounded familiar. Gershwin. She leant on the piano top, listening as he began to sing: '*One day he'll come along, and he'll be big and strong, the man I love.*' She blushed.

'Do my erotic proclivities embarrass you, Princess?'

'No.' Too quick and defiant. 'It's just the whole thing, really,' she mumbled.

He paused in his playing. 'The "whole thing"? What "whole thing"? Sex, you mean?' He sounded like a sadistic tutor making mincemeat of an undergraduate. 'And why's that?'

I'm damned if you're going to make me cry, she thought as she stared stubbornly at the keyboard.

'I just don't like it.'

'"It"? Why don't you like "it"?' She shrugged. He continued to play. 'Ah – it's a feminist issue, and you have an ideological objection to penetration. Yes?'

She was spared the effort of answering this by the sound of footsteps. The door opened and her father entered. He stopped in surprise, no doubt at the improbable sight of a young man in a biretta playing Gershwin in his vestry. He looked at Mara and raised an eyebrow.

'This is Andrew. A friend from college.' She hated making introductions. 'This is my father.' She made some kind of awkward gesture. And thank God he'd come in when he had. Andrew stopped playing and turned. Mara watched in fascinated shock as he gave her father an unambiguous once-over. The knowledge that he was only doing it to embarrass her in no way lessened her confusion.

'That's a fine organ you've got there, Mr Johns.'

'Yes. We're extremely fortunate.' How can he not have heard the innuendo?

'But does it get the loving care and attention it deserves?' Andrew played another idle chord, still looking at her father.

'We do our best.'

'But are you satisfied? When did you last feel the foundations shake with a really good fugue?' Mara was about to intervene to protect her father, when she glimpsed a look of amusement on his face. He knew perfectly well what was going on.

'That was you I heard earlier, I take it?' Andrew inclined his head. 'Impressive.'

'Years of practice and a natural bent, Mr Johns.'

There was a pause, and at length Andrew turned back to the piano and played on. Somehow the balance had shifted.

'Well,' said her father, 'my wife sent me to say that tea is ready. I've got a couple of things to do here, so I'll be along later.' This was an unmistakable dismissal, and Mara and Andrew started to leave. 'Andrew,' he called him back.

The two men stood staring at one another, and Mara's heart began to race. 'The biretta.' Andrew took it off with a grin and left. Mara followed, and by the time the two of them were in the churchyard, they were both snorting with suppressed laughter.

'You're such a queen.'

'I don't know *what* you're talking about.' He linked his arm through hers again and they began to walk back to the vicarage.

Suddenly he stopped. 'Is this where your sister's buried?' For a moment she almost denied it. 'Show me.' She continued to hang back. 'Please, Mara.' She had never heard him ask like this before, and she turned and led him in the direction of the new graves. It was just getting dark, and the white headstone seemed to gleam in the dusk. They stood in silence, and she dreaded some disparaging comment on the words. He spoke:

> '*I can but trust that good shall fall*
> *At last – far off – at last, to all*
> *And every winter change to spring.*'

She felt herself starting to cry at the bitterness in his tone. 'Oh, can't we drop the clever quotes just for once?'

'Have you read *In Memoriam*?'

'Stop thrusting Tennyson down my throat!' she burst out. 'Don't tell me what to read. It won't help. Nothing does.'

'Oh, I don't know. A bit of poetry, a bit of music, a bit of whisky. They all help a little.'

'Well, you've managed. You've made me cry,' she sobbed and stumbled off between the graves. He caught up with her, putting an arm round her shoulders. She was too miserable to thrust him away. The blackbird began whistling from the church roof again. Their feet sounded on the road. After a moment he spoke:

'When I was seventeen, my best friend was killed in a car crash.' Shock ran through her. His tone was so casual. 'Pissed out of his skull and not wearing a seat-belt. He hit a lorry head-on and was killed instantly. Stupid bastard.' Mara glanced at him. At that moment the village street lamp came on, casting light across his face, and she thought, This is what grief looks like so many years on. Does it never fade? She felt fresh tears falling, this time for him and his loss, and slid her arm round his waist. For a second his grip tightened. They walked back in silence to the vicarage.

It was ten o'clock. Andrew yawned and looked at his watch. He was going to go. Her parents had already set off and she would be left all alone in the big creaking house. All her childhood fears were lurking in the garden, ready to press their goblin faces against the windows as soon as he drove off. She watched him pick up the whisky bottle, then put it down again.

'If you drink any more you won't be fit to drive.'

'I know.' He drummed his fingers on the kitchen table. 'Can I stay the night?'

Her heart leapt. 'What about your brother?' Keep the smile off your face.

'I'll give him a ring.'

'OK.' She tried to sound indifferent. He made a brief phone call and went to collect his things from the car.

'You're pleased,' he said as she showed him to the guest room. 'Not wise. I haven't finished with you yet, Princess.' He dropped his bag and she saw his eyes scanning the room, measuring it up against his tyrannical code of good taste.

Unnerved, she said: 'If my mother were here, she'd apologize for that trunk.' He looked at her coolly, and she babbled on. 'It's just things from my grandmother's house waiting to be sorted through.' Aunt Judith's summer dresses which Mara had never bothered to look at. But she had caught his interest.

'Let's have a look.' He had the lid open before she could stop him. 'What about this?' He pulled out a dress. Blue-grey with a full circle skirt. 'A dress to impress a future mother-in-law.' He looked at her slyly. 'Why don't you wear it to Rupert's?' She blushed with fury.

'I suppose my mother told you that?'

'Yes. She likes me, you see. She tells me things. Try it on.'

He held it up against her and she wavered. It was beautiful. He was waiting, watching to see if she was still too embarrassed to undress in front of him. Hah. She began to strip off defiantly. He returned to the trunk with an amused look on his face and continued to sort through the clothes. She saw him pulling out a flying jacket. Yes. Aunt Judith had been a pilot, hadn't she?

'Try it on,' she said. He did. Suddenly the mood changed into a childhood dressing-up game. She twirled round making the full skirt swing out.

'What do you think?' They laughed at one another, then dived back into the pile of clothes. Sun dresses, ball gowns, slacks. They ended by pulling different ends of the same garment. It was a black satin dressing-gown, Chinese, with a dragon embroidered on the back. He pulled it from her.

'Mine!'

'Give it back, you big pansy. Ow.'

It was an idle blow, but one with a lot of practice behind it. The silk dragon seemed to writhe as he shook out the folds of satin.

'Just right for seducing a bishop's son in.'

'Shut up!' She snatched it back from him and held it to her burning face, feeling the heavy satin cold against her cheek.

Andrew began pulling out the old newspapers that lined the trunk and reading bits to her. Copies of the *Church Times* from the fifties. She took off the dress and slid into the Chinese robe. He looked up.

'Come here.' He unravelled her plait and ran his hands through her long curls. 'Perfect. Rupert's a lost man.'

'How would you know?'

'Don't be cheap, Mara.'

He went to fetch the whisky, and the two of them sat among Aunt Judith's clothes getting drunk.

The night wore on. Mara drank less while Andrew drank more. His head lay in her lap and he talked to her about his dead friend, his brother and his Ph.D, then started singing her some Elizabethan love songs. She stroked his forehead, running her hand through his dark hair and memorizing his face. I could draw him, she thought. I know I could. She smoothed his eyebrows with a fingertip, listening to his beautiful voice as he got more and more drunk. At last he noticed her full glass.

'You're not keeping up with me, Princess.'

'I know. Look, Andrew, can I ask you something?' There was a silence.

'Oh God.' He sat up slowly and looked at her. 'What?' She saw what he was thinking.

'Can I draw you? Now, I mean?'

'Draw me?' He looked blank. 'OK.'

She got to her feet and stood for a moment looking down at him. 'What made you think I wanted your body?'

'The fact that everybody does.' He grinned and poured some more whisky.

When she returned with her pencils and sketch-book, he was lying on the bed. She pulled up a chair and giggled nervously. She wondered whether she had sobered up too much to make the attempt. What if the drawings were terrible? Dare she risk his caustic criticism? She reached for her glass and took a gulp.

'Get your clothes off, then,' she said, sharpening a pencil. It was intended as a joke to relieve the tension, but he sat up immediately and began to call her bluff. 'No. Don't! I was only kidding. Andrew. *Andrew.*' But it was too late. Oh God. She covered her face with her hand. He was naked.

'Draw me.'

Her eyes skimmed nervously over his body as he lay there. Oh, God. She was giggling again. But gradually she found her embarrassment giving way to technical interest: perspective, light and shade, capturing those long, lean lines. You're beautiful, she thought. And you know it. She smiled as she drew his cock. Well, if she had ever wanted proof he didn't want her body, she had it now. She caught him grinning. The moral outlook of a tom-cat. She continued sketching, moving the chair, drawing him from different angles. She had not known anyone could be this drunk and still be able to quote poetry. He was reciting obscene chunks of Rochester to her with laboured precision.

She interrupted him: 'Turn over. I want to draw your back.' He laughed and rolled over.

'My arse,' he said, and passed out. She made a couple of quick sketches and then tried in vain to rouse him. Would he be all right? Stories of drunks choking and suffocating filled her mind, so she covered him up where he was sprawled, turned out the light and lay down beside him. Through the night she heard the sound of his breathing, felt the warmth of his thigh against hers, until at last she drifted asleep as the first birds were beginning to sing in the grey dawn.

The train went clattering through the Home Counties. Mara watched the countryside pass by the window. She had grown up not far from here, and the towns and villages were familiar. Canals, bridges, smooth chalky fields and hills, beech woods. The train had already bumped through the village where her father had been vicar almost ten years before. Rupert's father was now bishop of this diocese, although he had not been then. Her heart contracted a little with dread or excitement. She was on her way to the palace. At her feet were a bunch of flowers for her hostess and an overnight bag containing the grey dress. And the Chinese dressing-gown, but only because it was so much less shabby than her old one. She banished Andrew's smirking face from her mind. He had bet her his next term's grant cheque that Rupert would propose to her during her stay, and although the suggestion was completely ludicrous, she was unable to dislodge it from her thoughts.

The train pulled into a village station and drew to a halt. One more stop. They waited in silence. Somewhere further up the platform a door slammed. Mara's mind wandered back to Andrew. She remembered how he had woken that morning a few days before – suddenly, his whole body tense, eyes wide open as though he had been punched awake. Then he had seen her and laughed in relief.

'God, I hate that moment so much.' He yawned and stretched. 'Waking up hung over in a strange bed, trying to remember, then thinking, "Oh Christ. I did *what*?"'

'Why do it, then?'

'Why?' He grinned into the pillow. '"All this the world well knows; yet none knows well to shun the heaven that leads men to this hell."'

'You're incredible. You pass out quoting. You come round quoting.'

She smiled now at the memory. The train jolted and began to trundle out of the station. She watched the landscape gather speed and race past. They had spent half the morning in bed with the newspaper, drinking coffee, talking, doing the crossword.

'I could get used to this,' she said. 'It must be quite nice having a lover.'

'Ah yes, but think – if you had a lover, you'd have to have sex, Princess. That's the whole point, you see.'

'Then I think you must be my ideal man.'

'You're in deep denial, my girl.'

She watched him as he concentrated on the crossword, frowning and tapping the pen against his teeth. Their bare shoulders were touching. 'I reckon I could fall in love with you.'

'I'm sure you could.' He was filling in the remaining words rapidly. 'If you weren't already in love with Johnny Whitaker.' She jumped in shock at his words.

'And are you in love with Johnny Whitaker, too?' she retaliated.

'I think that's rather a fancy word for what I feel.' She reddened. 'Don't romanticize it. Or him, for that matter. He's no angel.'

'I know.'

He turned to her and raised an eyebrow. 'How can you say that! Isn't he generous and intelligent? Isn't he the most amusing man you've ever met? And wasn't he wonderfully kind to you last term when you were cracking up? Nobody really understands you the way Johnny Whitaker does.' She clamped her mouth tight in anger. 'Here's a little question for you: if he were five foot five with three chins and a beer gut, exactly how understanding and kind would he be then?'

The train rocketed into a tunnel, making her ears pop. She stared at her face reflected in the darkened window. She had not deigned to answer his little question, and she could feel it nagging away in her mind like an unopened bill. Maybe she should have asked in return, 'Well, what if he still looked as he did, but was a brainless, humourless twat? What would you feel about him then?' But if the non-fancy word that Andrew had had in mind was 'lust', then she supposed he would feel exactly the same. The train burst out of the tunnel. She blinked in the sudden light, and saw the fields giving way to houses. They were slowing down. Oh, God – we're here. Panic clutched at her stomach as the train swayed into the station. There was Rupert. She saw him scanning the carriages as they drew to a halt. She felt a wild impulse to jump out on to the tracks on the other side, but at that moment an express train went scything past, shaking the carriage. Pull yourself together. It's only Rupert, for God's sake. She opened the door and got out.

He caught sight of her almost at once, and was beside her, kissing her cheek, taking her bag. She let him carry it to his car for her, too jittery to make an issue of it.

'I thought we might go home first and you can meet my family,' said Rupert as the car pulled out of the station car park. 'Then we could go and look round the cathedral, or go for a walk, or something. Whatever you like.' He sounded on edge too.

'Fine.' Her fingers were laced tightly together.

'I forgot to say – my parents have got a few people coming for dinner tonight. Clergy. Politicians. Local big-wigs. You know the kind of thing.' Oh, no. Her worst fears had not come up with anything this bad. 'Stuffed shirts, the lot of them. But don't worry – we can escape afterwards and go out for a drink somewhere.'

'Fine.'

He looked at her and asked, 'Are you OK?'

'Yes.' She made herself smile. 'I'm fine.' Stop saying fine. She stared out of the car window, realizing in dismay that she was about to cry. The landscape wavered through the tears as she tried not to blink. Then suddenly she was distracted by a familiar turn in the road, and the sight of the wooded hills rising beyond the fields.

'This is Chestnut Walk,' she exclaimed.

'You know it?'

'I grew up near here.' There was the footpath going up through the avenue of trees. 'Oh, can we stop for a moment?' He pulled up, and she opened the door and got out. In the distance she heard a train rattling across the fields. Rupert got out too.

'Well, we could go for a walk now, if you like.'

'What about your family?'

He shrugged. 'Would you like to?'

She nodded. They left the car and began to make their way up the path under the chestnut trees. The buds were just bursting, and the way ahead looked like a pointillist painting. Her heart grew lighter as they climbed. The ordeal of meeting his parents was deferred a little longer. She did not even mind when Rupert took her hand and drew her arm through his.

'These are the strawberry woods, you know,' she said. 'I'll show you where they grow. We always used to come here in the summer to pick them, and then one year an old man saw us and showed us a secret place where there were hundreds.'

He was smiling down into her face. 'Did you have a happy childhood?'

She looked away. 'Not really.'

'Was it partly your father's job?'

'Among other things.' There was a slight breeze. They were passing under a beech tree, and the new leaves fluttered. She watched them in the sunlight. They were still pleated from their cramped buds, and they trembled like newly hatched butterflies waiting for their first flight.

'My father was a bit remote while we were growing up,' said Rupert. 'But then I went away to school, so I didn't notice it too much.' Yes. A frightfully pukka establishment. She had heard scurrilous stories about it from Andrew, who had been there too.

'You were Head Boy,' she said. He paused and gave her a Head Boy look.

'Have you been talking to Andrew Jacks?'

'Yes. Do you know his brother?'

'Alex? Yes. We were in the same year. Went up to Oxford together.'

'What's he like?'

'Oh, bright. Ambitious.'

'In what way?'

'Well, academically. Why?'

Mara shrugged. She had the feeling that Andrew's relationship with this bright, ambitious older brother might explain a good deal. A chiff-chaff called in the distance and they began walking again.

'Is it true you used to make Andrew polish your corps boots?'

But Rupert was not going to be drawn into a discussion of the fagging system. 'Andrew tells a good story,' he said drily.

'Don't worry. He says you always played with a straight bat.'

'I certainly did.' Despite Andrew's persistent promotion of a rather different style of batsmanship, thought Mara. 'He was a bloody nuisance.'

'You *swore*, Rupert!'

'It's not funny.' But he was smiling.

'Did he pursue you to Coverdale, do you think?'

'No. Pure coincidence. He was as surprised as I was.' Hmm. No coincidence was likely to be totally pure with Andrew. 'Anyway, I'm safe now,' he said. 'Let's face it, I'll never stand a chance with Whitaker around, will I?'

Was he sounding her out? She blushed and tried to find something else to say. 'Why are you and Johnny friends? You're so different.'

'That's probably why, I suppose. That, and circumstance. We were sent on the same urban placement in our first year.'

'Ah – the dreaded Bishopside experience.'

'You know about it?'

She nodded. Bishopside was to the average Coverdale student what Nineveh was to Jonah: a damn good reason to take off immediately in the opposite direction.

'Did you enjoy it?'

'You know, I did. In a way. It was certainly eye-opening. Home from home for John, of course. There were times when I was very glad to have him around.'

'Why?'

'Oh, he's just more streetwise than I am.' She could see his thoughts were elsewhere, and was not surprised when he paused again and said, 'Coming back to what we were talking about earlier – I know vicarage life can be tough in some ways. But you have to admit it's not as bad as it was thirty-odd years ago. When my parents were getting married the vicar's wife took my mother to one side and gave her a pep-talk: "Never wear trousers," and, "Nothing must come between your husband and his ministry." It's not like that any more.'

Was he leading up to something? The fear that he might be drove her to be more forthright than usual. 'But it's not like being married to a bus driver or a doctor, is it? You can't escape from the job. You marry it. Look at your mother – she's got to be a charming hostess to the stuffed shirts tonight.'

'Yes, but that's just her. She enjoys doing it.'

'But she couldn't get out of it, could she? She could hardly hide in the bedroom and leave your father to do it all.'

'No, but –'

She talked him down although she could see he was growing angry. 'There'd be a constant pressure on you to conform. People's expectations, bitchy comments: "It's a pity his wife doesn't support him in his ministry." A thousand tiny things hemming you in. I know what it's like.'

'But I'd fight passionately for your right to be yourself!' There was a stunned silence as they both took in what he had just said. 'That is . . . I mean, if I were . . . if we . . .' The wind ruffled the new leaves, and he clapped a hand to his face and laughed. 'Oh, no.'

'It wouldn't work!' said Mara in alarm.

'Look, give me a chance to propose first, will you?' He was overcome by laughter again. 'I can't believe I'm saying this. I wasn't going to. Not now, I mean.' He paused. His face became serious. 'But having said it –'

'But it wouldn't work,' she pleaded. 'You're always trying to change me.'

'Nonsense.'

'And you're always saying "Nonsense"!' He opened his mouth and closed it. The breeze whispered in the branches. They stood facing one another under the beech trees. Her heart was racing. 'You're mad, Rupert.'

'I know.'

'There must be dozens of more suitable girls.'

'True. But none I'd die for.'

She felt tears in her eyes. Nobody had ever said things like this to her before. She remembered her cousin's mocking words: 'You're so ugly no one will ever want to marry you.'

He took her in his arms. 'Mara, I'm sorry.' She felt his hand stroking her hair. 'I'm sorry. Please don't cry, Mara. I don't want to put any pressure on you. I know this isn't a good time. I'd just like to think you haven't ruled out the possibility altogether.' She nodded against his shoulder, not trusting herself to speak. He bent his head and kissed the tears away. She was trembling. 'Come on,' he said. 'Show me where the strawberries grow.'

She sniffed, and began to walk along the overgrown path. 'They won't be out yet, of course,' she said. The path branched off and curved round the side of the wooded hill. Her eyes searched through the undergrowth as she walked. 'They grow all along here.' She pointed. 'But if you go down the bank instead, there are hundreds which nobody ever sees.' They climbed down the slope. 'Look, these are the leaves.' They sat down amongst them.

'We'll have to come back in the summer and pick some,' Rupert said.

She smiled and lay back looking up at the sky. Her heart was beating fast and light at the thought of him wanting to marry her. He was lying beside her propped on one elbow watching her face. She turned to look at him, and he leant over to kiss her. She closed her eyes and let him, hearing the wind all around in the young beech leaves. His tongue moved in her mouth and gradually she felt her breath coming faster, every joint slackening, her arms going round his neck. At that point he raised his head again and laid a finger on her lips as if to say that was enough. They lay gazing into one another's eyes. It was like a dream. She had never been kissed like that before – out of tenderness, not lust. She touched his face.

'Rupert . . .'

'Mara . . .?'

'You can if you want to.'

'Can what?'

'Make love to me. If you want to.'

'No!' The sharpness of his tone jolted her. She took her hand away. 'I mean, of course I want to, but no, I'm not going to. Not just like that. Have some sense, Mara. You don't want to rush things, do you?'

'I'm sorry.' He kissed her burning cheek.

'Besides,' he said with a smile, 'never the time, the place and the contraceptive device all together.'

'You're so *sensible*, Rupert.'

'I should think I am! Do you *want* to get pregnant?'

'It's not automatic, Mr Fertile.'

'But there's a good chance! You know, Mara, you're terminally reckless.' Like mother, like daughter. Maybe I should have listened to the doctor. She put a hand over her guilty grin. He was smiling down at her. 'I won't sleep with you unless you marry me first,' he said. 'You wouldn't respect me.'

'Aren't those supposed to be my lines?'

'I know. It's the Church. It's made a woman of me.' His eyes defied her.

'It has?' And, drunk with the moment, she laid a hand on his groin.

'Don't!'

He gripped her wrist. She watched his face, waiting for him to push her away. Her lips were parched. They lay motionless.

'Don't?' She moved her hand and his grip tightened, but still he did not push her away. He rolled on to his back and she felt his hand sliding until it was pressed flat on hers.

'Don't stop . . .' She began moving her hand again, watching his face. Am I doing this right? His eyes were closed and she saw his lips moving, murmuring, 'Oh God, oh God.' He was undoing his belt and flies. She slid her hand down inside and met naked flesh. 'Mara . . .' He lay like the Cerne giant, sprawled out on the chalk hillside among the strawberry leaves. She watched his beautiful face, like an athlete's rounding the final bend. 'Oh God, oh yes, oh yes.' Down the home straight. Her own heart was pounding like the sound of running feet and she heard his breath coming short, saw his face contorting as he hit the tape: *'Ah . . . God . . .'*

For one second he lay still, then she saw the excruciating bliss dissolve into despair. His arms went over his face.

'Oh, no.' She slid her hand away. 'I can't believe I just let you do that.' He sat up abruptly and she looked away in shame as he sorted himself out. Why hadn't he stopped her? She sat up miserably, tainted by his guilt. *To shun the heaven that leads men to this hell.*

'I'm sorry.'

'Sorry! Mara, if you had any idea the struggle I have keeping my hands off you –' She shrank back from the savagery of his tone. He shut his eyes for a moment, then said more quietly, 'Sorry. My fault. I should have stopped you. I'm just a lusting fool.' He got to his feet. 'Come on. We'd better go.'

She stood up and they climbed back to the path and began to make their way to the car. The leaves were a green blur through her tears. How can I have misjudged it like that? she wondered. He took her hand. 'I'm sorry, Mara.'

They walked back through the tunnel of chestnut trees. There was the car. In no time at all she would be meeting his mother. Hello, Mrs Anderson. Sorry we're late. I was trying to seduce your son in the wild strawberry patch. Her tears turned to an awful bout of internal giggling. She bit her lips, Rupert's eyes were on her.

'You're laughing, you dreadful girl.'

'Sorry,' she gasped, but he was laughing too.

He whirled her round and hugged her. 'Oh, Mara. I feel like I'm sixteen.'

'Is that what you got up to when you were sixteen?'

'Well, didn't we all?' He grinned at some recollection.

'What?'

'I got caught with my trousers round my ankles once. By the girl's father.' A day of revelations!

'Oh, no! What did you say?'

'"Oh, Major Cartwright – you must have a terribly bad impression of me!"' Mara laughed out loud. 'He rang my father of course, and I was gated for about two hundred years. Stop laughing. And don't tell me you haven't done that before, young lady.'

She blushed. 'Well, I haven't.'

He looked at her in amazement. She saw some question rising to his lips which he did not ask. Instead he lifted her erring hand and kissed the palm. 'Save it for me, Princess.' They walked back to the car in silence.

It was not until they were drawing to a halt in front of the palace that Mara realized he must think she was still a virgin. There was no chance to tell him, for at that moment a woman appeared in the doorway to welcome them. His mother. They climbed out of the car, and Mara looked out across the smooth wide lawn. A peacock and two peahens were walking gracefully under a distant cedar tree. Their ugly yowls echoed through the grounds as Rupert led Mara up to the house. 'No-oo, no-oo.' They sounded like the cries of lost children.

Easter Term

CHAPTER 20

The bells chimed three. The sound quivered over the City. Spring always came late to this place. The steep riverbanks were still dull – grey bark, dark ivy – but soon the buds would burst, and the leaves would shoot out lush in the sheltered ravine of the river.

Mara was sitting on the parapet of the old bridge, her back to the cathedral, legs swinging over the edge. She watched the late afternoon light on the water and wondered whether Andrew's train had arrived yet. She was torn between wanting to see him and dreading it. He would persecute her until he got the truth about her stay with Rupert, and yet there would be some relief in confiding. Her body felt hot. Oh, God. How have I got myself into this situation? Rupert the sensible and bossy suddenly becoming Rupert the passionate and romantic. She had honestly tried to make him see it wouldn't work! But then she had muddied the waters so disastrously by her physical response to him that he became convinced it was only a matter of time before she changed her mind. She drummed her heels against the bridge in desperation. How could she have been so stupid? It was the spring air. It was his tender, gallant words – expressions she had been starved of all her life: someone to love her, to die for her. And if he had made love to her there among the strawberry leaves, she was sure she would have been lost. Instead they had gone back to the palace.

'*The palace.*' She said it out loud, then mentally hurled herself from the bridge with an echoing scream. His family. Such *wonderful* people. She could tell from the way they had tried to accept and involve her that she had been billed in advance as a Very Special Friend. She could also tell that Mrs Anderson was wondering whether she would have to take Rupert to one side and say, 'Of course, darling, we'll welcome any girl you choose as a daughter, you know that. But perhaps the time isn't quite right.' And then to compensate for her anxieties, Mrs Anderson had made an even greater effort with Eleanor and Morgan's rather awkward daughter. Mara had been made privy to Rupert's sister's wedding-dress fitting. Her opinion had been sought, and she knew – oh, death! – that in due course a thick, white, bevel-edged invitation card would be sent to her. The Right Reverend and Mrs Gordon Anderson request the pleasure. The ceremony in the cathedral, the marquee on the palace lawns, people looking at her and Rupert, thinking – saying, even? – *the next*. Mara saw the bride's bouquet being tossed and falling in eternal slow motion into her unwilling hands. The next. And I would be locked into a life of ghastly dinner parties.

Rupert, it turned out, had shielded her from the full horrors of what lay ahead that evening. He had failed to mention that the colour of several of the stuffed shirts was purple. There was something particularly dreadful about four bishops at a dinner table. Their combined urbanity made her want to eat her cork mat quietly to see if they would say anything. There had also been a cabinet minister, someone high up in the Arts Council, a master of a Cambridge college, and a barrister. And their wives. Liberty prints, crisp blouses, silver brooches. She had behaved herself to the point of insipidity. Maybe they thought she was shy. A nice girl. Terribly clever. A bit shy, but I'm sure Rupert will be good for her. Her father's a clergyman, you know. Good God – she had even behaved herself when they had got on to women's ordination, and the cabinet minister had suggested – arf-arf – that the neatest solution was to delay having women priests until the women themselves could reach a unanimous decision on what to wear in church. She had opened her mouth, but then seen Rupert's anxious eyes on her, and managed not to say, 'I thought bitching about vestments was an exclusively male preserve.'

This is what it would be like if I married him, she thought: anxious glances across the dinner table preventing me from speaking, until at last one day I explode, taking out half the vicarage dining-room with me. Eventually the last guests murmured and brayed their way to the front door and drove off. She and Rupert were left alone in the deserted sitting-room. The other Andersons had discreetly vanished. Rupert began kissing her again, but now it was all different. The lingering memory of the arf-arfing cabinet minister inhibited her. The sofa cushions still bore the dents of right-reverend backsides, and polite expensive scents hung in the air. As his kisses became deeper, his hands bolder, she began to feel relieved that Rupert was one of the honourable evangelical few who believed that sex was for marriage only. But after a while she realized he had no intention of stopping. What if he'd slipped out to a chemist's while she had been changing for dinner? What if his pockets were now bulging with condoms? Outside, behind the quiet folds of chintz curtain, the peacocks called 'no-oo!', and when Rupert's hand strayed past her stocking top she pushed him away in panic.

He kissed her gently. 'You're right. I'm sorry.' He kissed her again, and laughed. 'It's just . . . Mara – you're irresistible. I can't help myself.' But he respected her decision, and they had gone to their separate beds.

What had made him relax his principles? Was it just lust? Or had he sensed that this would be the only way of persuading her to marry him? The two became one flesh. She might well have mistaken passion for love if the context had been right. Strawberry woods, yes; palace drawing-room, no. As he kissed her one last time at the foot of the stairs, she knew he was honouring her for her self-control. He could not see that it was really terror of being trapped in his home and his image of her as his virgin princess. The following day as he drove her back to the station, she had tried to explain that she was not actually . . . that she had in fact . . . slept with people before. Twice. Actually. She watched and saw his love flex and expand to incorporate this: that she was young, that she had made mistakes (who hadn't?), that she had been hurt. He had thanked her for telling him, and, suddenly, what she had intended as a means of disillusioning him, had turned into the kind of appropriate confession of an almost fiancée. Oh, Rupert! What was she going to do about him?

She heard her voice again, pleading with him: 'Look, Rupert, I really did mean it when I said it wouldn't work. I couldn't be a vicar's wife. I know I've given you the wrong impression, but –'

'No, please. That was entirely my fault. I should never have said anything. All I want to know at the moment is that you . . . well, that you'll at least bear it in mind. Don't decide irrevocably. Please, Mara. I love you.' And maybe because he had said that, or because she was escaping, going home, or even because they were at that moment passing the strawberry woods again, she whispered, 'All right.'

Oh, why had she been so weak and stupid? Rupert was off skiing now with a group of friends. Maybe a fortnight in a chalet with half a dozen double-barrelled names would bring him back to his senses.

Then a voice drifted into her mind. It was a moment before she could place it. Tom. At the friary: *'What do you want, Mara?'* Actually, she thought, I want to paint. And for one light-headed moment she felt her spirit rise up and go whirling over the river. Air

261

and space and depth. How would she do it? The moment passed. She stared out across the water. What does a bird see? What would its map of the City be like? A network of paths above rooftops where she saw nothing but emptiness? How could she paint that, create that sensation of climbing on the wind, or spiralling down round a building's edge? She sighed. It was impossible. Then she was ashamed of her cowardice. What made her so unwilling to attempt something if she was not sure she could excel? Maybe she could try the idea out on Andrew. If it could survive his relentless deconstruction, maybe it was possible. But she knew she would not dare. She had never shown him the sketches she had made of him. He had not asked to see them, and she did not know if this was because he was not interested, or because he had been too drunk to remember anything about them.

The bells chimed four. In the distance she heard someone whistling. A workman? The sound carried clearly through the quiet afternoon. She glanced round and saw a man appear on the path that led down to the far end of the bridge. He continued whistling, and she watched his easy strides as he approached. She was about to turn away – he was close enough now to see her watching – when he raised an arm and waved. Johnny. She started as she recognized him. Suddenly it occurred to her: I've been trying to make myself forget him. I've just been using Rupert. But there was no time to do anything with this thought. He was beside her, saying, 'Thinking of jumping?'

'No.'

'Get down, then. You're frightening me.'

He reached out, and she swung her legs round and slid down into his arms. He hugged her tight for a moment. Surely he would feel her heart pounding, even through all those layers of winter clothes.

He was looking down into her face. 'Going back to college?'

She nodded, remembering to breathe again, and he released her. They began walking.

'You're back early,' she said. Her voice had an inane, blurting quality, but he appeared not to notice.

'Yes. Overdue essay. "The Charismatic Revival". I've been to all the libraries, and I'll tell you a funny thing, Mara: someone's got every single book I need.'

'Me. Sorry.' They had been on her shelf since her first term, she thought guiltily. She pictured him chasing from library to library and encountering her name at every turn. The college was almost in sight. 'If you come up now, I'll get them for you.' Nightcap, etchings, whispered a lewd part of her mind, and she blushed. He merely said thanks, and they walked on a little in silence.

'Did you have a good Easter?' he asked.

'Yes. And you?'

'Not bad. I've been in Basel.' She looked up in surprise. 'On a Mission.'

'What – converting people?' she asked in distaste.

'Why, aye. Scalp-collecting. Thrusting our beliefs down people's throats,' he agreed cheerfully. 'Christianity is a proselytizing religion, sweetie.'

'Yes – only think of the Crusades.'

'Of *course!*' He struck his forehead. 'I was forgetting the Crusades.' She coloured. 'And let's not forget Jesus's last words to his disciples: "Go into all the world and *learn from other people.*" Don't be so bloody wet, Mara.'

She laughed in amazement. 'You mean to say you enjoy it? Door-knocking and all that stuff?'

'Yes. And you know something else? When I started my training, I thought door-knocking and that stuff was the whole point of being a vicar. I'd worked out that "gospel" was supposed to mean "good news", and it all seemed pretty obvious: *Tell people.*' There was a silence. Don't let go of that, she wanted to say. If you lose that, you'll have nothing left. It'll tear your heart out with it.

'Anyway,' he said, shaking off his bitterness, 'it's not a question of enjoyment. We all have to go. All part of the training. We went to Basel, the other lot went to Watford. It's just the luck of the draw.'

'You landed on your feet, then.'

'It was OK. I must have put on about a stone, though. They force-feed you. A different home for each meal, and you're always greeted with the words, "We thought you'd be hungry."'

She tried to picture him eating polite dinners with diplomats. 'Was it terribly refined?'

'You bet it was. Even the children scared me. I had to preach to them on Easter Sunday. "Well, boys and girls. This is a difficult question: can any of you remember any of the words Jesus spoke while he was on the cross?" All these hands shoot up. "Yes? Little boy on the left." "*Eloi, Eloi, lama sabach-thani.*"'

Mara laughed. 'You're kidding! What did you say?'

'"Yes, yes. *Apart* from that." I don't suppose I knew who Jesus *was* at that age.'

'Surely you were sent to Sunday school?'

'I was expelled. Something to do with setting fire to hymn books.'

She smiled. Maddy and May would disqualify him for lying again.

'How's my friend Rupert, then?' he asked after a moment.

She blushed, hearing from his tone that they had discussed her. She tried to answer casually. 'He was OK when I last saw him.'

'So you're a couple these days?' She could not look at him.

'No.'

'No? That's not what Rupert thinks.' Oh, *God*.

'Well, he should. We agreed,' she said belligerently.

'Maybe he needs reminding, sweetie.'

'I've tried to explain!' she burst out.

He laughed. 'You'll just have to be patient with him, I'm afraid, Mara.' They were nearing the college main entrance. 'What women don't realize is that men can be incredibly stupid. Take the word "no", for instance. I keep having it explained to me, but somehow I can't hold the concept in my mind for more than about thirty seconds.' What if it were reinforced by a knee in the groin? At that moment Nigel appeared, about to step out into the street for a cigarette. Another man who had never got to grips with the 'No' concept.

'Hello, darling. You're back. Got a kiss for me?' He thrust his face up close and laughed as she recoiled. His eyes slid from her to Johnny, then back again. 'Been for a little walk, eh? Well, I hope he's been behaving himself.'

'More's the pity,' Mara heard herself say. Shit. She'd always dreaded being sucked into the smutty vortex of Nigel's thought. There was an interesting little pause, then both men laughed. Mara watched out of the corner of her eye as Nigel semaphored a swift message of encouragement to Johnny in those all-male coded gestures which any woman can read at forty paces. Johnny was grinning broadly. There were footsteps coming along the corridor. It was Andrew. Her scowl changed into a smile. Nigel swung round.

'Oh, *God*,' he said in disgust.

Andrew came across and stood between Mara and Johnny, and put an arm round each of them. 'Hello, beautiful people.' He kissed Mara's cheek. 'And hello, Nigel.' Mara felt the jagged hostility running between them.

Nigel rounded on her: 'I don't know why you waste your time on him. He's as bent as a nine-bob note.' She was too stunned by the loathing in his voice to respond. By the time she had collected her wits, he was renewing his last term's attack on her diet. 'You make sure you're in for your meals like a good girl. I'll be watching you.' He ran his gaze over her. 'Mind you – you've already got a bit more flesh on you. That's what I like to see.' His eyes flicked back to Andrew and he evidently caught some expression there which incensed him. 'Listen, *duckie*, how would you know what men like?'

'Actually,' said Andrew, 'I know exactly what men like, *duckie*. Let me educate you.'

Nigel gave a whole-body shudder and retreated hastily out on to the street, saying, 'You disgust me. You really disgust me.' Mara saw the cigarette lighter flare as the door swung shut.

'That's what you call de-camping,' said Johnny.

Andrew gave him a withering look, and the three of them began to climb the stairs. Mara reached out and took a handful of her mail which Andrew had collected from the common room. She leafed through them absently, bank statement, overdue library book, a couple of things forwarded from her Cambridge college. Her mind was still turning over the scene that had just taken place.

'Do you suppose Nigel's worried about his own orientation?' she asked as she opened her door. They followed her in. She began to be amazed at her audacity, and regretted speaking her thoughts out loud.

'What's this?' Andrew was looking at her in mocking wonder. 'Do I detect the first faint glimmerings of street wisdom?'

'You think I'm right?' She glanced at Johnny and read confirmation there. 'But he's always so disgustingly heterosexual.'

They both laughed rather too long and hard at this, and she scowled down into her pile of letters. One bore her mother's handwriting, and she opened it. A welcome-back-to-college card. She went and propped it on the mantelpiece under the ornate mirror.

'Disgusting heterosexuality is often a front for ambivalence,' she heard Andrew say.

Johnny laughed again, and she turned and saw him lay a friendly arm across Andrew's shoulders. 'True,' he said. 'But not always, I'd like to think.'

'Duckie,' said Andrew.

They were grinning at one another. Mara went back to her pile of letters, feeling slightly excluded. A postcard. Snowy mountains. Oh, no. She looked at the other side and blushed. From Rupert. She turned her back on the two of them to read it. 'Having a wonderful time, walking, skiing, looking for wild strawberries and thinking of you. Much love, Rupert.' She clutched it to herself. Had Andrew read it? Probably.

She glanced in the mirror to see if he was smirking at her, and froze. He and Johnny were kissing. She watched with the detachment which comes from profound shock. Almost at once she saw Johnny pull away – in confusion, she thought – and shake his head. 'Don't,' she watched his lips say. The two stood still for a moment. Andrew's hand on Johnny's shoulder clenched into a fist. It looked like despair. They stood, Andrew with his back to her, neither moving. Mara was still frozen, trying to take in what she was seeing, when Johnny raised his eyes and looked directly at her in the mirror. The spell snapped. She looked away and fumbled with her letters again. After a moment Johnny asked, 'Where are these books, then?'

'Over there.' She gestured blindly towards the bookcase. He crossed to it and took down half a dozen volumes. She did not dare look at Andrew. He must have seen her confusion, and would know how to interpret it. Johnny thanked her and left quietly. His footsteps disappeared down the stairs.

'Have I disgusted you as well, Princess?' She made herself face him, and realized from his expression that she was going to pay dearly for what she had seen.

'No.' Her voice sounded high and defiant in her own ears. 'I'm not disgusted. I'm . . . I suppose I'm shocked.'

'You're shocked. Why are you shocked, Princess?'

'Because . . . I don't know. I've never seen men kissing before.'

'Jesus. What did you expect?' She said nothing. 'Just grow up, Mara. I know you'd like homosexuality to be a chaste and cerebral thing. That would be nice, wouldn't it? But stop and think for a moment. What do you suppose men like me actually *do*? No, come on – I'm interested.' He waited, but she still made no reply. 'You know, of all your unappealing characteristics it's your wilful naïvety that pisses me off most.'

Tears gathered in her eyes. There was nothing she could do but stand and take it. She knew now he had been lying – love was not a fancy word for what he felt. The mirror had shown her not only his passion, but the pain of rejection. Now, at last, she had the means to wound him as he had wounded her, but she found she loved him too much to do it. He watched her tears dispassionately.

'Poor Princess. Trying so hard to be broad-minded.' He turned his back on her and left the room. She felt numb. The scene rose up again and again in her shrinking imagination until she no longer trusted her interpretation of it. Did this mean Johnny was –? He couldn't be. She thought of how he had pulled away and shaken his head; but had that really meant, 'Sorry – not a chance'? Might it not have meant, 'Not now'? Even 'Don't' could mean 'Don't tempt me'. Maybe that was why he had defended Andrew against Hugh and the Coverdale Group that time in the bar. She crossed miserably to her desk and sat down to work, trying to forget what she had seen. It was a long time before she managed to lose herself in her writing. It was the piece Dr Roe had asked for at the end of last term, and it was almost complete. The hours passed slowly. She could hear Andrew moving around next door, and hated being at odds with him. He's my best friend, she thought, and yet I daren't go and knock on his door.

At about nine-thirty she heard him leave his room. She held her breath, waiting for him to pass along the corridor. Instead, there was a knock. He came in with his whisky bottle and two glasses.

'Why do you let me do that to you?' he asked, sitting on the edge of her desk and looking down at her. She shrugged, unable to tell him. 'Jesus, Mara. You're such a victim. It brings out the worst in me.' He poured them both some whisky. This was as close to an apology as she could imagine hearing from him.

'Are you lovers, then?' she asked.

'Of course.'

There was a long, long silence. He's lying, she thought.

'No you're not.'

'Fuck it.' He grinned and raised his glass. 'To the *disgustingly heterosexual* Johnny Whitaker.'

She grinned back and with a long sigh said, 'I'll drink to that.' It's not that I mind for myself if Johnny's gay, she told herself. I'm just glad I've been spared the agony of reordering my world yet again. 'Why did you bother trying?'

'Who dares, wins.'

'Who dares, gets his face smacked, I'd have thought.'

'No. He's a big softie. And a bit too cocksure of himself to feel threatened. And now . . .' – he smiled – 'it's your turn to be cross-examined.'

'No. I'm not telling you.' She wrapped her arms round her head.

'Aha. So Rupert proposed.'

'I'm not telling you.'

He laughed and unwound her arms.

'At the palace? Did he seduce you? Yes he did. Don't lie. How big is he? Go on – approximately. This big? Did you come?' And so it went on.

By the end of the evening he had extracted from her a good deal of what had taken place. Mara found that talking to him clarified her thoughts, although she squirmed and squirmed at his perceptive mockery. After he had gone back to his room, her resolve was no longer wavering. She would extricate herself firmly and kindly before Rupert took to loitering outside jewellers' windows with smouldering credit cards in his pocket.

Term began. The exam season loomed like the Day of Judgement. A sort of eschatological fervour took hold of the undergraduate mind, and the libraries began to hum like generators. Mara observed two kinds of response to the approaching crisis. Some undergraduates drew up revision timetables and worked diligently to plan. Others refrained for fear that the process would reveal that there was not enough time to revise everything properly. The latter group was to be seen in the bar, at street corners, over coffee, lingering, deferring and procrastinating in a variety of ingenious ways, talking all the time about the amount of work they still had to do. Mara, who had always been a slogger, watched the antics of Maddy and May in disbelief. If they were worried about exams, why didn't they work? If they weren't, why didn't they shut up? She thanked God that exams were now for ever behind her.

The days went by. Mara noticed one sunny morning as she walked along the riverbank that she was feeling . . . happy. Don't say it, warned a voice inside her. She felt like someone who had once upon a time stepped out on to a wonderful green lawn only to find it was the duck pond and had never quite trusted grass since. Only believe, said another voice. It will take your weight. She was beginning to inch her way out across the broad grassy plain.

Late that evening the ground gave way under her again. Mara rounded a corner in Jesus College and there was Joanna. They both leapt back in shock at the sight of each other, then Joanna turned and disappeared through a doorway out on to the street. Oh, God. Oh,

God. Mara leant against a wall trembling. I knew she'd come back. Calm down, said Andrew in her mind. Breathe slowly. She concentrated. In. Out. After a while the truth dawned. Andrew had succeeded. Joanna was not going to pester her any more. Only believe, whispered the voice again. Mara hurried up the stairs to find Andrew.

'What's wrong?'

'I just saw Joanna.' Her voice was shaking.

'So?' He poured her some whisky. 'What did she do?'

'She ran off.'

'I told you.' He looked so smug that she forgot her fear. 'Admit it: I'm omniscient as well as omnipotent.'

'Well, you'll just have to wait till a vacancy comes up in the godhead, won't you?'

'Don't try to be clever, Mara.' She wondered whether one of the reasons why he served such good whisky was so that his guests would have to think really hard before throwing it in his face.

'You haven't managed to stop her hanging around college, though.'

'I didn't try. She comes to the college prayer meeting. And to Coverdale to worship at the feet of Johnny Whitaker. Who am I to discourage such piety? Anyway, you've got to face her. You shouldn't let her have this kind of hold over you.'

'I know. I can't help it. It's all bound up in –'

'In . . .?'

'I don't want to talk about it.'

'OK.' She stared in surprise, and he smiled. 'I'll give you a few weeks' grace. Let's get drunk instead.'

'What?'

'Come on – the chance to get pissed without the threat of sex.'

He poured them both more whisky and she drank cautiously, wondering what he was playing at this time. As the evening wore on, it seemed that he had nothing more sinister in mind than singing her torch songs and playing endlessly with her hair. At last he fell into a deep, drunken sleep. She lay listening to the night wind rustling in the trees and the cathedral clock counting out the quarters as they passed. Is this the only man who will ever fall asleep in my arms?

The revision period toiled on. Maddy had chosen this time to

269

embark on an intense love affair. Mara was introduced to the object of her passion, a tall Irishman called Kieran with a wicked smile; and she had to admit that as displacement activities went, this one probably had hoovering behind the wardrobe beaten hollow. Poor May was entirely left out by this obsessive relationship, but instead of using the unexpected free time to study, she took to calling in on Mara and preventing her from working too. On one particular evening she knocked on Mara's door and found Andrew already there with his whisky glass. She gave a great display of hesitating.

'Just come in, will you?' said Mara impatiently.

'Is it safe?' whispered May. 'Or is he in his Gestapo mode?'

Andrew raised his eyes from his book and looked at May in distaste. After a moment he turned to Mara. 'I blame you for this, you bitch. Everyone was scared of me till you arrived.'

May giggled, and sat on Mara's desk. Andrew returned to his book disdainfully, and Mara wondered how long it would be before he was driven from the room in disgust.

'We all dread his practical criticism classes,' said May, picking up a paper clip and unbending it. 'He made someone cry once.'

'She hadn't heard of Derrida,' said Andrew, without looking up from his book; as though it was nothing to do with him – tears and humiliation were the inevitable result of this kind of ignorance.

'I can't take Derrida seriously,' said May. 'It sounds like the chorus of a folk song. Derry derry da de dum dum da,' she sang.

Andrew was struggling not to smile. 'Be grateful to me. You've heard of him. At least you won't get through your degree unscathed by any knowledge of critical theory.'

'Oh, I don't know,' said May, beginning to clean her nails with the unbent paper clip. 'It's my ambition. I just let your classes wash over me.'

Mara listened to the conversation in growing disbelief.

'I've noticed.'

'Does it hurt your feelings?'

'No. If you're happy with a Lower Second and a nice girls' grammar school close reading of the text, it's fine by me.'

'Well, not everyone's daddy can afford to send them to a poncy public school,' said May. 'Only I expect you were a scholarship boy, because you're so terribly, terribly clever.'

Mara was convinced that Andrew would now pick up his whisky and stalk out; but although he did not deign to answer May's observation, he remained where he was and read on. Mara wondered whether after years of intimidating everyone with his cold intellectual bullying, he found he rather liked being treated with disrespect.

'I came to ask you for a word, Mara,' said May.

'A private word, you mean?' asked Mara,' glancing at Andrew.

'Oh, no. A word which you couldn't put in an essay on Marlowe.'

'A what? Why?' Mara stared at her, baffled.

'It's a running bet I've got with my tutorial partner,' explained May. 'To liven up the tutorial. We take it in turns to pick an impossible word for the other one to work into an essay without the tutor noticing.'

'Such as?'

'Oh, "candy floss" in an essay on Restoration Comedy. "Telephone box" in Fielding. That sort of thing. We've been doing it since November.' Mara glanced at Andrew again, and saw he had abandoned all pretence of being uninterested.

'Good God – and your tutor hasn't noticed?' he asked.

'It's Dr Walden. I don't think he's noticed we're in the twentieth century,' said May.

'True,' conceded Andrew. 'But don't *ever* try it on me, curlylocks.'

'Or you'll put me on detention.' He gave her a look, and she fluttered her eye-lashes at him. 'Well, what do you think? So far I've come up with "wart hog" or "sweat gland".'

There was a thoughtful silence.

'"Speculum",' said Mara.

'"Smegma",' said Andrew. There was a pause. May eyed him. 'Look it up later,' he said kindly.

'How incredibly puerile,' May replied.

He's right, thought Mara. She doesn't know what it means. It was a relief to see him using his nasty perceptive eyes on someone else for a change. She smiled as she put the kettle on for coffee.

After a moment May went and sat down at Andrew's feet on Mara's new rug and began to fiddle and plait the tasselled edge. 'Can you just *remind* me about post-structuralism?' she asked. 'In case I ever want to refer to it in passing.'

Mara watched, and saw him relent. She turned away to hide another smile. No man can resist it, she thought. Explain it to me. Educate me. What is the off-side rule in rugby, exactly? I can't seem to understand how to fill this form in. Save me, fulfil me, enrich my life. He was a good teacher, though. Clear, imaginative, concise. May sat plaiting and stroking the rug fringe, listening. Mara poured the coffee.

'No, no – forget about intentionality. Look, let's take a text you're familiar with.' He paused and looked at her sharply. 'Are you still letting this wash over you?'

May gazed up at him. 'No, honestly.'

Mara caught the look and stopped in the middle of what she was doing. Good God – she's in love with him.

But then May sighed, and added, 'I just *love* hearing you talk, Andrew.' This remark signalled the end of the lesson. Andrew returned to his book and closed his ears to her pleas and apologies.

'I'll be good, Andrew. I promise.'

'No.'

She pulled at his book. 'How am I going to get a First, if you won't help me?'

'Too bad. You fucked your chance up, young lady.'

'Please please please. You're my last hope now I've given up prayer.'

'Given up prayer?' said Mara. Was May rebelling against the faith of her fathers, too? Perhaps it was *de rigueur* for vicars' daughters.

'Oh, not seriously. I just can't bear going to the college prayer meeting now the tapeworm has got her claws into it. She . . . well. I don't go any more.' May fumbled to a stop and glanced anxiously at Andrew. Mara realized that there must have been a tacit agreement that nobody was to mention Joanna in her presence.

'I imagine we're talking about Joanna,' she said. May's eyes darted back to her nervously. 'It's all right. I can cope.'

'Well . . .' May hesitated, but then venom got the better of her. 'It's like a seance these days. We're always waiting to hear what the Spirit has to say, and it's always bloody Joanna who gets a message for us from the Lord. She sits there like Gypsy Rose Lee in her headscarf and says, "I think the Lord's saying blah blah blah."' Andrew laughed. 'I know it *sounds* funny, but it's horrible. It's like she's put a spell on everyone. Nobody's allowed to challenge what she says because she's only a mouthpiece for God's message, and if you argue then you're blaspheming against the Holy Spirit.'

'So what's God saying to the undergraduates of Jesus College?' asked Andrew. 'I hope you're paying attention, Mara. There's got to be a footnote for your thesis in here somewhere.'

'Yes,' agreed May. 'You can put, "I owe this insight to my colleague May Poppett." Well, according to La Joanna, God's telling us that he's doing a new thing, and that if we're faithful in prayer and fasting, then he's going to work mighty miracles in our midst.' Mara began trembling. She folded her arms tightly. May went on. 'This is part of a worldwide outpouring of the Spirit, says Joanna. God's giving the established churches one last chance to jump on the bandwagon before he washes his hands of them all and sets up a new restored church. With her on centre stage, of course. I just can't –' May caught sight of Mara's white face and stopped, appalled. 'Are you OK, Mara?'

There was a tense silence. I will not let her have this hold over me. I *will not*. She struggled to reassure them, to show she was in control. They waited, then Andrew slid his whisky glass across the desk towards her, and to her surprise she found herself almost smiling.

'I'm fine.'

Later, when they had both gone, Mara sat trying to make herself think about what May had said. But I can't. A few weeks' grace. Make the most of it. He'll force you to face it in the end. The Church of the Revelation. Leah. Hester. She felt powerless, as though there was a straitjacket on her soul. I'm not ready.

She stood up and began to get ready for bed, turning her thoughts deliberately down another path. May and Andrew. Had she imagined May's look, or was everyone she knew randomly and disastrously in love with the wrong person? This thought led her straight to Rupert, and she frowned. When he had returned from his skiing, she had made her position clear, sliding from his embrace, avoiding his kisses. She had found this harder to do than she had been expecting. A picture of him at the beginning of term came into her mind: bronzed, hair bleached by the sun, standing in her room saying, 'You have no idea how much I've missed you, Mara.' She felt a flicker of lust at the memory. But she had remained adamant. He had taken it on the chin, of course. A gentleman to the last. From her point of view the whole thing was over, but as the weeks passed she began to fear that he saw it as only a temporary cooling-off period. Perhaps he was allowing her time and space, confident that she would come back to him in the end? Well, she couldn't help what he thought. She climbed into bed.

As she drifted off to sleep, she thought again about passion and unrequited love. May and Andrew; Andrew and Johnny; her and Johnny; Rupert and her. Why couldn't she love Rupert? Handsome, intelligent, and – most astounding of all – in love with her. Why not? Why did it have to be Johnny? Was Andrew right yet again? Was she turning him into an angel? Probably. Wasn't it just like the kind of desperate idealizing love she used to feel for Dewi? But admitting this did nothing to change her feelings. And who could tell what Johnny was feeling? If he was in love with anyone, there would be no way of knowing. His behaviour was irredeemably flippant. She had met him in a corridor the day after she had seen Andrew kissing him, and he had only laughed at her embarrassment.

'Worried about my orientation, sweetie?'

'No.' She had blushed furiously.

'Well, I'd always be happy to reassure you, Mara. You know that.' His tone and expression had been so serious that for a moment she had missed his meaning. She thrust him from her mind. Bastard.

Her thoughts wandered to her thesis. She remembered thinking months ago that fanaticism was like being passionately in love. A crush on Jesus. 'She talks about the Lord as though he was her boyfriend.' That's what May had said about Joanna. The Principal floated into her mind. 'I've decided, on the whole, it's better that I don't offer Miss Smart a place at Jesus College.' Thank God. Thank Andrew, that aspiring fourth member of the Trinity. The Principal drifted away, and two Quaker women appeared, arrested for preaching in the seventeenth century:

'What is your husband's name?'

'We have no husband but Christ.'

Whipped till the blood ran down their backs, but singing praises with every lash. Then it was Hester. Silently rocking, refusing to name the father, refusing medical advice to have the thing aborted, refusing to believe the missing brain would not grow, that the child would not be healed, refusing to believe it was dead. Singing praises with every lash. The coffin no bigger than a shoebox. A monstrous birth. That's what they called it in the seventeenth century. That was the fate of heretical women who coupled with Satan. A child half fish, half human. Monstrous. Her mind filled with drifting bodies, pallid, flippered, eyeless, their silent mouths opening and shutting. 'Not one of these shall fall,' said a voice. The things drifted peacefully on currents she could not fathom.

CHAPTER 21

Mara looked at her watch. Seven minutes to go. If she set off now and walked at a reasonable pace, she would arrive at her tutor's door just as the clock was chiming ten. She fiddled nervously with the end of her plait, then gathered her things together. What would Dr Roe think of the piece she had written? Was it substantial enough to warrant a transfer to Ph.D? At this question Mara felt a wave of nausea. Not just anxiety about failure, she realized. Part of her was afraid of success. If the tutorial went well, she might find herself on some academic motorway, speeding off in the wrong direction without a turn-off in sight. She left her room hurriedly and began to run down the stairs. Oh, God, she thought to herself. I wish I'd never started. Scared to go on, scared to give up.

She was about to cross the landing which led to the last flight when the Principal's door opened and Johnny stepped out.

'Yes. All right. I understand,' he said.

From inside the room she heard the Principal's voice saying drily, 'I sincerely hope you do understand, John. Goodbye.'

The door shut and Johnny turned and saw Mara. He drew a finger across his throat and grimaced.

'What? What happened?' she whispered, but he shushed her, and they went down the steps in silence.

'I'm in disgrace,' he said as they emerged on to the street.

'Why?'

He paused to light a cigarette. She watched him inhale deeply, then blow the smoke away into the morning air. 'Someone tripped over my feet in the hallway on the way to chapel this morning.' She stared. What was he talking about? He grinned at her. 'Looks like I didn't make it back to my room last night after all.'

Her eyes widened. 'You were drunk?'

'Mmm-hmm. I was out with some old workmates. Last thing I remember was my brother saying, "Ha'away – let the bugger lie. It won't be the first time." They must have dumped me in the doorway.' He continued to smoke, watching her appalled reaction in amusement.

'But why?'

He shrugged. 'They probably didn't fancy carrying me upstairs.'

'No,' she said impatiently. 'Why did you do it?'

'Why?' He laughed and took a step closer. His hand slid round her waist. 'Well, why do anything? Because it feels good.' And he bent down and kissed her full on her astonished lips.

'Excuse me,' a voice behind them said. They stepped back swiftly from the open door. The Principal! Mara's face burned as Johnny backed off, grinning, down the steps, hands raised like a footballer caught making a dubious tackle. Honest, ref, I hardly touched her!

'We don't have to ordain you, John.' Definitely a yellow card, although Mara suspected the Principal was struggling not to smile.

'Ah, but you probably will. Think how much the Church has spent on my training.' He winked at Mara and set off down the street to Coverdale Hall. She heard him whistling as he disappeared. Good God. She turned back to the Principal open-mouthed. They stood for a moment in silence as though they both felt something ought to be said. Then the bells started to chime.

'I'm late for a tutorial,' she blurted and, turning, fled down the steps. Oh, God. He kissed me. I can't believe it. He's gone mad. And what's he playing at, twisting the Principal's tail like that when he's already in trouble? She slowed down a little to catch her breath, turning up the cobbled lane which led to Palace Green. 'He's struggling with his sense of vocation,' she remembered Rupert saying. But surely he wasn't trying to solve the problem by getting himself thrown out? She was approaching the Divinity School, and worries about Johnny gave way to fears for herself. What was Dr Roe going to say? She climbed the stairs and paused in front of the door trying to catch her breath and compose herself. She knocked and entered, apologizing.

'Don't worry. How are you?' She gestured for Mara to sit. 'I was sorry to hear you've been so unwell.'

Mara sat, feeling hot and grimy. 'I'm a lot better now, thank you.'

'Good.' Dr Roe gave her a steady assessing stare, then reached for Mara's paper. Mara glimpsed some pencilled comments in the margin. 'Now then . . .' But at that point the phone rang and Mara was left in horrible suspense. Now then, this is an excellent piece of work, or Now then, I'm afraid this really won't do at all, will it?

'Actually, I've got a student here, Alex,' Dr Roe said. 'Could you ring me back in about –'

A man's voice on the other end cut her off. Mara caught snatches of rapid-fire monologue. It sounded like a request for Dr Roe to reserve some books for him in the university library. Tell him to bugger off and do it himself, thought Mara. Dr Roe tried to interrupt before deciding that compliance would be a quicker way of getting rid of him.

'All right. What are they?' She reached wearily for a pen and began to jot down the titles. A minute or so later Mara heard the voice at the other end say, 'Got that? Great. Thanks. Bye.' There was a click, then silence. Dr Roe stared at the receiver for a moment as though expecting it to apologize to her on behalf of the caller, then she hung up.

'An old friend,' she said grimly. 'Now, where were we? Ah, yes.' She began leafing through the pages in front of her, saying 'hmm' in an ominous way. 'Well . . .' Mara braced herself. 'This is really very good. Overall, yes, excellent. One or two small points, however. Perhaps we can go through it together? Do you have a copy there?'

'Yes.' Mara crossed her legs nervously, accidentally kicking Dr Roe's desk with a smart rap like a karate expert. They began to work through page by page. Mara's mouth was dry. *One or two small points.* She knew from her Cambridge days that the most humiliating, soul-gutting criticism could lurk behind this mild phrase. The two small points could turn out to be 'style' and 'content'. But after a few minutes it dawned on her that Dr Roe was actually pleased with the piece. The reservations really were small. Well, thank God. Mara managed to talk quite sensibly with her tutor about fundamentalism, early Quakerism, Methodism, feminism, deism, even antinomianism, until the bells chimed quarter to eleven. At this point Dr Roe stacked the pages neatly back together. 'I wonder if I might keep a copy of this, Mara?'

'Yes, of course.' Mara could feel her face burning with the after-glow of intense academic activity.

'You might think about trying to get part of it published.' Mara nodded, thinking she never wanted to see the bloody thing again in her life. 'Now, how are your thoughts developing? I'm assuming you'll want to transfer to a Ph.D, of course.' There was a pause. Dr Roe seemed to catch some expression on Mara's face. 'Or won't you?' Mara tried to make herself say yes swiftly and convincingly.

'I don't know any more,' Mara heard herself croak. She cleared her throat as if to go on, but could not think how to explain.

'What do you really want to do, Mara?' That question again. Mara felt her hand groping around behind her for the end of her plait.

'I think I'd like to paint.'

'Paint? That's interesting.' Dr Roe sat forward. 'Did you do art at school?'

'Yes. Then I had to choose between art college and university.'

'And do you think you made the right choice?'

'Probably. But recently I've started to want to paint again. It's probably a reaction, or something. A phase.' She ended on a gasp.

'I had no idea,' said Dr Roe at last. 'But as you don't seem entirely certain at the moment, I wonder if it might be best to keep your options open? I think we should proceed *as if* you were going to do a doctorate – for the sake of getting the grant form off in time, if nothing else. You could always cancel your application later. How does that sound?'

'It sounds sensible. I'm sorry. I'm just being stupid.'

'No, no. I'm sure you're not.' Dr Roe smiled, but Mara still wished she had kept her mouth shut. At least she hadn't blurted it out to Andrew. She winced at the thought. 'I don't suppose . . . No, of course you won't have any of your work with you today.' It was a question. Mara shook her head. 'I'd love to see some.'

'Well . . . I suppose I could bring my sketch-book.' They both heard the ungracious reluctance.

'Well, pop in any time. I'd be delighted.' The invitation was sufficiently non-specific to ignore. 'We need to work out a research proposal. Think it over and come back in about a week.' They fixed a time and talked a little more about grants and references. 'Well, good.' This was the prelude to a dismissal. Mara got to her feet. 'Ah, I knew there was something else. Have you been following the court case about that sect? What's it called? The Church of the Revelation.' Mara went cold. Dr Roe was leafing through some papers on her desk and did not see her reaction. 'I know you aren't looking at modern sects, but I thought you might find this interesting. Ah, here it is.' She handed Mara a page torn from a Sunday paper. 'A lot of parallels with the piece you've just written.'

'Thanks,' said Mara, folding it swiftly and plunging it into her bag. She crossed to the door, and they said goodbye. Sweat was forming cold on her forehead as she ran down the stairs. She had caught a glimpse of the leader's face smiling up from the newspaper photograph before she had stuffed the thing out of sight.

She was out on Palace Green. Memories of the Church of the Revelation came pressing in on her from all sides, whispering voices, clutching, praying hands. She began to walk down the lane beside the Divinity School. Her fingers twitched to tear the article to shreds. I won't read it. I can't. She turned down the road that led back to Jesus College. You're a fool. Your few weeks' grace must be up by now. Better to read it now on your own than endure Andrew's interrogation. It's only a matter of time before he does it. She sat down on the low wall. Not yet. I'm not ready. But her hand was already groping in her bag. She smoothed the paper and there was the leader's face smiling up at her. His name: Roger Messenger. Of course. She began reading with greedy hatred. It was an even-handed, well-researched piece, but it was all there. The beginnings of the sect in the early, heady days of the charismatic revival; the meetings in the room above the village library; the healings, the glossolalia, the prophecies; the rift with the local church. That was just after she had left. Then the setting up of the community, the money which flooded in as God had promised it would, people leaving their jobs, selling their homes to join the Kingdom way of life. The building of the new church centre, the setting up of the hostel in Israel.

Mara's eyes ran swiftly down the columns. A brief biography of the leader. Working-class boy makes good. Successful entrepreneur. Fast cars, women, drink. Finding it all hollow, then finding Jesus. Hearing the voice of God saying, '*I am raising you up to restore my church.*' The years of success. Then the scandals. Acrimonious fights over money with those who wanted to leave the sect. Accusations of brain-washing, of splitting up families, of dubious business deals. And then recently a court case. He had been accused of having sex with minors. The words sprang out. Oh, God. Distraught parents, bitter recriminations. His wife stood by him throughout. The young women at the centre of the case refused to testify. Mara finished the article, hands quaking with rage. He'd got off scot-free. She raised her eyes and stared blankly at the buildings opposite. How could she know he was guilty? Hester had said nothing. And yet Mara was sure to the roots of her being that this man was a seducer, a disgusting goat of a fornicator. As she sat asking herself why, a memory rose up before her unwilling eyes.

She went to him. To his house after school. She asked him about that sermon on the role of women. She was seething. 'I'm still confused,' she said. 'I can't believe it.' And she saw his gentle smile, heard his voice: 'Mara, that's because you're still angry with God for making you a girl, not a boy.' She jumped. She had never said that. How had he guessed? 'God knows what He's doing, Mara. One day you'll meet the man God's chosen for you, and believe me, you won't have problems with submission then. It's natural. You'll find it a joy and a blessing. But you'll never be happy if you go on fighting God.' And then he had prayed for her. Made her kneel in front of him. Laid his hands on her head, prayed that God would heal her damaged emotions, set her free to be the woman he had created her to be, and teach her to accept and love the body he had given her. And she had begun quivering. 'You feel that? That's God's healing power at work, Mara. Don't fight it.' Like the bloody seventeenth-century Quakers. And then – Mara sat appalled at the memory – he had actually reached down and laid his hands on her breasts, still praying the whole time! Good God! She clamped her arms across her chest as though she could protect herself from him after all these years. And had she smacked his handsome flash git face and walked out? No. She had knelt there, trembling, believing that God was healing her.

He had told her to come back again, warning her that the Devil would try to snatch back the blessing from her, and that she needed to be under the protection of his spiritual covering. At the time she believed him. She really believed it was true. Too bad for him she cracked. That sermon the following week on crucifying the intellect had been too much, and she had walked out of the whole thing for good. Un–rogered.

Then Mara's mind turned to Hester who had not escaped, who had borne his child, yes, his, although she would never say. She had gone on believing in him to the end. Hester, who was dead and rotting away. Mara's hand crushed the paper face. Fuck him. And Leah, that foul bitch. Whispering to Hester the whole time that it was all the will of God. Mara stood up and ran back to college.

The bells chimed. She stood at her desk, breathing hard, trying to fight down the rage which was mounting in her. There was a knock at the door and Andrew came in.

'Hello. Good tutorial?' He caught sight of her face. 'What's wrong?'

'This,' she snarled, thrusting the crumpled article at him. 'Have you seen this?'

He glanced at it. 'Yes. It was in one of the Sunday papers, wasn't it?'

'That's him.' She jabbed with her finger. 'The leader of the sect my sister was in.'

'Yes. I know.' This knocked the rage out of her completely.

'How do you know?'

'Well, you said so last term. After the Valentine party.'

She couldn't remember. She looked down at the paper again. 'I'd forgotten his name. What he looked like. Everything. Dr Roe gave me this. She thought I'd find it interesting.'

'And do you?'

'No. I find it disgusting. I hate it. I only read it because you said you'd make me tell you about it.'

'Well, tell me about it, then.' His voice was surprisingly gentle.

There was a long silence.

'I was in it, too.'

'Yes. I guessed.'

'I left. I couldn't stand it.'

'Why not?'

'All that stuff about male headship. Women submitting. Crucifying the intellect. I couldn't stomach it.' She stopped.

'Go on,' he prompted.

'I . . . He . . . he laid hands on me once.'

She watched his mind leap ahead. 'Where did he lay them?'

Praying hands. Preying hands. She pointed without a word. It was the first time she had ever seen him look shocked.

'You're joking! But that's all?'

She nodded, but even as she did so another memory flashed into her mind. She stared at Andrew in disbelief.

'What?' he asked in alarm.

'I've just remembered something else.' He waited. She felt as if she was dreaming. 'I was kneeling. Facing him. He was standing up. He had his hands on my head. He . . . sort of hugged me to him.' She could feel the buckle of his belt digging into her forehead and his hands massaging her scalp.

'He made you go down on him?'

'No. Just . . . you know, rubbed himself against me.'

'Jesus! This is sick, Mara. How old were you?'

'Seventeen.'

'Didn't you tell anyone?'

She shook her head. 'Oh why didn't I? I should have done. Oh, God. If only I had, she'd be alive today!' She burst into tears.

'You can't know that.' He put his arm round her shoulders as she wept horrible hacking sobs. Oh, Hester.

'I don't care about me. But if he made Hester – she had a baby and I know it must have been his. I could have stopped it. It doesn't matter about me. I deserved it. But she was good –'

Andrew shook her. 'Stop it, Mara. Don't say things like that! Why did you deserve it?'

'I just did,' she sobbed. 'I feel so dirty.'

'You're not. He was using you. Nobody deserves that.' He cradled her in his arms, trying to calm her.

'I'm sorry. It's my fault.'

'No it wasn't. He was abusing his position. You trusted him. Of course you did – he was a minister. It wasn't your fault, Mara.'

'Maybe he thought I wanted him to do it.'

'What if you did? He was still to blame. It's still an abuse of power.' She felt his hand turning her face to look at him, but she couldn't meet his eye. He stroked the tears away.

'I'm sorry.'

'Ssh. Don't keep saying that.'

'And there was this girl. Leah. I hated her. If it hadn't been for her, then maybe I could have persuaded Hester to leave. She controlled her. I was a child of disobedience and they wouldn't let Hester talk to me. And they wouldn't let her have an abortion. Andrew, that baby had no brain, and they kept on and on that it would be healed. A testimony to God's healing, it was supposed to be.' She flung his arms off her. 'Don't try to placate me! She was my only friend and they took her away from me! That's the kind of god I'm supposed to believe in? I'd rather burn in hell.'

'Well, what if there's another kind?' he asked. '"Merciful, slow to anger, abounding in steadfast love"? Come on, you're an English graduate. What about getting back to the primary material? Forget the rest.'

'I can't,' she wept. 'I've lost everything.'

'That's traditionally held to be a good starting point.'

She stopped crying in mid sob. 'You're telling me to read the Bible? But you're not supposed to believe any of this.'

'Just a bit of role play. It's all part of the therapy.' No it's not, she thought. 'Come on, tell me about your tutorial instead. Was Dr Roe pleased with your piece?' She nodded and gave another hiccupping sob. He made some coffee for her, chatting casually, making the world normal again. 'She's an old friend of my brother's, you know. They were undergraduates together.'

Ah, she thought, Alex. 'He rang in the tutorial, I think.' Her voice sounded thick and strange. 'Made her order him some library books.'

'Typical. He's coming up later this term to examine some poor sod's Ph.D.' He shook his head pityingly. 'Alex has never quite mastered the distinction between a viva and a vivisection.'

'Then he said "Great-thanks-bye" and hung up. As if it was one word.' Andrew laughed. The kettle boiled and he handed her a mug. She drank, listening to him as he gunned down various members of the college and university with idle sarcastic insights. Her mind kept going back to what he had said about God. So much for your brave atheism, she thought.

'Whitaker's in disgrace by the way,' he said, moving on to tittle-tattle now.

'I know.'

He looked annoyed. 'How do you know?'

'I saw him on my way to my tutorial. He told me.'

'You're blushing. What did he do? Lay hands on you?'

Well, he obviously thinks I've recovered if he's making jokes about it already.

He glanced at his watch and stood up. 'I'd better go. My last First Year practical criticism class. Jesus, they're Neanderthal. I should get intellectual danger money.' His eyes were searching her face as he spoke, as though checking to see if she could be left safely.

'I'm fine now.'

'Good.' He smiled and went out.

When his footsteps had died away, Mara made herself look again at the crumpled photograph. He was right. It was an abuse of power. Roger smiled on. What went on in a mind like that? Had he no consciousness of sin when he fondled a teenage girl who had come to him for counselling? What twisted holy logic had justified his actions? That he was healing her with his caresses? That 'to the pure all things are pure'? It would have been better if it had been a yielding to passing lust. At least that left room for repentance. But wilful self-deception of that order was obscene, monstrous. She shuddered. I was too ashamed to tell anyone. They wouldn't have believed me. She's imagining it, they would have said. Over-reacting.

Asking for it, going to his house like that, alone. I couldn't have told anyone. But now the implications of her silence spread and spread, like blood seeping through the folds of a bandage. Oh, God. What if Hester had suffered months and years of degradation and abuse all in the name of Jesus? 'It's God's power at work. Don't fight it.' Submission. Kneeling. Service. She felt a wave of nausea. This terrible egomaniacal guilt. She saw it squatting like a toad on her mind, glutted on grief, trailing its ooze of self-pity over every thought. *I alone could have prevented this. I, I, I.*

But Hester had seemed happy when she last saw her. Deluded, but at peace. Rocking in the rocking chair, her eyes shining with that closed-in contentment Mara had seen in other pregnant women. 'We mustn't upset Hester,' her mother had whispered. 'She has enough to think about without us asking questions.' Hester's decision to leave the community and return home was seen by their parents as a hopeful sign. The sect must be losing its influence. Hester was coming to her senses. But then Leah arrived too, smiling, ensuring that Hester's faith didn't waver. Mother had made her welcome – 'Anything that makes you happy, darling' – but their father had not been fooled. After two days he had asked Leah to leave, looking as grim as Uncle Huw could have done.

'But darling – she's one of Hester's friends! It seems so inhospitable.'

'I will not have that girl in my house!'

But the damage had been done.

Mara realized now that Hester had probably been sent home to avoid a scandal, especially if there were under-age girls in the same state. I should have said something, she thought. Oh, maybe I could have persuaded her if I'd told her what Roger did to me. But deep down she knew her words would have been powerless. It would have been like arguing with the moon. Fanatics were untouchable. And Mara was glad she had not made the attempt. She couldn't bear the guilt of having robbed her of her faith. At least she died in ignorance and trust, even if it was all lies.

Suddenly she could stand it no longer. She tore up the page and threw it away. Five minutes later she was out heading for the woods, running, running, trying to forget.

The days passed. A green haze crept over the City. Sycamore, lime, chestnut, beech. Down at their roots the giant hogweed began to shoot up in the carpet of wild chives. The riverbanks reeked of garlic. Tension mounted in the colleges and libraries, spilling over into student pranks and water fights, and once in a while turning into sickening blur, high-speed despair, handfuls of aspirins washed down with vodka.

Mara was in the library chasing up an elusive volume, untouched by the angst around her. She fiddled around with the card catalogue, then crossed to the main desk to fill in an inter-library loan slip. A young man was standing a couple of yards away, drumming his fingers impatiently on the counter while the librarians were busy with other things. His manner reminded her of Andrew. She watched as his fingers moved rapidly, nailing that tricky cadenza. He looked at his watch in exasperation. It's Andrew's brother, she thought suddenly. Up to examine someone's Ph.D. It has to be. Same height and build, same colouring. His dark hair was cropped aggressively short, and Mara thought she could see why. If he left it, it would grow into cissy curls. She felt herself starting to grin. Suddenly a pair of cold grey eyes were on her, about as chummy as a border searchlight. She coloured and bent her head and filled in the form. God, I'm glad he's not viva-ing me. She left the library and headed back for college.

It was too beautiful to work. She made her way to a bench by the river and decided she could afford to take some time off. She had submitted her grant form and there was no pressure on her to work any harder than usual. Happiness was creeping up on her again. She took out her sketch-book and began drawing the old bridge. Its arch was reflected into a perfect circle, and behind it the cathedral tower rose up above the green wooded bank. Her pencil moved swiftly. The sketch book was hidden in an open file which could be twitched shut whenever anyone walked past. She had done a lot of shifty sketching like this over the last few weeks, sneaking out her pencil in libraries or in the corners of crowded rooms, stealing an expression or posture when no one was noticing. She flipped back through the pages. At the front were the pictures of Andrew she had done during the vacation, then Maddy and May lounging around their room pretending to study. She had even caught a fleeting likeness of Maddy kissing her Irishman. Then there was Rupert talking in the quad, glimpsed through a library window. And Johnny, reading at a library desk like a chained bear. I captured that perfectly, she thought with satisfaction. The next picture was even better. Johnny, a moment or so later, gazing into space, mind wandering. Mara bit her lips. Even from the other side of the library it had been patently obvious where his thoughts had wandered to.

The rest were mostly of strangers. She passed over them quickly. Then scenes from the City. Narrow cobbled streets, bridges, the cathedral looming over rooftops, the castle. She returned to the sketch of the old bridge. It's like a secret love affair, she thought. I fill every spare moment sketching. I think about it the whole time. Everything I see I view in terms of pencil on paper. This book is my love letters. I can't bear to be parted from it.

Someone was coming along the path behind her. Mara shut her file on the sketch-book. The footsteps passed by. Mara glanced round to see if she was safe. Joanna. Mara clutched the file to her chest. The girl had not seen her. Mara held her breath till she was out of sight. Which way was she heading? In another moment Mara saw her reappear on the bridge. Off to Coverdale Hall. The hair on Mara's arms was standing up. I don't feel scared of her any more, she thought. I only hate her. Was that an improvement? But was it fair to blame Joanna for something another girl had done to Hester? No. Mara smiled. But life isn't fair.

She was still gripping her file, watching the empty bridge. I bet she's going to look for Johnny. Sometimes she felt that the girl had no real existence. She was nothing but a horrible outward manifestation of Mara's darker self. How else could she have predicted what she was going to do all the time? Although she hadn't foreseen that Joanna would obey Andrew rather than the Lord. Aha – the Lord had changed his mind, of course. Joanna was no longer being commanded to convert the reprobate Mara Johns. The flexibility of fanaticism was astounding.

If only she would stop hanging around college, though. The mini-revival in Jesus College was beginning to attract the attention of the staff. A combination of Joanna's 'special ministry' and the approach of exams seemed to have whipped up a virulent kind of charismatic fervour among the undergraduates who still attended the prayer meetings. What amazed Mara was the reluctance of the more sensible people in college to challenge what was happening. Several Coverdale students had begun attending to try and steady things down, but as far as Mara could tell, they were unable to decide how they should act. Even Rupert – that yardstick of all things sensible – was holding fire. Perhaps he did not want to end up in the pharisees' camp by dismissing the Holy Spirit as the work of Beelzebub. After all, who was to say that the gifts of the Spirit were confined to the pages of the New Testament? What if there was something in it after all? But why couldn't they see Joanna for what she was? It worried her that both she and May seemed to have more insight at this point than grown men training for the ministry. An insight born of the worst kind of sexual competition, but so what? It was better than being blinded by a holy-holy appeal to male vanity. And so Joanna was holding sway as prophetess, and calling the student body to repentance and baptism in the Spirit.

Mara's one comfort was that Johnny didn't seem to have been taken in by it. He had alienated a further section of Coverdale Hall by his irreverent attitude. Mara had been in Coverdale common room one lunchtime and heard a serious discussion about the problem in Jesus College being turned by Johnny into an impromptu skit on charismatic prayer meetings. The laughter drew a larger crowd and Mara could see that by no means all the spectators were amused. Rupert had tried in vain to stop him, but had ended up as his unwilling stooge.

She could see that it was funny, but it was too near the bone for her to laugh. She could also see that several people found it not only offensive, but very upsetting. Satirizing the ridiculous was one thing, but mocking someone's beliefs was another. Couldn't he see what he was doing? She feared he could, but that he didn't care. What would dear Joanna have thought if she'd been privileged to witness this performance? Would he still be the man God had set aside for her? Probably.

Mara thought back to the previous night when Joanna had turned up in the bar and hovered on the edge of their group, waiting to be bought a drink. Maddy and May sat with a thought bubble visible over their heads: *I'm not bloody well buying her one*. Rupert and Johnny still hadn't seen her, and in the end Andrew leant forward with a smooth Borgia smile and said, 'Let me buy you a drink.' Joanna asked for wine, eyelids batting in fear, not knowing what he was playing at. Bastard, thought Mara with a smile.

The situation had already been unpromising without Joanna's fluttering and sparkling. Mara could not be in Rupert's presence without wanting to scream. She could tell he was trying not to say 'nonsense' or boss her about. Johnny was in a black mood. Maddy and May were needling him persistently.

Mara sighed impatiently. Why do I go over these scenes so compulsively? It's like binge eating, watching Joanna over and over again in my mind until I make myself sick. The girl wormed her way at last into Johnny's attention, beseeching him with her big eyes, Mary at the feet of Christ. Mara kept hearing snatches: 'The Lord says . . . exams . . . not coping . . . need to talk to you.' Johnny was caught between her and Maddy's and May's infantile sniping. Andrew was watching with amusement, waiting as Mara was for the explosion. What had finally caused it? Ah, yes. Maddy saying,

'I bet his idea of foreplay is to say "Brace yourself, pet."'

Well, he would normally have played up to that one, but instead he rounded on Maddy: 'Right. That's it. One more comment like that and you're out of here.' Mara saw Maddy's red face, felt the nasty silence again, then saw – ugh! – Joanna lay a calming hand on Johnny's arm. Like a patient wife controlling her impulsive husband in public. Johnny turned and stared at her in disbelief.

'*Noli me tangere,*' said Andrew, and Mara laughed before she could stop herself.

Johnny's eyes were on her at once. It was like looking down the barrel of a gun. Then he picked up his drink and walked out. Maddy was almost in tears, and Rupert steered the conversation into less stormy seas. After a while Joanna left. She's going to go and find Johnny, Mara thought. Yes. She stood up and left the bar with a calm joy in her eyes. The Lord had told her to do it.

Mara gazed up at the sunlight through the April leaves. The bells chimed half past twelve and she stood up and headed back to college. She wondered for the thousandth time whether her hatred of Joanna was really nothing more than sexual jealousy. Two unbalanced young women after the same man. Why tart it up with cosmic significance?

She was almost back at college. Her thoughts stole back to Johnny. She was feeling guilty: she and Andrew – the two smart-arse postgrads cracking Latin jokes and sniggering. At the same time she was infuriated by Johnny's stupid behaviour, which was sending a series of frissons through the college. Why does it matter what he does? nagged a voice in her mind. Why are your standards for him so exacting?

The smells of college lunch wafted out as she opened the door. After collecting her post she joined the lunch queue. Pizza with rice and chips. She felt someone pushing in behind her.

'God, another starch trip.' It was Andrew.

'You can piss off,' called Nigel from across the kitchen. 'I don't cater for your sort.' Andrew and Mara went and sat near the window. She began to open her letters. One was from her mother. Mara's heart pounded. She had asked for a picture of Hester. Her fingers trembled as she opened the envelope. Andrew was reading an article as he ate and not paying her any attention. She pulled the letter out. Three photos. The first was of Hester. Mara stared. A girl smiling in a garden. It was a good likeness, but meant nothing to her. It could have been a stranger. The next was a black and white portrait of a woman, probably one of the mad aunts. Mara traced a resemblance to herself, but as the woman was in Victorian fancy-dress it was difficult to be sure. She was seated at a piano, and a man was standing behind her wearing a twirling false moustache, hand resting on her shoulder. Mara was just turning it over to look at the back when her eyes fell on the third picture. Dewi! Good God. Where had her mother got this from? Dewi. She had worn her memories of him to rags, and now here he was again. It must be one of the last pictures taken of him before he disappeared. It looked as if someone had called his name, then taken the picture as he turned. Utterly characteristic. Level, offensive stare –

The picture was whisked out of her hand. 'Mmm, *mmm*. Who's this? A relative?'

'Cousin.'

'God, he's like you. Introduce me.' She grinned in spite of herself.

'You wouldn't want me to.' A more violently homophobic male it was difficult to imagine. Calling Dewi a poof was his sisters' ultimate weapon. It could only be safely employed from the window of a rapidly departing car, or in adult company at a range of two hundred feet. 'Besides, I can't. He's disappeared.'

'Disappeared? Is that a family euphemism for doing time?'

I could believe it, she thought. 'Well, he's a missing person with the police, as far as I know. He just vanished.'

Andrew was looking at her in amazement. 'Don't you *know* what happened?' She shook her head. 'God – your family, Mara.' He handed the picture back. 'Pity.'

Mara began to read her mother's letter as she picked at her chips. *I thought you might like this picture of Dewi I found the other day.* No explanation. Mara sighed in exasperation. The other photo turned out to be of Aunt Judith with one of Grandpa's curates. *It reminds me of that sepia picture of you and Johnny.* Mara could see why. She peered again at the moustachioed man, then returned to the letter. *'I can remember the Victorian soirée where the picture was taken. Judith was killed shortly afterwards. We still don't know how the accident happened. She was such a good pilot. Poor Judith. She was a real sister to me in many ways.'* What's she on about now? wondered Mara. 'She was my cousin, really, of course, as you probably know.' What? 'Mummy and Daddy brought her up as their daughter because Aunt Daphne wasn't married. It was all a bit complicated in those days, I'm afraid.'

Bloody hell! Mara tried to keep the stunned disbelief off her face in case Andrew saw it. So Grandma had been right at Christmas when she said, 'My niece, Judith.' Mara had assumed it was just another slip of the tongue. Her eyes scanned for the inevitable phrase – yes, there it was: 'It's not meant to be a secret any more, although it was at the time. I was never told who the father was. One simply didn't ask that kind of question.' So Judith was Aunt Daphne's daughter. Who was the father? Now Grandma was dead there was probably nobody who could tell her.

Mara abandoned her lunch and went back to her room, leaving Andrew still deep in his article and his starch. She propped the photos up on her desk and began to work under her various relatives' gaze. From time to time she glanced up and caught Hester's smile or Dewi's pale mad stare. She was grinning to herself at Andrew's drooling appreciation when a thought struck her. What if Dewi was gay? Was that what her father had been implying at Easter? It would explain why Dewi had left home. No room for nancy boys on that farm. She could almost hear her uncle roaring, *'No son of mine . . .'* My family.

The bells chimed. Mara was feeling restless. She tossed down her book and crossed to the window, staring down at the green riverbank. It was a beautiful mild evening and there was a voice in her conscience nagging away about Johnny. She turned and looked around the room. The row of relatives seemed to accuse her. Go and apologize. She gave in, and picking up her sketch-book in its file so that she would have something to clutch, she set off for Coverdale Hall. The voice in her conscience now changed its tune and began to suggest that she was just using any old excuse to go and see Johnny. She stifled it impatiently and climbed the last twisting flight of stairs to his room. She paused in the corridor. There was a sweet smell lingering in the air. Honeysuckle. She froze. Joanna wore honeysuckle perfume. Was she in the room with Johnny now? Mara felt her scalp begin to prickle. Well, I'm not letting her drive me away. She strode towards the door and rapped. There was a swift, furtive movement in the room, then silence. Mara stood, heart pounding. He was in but not answering. Was –? Her hand went to her mouth. She was in there with him!

Mara turned and retreated swiftly along the corridor and down the stairs. That furtive sound – if they were both in there, then there could be only one reason why he wasn't answering the door. Her face burned with mortification, and she heard her mind mumbling oh no, oh no, over and over again. She stood in the silent stairwell and tried to compose herself. A blackbird was singing down in the gardens below. The sound floated in through an open window on the warm evening air. No. Johnny was not in the room. Joanna had got in somehow and was waiting for him, the way she had got into Mara's room once. Johnny would come back at some point tonight, drunk even, and find her waiting . . . in his bed! No. Stop being such a bitch. You're projecting. She grinned guiltily and continued down the stairs. But oughtn't Johnny to be warned? Her conscience jeered. She was passing Rupert's room when the door opened and he stepped out. His face lit up.

'Were you coming to see me?'

She couldn't bring herself to crush him. He invited her in and made her coffee, talking to her happily while she tried to forget about Joanna. After a minute or two she realized that Rupert was asking her something.

'Mara, I don't suppose you're going to the June ball?' *The* ball to be invited to, if you knew someone who could get hold of a ticket. In the castle. 'Because I've managed to –'

The door crashed open. Johnny. Rupert stood up and swiftly cut off the most articulate stream of bad language Mara had ever heard. The two of them stepped out into the corridor, but Mara could still catch scraps of conversation through the half-open door.

'She's got into my room somehow. I've had it up to here with that girl!'

'Well, ask her to leave, John.'

'She says she wants' – something something. Mara strained to hear. 'Get rid of her for me before I throttle her. I don't care how you do it, just do it, man.'

Mara felt a surge of horrible triumph as though she had somehow stage-managed the whole thing. She heard Rupert going off along the corridor, then Johnny came back into the room.

'Sorry,' he said curtly, crossing to the sink. He had been out running. Mara watched as he stripped off his shirt and dropped it to the floor. He began throwing water on his face, breathing hard. He was standing with his back to her, both hands resting on the sink. Quick! She whipped her file open and began to sketch rapidly. Back, shoulders, arms, neck, those muscles – bloody hell. She scribbled for as long as she dared, then closed the file and sat absently chewing the pencil. Only just in time. He turned and fixed his eyes on her.

'Laugh and you're dead, Mara.' She sat, teeth clamped on the pencil, mesmerized. That's how I like 'em, said the fishwife, hard, hungry and sweating. Mara took the pencil from her mouth and tried to get a grip on herself.

'Joanna?'

'Yeah.' He rubbed a hand over his face. 'The girl's mad. Why me, for God's sake?' Even a prophetess needs her bit of rough. Mara bit her pencil again to stop herself saying it. 'I mean, I knew she had a thing about me, but –' He broke off.

'But then,' continued Mara obligingly, 'who hasn't?'

'That's not even funny, Mara.'

'No. Sorry.' The paint on the pencil crackled under her teeth. Johnny crossed over to her and put out a hand.

'Let's see, then.'

She jumped. 'See what?'

'What you were drawing.'

'Oh, it's nothing.' Her voice was casual, but her fingers were clamped on the file. 'I was just doodling on my notes.' He leant down and twisted it from her grasp. The pictures of Andrew! She leapt up.

'You can't. Oh, give it back. Please!'

He laughed and held the file above his head out of her reach, and in her frantic efforts to grab it she walked straight into a hard, sweaty embrace. She tried to step back, but it was no good. His mouth was inches from hers.

'Oh, God,' she heard herself say. A pulse of lust went through her. They stood motionless, locked together. Oh, God. Then he grinned and kissed her slowly on the lips.

'Mmm. Some other time, maybe.' He handed her the file, and she snatched it and fled.

She managed to get back to her room before the tears of humiliation spilled over. It wasn't fair! She'd worked so hard at hiding her feelings from him. There'll be no pretending now. I'm like Joanna, she thought. Mara felt a rush of sympathy for the girl. Was she crying in her room as well? Two of them in the space of five minutes, Johnny must be thinking. Shit, what did I do? They're throwing themselves at me. Mara licked her parched lips and tasted salt. Another horrible twist of lust clenched her stomach. Was this what had happened to Aunt Daphne? And to her mother?

The blackbird was still singing in the garden below. Mara crossed to the window and looked down. It was getting dark. She wondered whether the same problem was being dished up again and again to every generation of her family until someone at last solved it. She heard her father's voice: 'Someone somewhere has to break the pattern.' I can do it, she thought with a sudden hardening of her heart. I'm good at this. Renunciation, despair – my most familiar sustenance.

CHAPTER 22

The birds were singing outside when Mara woke. She went across to the window. It was a fine mid-May morning. She looked down at the steep bank. The river was almost screened by leaves now. Who would believe it could get this green? As she watched she could feel a thought twitching in her mind. Something about today. Something special. Then she laughed. My birthday. I'm twenty-two. She flung the window up and sat with her arms on the sill looking out. What a blue, blue sky. The whole world looked rinsed and sparkling. Hester used to call this birthday weather. Mara tensed herself, waiting for the rush of pain at this thought, but it did not come. Instead she felt strangely happy, as she had done that windy day at home in the vacation. Hester might have been just across the landing in another room, about to come in and say happy birthday and sit with her watching the beautiful morning. Mara had been dreading this day. The first birthday alone. Maybe these stretches of glee would go on occurring from time to time, like unexplained remissions in a long illness. Or else the wound was beginning to heal. She stood up and went to take a shower. No use picking at the scab to see if it would still bleed.

The hot water beat on her face and ran down her body. Her hair grew wet and heavy, sticking to her back as she began to wash it. A good bright day for drying it, anyway. A good day for many things. No. She thrust the thought of Johnny firmly from her mind. She had been avoiding him for a couple of weeks now, and she knew he had noticed. Once he had blown her a lascivious kiss across the theology section of the university library and laughed out loud when she stuck up two fingers in return. People had turned to see what was happening, and she had ducked between the rows of bound journals and hid.

The thing she hated most was the sense that she was no better than Joanna in all this. What *had* Joanna been up to that night, exactly? She 'had only wanted to talk to Johnny', according to Rupert, who had done what Johnny asked and got rid of her.

Mara winced at the memory of the verbal flaying she had once received from him. His words must been been effective in this instance too, since Joanna was no longer trying to climb into Johnny's trousers and establish the Kingdom of God there. She was pursuing the friendly gorilla instead, the one that Mara had washed up with at the college ball. Poor boy. He had been won over by Joanna's special ministry to Jesus College, and now spent long hours closeted with her in intense prayer, waiting for the fire of God to fall. He had clearly proved more pliable than Johnny.

Mara smiled as she stepped out of the shower. She knew her caution was probably unwarranted. Other than teasing her, Johnny wasn't going to take advantage of her accidentally disclosed lust. Mara repressed a voice in her mind which sighed, Unfortunately. She wrapped a towel round her head and went back to her room. No, he was altogether too ... well, 'decent' had to be the only word. Decent, my arse, said the fishwife. About as decent as a prize bull after a winter in the barn. Nonsense, retorted Mara. Now, what am I going to wear today? Something a bit special.

She went to the wardrobe and drew out another of Aunt Judith's dresses. Cornflower with a hint of lavender, she decided. The soft cotton was sprinkled with tiny white polka dots. It had a full skirt and a wide belt of the same material. She began whistling as she towelled her hair dry. *Now is the month of maying, when merry lads are playing.* A fist hammered on the wall.

'Shut up, you stupid bitch. I'm trying to sleep.'

She glanced guiltily at her watch. Twenty to seven. She had forgotten how thin the wall was. As she ran her fingers through her hair, to separate the curls out, an interesting thought struck her. She had heard a wide range of instructive things through that wall, from obscene language to sixteenth-century Spanish motets, but never the sound of bedsprings *in extremis*. Either Andrew did whatever it was men like him did – which she could never quite bring herself to imagine – elsewhere, or he was as chaste as she was. Hmm. Elsewhere, presumably. But where? Not public conveniences, surely? Not someone as fastidious as Andrew. But this might be another failure of the homophobic imagination. Or the female imagination. She began to whistle again as she wondered. *Each with his merry lass, a-sporting in the grass.* Another exasperated sound from the other side of the wall silenced her. A moment later Andrew came into the room in his silk dressing-gown.

'Right. I'm awake, so you can bloody well make me some coffee.'

He sat on the desk scowling into the sunlight. Mara put the kettle on with a smile. 'What are you so cheerful about, you cow?' Shall I tell him?

'It's my birthday.'

'It is? Why didn't you warn me? Happy birthday. How old?'

'Twenty-two.'

He got up and hugged her. 'Why didn't you tell anyone?'

'I don't want any fuss.' He laughed and kissed her cheek.

'Too bad. I'm going to take you out to dinner. Not tonight, though. I've got a concert.'

'Or tomorrow night. Aren't we supposed to be dining on high table?'

'Shit. I'd forgotten.' He sat on the desk again. 'You'll hate it, you know. We're supposed to be the Principal's model postgrads and impress the old farts from the college council.'

'Maybe I won't go.'

'Yes you bloody well will. If I'm going, you're certainly not getting out of it.' He pointed at her dress suddenly. 'I recognize that. Part of the mad aunt's wardrobe.' She whirled round for him and he nodded in approval. 'It needs a wide-brimmed hat. White.'

'There wasn't one.' She paused, and looked at him. 'I thought you were too drunk to remember anything.'

He was smiling his hateful feline smile. Surely he couldn't remember posing nude for her? No. Impossible, or he would have demanded to see the pictures by now. She began spooning coffee into the pretty blue and white mugs her mother had bought for her. When she turned round again Andrew was leafing through her sketch-book.

'Give me that!' she cried. He pushed her away.

'Just checking to see if you've done anything new since I last looked.'

'You sneaky, slimy little git!'

'You shouldn't leave it lying around.' But her anger had already dwindled. She stood plucking at her dress, watching fearfully as he turned the pages. 'Can I have this one?' It was the picture of Johnny stripped to the waist.

'No.'

'Cow.' He continued to leaf through. What did he think of them? Her heart thumped. At last he looked up. 'This is what you really want to do, isn't it?' Her hand fumbled in her damp hair. She nodded. 'What's the problem, then? You don't have to do a Ph.D, you know. Grant applications aren't the law of the Medes and Persians.' She could feel her hand starting to tug at her hair. He was watching her in amusement.

'Yes, but I ought . . .'

'You believe in a very strange god, Mara.'

'I don't.' She felt insulted. The god she so faithfully didn't believe in wasn't at all strange.

'You don't think irrational sadism is an odd quality for the Divine Being to possess?' She looked blank. 'Listen. God creates a woman and gives her the ability to draw like an angel. He fixes it so that there is nothing in the world she would rather do than draw, then he damns her in perpetuity if she picks up a pencil.'

Mara stared at him. He's right. That is what I believe. She turned away and faced the window in amazement. She saw the beautiful morning, heard the birds singing on the riverbank, the bells chime. Someone somewhere was laughing at her. She put her hand over her mouth to stop herself joining in. It was a theological gaffe of stupendous proportions. So that was the angel's message. For an instant she saw it again in her memory, like sunlight flashing off a distant window, the fierce eyes, the wrathful joy. Wrong. Wrong, wrong, wrong, you fatheaded finite fool. How can you even have thought it? She remembered Andrew's earlier words: What if there's another kind of God? Gracious, slow to anger. She heard herself laugh.

'I don't believe this,' said Andrew. 'It's seven in the morning, and we're talking theology. Give me my coffee, for Christ's sake.'

It had turned into a hot day. After lunch Mara sat with Andrew in the shade of the cherry tree on Coverdale lawn. She was wearing a white broad-brimmed hat which Andrew had bought for her as a birthday present. He was tucking cherry blossom into the peter-sham trim. She sat patiently. There was a clack of croquet balls from the next lawn behind the high wall, and up above the swallows dipped and nattered. It was the blissful hour before exams or revision started again for the afternoon. At any moment Maddy and May would appear, wailing, 'Oh, God – I couldn't answer a single question!' and then waste the whole afternoon in post-mortems.

'There,' said Andrew at last. He held her at arm's length. 'You look beautiful.' She felt herself flush with pleasure.

'You said that to me once before.' She knew as she spoke that she would regret it.

'It was true once before.' He picked up the book he had brought with him and opened it. 'The rest of the time you just look indescribably bad-tempered and plain. Like a partially resurrected Jane Morris with a hangover.' He lay down and rested his head in her lap.

'But that's twice in one academic year!' He ignored this quip. She looked down at him, enjoying the black of his hair against her blue dress. His eye-lashes flickered slightly as his eyes moved across the page. Pity she didn't have her sketch-book.

'You're beautiful all the time,' she said. He made no reply, taking it as his due, but she knew he was waiting for the sting in the tail. What would annoy him most, she wondered idly. A bee droned past them.

'In a slightly prissy Little Lord Fauntleroy kind of way.'

She yelped as he pinched her leg. He continued to read, and she tilted her head back and looked at the blue sky behind the blossom. Anyone could be beautiful on a day like this. Even the students leaping and catching their Frisbee seemed more lithe and graceful in the sunshine. Mara watched them as they played. Creation, preservation, and all the blessings of this life. She looked down at Andrew again.

'What kind of God don't you believe in, then?'

'Any kind.' His eyes continued to travel down the page.

'Be more specific.'

This made him look up disdainfully. 'You, my girl, are philosophically crass. A discussion of qualities pre-supposes existence. I'm an atheist.' He returned to his book. 'And don't wheel on the ontological argument.'

Mara watched as a small shower of petals fluttered down from the tree. She could never quite remember what the ontological argument was. It was like the spare keys to the house: important, but for ever being mislaid. Andrew was smiling as he read. He knows I don't know, she thought.

'I've got a theory about your atheism,' she said.

He read on as though he had not heard. She was beginning to feel like Miss Bingley in *Pride and Prejudice* remarking on the evenness of Mr Darcy's lines. She watched one of the young men leaping for the Frisbee, but it floated up high on some unknown path of its own and lodged in the branches of the hawthorn tree. A different shower of petals fell. Various missiles were hurled up, but the Frisbee was stuck. It hung there, pale yellow, like some strange fruit amongst the blossom. The fruit of the knowledge of good and evil, thought Mara, watching their attempts to dislodge it.

'What's your theory about my atheism?'

'It's not as rigorously intellectual as you pretend. I bet it's rooted in something deeply uncool, like personal experience.'

He sat up and treated her to his most unpleasant stare. 'Are you gambling on the chance I won't make you cry on your birthday, Princess?' Aha. She must be close to the truth. *I can't believe in a God who would let this happen.* Something as unsophisticated as that? 'What sort of "personal experience"?' She heard the insulting inverted commas. The death of his friend. She dared not say it.

'Something to do with the Church? Maybe you were molested by a priest.' At this point they saw Johnny walking towards the group under the hawthorn tree. They watched him in silence for a moment as he talked with the other students.

'You never know,' said Andrew thoughtfully. 'That might drive me straight into the bosom of Anglicanism instead.' He turned and looked at her. 'It would depend on the priest.'

'Stop drooling. Anyway, he's not a priest.'

'No, but he will be. Don't get your hopes up.'

She blushed. Some such thought had been lying around unacknowledged in the back of her mind. If he doesn't get ordained, then maybe . . . Andrew grinned, seeing his bolt hit home.

There was a cheer from the other end of the lawn. Mara and Andrew turned back. Johnny was standing on the top of the high wall, sure-footed and fearless against the sky.

'Over there,' called the students below, pointing to the Frisbee.

'I see it,' he said. He began to walk towards the hawthorn tree, keeping his audience entertained with a pantomimed tightrope walk and a spoof commentary on his progress. Impersonations of several well-known sports commentators carried across to where Mara and Andrew were sitting, and even Andrew was betrayed into a smile. Johnny reached the tree, leant out and retrieved the Frisbee, then sent it whizzing back to its owner. After a brief conversation with the croquet players on the other side of the wall, he leapt back down amidst laughter, cheers and cries of 'Don't do it, John!'

'Jesus,' said Andrew in disgusted admiration. Johnny caught sight of them. Oh, God, he's going to come and talk to us. Her heart began to race as he crossed the lawn to where they were sitting. Bad enough to face him alone, but infinitely worse with Andrew's eyes on her. Fortunately a distraction arrived at that point in the form of Maddy and May. They swooned down theatrically on to the lawn and howled about the brutality of the exam system. Johnny laughed at them and sat down. May stationed herself close to Andrew and began to make a daisy chain.

'I wonder what kind of degree I'll get,' May said.

'A nice girly Lower Second. You're only moderately bright, and you do bugger all.'

'Smack his face,' ordered Maddy.

'What if I worked really hard for the next two years?' persisted May.

He shrugged. 'What if you had brains? Who knows?'

May flushed, but she carried on with her daisy chain nonchalantly. 'Well, who cares?' she said. 'Joanna might be right. The Second Coming could've happened by then.' But her face said, Only moderately bright? I'll show you.

Mara glanced at Andrew and caught his eye. There was a flicker of amusement there. Interesting. So he cared enough about May to try and spur her into studying. Another figure joined the group. Mara looked up and saw Rupert standing there against the sun. She shaded her eyes. He smiled down at her.

'You look ravishing.'

She blushed and smiled back as he sat down beside her. Her eyes fled to Johnny and instantly away again. He was watching her. Andrew chose this moment to lie down and rest his head once more in Mara's lap.

'Comfortable?' asked Johnny.

'Mmm, hmm.' Andrew was deep in his book again. Mara gazed off towards the hawthorn tree, feeling Johnny's eyes still on her. At this point Maddy asserted herself, evidently dissatisfied with the way the male attention was being shared out.

'I used to have a hat almost exactly like that once, only it blew away and a bus ran over it. I wept for weeks because I loved it to bits.'

'Oh, well,' said May airily. 'It's better to have loved and lost than never to have loved at all.' She reached over and draped her daisy chain around Andrew's hair. He brushed it away as if it were a fly.

'Hah,' said Mara, inadvertently drawing the group's attention back to herself.

Andrew lowered his book. 'Does that grunt mean you take issue with Tennyson here?'

'Yes,' said Mara. 'You might just as well say it's better to have got drunk and fallen downstairs and broken your leg than never to have got drunk at all.'

There was a short pause.

'Well, isn't it?' asked Johnny. Andrew laughed, but Rupert most decidedly did not.

Mara could read hostility in his expression, but before she could analyse it Joanna appeared. Mara stiffened. The girl said hello and sat on the edge of the group. She had the gorilla in tow, and he sat beside her like a man under an evil spell. Mara could have wept for him. She had not realized it had got that bad. All his animal high spirits had vanished. Impossible to believe it was the same man she had washed up with. He was staring at the ground. He must have swallowed Joanna's story whole, believing he could help her, that nobody had ever really listened to her before. He was trapped.

Mara felt Andrew stroking her hand. Her fist clenched into a tight ball. Andrew smoothed the fingers out and kissed her palm. He smiled up at her and shook his head: She's not worth it. Mara smiled back. He was right. She let him lace her fingers together with his, and looked up in time to catch May's eyes swerving away. Oh, hell. She's probably sitting there hating me.

Her suspicions were confirmed a moment later when May said to Rupert, 'Do you think getting drunk's a sin?' She was venting her anger by stirring up trouble.

'I suppose it depends on the circumstances,' he replied, barely managing to be diplomatic. Johnny sighed and lay back on the lawn looking up at the sky.

'Good God. Situation ethics,' said Andrew, adding his mite. 'What's happened to you, Anderson? You always used to be a man of absolute values. Surely the Word of God is quite clear about sin?'

'It says that anything which doesn't spring from faith is sin.' This was an unexpected offering from Joanna. She was casting her eyes down modestly, saying to the gorilla, 'Doesn't it, Dave?' Rather ostentatiously flashing that 'imperishable jewel of a gentle and quiet spirit' that St Peter talks about, thought Mara. Johnny lit a cigarette and lay back with his arm over his face in the sunlight. Mara watched the smoke drift.

'Oh, what *is* sin?' said Maddy impatiently.

'Said jesting Pilate,' interjected May.

'That was truth, dumb-dumb,' said Maddy. 'Everyone knows definitions of sin are culturally conditioned. It's all relative.'

Aha, thought Mara. She's sleeping with her Irishman and feeling guilty about it. Andrew began to play with one of Mara's curls, twining it in and out of his long fingers. He was looking at Rupert and smiling maliciously.

'You didn't answer my question.'

'Because I don't think you're interested.' Rupert was very angry indeed.

'Oh, but I am.' Andrew was playing languidly with her fingers now, still smiling at Rupert, who met his gaze with level antagonism. 'Come on – let's hear the fruits of three years' training. What is sin?'

Am I missing something again? wondered Mara.

Then Johnny sat up and said, 'I'll tell you a story.' Maddy and May clapped their hands and squealed like excited three-year-olds. Johnny began: 'When I was about eleven and my brother Charlie was about thirteen, we were both given air rifles.' Maddy and May gasped and clutched one another. Johnny went on good-naturedly against the backdrop of their mockery. 'We were out in the woods on a sunny day –'

'A bit like this?' said May.

'A bit like this, and there was a bird singing its heart out on the top of a tree. Charlie said –'

'What sort of bird?' interrupted Maddy.

'No idea. Charlie said, "I bet you can't hit it." So I took my gun . . .' They all watched as he mimed the action. Eleven-year-old concentration, the careful aim, the finger on the trigger. 'Bang. Then there was silence, and we watched the bird falling down through the branches.' They all sat still on the lawn. Mara heard the silence after the echoing shot, then the sound of the small body dropping through the summer leaves. She felt cold.

'The poor bird!' said Maddy for all of them. 'I bet it was a robin. You're horrible, Johnny!'

'Yes.' He drew on his cigarette and did not smile.

'But why did you do it?' asked May.

'Because I could.' There was another silence. The words cast a shadow.

'Well, well. Arguably the best working definition of sin since the Reformation,' said Andrew. 'I see the Church hasn't wasted its money entirely.'

He got to his feet and the group began to break up. Maddy and May went reluctantly back to their room for more revision, May with a look of steely determination which was not lost on Andrew, judging by his smile. Joanna left, too, clutching the gorilla's arm and talking earnestly to him. He looked dazed and unhappy as he allowed himself to be led off.

I can't bear it, thought Mara. Has no one else noticed what's happening to him? She looked round and saw Rupert disappearing into Coverdale Hall. She ran and caught up with him in the corridor.

As he turned, she said without preamble, 'I'm a bit worried about –' Shit, what was his name? She couldn't say 'the gorilla'. 'You know, the one with Joanna. He looks terrible.'

'David? Yes.' Rupert paused. She watched in astonishment. He was almost visibly counting to ten. 'I've decided you were right about Joanna all along, Mara.' His tone was repressive, implying that *in this one instance* she was right, but her behaviour in general was still totally reprehensible. 'Several of his friends are worried, too. Apparently he's not doing any work, just spending hours on end talking to Joanna. They went and had a word with the Principal about it this morning, in fact. It's all got totally out of hand. Another girl passed out in one of her exams the other day, and it turns out she's been fasting. They've all been doing it.' He glared at Mara as if were her fault, somehow. There was another pause.

'Are you ... You're not mad at me for some reason?' she ventured.

'No,' he said tightly, looking away from her. She was at a loss, then suddenly he said, 'I'd be a whole lot happier, though, if you paid me even one tenth of the attention you pay to Andrew Jacks.'

Her mouth dropped open. 'You're jealous!' With a moment's warning she would have had the wit not to say this.

'Well, what the hell do you expect?'

'But why?'

'Don't be stupid.'

She blushed in indignation. '*You're* the one who's being stupid! He's gay, for God's sake. It's nothing. You must know that!' Her mind was rapidly replaying the scene on the lawn, Andrew's fingers twined with hers, his hand twisting her curls. So that was what the bastard was playing at. It was all aimed at annoying Rupert. Mara felt a complete fool. 'I'm sorry,' she muttered. 'It didn't occur to me.'

'I know. That's what pisses me off the most.'

Her eyes widened. 'Strong language for you.'

He took a step closer in the empty corridor. 'Strong feelings for me, too.' He pulled her into his arms and began to kiss her in a most ungentlemanly manner. She clutched at her wonderful hat to stop it from being knocked off. *Dash it! Rupert was going to teach the girl a sharp lesson, all right!* At last he released her.

'Take *that*,' she said, putting a wondering hand to her mouth.

'Precisely.'

He adjusted her hat for her and with his slight bow, turned and walked off. She stared after him, and at the foot of the stairs he looked back with a smile. Oh, oh, oh, it would be so easy to give in! Maybe I could tolerate all those church services with that kind of servicing from the vicar. She ran off along the corridor laughing to herself, but as she rounded the corner she saw Johnny loitering in the doorway.

He had a wicked grin on his face. 'All clear now?' He'd seen! Her cheeks flamed. She pushed past him without a word and went out.

Mara was in the bath three-quarters drunk, but it was under her mother's instructions, so that was all right. She raised her glass. The wine glowed like garnets. *Look not upon the wine when it is red*, she thought. *At the last it biteth like a serpent, and stingeth like an adder. Yea, thou shalt be as he that lieth down in the midst of the sea, or as he that lieth upon the top of a mast.* That's what the Word of God has to say about being drunk, my friends. But Mother had sanctioned it. She had sent a birthday cheque with a note saying, *Pamper yourself, darling. Buy some wonderful bubble bath and a really nice bottle of wine.* She probably didn't mean her to enjoy them simultaneously, but what can you do if all your friends are out or revising? Birthdays must and will be celebrated. *You're too much like your father,* her mother had written in her letter. *You think it's a sin to treat yourself.* True, thought Mara. But you don't pamper yourself, either, mother. You only pamper everyone else. The front of the queue, the top of the milk. You spend your whole time plumping up this world's cushions for other people. When did you last open a nice bottle of wine just for yourself? Mara drained her glass. Unlike Andrew. Now there was a model of high-minded dedication to self-indulgence. She pulled the plug and climbed dizzily out of the bath. Pity he had to be at this concert. She began to dry herself. She pulled on Aunt Judith's black satin dressing-gown – Judith had evidently been a woman who could pamper herself – and floated back to her room.

It was dusk. She poured another glass of wine. Well, I'm not going to have to make conversation. She sat at the window and breathed in the warm air. A dozen spring smells. Blossom, warm grass. The bells chimed. She drank. Ah. The leaves fluttered. That's a robin I can hear. The night had garlic on its breath. Wild chives deep down on the riverbank. Mara unpinned her hair and felt the long curls slide free. I'm letting my hair down and there's no one to see. She finished her glass. Leave me alone, she said to her conscience. What's wrong with a bit of hedonism? A pewful of Johns ancestors creaked forwards in the chapel to pray, not kneeling as Anglicans do, but bending over as if in pain, elbows on knees, heads in hands, despairing of the grace of God.

Mara stood up carefully. I'm an old campaigner. I know all about you, she said to her conscience. You're easy enough to trick. She crossed to her bookcase. All she needed was a book in her hand, one she ought to read, but didn't want to. She steadied herself. Never before had books looked so intensely book-like, so much *themselves*, platonic forms of books from which all other books derived their book-likeness. Tennyson. She took the volume down. *In Memoriam*. She grabbed the bottle of wine and slid down on to the rug. Not so far to fall. She leant back against the armchair and poured another glass. Now, then. Let's get this bugger read. She pored over the tiny print. Where's it got to? Aha.

> *I held it truth, with him who sings*
> *To one clear harp in divers tones,* [who was that?]
> *That men may rise on stepping-stones*
> *Of their dead selves to higher things.*

Her conscience went purring into its basket and curled up. She drank. The light of the table lamp glinted in the wine, red, red, red, rubies on a chalice. *Look not thou upon the wine* . . ., Yes, but then again, *Use a little wine for thy stomach's sake.* You see? *And for thy often infirmities,* says the Good Book. Tennyson slid from her slack hand. She closed her eyes and laughed. Lying in a warm ocean, tide rising higher, higher, lapping at her neck, her chin, up to her ears. *As he that lieth down in the midst of the sea.* Footsteps. Andrew coming back. So what? She'd seen him in a worse state. Knocking at the door.

'Come in.'

She opened her eyes. Johnny. Standing over her. Laughing. She sat up. The room wheeled round. Too far out, way out of her depth and drowning. Maybe if she kept her head still . . .

'Any left?' He'd got a glass from somewhere and was sitting down beside her. She tried to pour some for him, but he wasn't holding the glass steady. He took the bottle from her and poured his own.

'Sorry,' she said. 'I'm a bit drunk.'

He laughed. 'I'm not likely to cast the first stone.' She laughed too. 'I'm not above taking unfair advantage of you, mind.'

'How?'

'You see if you can work it out, sweetie.'

She waited. Her brain moved slowly, homing in on the thought. 'Oh!' She blushed. 'That's all you ever think about, Johnny Whitaker.'

But he only laughed again. She tried to sit up and pull her dressing-gown together. Her head was spinning.

'You know, that's the first time you've ever said my name.'

'It's not.' But it was.

'Say it again.'

'Johnny.'

'That's reassuring. And again.'

She felt herself starting to giggle. 'Johnny.'

'Sure you've got that? I'd hate you to say Rupert by mistake.' She made as if to push him away, but his hand caught her wrist. She felt it slide slowly up her arm inside the gaping sleeve. His fingers moved on her bare shoulder. He was watching her face. 'This is OK, isn't it, Mara?'

'What is?'

He struck his forehead and laughed again. 'You're not concentrating.' She looked at him. He took the glass from her and put it to one side. 'Now – are you listening?' She nodded. 'I want you, Mara.'

She waited. He waited.

'You mean . . . sex?'

'I don't believe this. Yes.'

'You can't!'

306

'I can.'

'You mustn't, then.'

'Mustn't I? Just a kiss, then. Yes? No?'

'Well . . .'

He bent his head down. Fool! Oh, God, let this go on for ever. His hands in her hair, his tongue hard in her mouth, thrusting again, again. The satin slipped from her shoulders. She was on her back. I don't care. I don't care. She clutched him, dragged out to sea on a fast tide. Useless to fight. Fight. Fight it, you fool. He'll hate you for letting him do this. I don't care. His teeth were at her throat, at her breasts, his hands laying her bare. She could hear his voice a long way off laughing at her. 'You like this? Is this good? Hmm? Say my name.' She was shivering as his fingers parted and slid. I'm burning up. I'm going to die. She was crying. 'Just let it happen, flower. Trust me. Let it happen.' His fingers slid deeper and at last she came, weeping shuddering, crying his name.

She was lying on the seabed. The ceiling billowed overhead, coming and going like silent waves. I'm lost. Not a sound, just the roaring silence of the sea.

Then another noise. The jingle of a buckle. A zip. It jolted her half-sober. He was tugging at his shirt.

'Johnny, you can't do this.'

'Like to bet?' He was lying beside her. She struggled to sit up, but he pulled her back down and kissed her.

'But you said once you couldn't lead a double life.' The argument was slipping from her. He was kissing her words away.

'I was lying.'

'You weren't.' His hand slid down over her stomach.

'Then I've changed my mind,' he said. 'Come on, sweetie, don't do this to me.'

Well, I tried. His tongue was deep in her mouth. It's his fault. I tried. He was nudging her knees apart and a sudden panic rippled through her. She pulled away.

'You'll hate me for this tomorrow.'

'That's nothing to what I'll do if you throw me out now. Come on, don't worry. You'll enjoy it. It's like smoking a cigarette, only it's tax-free and better for you.'

Don't giggle, you fool. But the laugh escaped, disastrously. He was on top of her, kissing her till her mouth and tongue felt raw, pinning her down, parting her legs. He doesn't believe me. Terror washed cold over her. There's nothing I can do. He's too strong.

'Don't! Oh, please don't make me!' she cried. His hand went over her mouth. He was saying something, but she bit and clawed at him, past hearing, past reason. He pulled away and stood up.

'Jesus *Christ*!'

She was lying at his feet. He towered over her, cursing and shaking his bitten hand. She cringed back. He tucked his shirt back in and did up his flies.

'Get up.'

She lay there, weeping, slack and slippery with lust. He reached out and dragged her to her feet. She tried to clutch the dressing-gown round her. He was speaking softly, but his voice was cold with rage.

'I've got two things to say to you. Firstly, a piece of advice. Another time, if you're going to say no, try saying it a bit sooner. Before the man's got his trousers down, if you can manage it. It's so much better manners. Secondly, you just keep out of my fucking way from now on.'

The door slammed. He was gone. Oh, God. Oh, God. The floor was slithering under her. I'm going to be sick. She stumbled to the bathroom and threw up, trying miserably to hold her hair back as she retched. Down below on the street she heard the main door of college slam. I've lost him. She sat weeping on the cold floor in the dark.

CHAPTER 23

It had been a long night. Hour after hour of shivering, of seeing Johnny's face looming up close in feverish half-dreams, then vanishing again. He was laughing at her, saying, 'You like that? Say my name.' Then his face darkened with rage. 'Stay out of my fucking way from now on.' She did not know when she had finally fallen asleep. It was all quiet now. Andrew must have gone out. Everyone else would be revising or sitting exams. All she could hear was the sound of distant traffic and the faint cries of the swifts and swallows circling in the sky. I must be strong.

She sat up. Her head throbbed so viciously that she began to cry. Aspirins. Water. Don't be a fool. She stood up and pulled on her dressing-gown to cover up her horrible naked body. The satin felt slippery and cold like the memory of lust. I must have a shower. I feel filthy. Disgusting. It was like the first time. That horrible boy in the lay-by. Forcing himself on her. She found some aspirins and looked around for a glass. Two wine glasses stood on the hearth where Johnny had put them last night. Her own was still half full. Oh, how have I let all this happen? I should never have trusted him. But how was I to know he'd do something like that? She felt in her body the physical memory of being overpowered, the terror, the useless struggle, his hand clamped over her mouth. But he was my friend. Why do I always trust the wrong person? Tears began to roll down her face. And now I've driven him away. It always happens. Every time I love someone, I lose them. It's like a curse. She took a mug and went to the bathroom. The smell of expensive bubble bath lingered sickeningly. Oh, mother, she sobbed. I want to go home. She caught sight of herself in the mirror as she filled the mug. There were ugly red marks on her neck. Love bites. Oh God. Everyone will see and know. I'm a slut. She gulped the aspirins down and sat on the edge of the bath. Her stomach felt as though barbed wire had been pulled through it. She showered and crept back to her room.

The sunlight hurt her eyes. Another scorching day. She opened the wardrobe, Aunt Judith's light summery dresses hung in a row, pretty colours, sweetheart necklines. I can't wear these. But she had nothing else cool enough. She pulled out one dress after another until she was sitting weeping in a pile of clothes. There was the white dress with the pink rose print which she had been looking forward to wearing. She held it up, then threw it aside. It was too pale. She would feel her shame seeping out and blotching it like sweat or menstrual blood. Oh, why am I so pathetic? It was nothing. We didn't even do it. Everyone else is sleeping around the whole time. Why do I feel so defiled? She stood up. I must go and shower. Then she remembered she already had, and sat down again with a sob.

The bells chimed half past ten. A year ago I was sitting my Finals. Hester was in the last week of her life. A year from now, ten years from now, twenty, I will be looking back on this morning. *A thousand years in thy sight are but as yesterday when it is past, or as a watch in the night.* Her mind groped despairingly towards the faith she had once known, and for a moment it seemed to snag on something. She thought she heard the echo of a fleeting chord, a tune she had once known but had forgotten. The long scar in her arm seemed to tighten. I'm too weary to go on with it any more. But even as she thought this, she felt a strange calm descending. She was still sitting among the discarded clothes. Her hand pulled a black and white gingham dress from the pile. It would have to do. She rubbed the tears away and began to get dressed. Maybe if she wore her hair down and pulled it forwards the marks wouldn't show.

She filled the kettle and started to put the dresses back into the wardrobe. It will all pass, she thought. Somehow or other. But her resolution drained away at the thought of seeing Johnny. How could she ever face him after last night? She leant her throbbing head against the wardrobe door. I still can't believe it. I was saying no. I truly was. He didn't listen to me. Saying no? Like hell you were, sneered the fishwife. On your back with your legs apart. Let me forget it, she pleaded. But she could not banish the image of herself whimpering and writhing under Johnny's expert fingers. He should have gone the moment he realized I was drunk. You weren't so drunk you didn't know better. But I told him. I *said* he mustn't. Oh Johnny, oh Johnny! mimicked the fishwife.

As she stood trying to calm herself, she heard footsteps. She froze. The footsteps were at the door. They went past. It was only Andrew. She could have wept with relief as she heard him let himself into his room, walk to his desk, put some books down. The wall was so thin she could follow his every move. Thank God he'd been out last night! He'd have heard everything.

She listened. He was walking back towards his door again. Supposing he was coming to talk to her? He'd see the marks. He'd make me tell him. Her hand scratched at the wardrobe door as though she thought she could scramble in and hide. But the footsteps passed along the corridor and down the stairs. Weak tears slid down her cheeks.

She made some coffee and sat at her desk to work. The print swam before her eyes and she fought back a wave of sickness. Concentrate. There were footsteps on the stairs again. Johnny. Better to get it over with. There was a knock at the door. Her voice shook as she answered.

It was Rupert. She half rose. He was coming towards her, his smile turning to concern.

'Are you all right, Mara? You don't look well.' She steadied the chair as it tipped backwards, and made herself stand and face him.

'Just a hangover. I'll be OK.'

A look of exasperation crossed his face. 'Oh, *honestly*, Mara.' She flushed. It's not as if I've never seen *you* drunk, she thought resentfully. The same idea obviously occurred to him, too. 'Yes, well. Know thyself, Anderson,' he said, smiling. She began to gather her hair back from her hot face to plait it. 'Actually, I came to ask you whether −' He stopped. His eyes were on her neck. Her hand flew up to cover the marks. He reddened and looked away. There was a dreadful silence. 'Who's the lucky man?'

'No one. Nobody you know. I was drunk. It was an aberration. I didn't intend −'

He broke into her babbling lies. 'Sorry. I have no right to ask.'

There was another tight pause.

'He wasn't lucky. I threw him out. It was nothing.'

Shut up, shut up, you little fool. Oh, how can I not have thought what this would do to him? Johnny's his closest friend. He was looking at the ground, then at the desk, unable to speak. She knew he was willing his eyes not to dart back to her neck and wonder who. She couldn't endure the silence a moment longer.

'What were you going to ask me?'

He ran his hand through his hair and half laughed. 'It doesn't matter.'

'Please.'

'I was going to ask you to the June ball. I managed to get a ticket.'

But now he wouldn't. Mara dragged at her hair. She had been intending to turn him down, but to have the invitation withdrawn like this was unbearable. She held her chin up, trying to prevent the tears of humiliation from brimming over.

He cleared his throat. 'Would you like to come?'

Now she was caught. Caught by his magnanimity and by her cowardice. If she said no, he would begin to think that last night had not been 'nothing' after all. He stood waiting. I mustn't say yes, she told herself. It's not fair to let him hope I'm changing my mind.

'I don't think I can, Rupert.'

'Because of . . .?' She shook her head. 'Then why not?'

'I've told you before why not.'

She saw a flash of impatience. 'It's only a ball, Mara, not a marriage contract.'

Her jaw tightened. *Only a ball*. Like Johnny saying 'just a kiss'. 'No. Sorry.' But he was going to argue. She knew that expression too well.

'Mara, I know you say you'd never marry a priest.'

'Yes.'

'Well, you probably know what I think about that.'

'Yes.' She waited stubbornly.

'I don't suppose – hypothetically, of course – that you'd marry a solicitor?'

Oh, God. 'Not . . . not if he'd given up his calling to the priesthood just because of me.'

'You won't marry me if I'm ordained. You won't marry me if I'm *not* ordained. Good God, what have I got to do? Are you saying you won't marry me, full stop?' He saw her expression. 'You *are* saying that. But I thought – you let me believe that . . .'

Was he remembering that afternoon in the woods and thinking, Maybe that was nothing to her as well? She waited for him to fling accusations at her, call her names, but he did not. It would have been better if he had. Anything would have been better than this white-faced honourable silence.

'I seem to have been incredibly dense,' he said finally.

Her tears spilled over. 'I'm sorry.' But there was a hard kernel of relief in her mind and she hated herself.

'I'd better go.' It was over. 'Sorry if I've been . . . um . . . too persistent.'

'It's OK, Rupert.'

She had a sudden dread of him saying, 'I hope we can always be friends,' and of herself finding it funny. She bit her lips hard. He kissed her cheek and turned to leave. Thank God.

He paused at the door and said in his usual voice. 'I don't suppose you've seen Johnny at all?'

Her hand flew to her throat again. 'Not since yesterday.' She managed to keep her voice level, but her gesture had already betrayed her. He knows. She flushed to the roots of her hair. He left without another word.

The smell of dinner came wafting in through the open window from the dining-hall below. Mara looked at her watch. She and Andrew were meant to be having sherry in the Senior Common Room before the formal meal, and she couldn't decide whether the ordeal of facing it alone was greater than the ordeal of facing Andrew. She pulled on the tatty academic gown she had borrowed from Maddy. She had refused on principle to buy the Cambridge graduate gown she was entitled to wear. Stupid traditions, she thought, scratching at what appeared to be a gravy stain. Andrew would be wearing his immaculate Oxford gown, of course, with its ridiculous long sleeves which looked as though they had been designed for the sole purpose of pinching rare books from the Bodleian without being caught. She could feel her natural belligerence returning. Curious eyes had strayed to her throat at lunchtime, but they had been repelled by her usual offensive stare. The worst ordeal seemed to have been postponed. A rumour was circulating that Johnny had disappeared. His car had gone and no one had seen him all day. She heard the sound of Andrew's footsteps and hardened herself to give as good as she got. He knocked and entered. She looked him in the face and realized with a sinking heart that he already knew. He must have been in his room last night after all. He drew close and ran a cool finger down her neck. She tried her blank stare.

'Tacky,' he said. 'Whitaker's workmanship, I presume?'

'Why ask? I bet you had your ear to the wall.' He did not deny it.

'Well, tell me all about it, then. Is he good? How does he compare with Rupert? Let's hear your verdict on their respective techniques.' He straightened her gown for her and tucked her hair back, successfully conveying the idea that she looked dishevelled and whorish.

She pushed his hand away and said tightly, 'We didn't do it, actually.'

313

'*You didn't do it, actually?*' She hated it when he repeated her words like this, like a tutor picking a clumsy phrase out of an undergraduate essay. 'Why not, Princess?'

'You wouldn't understand.'

'Why do women always say that? *You wouldn't understand.* It's so patronizing. How do you know I wouldn't?'

'We're going to be late.' She made for the door, but he pulled her back.

'No. Come on. Why wouldn't I understand? Because I'm incapable of emotional insight? Because I'm a man? Because I'm gay?' She snatched her arm away and left the room. He pursued her down the stairs. 'Why? Come on, why?'

She turned and burst out, 'Because you've got no conscience.'

'Ah, *conscience*, was it? That great preserver of chastity. Your conscience or his?' He caught her by the gown and looked into her face. Her hands clenched into fists. 'Yours? I respect you, Mara. And at what point did this conscience of yours kick into play? Before you'd got your skirt round your neck and his face in your cunt?'

'Shut up. Just shut up!' She wrenched her sleeve free and ran down the last flight of stairs. He caught her again on the landing outside the Senior Common Room.

'Just one small point of etiquette before we drop the subject. As far as I'm concerned, Mara, you can shag the entire University 1st XV. That's perfectly OK. Or you can decide at the last minute you won't do it, *actually*. That's also OK. But what isn't OK is bleating about your conscience afterwards. Nobody wants to know, Mara. It isn't interesting.'

Her anger mounted with every sneering word. She knew he was hurt and jealous, but he was not going to get away with this. 'Oh, just because you're not getting any, Queenie.'

He went white. 'Fuck you, you slut!'

Rage blotted out everything. She slapped his face with the whole force of her arm. The noise ricocheted smartly round the hallway. For a second she stood admiring the sound, amazed at what she had done, then she saw he was going to retaliate. She turned to run but he caught her by the gown at the foot of the stairs, hauled her back and slapped her so hard she cried out. They rolled on the stairs pulling hair, hitting, calling names, until a voice like a whip cracked across the landing.

'What the *hell* do you think you're doing?'

314

The Principal revealed in his wrath. Behind him a sea of astonished faces: the entire Senior Common Room and the old farts from the college council. They all stared open-mouthed at the model postgrads sprawled on the stairs.

'I will not tolerate this kind of behaviour from my students. Kindly conduct this altercation elsewhere.'

There was a swirl of black gown. He was gone. The silence was long and utter. Mara sat appalled. From below came the sound of the students rising to their feet as High Table entered, then the Principal's voice saying grace, the rumbled 'Amen', and finally the hubbub of talk.

'Oh, God,' said Andrew. He was laughing. A moment later Mara joined in. They laughed till they wept.

Mara pressed a hand to her stinging cheek. 'You really hurt me, you sod.'

'Tough titty. That's the nuts and bolts of sexual equality, my girl.'

'You hit me twice as hard as I hit you!'

'And that,' he said with his most fiendish smile, 'is the incontrovertible fact of male superiority. Come on.' He pulled her to her feet and led her to the nearest bathroom where they both splashed water on their burning faces. They were still shaking with laughter.

'You're the most immoral, nasty, vindictive bastard I've ever met, Andrew Jacks.' He looked up at her from the towel. She could still see the slap-mark on his face quite clearly, and her laughter began to tilt over into tears. 'Andrew, look, I'm –'

He laid a finger on her lips. 'Don't say it, Mara.'

'Yeah, yeah. Love means never having to say you're sorry.'

'Love means I get to treat you like shit and you always forgive me.' He leant forward and kissed her gently on the cheek where he had hit her. She locked her arms round his neck and he hugged her hard. They stood for a long time without speaking.

At last she said into his gown, 'Why do I love you so much?'

He stroked her hair and murmured, 'Because you're sexually disfunctional.' She shoved him away. He grinned, and straightened his gown. She watched him smoothing his hair in the mirror. 'Ready?'

What? Go down and join the meal? 'You're kidding! Andrew, we can't possibly!'

He put out a hand. 'Come on.'

She hung back. 'What will they think?'

'Who gives a bugger?' He clicked his fingers. 'Come on. Walk, or be dragged. You choose.'

315

Suddenly she thought, What the hell. I have nothing left to lose.

They went down the stairs arm in arm and entered the dining-hall to the barrage of hissing and spoon-banging which always greeted latecomers to formal meals. Mara slid into the nearest seat wishing she was dead, but Andrew observed the proper etiquette. She watched as he bowed sardonically to the Principal and to the Senior Man, then, raising a leisurely two fingers to the baying rabble, he took his place at the other end of the table. A lesson in Ph.D-level chutzpah. She saw him grin at her before beginning a conversation with the old fart on his left. He's the only man in the whole world I could spend the rest of my life with, she thought.

'That was *death*,' said Mara after the meal was over and they were back in Andrew's room. He grinned and put the kettle on. She thought again about the Principal's face. 'Ought we to apologize?'

'Oh, I'll drop him a note.' Hah, thought Mara. Like hell you will. He saw her expression and got out his fountain pen.

'Watch me.' She leant over his shoulder. Expensive notepaper. Naturally. *Dear Principal*, he wrote. *I cannot tell you how deeply I regret the scene you witnessed earlier this evening. I assure you it will not happen again*. He signed it and looked up at her. It was such a shameless piece of equivocation that she couldn't help grinning.

'Whisky?' She shuddered and shook her head. 'Oho. A hangover. So that was it.' She scowled. 'A little word of advice, Princess. If you don't want to screw them, don't get drunk with them.'

'I was drunk before he arrived,' she snapped.

He tutted at this. 'A little off-side, I fear, Whitaker.' He handed her a mug of coffee.

I'm going to cry, she thought in dismay. *A little off-side*. I can't bear to have it trivialized like that.

Andrew sat down on the bed beside her and said more seriously, 'Look, Mara, if you feel like this about him, why don't you sleep with him? Would it be so very wrong?'

'I knew he'd regret it. I don't want to be his sin. I don't want to be repented of.'

'I think you're underestimating the flexibility of the Whitaker conscience.'

'He would have regretted it,' she repeated stubbornly.

'All right,' said Andrew after a long silence. 'And now let's have the real reason. You were scared, Princess.'

316

She burst into tears. 'I wasn't!' she spat out at last.

'Of course you were. I've never met anyone as uptight about sex as you are, Mara.'

'I'm not!' she sobbed. 'It was him. He was ... Andrew, he's just too strong! He wasn't listening. I said no, but he wouldn't listen!' Her voice rose in terror.

'What – he raped you?' He was staring at her in amazement.

'He tried to. He was going to!'

'You're joking.'

'I knew you wouldn't believe me!'

'Oh, come on. I'm sure he's not above an opportunistic legover if you were drunk and seemed willing. But rape?'

'I said, "Don't make me," and he just put his hand over my mouth.'

'Well, maybe he thought I could hear through the wall.'

'You think I'm over-reacting!'

'Well, aren't you? You weren't raped, were you? He did the honourable thing.'

'You're on his side. You think I was asking for it!'

'I'm not on anyone's side, for God's sake.'

'You don't know what it feels like!' she shouted. 'To be ... to be overpowered. There was nothing I could do! He's five times stronger than I am.'

He put an arm round her. 'I know. Poor baby. I'm sorry you had a bad time.' He hugged her, waiting till her tears began to subside. 'You should have told him you were scared, instead of that crap about him regretting it. Well, so much for his legendary way with women. Either he didn't realize you were scared, or else he didn't care. I'm not sure which is worse.' He was angry.

'I don't understand you. You admit you treat me like shit, yet you mind if someone else hurts me.'

'Naturally. You're my whipping boy, not his. I've put a lot of effort into our relationship.'

'Well, *thanks*.'

'My pleasure. You're going to have to talk to him when he comes back, you realize.'

'I daren't.'

'You will, though. Or I'll go and tell him what you've just told me.'

'No!'

'Come on. He's not a monster.'

'He behaved like one.'

Andrew stood up and put on a cassette. Plainsong. She listened as the chanting voices wove their long, clear thread of music. He poured himself some whisky and let out another long sigh.

'You're sick of me,' she said.

'Don't be stupid.' He sat down beside her again and leant back against the wall. 'Come on,' he said, reaching out an arm. She rested her head on his chest listening to his slow heartbeat. The voices sang on, chaste and passionate, and her head rose and fell slightly with his breathing. She began to drowse. After a while she heard his heartbeat quicken. His hand began to smooth her hair back from her forehead. He took a mouthful of whisky and swallowed.

'For what it's worth, I do know what it feels like. I had a pretty rough initiation, as it happens.' She dared not move. His voice sounded calm, but his hand trembled slightly as he continued to stroke her hair. 'Some man I had a thing about. I probably made a nuisance of myself. I was sixteen. Anyway. I was drunk and he took me back to his place. Before I knew what was happening, he had a friend there with him.' He paused and drank some more whisky. 'Basically they just took turns. I imagine I was being taught a lesson.' He drew a deep breath and she felt the tremor at the end of it. 'Christ. I thought I was over this.' He was crying. He hugged her head close to him, not letting her look up and see. She lay still in his arms, weeping for him. Eventually she felt the tension leave his body. He wiped his eyes on his sleeve and downed the rest of his whisky. A moment later he let her sit up.

'Do you hate them?' she asked.

He stared down at his glass for a long time before speaking. 'No. Not really.' He looked up at her. 'In the end you're responsible for how you deal with what's happened to you.'

'But – no matter what it was?'

'I think so.'

'But that's . . . It's very harsh, Andrew.'

'Yes.' The tape ended with a click and they sat in silence. 'Look, Mara, you can waste your whole life hating and blaming. Yourself or other people. I'd just rather move on.'

'I can't.'

He shrugged. 'That's your choice.'

'It's not a choice. You can't say that! What if people have been hurt so much that they can't help themselves?'

'Then they need a saviour.' He stood up and crossed himself like a priest in a pulpit. 'In the name of the Father, and of the Son . . .' He poured himself some more whisky. She watched as he raised the glass sardonically.

I hate them even if you don't, she thought. *Taking turns*. I can't bear it. 'But are you happy?' she persisted.

He leant back against the desk and watched her in amusement. 'As a sandboy.' She saw a flicker of a grin. 'And I have great sex, Princess.'

'Stop boasting.'

'Another time,' he said, 'just knock on the wall and I'll come and take him off your hands.'

The days went slowly past. Johnny did not return. Various theories circulated about his absence. Mara bore them in silence. She began to wonder if Andrew was right. After all, he was a shrewder judge of character than she was. He has to be right, she said to herself. Johnny wouldn't have forced me. It was my fault for not saying how scared I was.

The exam period was drawing to a close and she found herself longing for the end of term. She had almost decided to abandon her research in order to paint, but she was held back by worries about money. If she devoted herself to painting she would starve. If she got a job to support herself she would have no time to paint. Apart from evenings and weekends, of course, but if she was only going to paint in her spare time, why not combine it with a Ph.D instead? She could return home to her parents, but the thought was more than she could bear. As her mind was tramping wearily round this circuit of possibilities after lunch one day, there was a knock on the door. She leapt, but it was only May.

'The kettle's just boiled,' Mara said. May made herself some coffee and went and sat beside Mara at the window. They both gazed down at the students sunbathing on the terrace and at the riverbank below them.

'Maddy's gone to revise in Cuchulain's room,' said May. This was her name for Kieran. 'Revise, ha ha. They're sleeping together, you know. Do you think it's wrong?' Only vicars' daughters could still ask that, thought Mara.

'I think Maddy thinks it is.'

'They're for ever springing apart when I come into the room. I refuse to knock on principle. Why should I? It's my room, too.' She began to pick at the blistered paint on the window sill. 'I have to trample noisily up the stairs so that they can unglue themselves from one another's orifices in time.' She's really upset about it, thought Mara in surprise. May sighed. 'Oh, well. It's that time of year, I suppose. The pheremones are all frolicking and the young man's fancy turns lightly to the thought of love.' There was a pause, and Mara discerned the faint spectre of Andrew hovering on the fringes of May's conversation. How would she work the topic round? They were both staring down at the riverbank and the wind ruffling the leaves.

'The silver lining is that I've been driven to revise for my exams by sheer boredom.' Mara smiled down into her mug. 'Who knows? I may even get decent results.'

'Whatever Andrew says,' remarked Mara helpfully.

'He's such a bastard, isn't he?'

'Yes.'

'But you like him?'

'Yes.'

'He likes you, too.'

'Yes.'

'I mean, he seems to like you a *lot*.'

'In what way?' asked Mara, no longer wishing to be helpful.

'Well, you know. He's always . . . touching you.' May was picking at the paint again. 'I mean, if you didn't *know* he was gay, you wouldn't realize, would you? Necessarily.' Mara made no reply. There was another pause. 'Do you suppose that anyone ever stops being homosexual?' Cured by the love of a good woman, thought Mara. I'd hate to be the one to suggest it to him.

'I think,' she said carefully, 'he'd find the idea a bit patronizing.'

May flushed. 'I meant people in general. I wasn't thinking of him in particular.'

'No.'

They fell silent again. May stealthily wiped away a tear. Mara's heart went out to her suddenly, but she didn't know whether it was kinder to say something or pretend she hadn't noticed. May covered her face with her hands and started to sob.

'Oh, I've hated this term so much!' Mara put an awkward hand on

320

her shoulder. 'I'm jealous of you sometimes, Mara. You're always so calm and aloof. Nothing seems to affect you.'

Mara's mouth dropped open in amazement. 'That's not actually true.'

May sobbed all the harder. 'I know. I'm sorry. You had a horrible time last term and your sister died. I shouldn't be jealous. I'm just selfish, I know I am, but I'm so miserable.' She buried her head in Mara's shoulder and clung on to her sobbing. Do women always blame themselves for their misery? wondered Mara.

May sat up and blew her nose.

'It'll be all right,' said Mara, feeling totally inadequate. 'Everything seems worse at exam time.'

'I know. I'm just being silly. I wish I was more like you. You're so clever. You always seem in control. And you've got the best-looking men in college running after you.' Mara disclaimed. 'It's true. And you're beautiful.'

'Actually, according to Andrew, I've only been beautiful twice this academic year. He says the rest of the time I'm indescribably plain.'

May giggled and wiped her eyes. 'He said that? Is that why you smacked his face?' Mara sighed. Too much to hope that the whole college wasn't discussing the incident. The phrase 'Kindly conduct this altercation elsewhere' had passed into legend.

'No. That was for something else.'

Before May could pursue this there was a knock on the door. The devil himself. He came in grinning and handed Mara a note. The Principal's reply. *My dear Andrew*, it said. *Your note was unnecessary. I have known you too long to harbour any doubts about the depth and sincerity of your regret.* Mara laughed out loud and Andrew whisked the letter back before May could read it. He looked down at her and raised an eyebrow.

'Not working, little one?'

May blushed. 'I was just going, *actually*.' She left with a fair assumption of nonchalance.

'Be kind to her,' Mara said.

'I am. In my way.'

'She's in love with you.'

'And with you.'

'*What?*'

'Oh, just a schoolgirl pash on the young Latin mistress, that sort of thing. Don't let it worry you.'

'Don't be ridiculous!'

'She adores you. Thinks you're wonderfully cool and aloof and beautiful.' Mara's hand flew to her mouth. Suddenly it sounded possible.

'Oh, God. What am I going to to do?' He smiled his hateful smile.

'Be kind to her, Princess.' He made himself some coffee while her mind tangled itself helplessly in the web of attractions that seemed to weave her group of friends together. 'She'll grow out of it,' he said, sitting down beside her.

'It's not sexual, though.'

'Isn't it? But then, the line's so blurred,' he said, trailing a finger down her bare arm. 'Don't you think?' She looked at him in dismay as a new thought formed. Then she saw he was laughing at her.

'Will you stop arsing around?' she said.

'No. Will you come and live with me in Oxford?' There was a pause as these words sank in.

'What? What do you mean?'

'I've decided to accept the research fellowship after all. Accommodation is part of the deal, and I want a flatmate.'

'Why are you asking me?'

'It's part of my long-term plan of humanizing you.'

'Why – but – um . . .' She put her hands over her mouth and laughed. 'How much a month?'

'Nothing. I get it rent-free. But if you'd prefer me to fleece you, I will.'

'What's in it for you?'

'I need an Aunt Sally. My psychological well-being suffers if I've got no one to victimize.' She realized she wasn't going to extract a serious answer from him.

'But aren't you worried I'll bugger up your morning routine?'

'I'll be issuing house rules, Princess. No banned substances, no answering back, and don't bring home any muscle-bound brickies.'

'Unless it's your birthday, and they're giftwrapped.'

'You cheeky bitch.' He stood up to leave. 'Let me know. Oh, this came for you, by the way.' He handed her a letter. The handwriting was unfamiliar. 'From the prodigal.'

Johnny! She flinched. Andrew laid a hand briefly on her shoulder and left. She tore the envelope open.

Dear Mara,

I'm sorry for what happened the other night. I didn't come round with the intention of trying my luck. I suppose I should have left as soon as I realized how drunk you were, but old habits die hard. I did warn you what I'm like. Anyhow, I'm sorry. It's not your fault I'm in a mess. I'm at the friary now trying to sort myself out, but I'll be back on Saturday. Will you come and talk to me? Forget what I said at the time. I don't really blame you.

Johnny.

She read the letter again, and then a third time. She could hear his voice speaking as she read, and tears of relief poured down her face. He was sorry. He didn't blame her. She raised her head and looked at the swimming green of the trees through her tears. I do still trust him. Oh, don't let me be wrong. The letter sounded so genuine, he might almost have been in the room pleading with her. Today's Monday, she thought. Five days till he comes back. She looked up at the blue sky and her heart mounted up on wings till the City lay spread beneath her like a child's toy. If I'm wrong now, then God help me. God help me.

CHAPTER 24

She woke in the sunlight to hear a robin singing down on the riverbank. The bells chimed six and Andrew's words came back to her: 'You are responsible for how you deal with what's happened to you.' Perhaps he was right? She was wasting her life 'hating and blaming'. She had assumed that by renouncing her faith she put herself for ever beyond the pale, outside the fold. But now it struck her that the fold might be far larger than she had supposed, and that she might, in fact, still be inside it. Well, I'm not bloody well going to church, she thought. She listened to her tone. She sounded like an angry child being bribed with a present: *I'm not opening it. I hate you all. I don't want it!* She smiled. Someone somewhere was laughing at her again.

She got out of bed and crossed to the window. Three days till Johnny came back. Her stomach tightened. She'd have to go and talk to him. She could picture his anger if Andrew got there first with his version. The wind ruffled the leaves of the copper beech on the riverbank. What was she going to say to Johnny? Her mind went over his letter again for the thousandth time. Doubts had started to creep in. *'I don't really blame you.* What was that 'really' doing in there? It implied the opposite: he *did* blame her. And maybe he was right to do so. To her dismay, her thoughts kept slithering back to that night. Those hard, slow kisses, his hand up between her thighs. A voice whispered, You should never have stopped him.

I can't face him, she told herself. Watching his hands as he lights a cigarette, knowing what those fingers have done to me. And to all the other women before me. When he grins at me, I'll think he's remembering. 'Mmm, mmm. Not as cool and sophisticated as you like to think you are, young lady.'

Later, as she sat at her desk working, she found herself thinking, I can survive. Only another few weeks and I'll be painting in Oxford and I'll never have to see Johnny again. She had accepted Andrew's humanitarian offer, and later that morning she was going to go and break the news to Dr Roe. She intended to write up her MA and submit it, because she found it impossible to abandon something she had undertaken to do. But after that . . . freedom. Would her friends all think her mad? Would her parents 'rather disappointed, but if that's really what you want to do, darling, then you must do it, of course'.

How do I know I'm right? she asked herself. As she wondered, a picture came into her mind. It was her moorland. She had not seen it for months. There was the dark winter heather and the pale sky leaning on the hillside. The earth beneath seemed to crackle faintly with expectation. The curlew's cry. Soon it would be spring. This is what she'd paint first. She saw the canvas. Two thirds dark for the steep moor and stream, then the top left-hand corner white for the sky, as though it had been torn back to let the light through. She held the picture in her mind. Strong diagonals, dark, light, dark, light. Space and depth and movement. It shone for her as though it was lit up from behind.

Does art have to be selfish to survive? she wondered. She remembered herself as she was when she first arrived in the City, vowing to remain alone and have no friends. She did not wish herself back. Maddy and May, Andrew, Rupert. Johnny, even. Well, if you invite people in, then they can't be blamed for making themselves at home.

She set off early for her tutorial, intending to wander along the riverbank and plan what she would say. She took her sketch-book to show Dr Roe. After a good deal of heart-searching she had decided not to tear out the pictures of Andrew she had done during the Easter vacation. Dr Roe would have to form her own conclusions, she thought, running down the flight of steps that led to the Principal's study. As she passed his door, her conscience began to crackle like a Geiger counter. She had never apologized. She carried on and the crackling doubled. She sighed and retraced her steps. With a bit of luck he'd be out. But when she knocked, he called her in. She entered red-faced with her sketch book clamped to her chest like a breastplate. The Principal raised an inquiring eyebrow.

'I came to say sorry about the other night.'

He inclined his head. 'Thank you, Mara.'

There was a silence. Was that it? Should she just turn round again and blunder back out? But by then she had already paused long enough to suggest that she had something else to say. She cast about desperately. He was not helping, and it occurred to her that he might be paying her back for all the times she had done the same to him.

She hit upon a handy idea: 'I also came to say goodbye. I'll be leaving at the end of this term. I've decided not to do a Ph.D after all. I'm moving to Oxford, where I'm going to paint.'

'Ah, yes.' He leant forward with interest and motioned for her to sit. 'I'd gathered that you were good at drawing.' She sat down and gawped at him. He gestured apologetically. 'One tends to hear these things in my position.' Hah. One bloody well tends to ferret them out, you mean. 'A courageous move,' he said in a drawing-out-the-interviewee tone. She made no response and after a moment he took a pair of half-moon glasses out of his breast pocket and put them on. 'It's good to take stock now and then. Do a personal audit, as it were, and be prepared to ask whether a complete change of direction might be called for. I try to make a point of asking myself that from time to time.' He lapsed back into silence, resting his elbows on the desk and joining his fingertips prayerfully. Mara saw the ghost of a mitre shimmering over his head. He roused himself. 'However, as often as not it's simply a case of waiting for the right thing to come along.'

'Or the Right Reverend thing,' agreed Mara.

He looked at her over the top of his glasses for what felt like twenty seconds. 'I think I'm going to forget you said that.' She hung her head, biting her lips in a desperate attempt not to laugh. When she looked up again, she saw a gleam of amusement in his eyes. He reached out and said, 'May I?' For a wild moment she thought he was asking for her hand to hold or kiss. Then she realized with a blush that he was indicating her sketch-book.

She was so flustered she unfused it from her chest and handed it over. The nude pictures! Well, sod it. Let him think what he likes. He adjusted his glasses and opened the book. She watched his face as he turned the pages. He was far too civilized to betray shock or surprise. He was looking with careful interest, sometimes smiling in recognition or amusement at the various students and City scenes she had captured. He was nearing the end. Pictures of Andrew sitting in his armchair reading and ignoring her. She had spent a couple of hours the previous night doing them. The Principal looked up and removed his glasses.

'Very good indeed. You have a real gift.' She mumbled something and began twiddling her plait. He put his glasses back on and leafed through the book again. 'What a wonderful record of the summer term. I think, however . . .' He removed his glasses and folded them carefully. She watched as his hand hovered with them above his pocket, and willed him to put them in. 'I think the pictures of Andrew are in a different class. I don't pretend to be a judge, but there's a certain detachment in the others. They're shrewdly observed, but . . .' – he unfolded the glasses again and made as if to put them back on – 'there seems to be a deeper level of insight and observation here. Possibly a greater emotional engagement?'

She blushed. This was what she had been attempting, but she was surprised it showed so clearly.

'Well, he's a good friend, I suppose.' The Principal inclined his head at this muttered declaration. It sounded so inadequate that Mara added: 'Actually, we're going to share a flat in Oxford.'

'Aha,' said the Principal with a smile. 'A fate you both richly deserve.' He rose to his feet. She got up too. 'Well, Mara, I shall follow your progress with interest. I'm sorry we're losing you, but I wish you every success. I've very much enjoyed having you as part of the college.' She flushed, thinking she detected irony. He put out a hand. She fumbled one out in return and he shook it warmly. 'Go well. God bless you.'

He really meant it, she realized. On impulse she said, 'Would you like a picture for your wall?'

'I'd be delighted, Mara.' He had to say that, of course.

She opened the book. Which one, for God's sake? After a moment's dithering she tore out the last picture in the book. Andrew reading. She thrust it at the Principal and escaped. As she ran down the stairs she imagined him peering at it through his glasses and thinking, Oh, dear, how unfortunate. Still, we can always put it in the box room, I suppose.

Mara met Dr Roe coming out of a meeting in the professor's study. They walked up the stairs together in silence. She could see that her tutor was upset. When they were in her room, Dr Roe said without preamble, 'This is awful. One of our First Years is going to fail her prelims completely. She hasn't turned up for any of her papers. Apparently the Lord told her not to.' Joanna. 'I can't believe anyone would do that. It sounds like . . . *fanaticism*. Like something out of your thesis. I gather it all started in a prayer meeting in your college. Did you go?'

'No.'

'People passing out and speaking in tongues and so on. You'll have heard about it, I'm sure.'

'A little.'

'And the Maths department's hopping mad because one of their brightest Second Years is barely answering a single question in his exams. Which they seem to think is *our* fault in some way, because he's a friend of hers.' Not the gorilla, thought Mara in dismay. 'What do you make of it all?'

'The same old story. Renewal spilling over into fanaticism.'

'Ah, so there's such a thing as genuine renewal, but it gets out of hand?'

'Maybe.' Do I believe that? 'Or else people exploit it for their own ends.'

'Yes,' said Dr Roe. 'I taught her, you know.'

'Joanna?'

'Yes.' There was a silence.

'What did you . . . make of her?'

'Nothing. That's just the problem. She always seemed . . . not sly, exactly. Evasive. I never felt I was making any kind of real contact with her. It was as though there was something *missing*. A sense of reality, maybe.'

'No. It's a different reality.'

'Go on,' prompted Dr Roe.

'A different universe. This world is just the stage for spiritual warfare. We're living in Armageddon. And she's the focal point for all the action.'

'That's what she thinks?'

'I'm guessing.'

'Delusions of grandeur. Isn't that a symptom of schizophrenia?'

'Possibly. I don't think that's the problem, though.'

'What is it, then?'

'Attention-seeking. On a cosmic scale.'

'Ah. Thank you. That's helpful. It's a pity it's outside your period, or you could include a chapter on it,' said Dr Roe. 'Anyway. Do sit down. Coffee?'

Mara nodded. She was surprised Dr Roe had confided in her. Maybe we could have been friends, she thought, now it was too late to do anything about it. As the kettle boiled, Mara tried to remember the first sentence of her prepared speech, but before she could find her starting place, Dr Roe spoke.

'I'm afraid I've got a confession to make, Mara. I'd have told you earlier, only nothing was certain. I've been offered a post in Oxford, starting this October.' Mara smiled. 'I'm really sorry to mess you around like this, but I do hope we can work something out. Maybe –'

'It's OK,' interrupted Mara. 'I came to tell you I've decided not to do the doctorate after all. I'm going to paint.' She felt her smile broaden. 'In Oxford, in fact. I'm sharing a flat with a friend.'

'Oh, wonderful!'

Mara shrank back slightly from her tutor's enthusiasm and said frigidly, 'I intend to finish the MA, of course.'

'Well, I'd be delighted to carry on supervising you informally.'

'Thanks.' She really seems pleased, Mara thought.

Dr Roe made coffee, and Mara noticed she was glancing at her sketch-book. 'Oh, I wanted you to see these.' She handed it over awkwardly. 'If you're interested.' Stop begging for affirmation, she told herself.

'I'd love to.' She watched nervously as Dr Roe opened the book. There lay Andrew in all his glory. 'Oh – Andrew Jacks!' she exclaimed. 'I wondered if you two knew each other.' Mara stifled a gauche explanation. 'His brother's an old friend of mine.' She smiled down at the picture and shook her head. 'That boy. He's *so* beautiful. How do you know him? Through college?'

'His room's next to mine.'

Dr Roe turned a page. 'I first met him when he was about fifteen. He used to come up to Oxford to see Alex.'

'What was he like then?'

'Oh, terrifying. Sophisticated. Incorrigibly gay, of course. He loved shocking people. Especially me,' she added with feeling. 'I was a terribly naïve eighteen-year-old. I can remember one party in particular. I must have spent about half an hour talking to this incredibly beautiful girl in a black leather miniskirt. Andrew, of course. I wondered what Alex was smirking about.' Yes, oh yes! 'I still couldn't believe it when I was told.'

'You don't have a photo, by any chance?' Dr Roe laughed and shook her head.

'He swans in here periodically and criticizes my taste. Calling me "Jane", like that, as if it were in inverted commas. I wonder why I put up with it.' Dr Roe continued turning the pages, smiling as the Principal had done at the pictures of the cathedral and the students.

'Actually,' said Mara, 'he's the one I'm sharing a flat with.'

Dr Roe looked up. 'You are? Wonderful. So he accepted that research fellowship, then. I wasn't sure he could bear to be at the same university as Alex.' This was an angle on Andrew which had intrigued Mara before.

'Why? Don't they get on?'

Dr Roe laughed. 'You'll find out soon enough. They compete. Over everything. Sport, music, number of publications, who they know, what they've read.'

Mara bit her lips. At last. This was the ammunition Rupert had failed to supply her with. 'At least they specialize in different fields,' she said, hoping to draw out more.

'Ah, yes, but they spend hours reading up the other's subject so that they can be casually erudite about it.' Mara covered her smile. Did they also specialize in different sexual fields, or were they constantly competing for the same lovers? 'But having said that, they're intensely loyal and think the world of one another. Although neither would admit it. It's all very childish.'

Dr Roe was almost at the end of the sketch-book. Mara remembered belatedly that she hadn't responded to the news of her Oxford appointment.

'Congratulations, by the way.'

'Oh, you'd heard.' Dr Roe coloured slightly. It was then that Mara caught sight of the ring. 'Paul's a registrar in Oxford. Our careers seem to have meshed at last. We're getting married in August.'

Having said congratulations once by accident Mara was at a loss. She tried to think what her mother would have said. *That's wonderful!* Somehow she couldn't get the words out. Dr Roe finished looking at the sketches and handed them back. 'Thank you. I love them. Especially the ones of Andrew.'

'Thanks,' muttered Mara.

'Just think,' said Dr Roe, 'you'll be able to introduce him to everyone as your live-in model.' A hint of unexpected malice. 'I look forward to seeing more of your work in Oxford.'

Mara gazed out of the window. This was supposed to be a farewell, but here she was tidying up loose ends and closing doors behind her only to find a new beginning. But I'm only good at break-ups and disasters, she thought. Did she dare trust herself to a new friendship?

'Would you ... like a picture? As a wedding present, or something?'

'I'd love one!'

'One of Andrew?'

There was a pause.

'Dare I? Yes. Why not?'

Mara tore one out: Andrew sprawled on the bed, naked, drunk and beautiful. What will Paul the registrar think? Or Andrew, for that matter?

Dr Roe took the picture. 'Thank you, Mara. I'll have it framed and hang it in my new rooms.'

Oh, God. Mara finished her coffee and stood up. 'Um, actually, Andrew doesn't know I've given you that. He may be . . . um, well . . .' Seriously pissed off, was what sprang to mind.

Dr Roe hesitated. 'Does that bother you?'

But then Mara thought of all the insults and humiliations she had suffered at Andrew's hands. 'Not particularly,' she said after a long pause.

Dr Roe looked down at the picture again, then up at Mara. 'Good.'

They both smiled slowly. Mara glimpsed what was in the other woman's mind: next time Andrew came swanning in to criticize her artistic taste, he was in for a small surprise. Yes, she thought, 'Jane' and I could get on extremely well. She said goodbye, and left Dr Roe still smiling.

On her way back to college, she saw Rupert coming towards her. They both hesitated for a moment before continuing. He had not spoken to her since the day he had walked out of her room, but she had seen him in the distance several times looking bleak with misery. He drew close and stopped.

'How are you, Mara?'

'Fine. How are you?'

'I'm fine.'

The bells chimed midday. They were both blushing and staring past one another down the street.

'I've just been to see Dr Roe,' Mara gabbled before the silence got too firm a hold. 'She's getting married in August.'

'Yes,' said Rupert, picking up the baton she had fumbled and dropped. 'Who'll be supervising you after she's gone?'

'Actually, I'm not doing a doctorate after all. I'm leaving.' This brought his eyes swiftly to her face.

'You are? Why?' *'I'm going to have a baby!'* blurted the anguished girl.

'I've decided to paint instead.'

He looked blank. 'Paint?'

'You know – pictures. I want to be an artist.'

'Really? But can you paint? I mean . . . Of course, that sounds wonderful. I had no idea.' She watched him trying to dig himself back out. 'And it's not something you could combine with doing a doctorate at all?'

'It's not a *hobby*.'

'Well, I'm sure you've thought it all through.'

'Yes, I have.' There was a dangerous pause, and then she saw him back off.

'Well, good. Are those some of your drawings? May I see?' She was too conscious of having wronged him to refuse.

'You can if you promise not to be shocked.'

'I *am* aware that artists use nude models, Mara,' he said irritably. She handed the sketches over and they both sat on the low wall. He opened the book, stared, then looked up at her open-mouthed.

'You said you wouldn't be shocked.'

'Yes, but . . .' He looked at the first picture of Andrew again. 'I assumed you'd been to life-drawing classes, or something.'

'Well, what's the difference?' She knew there was one, but that he wouldn't risk trying to define it.

He turned a page and adjusted his responses suitably, saying in a grown-up voice, 'They're very well drawn.' This was the tone her mother used when describing *Lady Chatterley's Lover* as beautifully written.

'It's the cross-hatching,' she murmured.

He shot her a suspicious look before continuing to turn the pages seriously, thoughtfully, not too fast, until at last he came to some sketches of other students (fully clothed).

'Phew,' said Mara for him.

He laughed. 'Shut up, you dreadful girl.' For a moment it seemed as if they were friends again. He went on turning the pages. 'I take it back. You really can draw. These are excellent, Mara. How do you do it? Look, that's Maddy exactly. And May. And me! Good grief. When did you do that?' All was going well until he came to the sketch of Johnny stripped to the waist leaning on the sink. Rupert reddened and fell silent.

'That was in your room, remember? When you were throwing Joanna out of his bed, or whatever it was. He'd been out running.' But her tone was too desperate.

'I remember.' He turned the remaining pages in silence, then handed her back the book. 'Thank you. They're very good, Mara.'

She mumbled something and wondered how she was going to get away.

'Where are you going to live? With your parents?'

'Actually, with Andrew,' she said, trying not to sound defiant. 'In Oxford.'

'Ah.' She longed to stand up and run off, but knew she owed it to him to see it through. Her feelings of guilt were hardening into resentment. 'I had no idea you could draw, Mara.'

It sounded like a rebuke and she was stung into saying, 'Well, there's a lot about me you don't know, isn't there?' He winced. 'Look, I'm just not a nice person, Rupert.'

'More sinned against than sinning,' replied Rupert. She opened her mouth as if to protest, but he went on: 'Look, Mara, at the risk of embarrassing you, I think I'm in a position to know how . . . passionate you are, and . . . What I'm saying is, it would be easy for a man to take advantage of that. I've a pretty good idea where the blame really lies.' When she made no reply, he put a hand on her arm. It took all her willpower not to fling it off and scream, 'You don't understand, you fool! I want him. I'd do the same again!'

'It takes two, Rupert.'

He removed his hand. They stood up. The pain on his face made her want to hurt him even more.

'Oxford,' he said, gathering his manners about him. 'You'll enjoy it. Andrew's got a research fellowship, or something, hasn't he? I was a student there. I still go up now and then to see friends.' She knew she was supposed to say, 'Oh, you must come and see us.'

'Oh, you must come and see us.'

'Thank you. I'd like that.'

He gave her his formal little bow and walked off. She made her way miserably back to college.

She woke, and a sudden realization jolted her out of bed. Today. Johnny gets back today. She showered and dressed and began to walk fitfully around her room. She didn't know what time he'd be back. She pictured herself having to knock at his door. Repeatedly. I'll wait till late afternoon, she decided. He's sure to be back by then. She went to her desk and fiddled desperately with her card file index. I know – I'll tidy my desk. Use the time profitably.

Almost at once she came upon the photographs her mother had sent her earlier that term. Dewi. Aunt Judith at the piano with the curate. She stared at the face under the elaborate hat. We have the same shape jaw. What was she like? How had she come to crash her plane on a clear, fine day when everyone knew she was such a good pilot? What am I not being told about her? Perhaps she was schizophrenic, or something. Maybe she had committed suicide. It's not supposed to be a secret.

Mara put the photograph down and picked up the one of Hester. She stared at the beautiful face for a long time. A year ago she had less than a week to live. What had been going through her mind? Had she stood staring out across Galilee towards those pink hills we loved in the children's Bible? *By blue Galilee, Jesus walked of old. By blue Galilee, wondrous things he told.* We always dreamed of going to the Holy Land together. But she went alone. She had found some new prophecy to cling on to, after the baby had died. Fed into her distraught mind by Leah. The Book of Revelation: the woman clothed with the sun and the moon under her feet. The dragon stood before her ready to devour her child when it was born, and she brought forth a man child who was to rule all nations with a rod of iron, and her child was caught up unto God. It was not really dead. And the woman had to flee from the dragon into the wilderness to a place prepared by God. And we were the dragon, thought Mara, remembering her mother's tears — her family and friends. Everyone who was opposed to the Church of the Revelation were the dragon and his angels, who fought against Michael and his angels.

Suddenly Mara saw what it must have been — postnatal psychosis. Not just another dose of whacky charismatic theology. No wonder their father had got Hester up to the psychiatric ward so fast. He would have recognized the signs. Mara had hated him for it. There was even a part of her that was glad when Hester discharged herself and headed out to the sect's hostel in Israel. But then one night Hester had gone out swimming alone in Galilee and drowned. How could that have happened? She was such a good swimmer. Yes. And Judith was such a good pilot. That's what Mara feared. Proof that both Judith and Hester committed suicide. But Hester left no note. Her sister's face smiled up at her from the photograph, captured for ever in a sunny garden. She felt herself starting to cry and picked up the photo of Dewi instead.

After a moment his face became a stranger's face. What would I think if someone handed me this, and I didn't know anything about him? I'd think he was dangerous. Unbalanced. Potentially violent. I wouldn't say, 'Excuse me, would you mind putting that cigarette out?' if he were in a no-smoking area. Where is he now? Would I still worship him if I met him again now after all these years? She was weeping again at the thought that her feelings for Johnny were just a rerunning of her feelings for her cousin. She loved them both and now they were both gone. Even if she went to talk to Johnny it would do no good. She'd ruined everything.

After a moment she began to remember someone else's tears. Aunt Susan. Why is she crying? We are in the farm kitchen. The dog. It has to be put down. Uncle Huw says so, and gets the gun.

'It's no good. She's in pain.' Then he turns and hands the gun to Dewi.

'You can't!' says Aunt Susan. 'You can't make him do it. He loves that dog, Huw!' Dewi stares, his whole face raw with disbelief. His hands shake on the gun. 'He's only thirteen,' cries Aunt Susan.

'He's old enough.'

There is a pause. We all stand in silence. I am crying too. Then Dewi turns blindly and goes out with the gun. He whistles and the old dog drags herself faithfully after him. Aunt Susan continues to cry and says, 'You can't expect him to do that, Huw. What kind of a father are you?' She goes on and on, until in the distance we hear a shot. Just one.

Then Huw turns to her. 'I will not stand by and see my son turned into a pansy by his mother.'

Mara uncovered her face and looked down at the photograph again. Why had her uncle said that? She searched her memory. Something about Dewi and another boy. Something she and Faye weren't supposed to know. She heard Faye's voice taunting, 'Poofter, homo,' saw Dewi's violent response. But what about all those girls in the village? A desperate attempt to prove himself? The pale, dangerous eyes stared up at her. I bet the whole family knows, but won't talk about it. They drove him away. She thought about her uncle, a hard violent man who had never asked himself what he might be turning his son into.

It was nearly three-thirty and she had not been able to stand the suspense any longer. She paused in front of Johnny's door, heart thumping. She knocked. There was no answer. But before she could decide whether to leave a note, there was a sound in the corridor behind her. She turned and saw Johnny's head appear through a small window.

'I thought I heard you,' he said. 'Come and look at this.' What was he doing out there? Driven by curiosity, she went and climbed through the window out into the angle of the roof where he was standing. Her heart was still pattering wildly. She looked around. Nothing but steep slates, chimneys, sky. Then he swung himself up on to a higher level and reached down a hand. She slipped her shoes off and scrambled on to the hot slates and let him pull her up. They were on a flat roof. She looked out.

'Oh!' The whole City lay spread out around them. She forgot what she had come for.

'I thought you'd like it,' he said. 'Like walking on the ice.' The asphalt was warm under her bare feet and she felt the summer air on her cheeks. We're on top of the world. Trees, riverbanks, rooftops, the cathedral rearing up over them, then off in the haze, hills and yellow rape fields. She looked down dizzily on to the college lawns below. Students sunbathing and playing croquet. 'They haven't seen us,' she whispered.

'Aye. They won't. People don't look up this high.'

'I do.'

'You're different.'

What a world! I can fly across it. She walked swiftly to the edge which dropped down to the street four storeys below, but before she could look over, Johnny seized her arm and jerked her back.

'Jesus Christ! Don't do that!'

'Do what?'

She tried to pull away, but he gripped her all the harder, dragging her towards him. Suddenly she thought, What am I doing up here alone with him? I walked straight into a trap!

'Let me go. Please.'

'You just don't think, do you?'

'I didn't realize. I don't want to. I'm saying no!' she cried.

He let go of her arm and said contemptuously, 'No one's asking you, Mara, actually. Just keep back from the edge.'

She flushed scarlet with mortification. 'Sorry.' She watched as he got out a cigarette and lit it.

'For once in my life it hadn't crossed my mind. I just wanted you to see.' He gestured around him. 'Would you rather go down?'

'No. It's OK.' She couldn't meet his gaze.

After a while he said, 'Well, thanks for coming. I just wanted to explain.' She glanced at him. He was looking away, smoking nervously. All his gestures seemed angular. She had never seen him stripped of his flippant manner like this. 'This term. It's just . . . Look, if I'd had my way, I wouldn't even have been here. It's the Bishop. I told him I wanted to leave. Mara, I'm not cut out for this. I don't fit in here, and I never will. But the Bishop wouldn't hear of it. Told me to finish my training, and that he'd talk to me again afterwards. I guess I came back at the start of term thinking well, sod you, Bishop.'

Her temper flared suddenly. 'So that's all I am – proof to the Bishop that you're not fit to be ordained?'

He flushed. 'Don't be daft. Look, OK, I went to your room that night feeling sorry for myself, mad about everything. I just wanted to talk, or go for a drink, or whatever. But there you were, looking so . . . I'm not trying to excuse myself, but bloody hell, Mara. I kept thinking, You ought to go, man. To be honest I was expecting to get my face slapped, not – mmm. Yes, well. There you go.' He stubbed his cigarette out and shrugged. 'Sorry. I did warn you.' His eyes followed the path of a pigeon as it sailed past them. 'And then there was the added incentive of buggering up Rupert's chances.'

'But he's your friend!' He flushed again and lit another cigarette.

'Not right now, he isn't. Did you have to tell him?'

'I didn't! He . . . he must have guessed.'

'Hah.' She quailed at the idea of what he would say if he knew she had told Andrew. 'Look, I'm not proud of myself, Mara, but I tell you – it wasn't easy just standing back watching him and knowing I wasn't in a position to do anything about it.' What was he saying? That he loved her?

'Why did you have to pick on me?' she burst out.

'*Pick on you?* Oh, great. I think I could be forgiven for assuming you didn't mind. At least to begin with.'

'I'm sorry.' He made a visible effort to control his temper.

'Yes. Well, you don't have to be. You're allowed to say no.'

'You're angry.'

'I've got no right to be, have I?' he said tightly. There was a pause. 'But you are.'

'Yes, I bloody well am,' he snapped at last. 'Just give me a break, Mara. I'm doing my best. It's bad enough being turned down like that without having to apologize as well. Jesus. No, don't cry, please, sweetie. I'm sorry. It's OK to say no. You might work on your timing a bit, that's all.'

'I was thinking of you!' she sobbed. 'I knew you'd feel terrible afterwards.'

'Nice of you. Another time leave the decision to me. It's my conscience.'

'I was scared.' There. It was out.

He stared in surprise. 'Scared? Why?'

'I don't know.'

'But what of? Of me?'

'No. Of − I hate it. I've only done it twice. It was horrible both times.'

'Oh, God.' He looked appalled. 'Why didn't you say, sweetie? I'd never . . .'

'I'm sorry.'

'Stop saying that! I'm the one who should be sorry.' He seemed close to tears himself. They stood looking at one another helplessly. Mara heard laughter from the lawn far below. 'Well, so much for salvation,' he said savagely. 'So much for the grace of God. You'd think some of it would've rubbed off on me after all these years, wouldn't you? You were drunk. Terrified. Begging me not to. And does that stop me? No. All I care about is whether I score or not.'

'But you did stop!' She couldn't bear the bitterness in his voice.

He dropped the cigarette and ground it out with his foot. 'Yeah. I could hear Andrew next door.'

'But − you would have done, anyway?' She was almost pleading. There was a horrible silence.

'I hope so.'

'I know you would,' she protested.

'You don't know anything about me, Mara.' He sniffed back the tears and wiped his hand across his eyes. 'God, I'm a mess, aren't I? I'm crying. I never cry. My whole life's a mess.'

'What will you do?'

'God knows. Go back and work for my father. Like the bloody prodigal son. Except he won't welcome me with open arms, that's for sure.'

It's wicked, she thought suddenly. He only wanted to tell people the good news. And he'd have been better at it than half of the self-righteous gits the church ordains without a murmur. She thought of the college chapel full of people who never went to church, all listening as he talked about the lost son and the grace of God. Why has he been made to feel so worthless?

'You're sure you're doing the right thing?'

'Don't start. I've had the Bishop, the Principal, Rupert, everyone all trying to convince me.'

'What will your family say?'

'"Well, our John, we told you. You – a priest? Never. You'll never change. You'll never make anything of yourself. Why can't you be more like your brother?"' She watched his profile. 'I should have listened.'

'You're scared,' she said suddenly.

'*What?*'

'You're scared of failing, so you're wimping out. You're just using sex and drink as an excuse.'

He stared at her, his astonishment rapidly giving way to anger. 'You take that back right now!'

'No. You've got no balls, that's your problem. No moral stamina. When have you ever seen something through to the bitter end just because it was *right*, not because you enjoyed doing it?'

They squared off. She had never seen him so angry.

'You're going to apologize for that!'

'If I'm wrong, why are you so mad about it?'

'Don't you get clever with me! I'm mad because it's not true.'

'You're a quitter.' She turned and started back across the roof.

'Don't you dare walk out on me!' But she swung herself over the edge and slithered down the slates. He was coming after her. 'Fuck you! You take that back.' She didn't answer, just put her shoes back on and slithered through the window while he swore and raged at her to apologize. She was back in the corridor. He stuck his head through the window.

'If I were you, Mara, I wouldn't stand there preaching moral stamina to me. It didn't take much to get you on your back.' She flushed scarlet and turned to run. 'No, wait. Mara, I'm sorry.' He came through the window and caught hold of her arm. She burst into tears. 'Don't cry, flower. Please.' He took her in his arms, and in another second they were kissing, gripped by a desolate, starving lust. Her knees were shaking. Do it. Just do it. Don't ask me. Their breathing filled the corridor. His mouth was burning at her throat, hands sliding up her thighs under her dress.

'Oh, Johnny.' He picked her up and carried her into his room, closing the door after them. They were on the bed. I don't care. Don't let me think. He had her dress undone and was pulling her knickers off, kissing her again and again, as if they both knew that one word, one moment's thought, and they would realize what they were doing. She tugged at his belt.

'Wait, Mara.' He crossed the room swiftly, opened a drawer and came back. He keeps condoms in his room! He was quick, but it took too long. Her lust vanished.

'Are you sure about this, sweetie?'

'Yes.'

'You don't have to, you know. I won't be mad.'

'I want to.'

He was on top of her, kissing her, murmuring her name. Oh, get it over with. She waited terrified, eyes shut as his fingers moved gently. Relax, relax. It can't be as bad as an internal examination. He entered her. Horrible, oh horrible. How can anyone say they like it? That ghastly churning feeling. Oh let it finish soon. He stopped.

'I can't do this to you, flower.' Nothing could be more humiliating than him abandoning the attempt.

'I want you to.'

'But you're hating it.'

'Please.'

He began moving again. She shut her eyes, willing herself to like it. He smoothed the hair back from her forehead, kissing her softly. It's not so bad, she told herself. Truly. It's . . . nothing. Just waves sliding in and out on a slightly boring stretch of coast. Gradually she began to relax. What was all the fuss about? Not horrible: neutral. Oh, whatever am I going to say to him? He thinks he's so good at this.

'You all right, Mara?'

'Yes, thanks.'

'Good. Not hurting?'

'No.' It reminded her of being crushed up against someone in a crowded train. A spot of conversation to help pass the time, to distance you from such embarrassing bodily contact. There was another lengthy pause.

'Nothing to write home about, though, is it?'

'It's . . .' Was there an adjective in the English language which combined truth with tact? She felt him laughing at her, and opened her eyes.

'You can say it, Mara. I won't be hurt.' She stared, doubting. 'Trust me – I've not started yet.' Not started? The whole thing had already gone on three times longer than she thought possible.

The fishwife appeared from nowhere: 'Well, get a move on, then, you lazy bugger.' He grinned, and suddenly, 'Oh! Oh, God! Johnny!' The bedsprings squealed with every thrust.

'This hurting?'

'No, it's –' Oh God, horrible. Her breath came in gasps. Or wonderful.

'Good, mmm?'

'I don't know!' Pins and needles down her arms. I must be hyperventilating. 'Oh, God!' She was losing herself, tumbling into an icy river, rushing downstream headlong over the falls, pounded down and down and down. I'm going to die. 'No!'

He stopped.

She opened her eyes wide. 'What?'

'You said no.'

'Did I?' They stared at one another.

Then he laughed. 'Oh, I *see*. We're going to have to work on that timing. I think "yes" is the word you were looking for.'

He was still laughing as he began again, but the moment had escaped her. Now all she was aware of was the bedsprings and the peremptory rapping of the headboard against the wall. And of him, laughing, grunting like a weightlifter. Had he no inhibitions? What if someone came to the door, for God's sake? Would he never finish?

'Mara. You're too much. This isn't going to – *ah!* . . .' She opened her eyes and saw him like a film of a man shot in the back and dying in slow motion. He collapsed on to her, laughing. '. . . last much longer. Sorry. Out of practice.' He buried his wet face in her neck and lay still.

She felt the hammering of his heart. Way down on the street below people were talking. The bells chimed half past. Half past *four*? How can it be? She lay looking at the ceiling, seeing the cracks feathering out across the plaster. A long-legged fly clung there, motionless. She fitted her breathing to his. They continued to lie. Had he fallen asleep? Her hands crept round him. His shirt was stuck to his back. She could still feel his heart beating against her. The swifts circled and cried in the sky, and she ran her fingers through his damp hair. You're all mine. But even as she thought it, she felt him slipping from her. He pulled away and sat up on the edge of the bed. She watched. He dropped his head into his hands. He's repenting. I knew it. I knew he'd feel bad about it. Why was I such a fool? Then she began to fear that it wasn't just repentance. What if she'd done what the Bishop and the Principal and Rupert couldn't do? She'd called him a coward, slept with him, and now he knew he wanted to be a priest. It was an own goal of spectacular flamboyance. He couldn't even bring himself to look at her. She sat up and began buttoning her dress. In a moment he would start trying to explain. She groped around for her damp knickers and pulled them back on. This is the most undignified moment of my entire life.

'Mara —'

'You don't have to say anything. I understand.'

'No, wait!'

But she left him on the bed and blundered out, hurrying back through the college, holding the tears in till she was safe in her room.

Andrew was waiting for her. His eyes took in her every detail.

'Shut up,' she said before he could speak. 'Leave me alone.'

'Good God. The lineaments of gratified desire. The man's an animal.' He steered her to the mirror and forced her to look at herself. She flinched. More love bites. And I've buttoned my dress up wrong. Oh, no! walked all through college looking like this.

'Were we careful, Princess?' She said nothing, hands fumbling to rebutton her dress. 'Because if not — speaking as a nice helpful little doctor's son — now's the time to do something about it. Not in four months' time when you discover you're pregnant.'

Her face burned. 'I'm not stupid. He used a . . .' She couldn't bring herself to say.

'He keeps . . . in his room, does he? That's interesting. With you in mind, do you suppose? Or just generally on the off-chance?'

'Andrew, go away. Just *go away!*'

'Did you enjoy it?'

She stamped her foot and screamed, 'Fuck *off!*'

'You didn't. Ah, I'm sorry.'

'Yes, I did!'

'So what's the problem, then?'

'He's going to be ordained,' she wailed.

'Yes, yes. We all *know* that, Mara.'

'But he told me he wasn't.'

'He tricked you! The *bastard*!'

'It wasn't that simple!'

'No? Ah. He screwed you, his conscience smote him, and all of a sudden he knew he wanted to be a priest after all?'

'Just leave me alone!'

'That presents us with a worrying angle on divine providence, doesn't it? Do you suppose a Calvinist would be forced to concede that God preordained an act of fornication as the means by which his purposes would be fulfilled?'

'Get out!' she sobbed.

'So. One of us has been shagged senseless by the great sex god at last. My congratulations. I fear the experience may have been wasted on you, but there it is. Oh, stop crying, for Christ's sake. It's not worth it.' He looked at his watch. 'I still owe you a birthday meal. What about tonight at eight? I'll meet you in the hallway, if you've managed to be civil to me by then.'

He was gone. She felt her face crumpling like a four-year-old preparing to howl. Then she thought, Oh, come off it. He's right. It's not worth it. You got what you wanted. She looked at her disgraceful reflection. Silly cow. So he's getting ordained after all? Too bad. A little voice wailed that she'd lost him for ever, but the rest of her remained adamant. Too bad. And somehow, try as she might, she couldn't wring a tragedy out of it. Despite her protests to Andrew, she had known perfectly well what she was doing.

She stared at the marks on her neck. To her amazement she caught her memory in the act of editing out the horrible bits of the experience and leaving something shudderingly delirious. Hard luck. He would be reverting to his celibate state again. His willpower had only faltered because he had doubted his calling. She knew he had spoken the truth when he said he couldn't lead a double life.

That's it, she told herself. It's over. And yet there was this stupid little hope budding. Maybe he loved her? Even if she starved it of light it would continue to feel its way faithfully upwards, telling itself that there must be a sun out there somewhere.

It was dusk. She and Andrew were walking arm in arm along the riverbank on their way back from the wine bar. The leaves fluttered overhead. It can't get any greener, thought Mara, and yet every day it seems to. This garlic smell will always remind me of the City. Andrew was humming. After a moment she recognized the tune and smiled: *Sigh no more, ladies, sigh no more. Men were deceivers ever.* She was drunk. She hadn't been able to eat a thing, and for once Andrew had laughed and ordered champagne instead of bullying her. She was worried by his magnanimity. She couldn't believe he'd finished with her yet. A bit more pointless sadism would have been reassuring. Mosquitoes danced in a cloud over the river edge. Now and then a fish jumped with a splash. The bells chimed. They reached the old bridge and stood leaning on the parapet, watching the cathedral and the water. The weir rumbled in the distance. Each different smell seemed distinct as she breathed the evening in. Ah – it's all a part of me, and I'm just a part of it. She thought of Johnny deep inside her and shivered. Andrew nudged her.

'Now how much did you enjoy it, Princess?' She put her hands to her burning cheeks. Did the man know everything? He laughed. 'It's nine-tenths in the mind, Mara. Sex is always better in anticipation or retrospect. "Doing a filthy pleasure is, and short," ' he quoted.

'Mmm. Not *that* short, actually.'

'I don't want to know, Mara.' She made no reply. There was a long pause. She waited. 'Minutes, rather than seconds, I suppose you mean.'

'Not telling.' He pinched her and she danced out of reach, laughing.

'Cow.' They walked along, bickering, until they reached the college steps. He stopped and kissed her cheek. 'Good night, sweet one.'

'You're not coming in?'

He shook his head. 'There are a couple of things I've been meaning to do.'

'Such as?' she asked. But he only smiled. She stood at the door and watched him as he walked off along the street, before climbing slowly up the stairs to her room in disappointment. Aha. But at least he'd be out if Johnny called, though. At this the wine began singing along her veins, and she ran lightly up the last flight.

CHAPTER 25

Johnny did not come. At last she gave up hope and went to bed. It was a long while before she drifted asleep. In her half-awake state she was aware of Andrew returning. There was music playing, and voices, then Dewi appeared. 'You've come back,' she said. 'Where have you been?' But then it was not Dewi at all, but Johnny. He was going to be ordained and she was supposed to have embroidered his stole, but she had not finished it, and now he would miss the service. 'You've wrecked his life,' they all said as she searched everywhere for her needle and embroidery threads.

She woke in the dark with a headache. The bells began to chime. She counted. Two o'clock. She pulled on her dressing-gown and made her way sleepily to the bathroom to get a glass of water. The light was on. Someone was already in there. She drew back at once but it was too late. She had seen. Andrew's mocking laughter pursued her back to her room.

Oh, God. She pressed her hands over her eyes, but the scene would not be banished. Andrew standing naked facing her. Another man kneeling in front of him. Every detail was clear in her cringing memory. White tiles, cork bath mat, Andrew's long fingers in the other man's hair. She heard footsteps crossing the landing, but had no time to compose herself before Andrew was in the room.

'You should lock the fucking door!' she shouted at him.

He laughed. 'Get used to it, sweetheart.' He was drunker than she had ever seen him. 'What do you think your life's going to be like in Oxford, hmm?'

'Get out! Get some clothes on!'

He lurched across and wrapped his arms round her. 'This is the real me you're seeing. Makes you think, doesn't it?' She tried to push him away, but he clung to her drunkenly, pressing his face up against hers. 'Makes you realize it's not going to be a nice cosy little rent-free sex-free love nest among the dreaming spires.'

'Go away!' she sobbed. 'You're drunk.'

'If you don't like it, try living off Whitaker instead. You can paint and think pure thoughts while he fucks you.'

'Please, go away, Andrew,' she wept as she tried to struggle free. 'Please.'

'No. It's time you heard this.' There was a movement at the door. The other man, clutching a towel round himself.

'What's going on?'

'Come in,' said Andrew. The man hesitated at the sight of Mara's tears. 'No. Seriously. She'd like another little demonstration, wouldn't you, Princess?' His tongue flickered in and out. 'You'd better learn fast, darling, because all men want it. Believe me. Even the nice straight ones like Johnny Whitaker.'

'Don't be a shit,' the other man said. He came in and began to haul Andrew back out of the room. 'I'm really sorry about this,' he said to Mara.

'Why?' asked Andrew. 'What are you sorry about?' They were at the door. Andrew grabbed him and began kissing him. He pulled away.

'Don't. Can't you see she's upset?'

Andrew laughed. 'So what? She's a blood-sucking parasitic bitch.' Mara pushed him out, slammed the door and locked it. 'Like every fucking woman on God's earth,' he shouted, pounding his fists against the wood.

She cowered on the bed weeping as he continued to hammer on the door and swear at her. The field mice were stirring in their room, but they had the sense not to emerge. At last the other man succeeded in dragging Andrew away. Their voices came through the wall. Arguing. Then silence. Music playing. It was Billie Holiday. Each footstep or creak of furniture made her cringe and clamp her hands over her ears. No sound seemed innocent any more. He was drunk. He didn't mean it, she tried to tell herself. No, said another voice in her mind. That's what he really thinks. You're a blood-sucking parasitic bitch. Was it really only this afternoon that she had slept with Johnny? The whole thing seemed to have happened in another age. If only he would come. Tapping softly on the door, carrying her back to bed and making love to her silently, over and over again. Johnny, Johnny. I've lost everything. She wept in the dark, longing for him, longing for sleep, trying not to think of the two men in bed only inches away behind the wall.

When she got up the next morning, she felt as though she had slept only five minutes in the entire night. There was no sound from

Andrew's room. She went down for breakfast with a strange, light-headed sensation, as though the world was being kept from her behind plate-glass. She collected some coffee and toast and sat down, but as she reached out for the butter, her hand suddenly looked odd to her. Then a bright stain of light appeared in front of her left eye. Oh, God. Please not a migraine. She dropped her head in her hands and watched in despair as her vision was swallowed up in angry flickering. Someone came up behind her.

'Hung over, are we? Tut, tut.' Nigel. She got up and made for the vanishing doorway.

'Migraine,' she said.

'Nasty. Go and lie down in a dark room.'

'I *know* that.' She began to cry in anticipation of what lay ahead. His arm went round her waist.

'All right. Come on, then, beautiful. I'll take you back.' She sniffed back the tears and let him lead her to the stairs. He gave her a squeeze. The lights were jangling and bursting in her head. 'Anything I can do?' They were on the last flight. She shook her head. He took the keys from her hand and opened the door. 'Now you lie down and get some rest.' She heard him drawing the curtains.

'Thanks, Nigel.'

'Yeah. Well, you can owe me one, darling.' She lay down. He went, and a moment later she heard him writing something on her door. 'Do not disturb,' she hoped. Someone came out of the next room.

'Good God.' Andrew. 'Joined-up writing.'

'Bugger off.'

She lay tense, listening to them.

'What's wrong with her?' Andrew asked. More scribbling. 'Ah. Migraine. With an "e" on the end, usually, Nigel.' He sounded half drunk still.

'I *know*.'

'Listen, can I bring someone to breakfast?'

'If you've signed them in.'

'I didn't get round to it.'

'Too bad, then.'

'I'll make it worth your while, darling.' Mara pictured Nigel recoiling.

'Who is it?'

'A colleague, Nigel. Just a colleague.'

'Oh, all right, then.'

'Nigel! Let me thank you properly.' A muffled protest. He knows I can hear, thought Mara. That's the only reason he's doing it.

'Get off, you pervert.' She heard Nigel's footsteps retreat rapidly down the stairs. There was a silence. She lay waiting for him to come in and taunt her again. The cathedral bells began to chime for mattins. Then she heard Andrew go back to his room. Voices. She pressed her knuckles into her temples as the flickering lights gave way to pounding. Nothing to do but endure. Footsteps went past her door then down the stairs. The Sunday morning bells pealed on and on, and eventually she fell asleep.

When she woke, it was after four o'clock. She moved her head gingerly this way and that. The worst seemed to be over. She listened for a sound from the next room, but heard nothing. A kind of dull reassuring peace had descended. All her hopes were crushed, but at least the terrain was familiar again. Sunlight was coming through the crack in the curtains and fanning out across the ceiling. There were people chatting down on the terrace below. Nearly the end of term. Thank God. I'll soon be gone. It felt like an echo of the mood that always gripped her at the end of the summer term at school: *Soon I'll be at the farm.* She lay trying to remember why she had looked forward to going there so much, and found herself drifting back to one summer when she was fourteen.

I'm lying on the swaying hay bales on the trailer as Dewi drives the tractor back to the barn. Willow warblers in the trees along the stream. Listen: the falling cadences, beautiful warnings – my tree, my tree, keep away. And somewhere up in the blue a lark filling the whole sky with song. I am searching for the tiny speck of bird, but I can't see it.

Back at the barn. We are unloading the bales and stacking them. My hands sting as sweat seeps into the blisters made by the baler twine. The bales are too heavy for me, almost, but I struggle to lift them, to help Dewi. Aunt Susan calls in the distance that tea is ready. I sit down on a pile of bales and Dewi comes up to me. He stands close and says, 'Kiss me, girl.' I kiss him quickly on the lips, then look away, face burning. 'No, kiss me properly. French kissing.' But I don't know how. I've tried to work it out from films and by sneaking glances at snogging couples. I have no one I can ask. 'You don't know what I mean, do you?' I shake my head in shame, still

348

looking out across the yard. 'Time you learnt, then, isn't it?' he says, and turns my face to him with his hand. I let him. I feel his breath. He's sucking at my lips, and then I feel his tongue slipping into my mouth. I flinch back, but he holds on to me. Touching tongues – kids do that for a dare! Surely grown-ups don't enjoy this? 'That nice?' he asks. If I say no he might be angry, but he might be angry if he thinks I'm lying. So I mutter, 'I don't know.'

'Want me to do it again?'

'I don't know.'

He does it again. I feel hot and strange as though I'm going to wet myself. He pauses and says, 'You're supposed to do it back.' I try, but then he puts his hands up my T-shirt and fingers me. I freeze, knowing I shouldn't let him. No boy's ever going to fancy you, Faye always says. Look at you – you haven't got tits, you've got corn-plasters. He stops kissing me and pushes me back on to the bales. The hay prickles my bare back. I roll my head and look away as his hands start to unzip my jeans.

'Dewi, Dewi,' calls Aunt Susan again. He pulls my shirt back down. I zip my jeans up guiltily and sit up. He smiles at me, knowing I won't tell. I watch him as he walks off across the yard. The barn is full of stealthy rustlings. I imagine the mice and rats staring at me, the farmyard cats, the owls in the gloomy rafters, the swallows in their mud nests, a hundred round eyes all staring, all feeling my shock, all wondering what will happen.

Mara sighed. And I never saw him again. He just walked out of my life and disappeared. And I've always blamed myself. Somehow I made it happen. I drove him away by loving him too much. By letting him kiss me and touch me like that. And the same pattern has gone on and on repeating itself.

Would Dewi ever come back? she wondered. How would his parents react if he did? What were her cousins like these days? The families had drifted further and further apart. Elizabeth now had three children, according to Aunt Susan's Christmas card. Faye was married, divorced, pregnant and living with another man. Mara wondered what it was like to be Aunt Susan, grieving for her lost son, despising her daughters for not making a better job of their lives than she had done, hoping the empty sherry bottles would not roll out of their hiding places when visitors called. But maybe they all pity us. Poor Eleanor and Morgan. One daughter dead, the other totally out of control.

There was a knock at the door. Andrew came in carrying a vase of flowers which he put down on her desk. Tears of relief brimmed over. He went and opened the curtains, then came and sat beside her on the bed.

'Poor baby. How are you feeling?' His gentle tone made her cry all the more. 'Ssh. It's all right.' He stroked her forehead. After a while she managed to stop sobbing. 'Well, are you still coming to Oxford with me?'

'I don't know.'

'You don't fancy being a fag hag after all?'

'It's not that.'

'Yes it is.'

'No – it's because you're so cruel. And manipulative. You treat me like shit, then you make me feel it's all my fault.'

'Oh, come off it. It's the sex. You're just a bit squeamish, that's all. You'll get used to it, Princess. Come to Oxford.'

'No.'

'Look, if you weren't so uptight, everything would be OK. You can't spend your whole life freaking out over every innocent little bit of fellatio you interrupt.'

'You . . . you . . .' she stuttered. 'I'm not taking the blame for this, you bastard.' He was laughing. 'That's exactly what I mean! You're always doing it.' She felt herself starting to cry again. 'I can't bear it, Andrew. One minute I think you're the only person who really understands me, and the next you say such terrible wounding things.'

'They go together. If I didn't understand, I couldn't wound.' He took her hand in his. 'Actually, you have a slight advantage here. I haven't a clue what I said.'

Her chin trembled. '"Blood-sucking parasitic bitch."'

He laughed and repeated the phrase admiringly, domesticating it for her. 'Well, it's a slightly muddled image, zoologically speaking, but not bad after a bottle of whisky.' He held her hand to his cheek. 'Come to Oxford.' Why do I always let him get round me like this? she asked herself. 'Please. I need you, Mara.'

'Yes. As an Aunt Sally.'

'No! As a *friend*.' He began kissing her fingertips. 'Oh, please. Don't be so unforgiving. What if I do the cooking?' She made no reply. 'What if I promise to lock the bathroom door?'

'What if you apologize?'

He dropped her hand. 'Don't let's be silly about this, Mara,' he said austerely.

She felt herself starting to smile. 'All right. But if I catch you at it again I'll throw a bucket of cold water over you.'

He considered this. 'Mmm. That might add an interesting *frisson*.' He got to his feet. 'Coffee?' She nodded and he filled the kettle. They fell silent for a while. Mara wondered if she would get hardened to his bouts of nastiness if she lived with him long enough.

'Why are you so horrible to me?' she asked.

He gave her his fallen choirboy smile and shrugged. 'Kismet. We were made for each other: you're a born victim and I have a sadistic streak a mile wide.' There was another silence. He wandered around the room, whistling softly through his teeth. At last he stopped and faced her. She saw his fingers drumming rapidly on the desk, at work on some complex piece of Bach. 'And because you took my man, you bitch.'

'Hah! So we're out in the open, at last.'

'Yes. I had some vague intention of being generous about it; but let's face it, darling, generosity is so bland compared with revenge.'

She reddened in anger. 'Well, I hope last night made you feel better.'

'No. It didn't. And now I can't decide who I hate more: you, or him, or myself.' The kettle boiled.

'But that sounds like remorse,' she said.

'Mmm. I thought I dimly recognized the feeling.'

'You know something, Andrew, for a hardened hedonistic atheist you've got a pretty sensitive conscience.'

'Vestigial.'

'I think you've got an ethical code after all.' He shrugged again. 'So why don't you just give in and admit you believe in God?'

'Because God hates gays.' Her eyes widened. 'It was a joke, Mara.' No it wasn't, she thought. 'Oh, don't take everything so seriously, for Christ's sake. You're so bloody demanding, Princess. You either idealize people or write them off. You're such hard work.' She knew she was. No wonder people tired of her. 'I don't want to be your honorary angel.'

'Sorry.' He grinned, and she realized he had tricked her into accepting the blame again. Good God – if he wrote off someone's car he'd get them apologizing for lending it to him in the first place.

351

'This bodes well for our co-habitation,' he said. 'You can be the one who wears the hair-shirt in our relationship.'

'And what will you wear?' she asked, itching to slap his smug face. 'The cat's pyjamas?'

'The trousers, Mara. The trousers.'

They went down for college tea arm in arm. Mara's ears were ringing from too many aspirins. Her legs felt weak. It was over twenty-four hours since she had eaten anything, and she could feel Andrew watching her as she collected a plate of bread and salad. They went out through the French windows and joined the other students on the lawn in the late afternoon sun.

After a while May appeared. 'Only two to go. Shakespeare and sociolinguistics,' she announced, bolting down her scotch egg salad and fantasizing about all the things they would do once exams were over. Mara listened to her rattling on about picnics and punting.

'Where's Maddy?' she asked when a long enough pause occurred.

'Oh, crying in our room, probably,' said May. 'I don't *mean* to be horrible, but she's been going on and on about it, and nothing I say makes any difference. It's her performance exam tomorrow. The accompanist keeps letting her down – not turning up for rehearsals, or arriving late and buggering off early. "Find someone else," I say. "There *isn't* anyone," she says. "I'm going to *fail*."' May flushed at the heartlessness of her impersonation. 'Well, I'm sorry, but she's been going on about it all week. Cuchulain's completely useless. He just strokes her hair.' I could stand that type of uselessness, thought Mara.

'Go and tell her I'll do it,' said Andrew. They both stared at him in surprise.

'You're going to do something *nice*?' asked May reverently. 'Aren't you worried your image will suffer?' This brought no response other than a raised eyebrow, so May got to her feet. 'Well, I'll go and tell her the wonderful news.'

'Do that, little one.' He smiled up at her and she coloured.

'You realize, of course, that if you weren't such a shit she'd probably have dared to ask you.' With this she walked off.

'True,' said Andrew. The students around talked and clattered their cutlery. Mara looked at him. He had his head tilted back and he seemed to be watching the flight of the swifts high above. Was he unhappy? He always seemed so self-sufficient. No one would dare to assume he was feeling lost and small and in need of comfort.

He turned and met her eye with a questioning look, and she heard herself saying, 'I just want you to know I think the world of you.' It sounded wooden. There was a burst of laughter from a group near by, as though they had heard what she said. She waited for his blighting response, but he only leant and kissed her cheek.

'Thanks,' he said.

I can't help him, she thought. But instantly she was ashamed of herself for being more absorbed by her inability to comfort him than by the fact that he was suffering.

A moment later he roused himself and stood up. 'Ah, well. I suppose I'd better go and be wept over.'

She got to her feet too, and they went back into the building. He waved idly and disappeared as she began to climb the stairs. Halfway up the first flight she was forced to stop, her head throbbing. She looked up to the top and saw Johnny there in a jacket and tie. Her face burned as he ran down to meet her.

'Feeling any better?' he asked. She nodded stupidly. 'I've just been up to your room. Listen, Mara, we need to talk.' She nodded again. He seemed horribly grown-up all of a sudden. Perhaps it was the tie?

'Um . . . now? We could . . .' She made a flapping gesture up towards her room. Why wasn't he embarrassed too, for God's sake?

'Sorry, can't. I'm just off to church, then I've got to see someone after the service. It'll have to be later.'

'Fine.' She aimed for a brisk mature tone like his. 'When?'

'About nine? We could go for a walk.'

'OK.'

'I'll meet you back here, then.' He grinned at her and raced off, taking the stairs two at a time. Her dying blush surged back at the suspicion that he only wanted to meet her in the hallway because he didn't trust her in a bedroom.

She stumbled upstairs and sat on her bed. This is awful! I know exactly what it's going to be like. He'll be sensible. 'I think we both know it shouldn't have happened, Mara,' he'd say. Kind, but firm. 'It's probably better if we just forget all about it.' But I don't want to forget, she sobbed to herself. Oh, I'm going to look so stupid and undignified. There must be some kind of civilized fornicators' etiquette. Well, ahem, we seem to have got a little carried away. No hard feelings, I hope? And then a well-bred silence, or a tolerant grin in passing.

She went across and sat at the open window. I'll be sensible, she resolved. I won't burst into tears. The shadows lengthened. All the students had gone from the lawn back to their revision. Or to church, Jesus College being the devout place it was. She watched the dark wine-coloured leaves of the copper beech and felt a twist of heartache for lost summer evensongs. *Lighten our darkness, we beseech thee, O Lord; and by thy great mercy defend us from all perils and dangers of this night.* Maybe I'll go back, she thought. Not here, though. In Oxford. She had an unexpected image of herself kneeling in a dim church and of Andrew sliding into the pew beside her. She saw his expression clearly: '*Well?*' Defying her to look surprised. Was he on his way back to God, too? *Our hearts are restless till they find their rest in thee.*

Johnny. Maybe his heart was at rest again now. She pictured him as she had first seen him, kneeling in the cathedral in a shaft of sunlight. She was just a part of his restlessness, like his drinking and bad language. Childish things that had to be put away. He'd be a better man for it. But not her man. She wouldn't ever lie with him in her arms feeling his heartbeat. Maybe it was all for the best. She would be in Oxford and he would still be up here in the north-east in his parish. It wouldn't work out. Their paths were always going to diverge. This year was just an accident.

She sat willing the time on towards nine o'clock so that she could get it over with. The bells chimed the slow quarters and she waited and waited.

It was four minutes past nine and she was in the hallway. From time to time she heard footsteps in the corridor or outside on the street and her heart squeezed tight with dread. She looked at her watch. Still only four minutes past nine. He'd forgotten. But then she heard feet leaping up the steps and knew it was him. She wiped her sweaty palms on her dress. The door opened. He had changed back into casual clothes, but she could see that he was still wearing his grown-up manner.

'Ready?' She nodded. 'Where shall we go? To the river?'

'Fine,' she said. They set off down the street towards the old bridge. She reminded herself to be sensible. 'How was your service?'

'All right, thanks.'

'Were you preaching?'

'No.'

An awful silence.

'I went to see the Bishop afterwards,' Johnny said at last. She glanced at him and he grinned. 'I told him a good friend had managed to talk some sense into me, and that if he'd still have me, I wanted to get ordained.' She had been right. She tried in vain to feel some kind of satisfaction.

'What did he say?' Her heart was racing and making the blood pound painfully in her head.

'He was delighted. "I'm sure you're making the right decision, John." Mind you,' he lapsed back into his own voice, 'he'd have to think that. I was turned down by the selectors three years ago and he overruled them. It's good to have someone who believes in you.' He fell silent. She knew she should say something affirming. 'Look, thanks for saying what you said, Mara. Sorry I bawled you out like that. I knew all along you were right.'

'It's OK,' she said unhappily. They skirted past a group of students having a noisy water fight and passed under the archway. It was a beautiful evening. As they walked down to the bridge, Mara saw the bats twisting and flickering against the sky. She could just catch their high-pitched cries. The shouting and splashing continued in the distance.

'Well, anyway, I'm grateful, sweetie. There aren't many women who stand up to me and tell me when I'm wrong.' They stopped on the bridge and leant against the parapet. He sighed. 'You have no idea how much better I feel. You know that bit in the Bible about the man who finds treasure buried in a field? That's what it's like. A lucky break, when I've done nothing to deserve it. Do you know what I mean?'

'Sort of,' she mumbled.

'Or like I'm doing what I was created to do. Getting ordained, I mean. Until I was converted I always felt a bit . . . I don't know, like a runaway train, or a mad bull, or something. All this energy, and no purpose, nothing to use it on.' He grinned. 'Well, nothing you could put on your CV, anyway. I must have reverted, this term. I'm sorry you got the brunt of it.'

'It's OK.'

'But now I feel . . .' He paused. 'I feel God laughing. Do you know what I mean?' he asked again. 'And everything inside me thinks *yes*! I know I'm not making a good job of it, but I want you to know how I feel.'

'Thanks.'

'Are you OK, Mara? I hope I wasn't the cause of this migraine.'

'No. It wasn't you.'

'Andrew?' She made no reply. 'Yeah. I thought he'd give you a hard time. I'm sorry.' She still said nothing. 'Do you want me to have a word with him?'

'No.' She stared down at a willow leaf as it floated towards the bridge.

They were silent again. The leaf passed under the arch. At last he drew breath. Here it comes.

'Listen, pet. Would you like to come to my ordination?'

'Your – but I . . .' She was too taken aback to respond.

'On the 28th,' he went on. 'It'd mean a lot to me if you did.'

'The 28th?' she repeated, grasping hold of the date in desperation. 'But I'm going home on the 24th. My mother's driving up to collect me. It's all arranged.'

'Well, couldn't you *un*arrange it? Or come back, even?'

'It's all settled,' she said, but seeing his hurt surprise she blurted out, 'I never go to church. I just couldn't bear it.'

'OK.'

'I just don't believe any more.'

'OK,' he said again, but she couldn't tell how he was reacting. She flung out one last attempt.

'It's not personal.'

'No.' They began to walk again, crossing to the far side and turning down the path which led to the bank. What was he thinking? She stole a glance and saw he was frowning. They walked on under the trees in the green garlicky gloom. Johnny led her to a bench under a vast beech tree and they sat. The bells chimed. Oh no, this really *is* it.

'Mara, I think we've got some talking to do.'

'I know.' Her voice sounded high and tight, not sensible; but she hurried on so that she wouldn't have to hear him say it. 'I think we'd better forget it ever happened.'

He looked bewildered. 'Why?'

'I think we both know we shouldn't have done it.'

'Yes, but –'

'I know you'll have to be celibate again.'

'True, but that doesn't mean I want to forget about what happened.' Something had gone wrong. They were saying one another's lines. 'Why ever would I want to forget, flower?' She saw a sudden look of dismay on his face. Was he blushing? 'I wasn't too rough for you, was I? Did I scare you again? Mara –'

'No,' she cut him off, blushing too. 'No, it's not that. It's just . . . Oh, I don't know. It just makes it all so confusing.'

'Confusing?'

She could feel she was painting herself into a corner, but somehow she couldn't stop. 'I mean, you're going to be ordained. I'm moving to Oxford, and –'

'You're doing what?' he broke in.

'Moving to Oxford,' she repeated.

'You're not! But you've got two more years of research here.'

'I'm giving it up. I'm going to paint.'

'Ah,' he said. 'I knew I'd seen you drawing. Why wouldn't you show me? What's the big secret?' She mumbled something. 'Is this what you really want to do, then?'

'Yes.'

'Well, that's great. Why can't you do it here, though?'

'Because I'm going to Oxford,' she repeated stubbornly. 'I'm sharing a flat with Andrew.'

'Hah. So that's his game.'

'Game?' Her voice rose aggressively. 'Listen, I like him.'

'Forget Andrew for a minute. Just tell me again what's confusing you?'

'It's just . . . I don't know. The distance, and everything. It would all just be too *complicated*.' Why am I saying this? I don't mean it.

'Well, you'll come back and visit, won't you?'

'I doubt it. It's usually a mistake.'

He seemed completely dumbfounded. She looked away, unable to bear his expression.

He stood up abruptly. 'Well, fuck this.' He set off the way they had come. She hurried after him.

'Listen, I didn't mean –'

'Don't worry. I've got the message, Mara.'

She tried to keep pace with him, but she was still too drained after her migraine and began to fall behind. After a moment he relented and waited for her. Oh, what have I done? What would he have said if I'd kept quiet? She kept opening her mouth to explain, then

357

finding no words. Tears started to brim over. They reached the college steps and she turned to face him.

'Johnny —'

'It's OK, Mara. It's your choice. Just so long as you've worked out what that bastard Jacks is playing at.'

'He's trying to help me,' she cried. 'He's being *kind*, for once.'

'Bullshit, Mara.'

'You don't know how much it means to me. The chance to paint, I mean.'

'Try explaining it some time, then. I'm not a bloody mindreader.' She bit her lip. When she said nothing, he shrugged. 'Well, sorry I *confused* you, Princess.' He lingered, but she still couldn't make herself speak. A group of students came out of the door and pushed past them. He turned and left. She watched him walk off down the street. 'Why can't you see I love you?' she wanted to scream. Instead she pushed open the heavy door and went up to her room.

She sat in the dark and wept. What am I supposed to do? I can't stay here just to be near him. It would be too pathetic for words. What if she'd got it all wrong again? Maybe Andrew was trying to scotch the chance of a relationship between her and Johnny? Oh, *what* chance for God's sake? Johnny had never once told her he cared for her. I'm not a mindreader, either! she thought. She tried to think of Oxford, her golden city, her new beginning, and found it was becoming just some tedious library-ridden town two hundred and fifty miles too far south.

CHAPTER 26

Exams drew to a close. Whenever Mara went out, she seemed to see students emerging from their last Finals papers to be met by friends and sprayed with champagne. It was like watching the same clip of film over and over again. She had seen it all before at Cambridge.

The glorious weather persisted till the very last paper, then it broke in a spectacular storm. Thunder cracked like gunshots, splitting the sky and rattling the City like a toy drum. Streets turned to rivers, flights of steps to boiling waterfalls. Mara had gone out after lunch in summer clothes and was drenched a few hours later. She crossed the footbridge carrying her shoes and waded up the river that had once been a steep lane. Half a dozen students were dancing in the rain in their underpants outside Jesus College and brandishing bars of soap. Idiots, she thought with a smile as she went past.

How was she going to work in this? Thunder ripped across the City. The power failed the instant she switched on her light, and she got out of her wet clothes in the eerie half-light and wrapped a towel round herself. The storm crashed on overhead now, no breathing space between flash and thunder. Oh, God, if only Johnny were here. On the floor. Wet skin, pounding rain, wild light at the window. And Johnny on top of her, hard and desperate . . . A knock! She flew to the door, but it was one of the field mice.

'Nigel says college dinner is cancelled tonight. The kitchens are flooded. Sorry to disturb you, only he asked us to let people know . . .'

'Oh. Thanks.' The girl retreated, smiling uncertainly. Mara shut the door and stood a moment without moving, then ripped the towel off and began drying herself viciously. Fool. He won't be back for more. Not after the way you've treated him. She pulled on more clothes and tried to work in the gloom.

The rain fell day after day. Mara went back and forth to the libraries checking footnotes and references, blocking out all thoughts of Johnny. She saw him now and then, and he treated her with an amused indifference which cut deep. She tried to believe that he was only doing this to mask his true feelings, but the act was too convincing for that. He'd never cared for her. Forget him. Sod him. The river was high and rain dripped heavily from the leaves. Everything was too green, too grey. Bedraggled bees crept into flowers. The birds sang on in the branches as though they were glorying in the wet.

Joanna's little revival vanished as though the rain had dissolved it and washed it away. Joanna disappeared with it, her task fulfilled. God had called her to testify against the satanic nature of academic theology by boycotting her exams, and she had been faithful to that call. The gorilla would be back to re-sit his failed papers, but Mara guessed Joanna would not. God never called people like Joanna to a task as mundane as revision. The prayer meeting was calm again, steadied by the ballast of Coverdale students and members of staff who had started to attend. Armageddon had been averted, but there were still plenty of casualties – May, who had given up prayer; the gorilla, who had looked like a bomb-blast survivor on the last day of term. And the cause of it all, Joanna, walked away without a mark on her. My God, thought Mara, someone somewhere will have to take the rap for this kind of thing. Forgiveness is not enough. There has to be justice.

The rain continued to fall. 'It's not fair!' wailed Maddy and May, lamenting all those parties and picnics and open-air productions. Let it come down, thought Mara. She had nothing to do but slog on with her thesis, trying to do as much as possible before she left the City. She decided to stay up for a couple of weeks after term ended. She could put the finishing touches to it in Oxford.

The days passed. Mara took a break from her work every couple of hours and walked up and down the room. Rain trickled down the window. From time to time her friends tried to coax her out of her room with invitations to go punting or to drive with them to the coast, but she always refused. After their footsteps died away, she cursed herself. Everyone was having fun except her. She missed the comforting sounds of evening study through the wall. Andrew seemed to come back late or drunk or not at all. Where was he going? And who were all those beautiful young men in dinner suits slinking around the corridor? Eventually it dawned on her that they must be the other three-quarters of Andrew's infamous barber-shop quartet, Parsons' Pleasure. Their reputation was founded – as far as she could tell – on their nicely judged blend of obscene lyrics and technical brilliance. They were in constant demand at every ball and party in the university. One night Mara heard them for herself. She woke at two o'clock to the sound of laughter and baying on the terrace below. Drunken voices called her name.

'*What light from yonder window breaks?*' Andrew's voice floated up above the caterwauling. She pushed the covers back and crossed the room. There was a cheer as she threw the window up. '*She speaks, yet she says nothing.* Like all women.'

'Piss off the lot of you!' More laughter.

'*Speak again, bright angel!*' And they began serenading her. She leant on the window sill and listened. Their beautiful voices filled the night. Too drunk to stand, but still in tune. She smiled down at them and could just make out their faces and the white of their dress shirts in the darkness. Then a light came on in a window below her and the concert ended abruptly in a bucket of cold water and a volley of bad language.

'Why are you hiding in your room like a sulky adolescent?' Andrew was sitting on her desk in his dressing-gown late the following morning, drinking black coffee.

'I'm trying to finish my thesis.'

'But why? You've got no deadline.'

'Because I want to.'

'What's wrong, Mara?'

She scowled down into her bibliography. Her hand began to fiddle with her hair.

'It's just . . . I don't know.'

'Look, it's Johnny, isn't it?' She nodded. I won't cry. This time I won't. 'Jesus, you're incredible. How can *anyone* make such a consist-ent balls-up of their life?'

'I don't do it on purpose!'

'Has it crossed your mind that you could actually tell him how you feel?'

'He's not interested. He – ow! Don't you hit me!' She ducked, but not fast enough. He slapped her round the head again.

'Toughen up, Mara. You're pathetic.' She was on her feet in an instant, arm raised, determined to land one good slap on that smirking face no matter what. But he was too quick. She stamped and swore as he taunted her, always just out of reach. In the end he wrapped his arms round her and pulled her down on to the bed. She lay beside him half sobbing, half laughing.

'Bastard.'

'Bitch,' he replied. 'Slag, whore, cow, slut – I think Roget's on my side, here, Princess.' He was lying with his head propped on one hand looking down at her.

'The whole world's on the man's side.'

'I know. Get reconciled, sweetheart.' He stroked her hair back from her forehead. Such lover-like gestures. She watched his face as he smiled and played with her curls.

'Don't you ever find women attractive?' she asked.

'Are you asking if I find you attractive?' He opened his dressing-gown and peered down at himself. For God's sake! 'Sorry – honest Peter says no. Why?'

'I just wondered.'

'Just idle curiosity, hmm?' He bent his head and kissed her softly on the lips.

'Don't,' she said faintly, heart starting to race. But he did it again, this time more slowly, just teetering on the extreme edge of what could be called brotherly. 'Don't play games with me. Please.'

'Games?' His lips were brushing hers. She could smell the coffee on his breath. Oh, God. 'Am I *confusing* you?' She jumped, remembering her words to Johnny. Andrew was smiling his malicious smile. 'This isn't making everything too *complicated*, I hope?' She shoved his face away and sat bolt upright.

'He told you!' Her voice shook with rage. 'I can't believe he talked about me like that!'

'Don't be stupid. Of course your friends talk about you.'

'What did he say? What – Oh, God. Tell me.'

'He seemed to be under the impression that I'm deliberately enticing you to Oxford to wreck his chances. "No, no," I said. "You've got it all wrong. It's her devotion to *Art*, not me, that's to blame. You're being sacrificed on the altar of her vocation, Whitaker."'

'That's not true!'

'I know it's not,' said Andrew. 'The truth is, you're shit scared of commitment. You don't believe in being happy. Whether you have the right to go around systematically inflicting unhappiness on the rest of us is an open question, however.'

'I don't! I do believe ... You ...' He laughed at her inarticulate anger.

'Want to know what he thinks of you?'

She clutched him, anger forgotten. 'Yes!'

He was smirking again. 'Ask him.'

'No. Tell me. Please.' She shook him in exasperation. 'Tell me, Andrew.'

'Shan't.' He stretched languidly and looked up at her with a sly grin. 'I'll admit I did give him a piece of disinterested, friendly advice.'

'That he'd be better off with you?'

'Precisely – I'm brighter, better looking, and I'm not certifiable.'

'And what did he say to that?'

Andrew laughed. '"Pity you've got a dick."'

'Well, only a very small one. Ow!' She was too slow again.

Andrew got to his feet. 'Go and talk to him, Mara.'

'I'll try,' she muttered, knowing she would not dare. He patted her cheek and left. A moment later she heard him singing as the bath filled.

> *Trip no further pretty sweeting,*
> *Journeys end in lovers' meeting,*
> *Every wise man's son doth know.*

It was the last day of term. The weather was sullen with occasional spiteful bursts of rain. An elegiac mood settled over the City. By now the worst – and best – was known. The degree results had been posted on noticeboards in Palace Green days before. The anxious crowds had gone for that year. No more eyes scanning nervously through the lists, no more squeals of delight, no more ashen disbelief. Raindrops trickled down the glass, blurring name after name as they meandered down from First to Upper Second to Lower Second to Third. The wind blew across the empty Green.

Mara paused on the old bridge and looked down at the brown fast-flowing river. It was over a year since Hester had died. She had meant to mark the day out in some way, to sit and think about Hester and reflect on death, but it had slipped past without her realizing, just as the actual day had done a year before. She pictured herself in her room at Cambridge on that evening. She had probably been revising her sociolinguistics. Turning the pages of my notes while she was drowning. Mara could not keep the two events together in her mind. They seemed so unconnected.

The water swirled under the archway. 'She won't have suffered,' people had said reassuringly. 'It's not an unpleasant way to die.' Liars. Snorting water into your terrified lungs, clawing, sinking, smothering, eyes bulging – this is it, I'm drowning, I'm going to die. Oh, Hester, there must have been a dozen better ways to go. Why did you choose drowning?

She checked herself. She didn't know that it was a choice. Perhaps Hester had been out swimming when a sudden squall hit the lake. Galilee was like that – winds whipping down the tunnel of hills and lashing the water up into a storm. The disciples in the boat. *Master, carest thou not that we perish?* Mara's hands gripped the damp stone of the parapet. Why am I so scared of the thought that she killed herself? The fear that I am destined to do the same? After all, we're cut from the same genetic cloth. A congenital propensity to despair. Oh, let it have been an accident. Oh, God, don't let her have died alone, lost and without you at the last. That's what I can't bear. Tears began to roll down her cheeks.

Hester, I can't believe you're gone. I keep seeing you disappearing round a corner or going past in a car. Yes, I know what it is. It's one of the stages of grief. I've read all about it, but I still have to stop myself from calling out and running after you. Maybe if we'd spent more time together I could believe in your death. Each day would drive it home; minutes without you like nails hammered into your coffin. Dead, dead, dead. But I keep forgetting that this absence is different from any other. I can't hold on to it. Whenever I think of going home, I've already wondered 'Will Hester be there?' before I remember. We should have said goodbye. I can't even remember when I last saw you. Was it this day, or that? It slipped from me. It was too ordinary.

Another sharp shower began. Mara walked back to college, the cold rain mingling with her tears.

The bells chimed three. Mara paused in her packing. The last note died away, and there was no other sound apart from the rain on the window. All her friends had gone weeks before. Her mother was due to arrive in about an hour to collect her. She would be late, of course. Mara knew of no one else with such a blithe innocence of the points of the compass. She felt a twinge of childhood resentment that her father was always too busy to drive anywhere for her. He never came to collect them from school trips. He never met their trains. It would have been nice, just once, to have him greet them at the door. 'Daddy's busy, darling.' Daddy doesn't care, you mean. Oh, leave it, she told herself. Surely you're reconciled to his indifference by now? The room was almost bare. Bookshelves empty, bed stripped, hatstand dismantled. Beside her was the pile of clothes ready to go into the trunk on top of the layer of books and files.

She picked up Aunt Judith's white party dress with the rosebuds on it. Poor dress, you deserve a better owner. Mara had worn it to the end-of-term party, and although it had looked beautiful, an odour of awkwardness and failure now seemed to cling to it. She could see the crumples on the skirt where she had clutched it during all those badly executed farewells. The bow on the bodice was limp, too. She could still feel herself fingering it, back to the wall as the endless goodbye dances went on. Rupert had asked her to dance, gallant as ever. Johnny had spent the time fooling around with Maddy and May, treating the college to his Elvis impersonations and avoiding Mara completely. She folded the dress. Into the trunk with it. She crushed the net petticoat on top, hearing in her memory the late night madrigals on the river, voices from the boats echoing under the old bridge, the singers' faces lit by the candles they were holding. The music had been so beautiful she had wept. Even the drunken rowdiness on the banks and bridge could not mar it.

All gone now, she thought. Maddy and May had come crashing in and out of her room for the last time. May had been full of her unexpectedly good exam results – 'take that, Jacks, you bastard' – and Maddy had talked of nothing but her imminent trip to Florence with Cuchulain. She'd miss them.

Mara folded and packed more of Aunt Judith's dresses. She wrapped her teapot carefully and put it in the trunk.

The rain still pattered on the window. She got to her feet and unhooked the mirror from the wall. You've seen a lot in your time, she told it as she wrapped it carefully in her cape to protect the gilt cherubs. For a second her face stared up at her before the black folds covered the glass. The final curtain coming down. She folded the grey dress which was exactly right for impressing a future mother-in-law. Rupert. Guilt had gnawed away at her, and when Rupert came to say goodbye, she couldn't help blurting out an inadequate apology.

'Look, I feel as though I've treated you really badly, and –'

'No, no, of course you haven't, Mara,' he broke in. 'If anything, I'm the one who behaved badly.' *Rupert could and would have the last apology.*

She smiled up at him. 'You're too good for me, Rupert.'

'Nonsense.' He took her hand and she saw him hesitating. Oh, God, not another declaration, please. 'You're not going to change your mind, are you, Mara?' She shook her head. 'So it was Johnny all along.'

'But we're not – I mean, there's nothing going on between us.'

'Yes. He told me that.' He was hesitating again. 'Mara, I don't think you realize how much –' He caught himself back. 'What am I saying? He's capable of pleading his own cause.' He waited to be prompted, but she couldn't open her mouth. 'Well, all the best with your painting.'

'Thank you.'

'We're still friends, I hope?' *'I'll never forget the sweet times we had together,' cried Rupert.*

'Of course.'

'You know, I had my life so beautifully organized till I met you, Mara.'

'Well, I expect you can lick it into shape again.'

'Maybe. I think I've changed, though.' They lapsed into silence.

'Your mother will be relieved,' said Mara at last, for the pleasure of hearing him say 'nonsense' one last time.

'Nonsense. My mother thinks you're wonderful!'

'Nonsense!' she said back. He grinned.

'Well, she'd have come round.' He squeezed her hand.

'Wish me well, Mara.'

'Of course I wish you well.' She felt tears in her eyes.

'Off to a lifetime at the beck and call of "twelve thousand bloody parishioners" twenty-four hours a day.' She smiled to hear her own words bouncing back. 'Of course, if I had any sense, I'd do what Johnny's doing and go in for industrial chaplaincy. No parish at all. No PCC, no Mothers' Union, no church bazaar . . .' She felt herself grow very still. Was he pleading Johnny's cause again? He kissed her goodbye and left.

Mara piled the rest of her folded clothes swiftly in the trunk. Oh, why did you have to say all that, Rupert? She knew he had meant well. All her hopes about Johnny – pruned back so ruthlessly – had come springing up again. Maybe it would be different, she kept thinking, maybe it would work if he wasn't a parish priest. The new shoots waited quivering when Johnny appeared at her door to say goodbye, but his casual manner soon blighted them. She was reduced to inarticulate muttering and they parted without her showing him her drawings or saying any of the things she had planned. Just as well, she thought. She imagined him having to say, 'Look, I'm fond of you, sweetie, you know that, but . . .' At least she was spared that. She felt herself starting to cry as she folded the Chinese silk dressing-gown, remembering Johnny's hands sliding the heavy satin from her shoulders that drunken night. She blotted her tears on the cold fabric. Toughen up, Mara. There's nothing special about unrequited love. It happens to everyone. Think of Rupert. She pictured him, poleaxed in orgasm on the hillside under the beech trees. The wild strawberries will be ripe now, with nobody there to pick them. She shut the trunk and sat on it. That's that. Only the books to return now. On her desk was the pile which belonged to Dr Mowbray and which she had shamefully never taken back to him. She picked them up and set off through the empty college to Coverdale Hall.

'I'm returning your books,' she said when Dr Mowbray opened his door. 'Sorry I've hung on to them for so long.'

He waved his hand as though nobody seriously expected books to make their way back to their owners in anything less than five years. 'I hope they proved useful.' She followed him into the flat and put the books on his desk. 'Coffee?' She glanced at her watch, conscious both of the time and of the fact that the last time he had offered her coffee she had refused very rudely.

'Um . . . yes, please. I'm afraid it'll have to be quick. My mother . . .'

'Of course, of course.' He disappeared and she heard him pottering in his kitchen. This room – it looks so different. In the gloomy summer afternoon it no longer looked like the quarters of an old seafarer. Her eyes skimmed over piles of papers and books. It all seemed shabby and sad without the golden touch of the lamplight. The wind had been wild and blustery that night months before. 'Set sail, set sail,' it had seemed to say, 'the whole world's before you.' Now it blew across the City in a weary wash of rain. It's all over. That was the sofa where Johnny had lounged. She turned away and tried to block out the pain. Her gaze fell on some old framed photographs on the opposite wall and she crossed to look at them.

Coverdale Hall students down the ages. She studied one from the late twenties. Stiff young men with centre partings ranked on the lawn. The buildings of Coverdale behind them looked unchanged, and she could see the cathedral tower looming over the rooftops. Dr Mowbray came back into the room.

'Admiring the rogues' gallery?' He rubbed his hands together briskly, and it occurred to her that he was the sort of man who had found women very difficult in his younger days. He chatted to her about the history of Coverdale Hall while the kettle boiled. Yes, he probably grew up in the all-male world of boarding school, Oxbridge and theological college. It must have come as a relief when he actually met women and realized they were essentially quite rational beings (*pace* Andrew Jacks).

'Of course, there was a strict teetotal line in those days,' he was saying. 'Ah, the kettle.' He vanished into the kitchen and came back a moment later with two steaming mugs. Suddenly he became the old sea captain again. She pictured him sloshing a tot of rum into the coffee as the kitchen pitched this way and that.

They drank and chatted about mysticism and Mara's MA. Maybe I've mellowed in the last year, she thought, remembering how nastily she had cut him off on the previous occasion. He's a nice man.

'Well, give my regards to your parents,' he said when she rose to leave. She nodded and smiled. He smiled back in a slightly startled way. She ran back down the stairs. Yes, definitely nervous of women. And rightly so – at any moment we could cast off our education and bay at the moon in primitive matriarchal blood rituals.

She made a detour and checked her pigeon-hole for the final time. One last overdue library book and a letter forwarded from her Cambridge college. She was puzzled by it. Foreign stamp. She peered at it as she climbed back up the stairs. Israel. Her heart jolted, and she ran to her room.

Someone in the sect. It had to be. She didn't know anyone else in Israel. She had received letters before, rebuking her for her unbelief, preaching repentance to her. Would they never give up? She crumpled it and made as if to drop it in the bin. But what if it were about Hester? She smoothed the letter, turning it over and over with trembling fingers, studying the envelope as though it would reveal the truth to her. Then suddenly she tore it open. A folded airmail letter addressed to Mara. Hester's handwriting on it. And a note. Mara fumbled with it.

Dear Mara, you won't remember me, but we were at school together. Mara turned to the bottom of the letter. From Beverley Henson. The girl with the healed leg. So she'd stayed in the sect and gone to Israel, too. Mara read on hurriedly.

I'm writing from the hostel where your sister was staying. I'm sending you a letter I found in her Bible. I haven't read it. I know I should have sent it to you last summer, but I was afraid. They would have wanted me to hand it over to them if I'd told them about it. They took away the letter she wrote to your parents. I didn't know what to do, so I hid it and waited till I could make my mind up. Now I know I'm leaving. I'll post this to you as soon as I'm out. I just wanted to say sorry. Please don't try to contact me. There's nothing I can tell you.

Oh, God. Poor Beverley. Mara began to weep for the other girl's suffering. At least she was out of it by now. She picked up her sister's letter. What fresh misery was about to spill out? Her hand tore the envelope open. She was shaking as she read.

Dear Mara,

This is to wish you well for your Finals. I've written to Mum and Dad and ask them to take me home. I tried so hard to carry on believing but I've no strength any more. I know you thought I was mad, but please try to understand. It all seemed true to start with, and then later it just had to be true, otherwise I had committed a sin too terrible to bear. Letting Roger do those things and believing it was God's will. But God does ask people to do strange things. You only have to read the prophets. Mara, that poor baby. It should never have been born, only they said it would be healed if I had the faith. Sometimes I wanted to kill myself, because I had let it die by not believing enough. Now I think it was meant to die anyway. Mara please pray for me if you feel you can. I'm so tired. I just want to come home. Sometimes I think there is still a God, only different from the one I tried to believe in. Bigger and cleaner and stronger, like the air. I hope he hasn't abandoned me. I have no framework any more. Nowhere to put anything. Please come and see me when I'm home. You're the only one who knows what it's like to lose everything. Don't hold all this against me. I never thought you were a child of disobedience like they said you were. I hope your exams go well.

> *Love,*
> *Hester*

Mara buried her face in her hands and wept again. She wept for

369

herself, and for her parents who had never received Hester's letter. She wept for Hester who had suffered so much, and yet could still spare a thought for her sister's exams; for Hester who had been coming home, but had drowned instead. Why oh why did you let her die like that? How could you let that bastard Roger Messenger walk free? What kind of a God are you that you let this happen? She saw Hester sinking, abandoned by God, one pale hand flailing above the waves, then nothing. She was coming home and you let her drown. And then in the midst of her raging grief a sense of calm drew near and nearer. A shining figure walking steadily across the waves, an outstretched hand pulling her up. 'Fear not, it is I.' She didn't die alone. A blast of joy hit Mara's soul and vanished. The gate of glory ajar for a fraction of a second, then slammed shut again. Angels and archangels and all the company of heaven. She looked in amazement around the empty room.

The bells chimed four. She scrambled to her feet and wiped away her tears. Her mother would be here any time now and Mara still hadn't taken her library books back. She snatched the carrier bag of old calf-bound volumes and ran down the stairs. Oh, Hester. At least I know now. It's like the sudden lifting of a life sentence. For my parents, too. Oh, quick. The sooner I've done this, the sooner I'll be able to tell them. Her hand was on the doorknob.

'Where are you off to in such a hurry?' Nigel. He came leering towards her as she stood at the main door, and she was surprised by a surge of affection for him. 'Off home, are we?' She nodded. 'Well, you be good, darling. I'll miss you. There aren't enough good-looking women in this place.' He slipped an arm round her waist and she remembered all the times he had been kind to her in his loathsome way.

'Look, thanks for . . . being nice to me, Nigel.'

He waggled his eyebrows at her as though her words were a polite euphemism for a shag in the broom cupboard. 'I'll be nice to you any time you fancy. Bye-bye, gorgeous.' He planted a kiss on her lips before she could dodge away. 'Give my love to the stud.' She flushed.

'And to Andrew?'

'Oh, hah, hah.' He turned to leave and on impulse she reached out a hand and nipped his retreating backside. He yelped in shock and she darted out of the door before he could catch her. 'You want a bloody good seeing to, you do,' he bawled along the street as she ran off. The fishwife raised her mighty arm in a clenched-fist salute.

Mara watched through the persistent drizzle, her mind still ringing with amazement at Hester's letter. It was as though she had been snatched back from the sect at the last moment. She thought of Roger Messenger and of Leah. You lost. And one day, one day there'll be a judgement. You won't walk free in the end.

She increased her pace and decided to cut through the cathedral to the library on Palace Green. She passed under the archway and through the cathedral close. There seemed to be a lot of clergy prowling about. She entered the cloisters and passed a group of elderly women wearing plastic rainhoods. Bad weather for a day trip. She rounded a corner and saw that a couple of them had strayed ahead and were peering through the window into what had once been the monks' dormitory. It was a curious window made of old fragments of glass, with random colours, bits of angels and saints and scraps of Latin. Mara went to admire it for one last time.

'Oh, look, and there's a gentleman in red as well,' said one of the women as Mara drew level. She grinned, thinking how odd the church must appear to outsiders. I wonder what's going on? she thought as she peered in. The room was crowded with clergy all talking and busy robing up. Their surplices were dyed green by the glass. No sound from inside reached her as she watched. It could have been a silent underwater scene. The rain pattered on the cloister roof overhead. Suddenly she saw Johnny. He seemed to be looking straight at her and she flinched back out of sight. Don't be stupid, she told herself. He can't see you. She inched back and looked through a red pane. Blood-red surplices. Johnny was laughing with another young man as they fixed their stoles cross-wise like Miss World sashes. Deacons. Of course – he was getting ordained on Sunday. It was a practice. They started lining up for the procession. Mara began to be aware of the two women again and their stream of uninformed chat.

'They've got suitcases. It must be the new monks arriving.'

Mara suppressed a giggle and they both turned to look at her. 'Actually, I think it's a rehearsal.' They focused at her with interest. 'There's an ordination here on Sunday.'

'Fancy that,' said the other. 'All those young men becoming priests.'

'And deacons,' said Mara, sensing she was being taken for an expert.

'We were wondering about the gentleman in red.'

'The Bishop.' The three of them fell silent and pressed close again as the procession started to move into the cathedral. Johnny was at the back. It must be in alphabetical order, she thought. Ah, God. I can't stand this. It all felt too symbolic, watching him from the outside as he was carried away from her into the Church. This was the real reason she had refused to go to the service. She was the one being sacrificed on the altar of his vocation.

'You seem to know a lot about it,' said the first woman. 'Have you got someone in there?' Mara bit her lip. Johnny was framed for one last second in the great doorway before he vanished from her.

'No,' she said. 'No one at all.' She turned and ran, leaving them to their speculation.

Rain crossed the City in grey waves. Mara returned the books and checked one or two last references. Tears kept trickling steadily down her cheeks like rain on a window. She unravelled her plait to let her hair hide her face. Hang on to yourself. Only a few more minutes and it'll all be over. Her heart was already escaping south as she made her rapid notes.

At last it was all done. She left the library and began to run back across the empty Green. The previous week it had been teeming with graduates in their furs and gowns. Would her mother have arrived? Mara paused. On impulse she turned and cut back through the cloisters. One last glimpse.

The cloisters were empty. She slowed to a walk, clutching her damp notes. Raindrops dripped from the stone tracery in flashes of white. The sky was brightening a little overhead. They had all gone. She turned a corner. All except one clergyman leaning in an empty archway watching the rain. He had his back to her and she stared, thinking how like a painting he looked. Calm and still, the man of God in the house of God. Then she saw the cigarette. Her heart jolted. Johnny. He turned and saw her.

'Hello, sweetie – I thought you'd gone ages ago.'

She shook her head. She shouldn't have come back this way. He was walking towards her. What if he asked her again to go to his ordination?

'My mother's picking me up this afternoon,' she gabbled, twisting her sodden sheet of paper. 'Any time now.'

372

'Give her my love.'

'Yes.' The rain mourned across the sky. He'd had his hair cut. 'I didn't recognize you. You look . . . right. Standing there like that.'

He looked down at his cassock and did her a mock curtsey. 'Like it? Funny, it feels right, somehow. I was just thinking that.'

She watched the smoke drift from his cigarette. 'I'm glad you're getting ordained. Even if . . .' Her courage failed.

'So I should bloody well think. You're the one who talked me into it, Mara.'

'I just meant even if we're ending up going down different paths.' Her hand tugged miserably at her curls, trying to straighten them out. 'I think you're doing the right thing. Sometimes you just have to make choices, that's all.'

'Is that right?' He was grinning at her as he smoked. 'I've always been one for having my cake and eating it. I mean, what's the point of having a cake and *not* eating it?'

'But that's not what it means.' He was still laughing at her. She turned away. Raindrops sparkled on the points of stone. She felt tears welling up. He stubbed out his cigarette and began fishing around in his cassock pocket.

'Here. Read this, flower. I was just going to post it to you.' He handed her a letter. She turned it over fearfully and saw her name and address in his writing.

'What does it say?'

'It's my attempt to explain. Without losing my temper, for once.'

'Explain what?'

'Ah, well.' He smiled down at her. 'You'll have to read it, won't you?' She stood irresolute, hearing footsteps enter the cloisters. 'The coffee shop's this way,' called a woman's voice. 'You didn't think you'd get rid of me that easily, did you?' She felt herself starting to panic.

'Look, I'm going to have to go, Johnny.'

'Kiss me goodbye, Mara.'

She flushed. 'I can't. I mean . . .' She gestured desperately at his cassock. He grinned. The footsteps and chatter were drawing nearer all the time. It would be those women again. 'Besides, I told you . . .'

But he laughed and took her in his arms. 'You might be confused about this, Mara. I'm not.'

'Johnny, no. Look, listen, someone's com-mmm . . .' The rest was lost. His hands were tangled in her hair and she could feel his cassock buttons digging into her breastbone. The voices fell silent and feet hurried tactfully past. His kiss deepened. This wasn't supposed to happen. She was trembling when he released her.

'Look after yourself, sweetheart.' He touched her cheek briefly and was gone.

She watched him as he walked away, whistling, down the long cloister. You should have said something. You should have told him how you feel. You missed your last chance and now you'll never see him again. The bells chimed overhead. She clutched the letter tight. I'm late. I can't open it now. The sound of Johnny's whistling followed her as she ran off, weeping, letter in hand.

She crossed the cathedral close and emerged on to the street. Her parents' car was parked outside Jesus College. She's here already. Mara thrust the letter into her dress pocket. I'll have to wait till I'm home. Stop crying, you fool, she told herself. Do you want to have to pour out the whole story? The college entrance wavered through her tears. She glanced up the steps and stopped in astonishment. It was her father standing there waiting for her.